All The Days

Elle Jayce

All The Days

ELLE JAYCE

Elle Jayce Publishing

Elle Jayce Publishing
South Wales, UK

www.ellejayce.co.uk

ISBN-13 978-1-7395850-0-6 (Ebook edition)
ISBN-13 978-1-7395850-1-3 (Paperback edition)

Cover Design and Illustration by @ValleyAndVale

For everyone in need of a happy ending...

About the Author

Elle Jayce lives tucked away in a tiny valley in Wales. She works in healthcare, and although she's always had a love for everything bookish—her father was an author and her first job was in a library —it wasn't until the lockdown of 2020 that she plucked up the courage to share her stories.

When not working or writing, she loves to paint, blow raspberries on her reluctant cat's belly, and go for beach walks with her hubby and a flask of 'I-promise-it's-not-G&T.'

(Obviously, it's G&T.)

♫

For the accompanying playlist to *All The Days*, follow Elle Jayce on Spotify!

instagram.com/byellejayce

facebook.com/byellejayce

tiktok.com/@byellejayce

Author's Note & Trigger Warning

In 2020, violent attacks toward women, especially in cities like London, reached epidemic proportions. Although completely fictitious, elements of the characters have been inspired by some incredible people. I hope that I've done them, and their experiences justice.

All The Days touches on the topics of anxiety, panic attacks, and the survival of a violent crime/stabbing. No overly graphic descriptions are given, but if these are subjects you find sensitive, please read with care.

Pg-13. Closed door. Mild Language.

Day 330
Wednesday

Most people saved their memories in a diary. I saved mine in a playlist.

I sat in the shelter of my car, watching the blackened sky, listing off possible songs for today's entry: *Purple Rain, Singing in the Rain, Set Fire To The Rain...*

The narrow streets of my little Welsh town looked deserted. I prayed for a break in the clouds and waited. Nothing. Heavy drops continued to thunder against the metal roof and pour down the windscreen, making the translucent blue eyes of my reflection cry a thousand tiny waterfalls.

Yup, today was definitely an acoustic, melancholy *Why Does It Always Rain On Me* kind of day.

In front of me, a yellow, sun-shaped sign hung above the entrance to the old school where my DAYS support group meetings were held. Coat slung pointlessly over my head, I made a run for it, barged through the doors and stood for a minute in the corridor to drip dry before making my way to the main hall. The scent of freshly baked cakes and a cheerful hum of conversation welcomed me in. Built for pure functionality, the hall was a bare brick square. No frills. One row of thin windows ran below the ceiling, placed there merely as a light source, not for enjoying the surrounding countryside.

I loved the logic and flexibility of construction. If something didn't work, you traced back to the source of the problem and fixed it, or if necessary, you ripped it out and started again. When done properly, you would never know there had been an issue. I wished the same could be said about humans. Then I wouldn't need a support group. Just a sledgehammer.

All the regular attendees were already seated in the circle of creaky chairs. They looked up to greet me with waves and nods. I barely had time to shake the mud off my clumpy work boots and find a seat before Andrew—one of the group leaders—began talking.

He introduced some new visitors who sat by his side, hovering on their chairs, ready to flee. Everyone smiled warmly at them in an attempt to ease their anxiety. We understood all too well the kind of terrors that had brought them here.

"So, Lara, how's things with you this week?" Andrew, and the rest of the group, looked at me.

I gripped the hem of my coat. "Fine, thanks. All good." A standard answer. I grinned to make it convincing. "Same old." Work. Try to sleep. Panic about not sleeping. Repeat.

Knowing me well enough not to press for further information, Andrew thanked me and moved on to the next person. "Ffion, how about you?"

"Okay, I guess. Up and down." She stopped chewing her nails to take a breath. "Some days, I feel like screaming and smashing stuff. I shouted at my partner yesterday. Who knows why. It doesn't make sense."

I nodded along. Nothing made sense to me either.

At the end of the meeting, the group's founder, Jenny, handed me a piece of her famous chocolate cake. Although retired, she still dressed the way she always had for work. Tweed jacket, shiny court shoes, pearls. A prim and proper teacher from a country boarding school. "Alright, my love?"

I idly pushed a crumb around my plate. "Yeah. Long week at work. We've finally finished an overdue renovation. Daniel's on the phone *all* the time."

"Ah. Him." With a pointed roll of her grey eyes, she took a bite of cake.

Jenny was not a fan of my boss, Daniel David, an architect who made up half of David Clarke Construction. To be fair, when I first met him, neither was I. Almost three years ago, I'd jumped at the chance to become his apprentice. Back then, the thought of moving to London and living on my own was an adventure. Nothing to be afraid of. Even so, I knew earning my place in a male-dominated industry would require toughening up. Which was why I'd resented the way Daniel's inky-blue stares knotted my throat. And how his mere presence made my cheeks flush, announcing my girlish emotions to the world in flashing neon pink.

Now, I'd moved safely back to Wales and become the manager of a branch office which had a four-hour journey and a country border separating me from Daniel, so things were... easier.

Distance helped.

"Men like him are hard to deal with at the best of times." Jenny tutted. "But with your connection, maybe it's time to think about being your own boss?"

It wasn't the first time the thought crossed my mind. But after everything Daniel had done for me, I couldn't leave.

I'd made a promise.

Jenny read my mind the way she always did. "You don't owe him anything, Lara."

My heartstrings tied themselves around my lungs. "Maybe one day." I hastily moved on. "So, what're the plans for the new fundraising? Anything I can do to help?"

"A few folks suggested the idea of being sponsored to face a fear." She twisted a stray silver strand of hair around her glittery nails. Jenny's bright taste in nail varnish was her form of a wild rebellion. "Nothing crazy like bungee jumping or skydiving, gosh no. We want this to be about ordinary things that become scary after a Day Zero event. I think Stuart wants to start driving again."

"Wow, good for him." I glanced at Stuart. He'd recently joined DAYS after being robbed while sitting in his car at traffic lights. It left him with a burn across his right cheek and neck. All for an iPhone. He hadn't driven since.

"How about you, love?" Jenny asked. "Any ideas?"

Since my Day Zero, everything scared me. "What about my version of *50 First Dates?*"

"That's brilliant!"

I choked on my cake. "I'm joking."

"Are you now?" Her eyes widened, wrinkling up her pale forehead. I gulped down more cake to avoid answering. "Funny how that's the first thing to pop into your head. Tell me, when was the last time you went on a date? Good-looking girl like you"—I laughed and swept a hand over my cement and paint-splattered overalls—"should be out getting wined and dined every weekend."

I had been out with one guy since moving home. It went well. Until I had a meltdown, fainted, and told him my history. Apparently, he couldn't deal with it. *Must be nice to have a choice.* Anyway, I didn't need another person trying to protect me. I definitely didn't need anyone else feeling sorry for me. All I wanted was to be my old self and for life to go back to normal.

No dramas. No complications. Simple.

I'd even made a step-by-step plan:

1. Move away from London. (Done.)
2. Find and rent an office. (Done.)
3. Build the business, possibly enter a design award. (Work in progress.)
4. Write my journal. (Pending.)(Sort of.)
5. Get back with my old band. (Nowhere near.)

I sipped my tea. "Wine-and-dine-type gentlemen are hard to find these days, Jen."

"True, true." Her eyes sparkled. "I can think of a few guys who'd be up for a date though. Sponsored. Purely to fundraise and help you overcome your fear, of course."

"Oh, of course!"

"You'll never know if you don't look."

"I don't have a problem with looking. I like looking. It's just..." Everything else. All the messy stuff that came afterwards.

I set my mug down as Jenny rubbed my shoulder. I knew exactly what she'd say next, so we chanted it together:

"Be brave. Be honest. Make all the days count."

That was the mantra she repeated at every meeting. It inspired the name of the DAYS charity and became a motto for the group. Simple enough to remember when in the grips of a panic attack. Cheesy enough to bring back a smile.

Sometimes, it was the only thing that kept me going.

Why Does it Always Rain On Me? - Travis

Day 332
Friday Morning

I skated in my socks over the smooth pine floorboards toward the kitchen where Olivia, my housemate, lifelong friend, and PA (so yeah, basically my right hand) had left a note on our fridge:

Gone for a run to Mum's house. Will spend the day with her... yay. Be back for tea. Fancy a chinese?
x Luv ya x Liv.

Giggling at the smiley face scrawled at the bottom of the message, I flicked on the coffee machine along with my dance party playlist and started cleaning. Due to the snug—that was an interior designer's way of saying 'tiny'—size of my traditional stone, two-bed terrace, it didn't take long to work through the entire house.

Being home alone got easier with each passing day. I no longer jumped out of my skin at every unexpected noise. However, by mid-morning, the rumbling coming from my stomach grew too loud to ignore.

Searching the kitchen revealed nothing but a box of cereal. No milk.

A supermarket trip was the last thing I wanted to do on my

day off. To summon up extra courage, I changed into a floaty skirt and my favourite cosy jumper. It didn't stop the handle of my front door from turning into a block of ice under my shaking fingers.

Were dry cereals really that bad? *Be brave.* I shook out my arms. Just a shop. Drive there, grab milk, come home. Easy. I'd be fine. If I got there before lunch, it wouldn't be too busy.

♪

It was busy.

Darting in and out of the cramped aisles, I grabbed the essentials (red wine included) while trying to avoid getting swept up by the crowds that drifted and pushed without warning like an unpredictable wild ocean I couldn't control. My stranglehold on the handles of my basket tightened further. Doing the shopping never used to feel like drowning. And logically, I should have felt safer here than somewhere quiet. Life often defied logic.

I earned myself a dirty look from the cashier by dumping everything onto the till counter. A shiver spread over my shoulders when the woman in the queue behind me let out a cigarette-smoke filled yawn. I held my breath, swiped my card, and marched for the exit without waiting for a receipt.

Drizzle slicked my hair the second I stepped out of the doors, instantly turning my freshly curled bob into a frizz ball. I'd forgotten my umbrella again. *Every time, why?* I moaned to myself, took a shortcut, running through a narrow gap between rows of parked cars, and it hit me. No, not the answer to my umbrella dilemma, but a large, painfully solid car door.

I collided with it at full speed, stumbled back a step and lost my balance. My left wrist smacked the ground sending sharp needles of pain up my arm, followed by red-hot stinging as my forearm and elbow scraped the tarmac.

In a blur of slow motion, I ended up sprawled across the wet, dirty car park. *What the hell? Wait a sec—* "Where's my bag?"

A male voice came from above, fuzzy inside my spinning head. I clutched my chest. Shock spiralled into heart-racing fear as my consciousness fell into the depths of my Day Zero...

Cold seeping through my veins... no air...

Stones cut into my back as he dragged me by the ankle over the rough gravel. My pain blended into numbness. I couldn't fight back.

Not this time.

The man had left his car and was about to touch me. Adrenaline took over. Fear drove me to act. I caught him off guard by using my injured hand to shove myself up onto my feet. With my right hand, I grabbed his outstretched arm, twisted it hard behind his back and pushed him, front first, against his car. He hit the side with a satisfying thunk.

Pain scorched my wrist, but I kept pushing.

This time, I was stronger.

This time, I was prepared.

I blinked over and over to focus, concentrating on my breathing to block out the thumping pulse in my ears. "No, no, no. Don't panic, come on. Breathe in. One. Two." Slowly, the relief of gaining control dulled my initial shock.

"Hey, it's okay." His calm reply startled me. I hadn't meant to say anything out loud. "I'm so sorry, you're alright, no need to panic. I was trying to help you up." He didn't attempt to break free, rather he quietly repeated the words, "It's okay, you're alright."

It should have been annoying, but like a steady tick-tock of a clock, his low voice filtered through my daze and stilled me, lifting my senses from the past to the present. Rainwater dripped off my fringe onto my nose. Some of the contents of my dropped bags were slowly rolling away. Thank goodness the wine bottle hadn't smashed.

A shudder of reality shook my core. I released the man, took a step back and pressed my face into my trembling hands.

Careless idiot scared me half to death.

"Oh. Umm?" I cringed as my mind struggled to produce words. "Argh. I can't believe I did that. Err, I thought you were trying to mug me. Oh..." I kept my face hidden, only able to see up to his waist through the gaps in my fingers.

"No, don't worry. It was my fault." He pushed himself upright, casually brushing off his long coat. "Hey, those were some moves."

He didn't seem rattled about being assaulted by a strange woman. He sounded amused. Impressed even. No trace of the anger I'd been expecting.

I massaged the pressure building in my forehead.

Tentatively, his biker boot-clad feet moved closer. "Please, you're hurt, let me help you." The soft purr of his voice oiled my tightly wound nerves.

Careless idiot with an unearthly deep voice.

Honestly, he could have been the guy who did those emotional voice-overs on movie trailers. Only without the American accent; his was English. Posh. Hugh Grant style.

Eyes still fixed on the ground, I waved in the general direction of my car and assured him I'd be fine, aiming for a calm, firm tone. What actually came out was faint and wobbly, so I quickly occupied myself by bending down to recover my shopping.

Another sharp twinge came from my wrist when I tried to move it. Grit stuck to the grazes on my palms. Lifting my sleeve uncovered patches of skin already turning into bruised, sickly shades of violet and lime. My assailant crouched beside me to pick up the second shopping bag. I could feel him watching my self-assessment. He definitely saw me wince as I tried to lift the refilled bag.

"I can't leave you here," he stated as if it were an obvious fact. "Your wrist might be broken and you're bleeding."

Out of the corner of my eye, I saw him point at my face. The burning sensation must have been from more than embarrassment. Touching a finger to my cheek confirmed it—I was bleeding.

Edging closer, he knelt on the ground next to me, boots creaking, slim black jeans soaking up water. He pointed again, this time at my wrist. "I really should take you to a hospital."

Every single one of my muscles jolted in response to the word 'hospital' as if I'd been plugged into a faulty socket. "No, please! You don't need to, look—" I held up my hand and spun it. Bad idea. I gritted my teeth against the pain. "No swelling, I can still move. It's bruised, that's all."

"Okay. I'm not going to force you." He lifted a hand, palm open, before gently placing it on my shoulder. I shivered at the touch but resisted the urge to attack him again. "At least let me help you carry your things?"

No longer believing him to be a mugger, I agreed with a nod.

He insisted on carrying both bags and gestured for me to lead the way. From what I could make out while still keeping my head down, his clothes were all grey and black. A plain jumper under a smart overcoat. Stylish but understated. *Nice.*

"You really don't have to do this. I'm fine," I told him, stealing a backwards glance at his tall frame. For every two of my steps, he took one long stride.

"I'm not leaving you," he said. "Not until I'm convinced. Which I'm not. Yet."

Something in those adamant but caring words made me smile. I risked another glance—Dark hair. Square jaw.

We got to my car and I opened up the back for him to unload the bags, then leaned in to retrieve some anti-bacterial wipes to clean my hands. They were still shaking. I wished he would stop watching me so closely. I *was* fine, I just needed a minute to properly calm down. Alone. That was all.

"Ah, good thinking." He swooped forward, making me jump

again. "Come on, take a seat and let me have a look at that cut. The top of the door must have caught you."

Before I had a chance to refuse, he decisively took the wipes—and the situation—in hand and made his way to my front passenger seat. I stood there like a lemon, winding the strap of my handbag around my fingers.

In the past, I would have objected to being told what to do, especially so abruptly by a stranger. But I'd since discovered that sometimes it was easier to let people help you. Even if I didn't think it necessary, it made them feel better. I wanted to crawl back into my shell of embarrassment, but if the situation were reversed, I'd be feeling mortified. So, I shut the back door and went to the driver's seat, resigned to accepting his courtesy.

Careless, but kind man.

And... oddly familiar. Ha! Maybe he was the voice-over guy?

Thanks to wet clothes, my clumsy entrance did not help to restore any of my dignity.

He apologised again while I tried to get comfortable, took a wipe from the packet, and swivelled to face me. "I have some medical training. Granted, it was a few years ago." He exhaled a low laugh. "But if it's okay with you..." The offer was left hanging.

If my mind wasn't wading through brain fog, I might have been able to think of another (polite) way to get rid of him. But then again, my face stung like a wasp with anger issues.

"Fine. I give in." I tucked my increasingly messy curls behind my ears and put on a well-practised smile.

I looked up. Straight into his eyes.

Good grief. Fresh panic of a different kind flooded my body. Heat zipped up my spine. I drew in a shamefully loud breath, meanwhile, he carried on without so much as blinking. With a face like his—chiselled greek-god, but pleasantly rough around the edges—he must have been used to my kind of reaction.

He supported my head in one hand, the span of his fingers reaching all the way from my chin to my ear, into my hair. The other began carefully cleaning my cut. His skin smelt like earth and the air after a thunderstorm. I swallowed, chewed my lip and tried not to move, thanking my throbbing wrist for providing a distraction.

Careless, but kind man with eyes the colour of chocolate and caramel and maple syrup and every kind of sweet, naughty thin—

"What's your name?" He squinted in concentration. Little lines appeared over his nose.

"Lara. Lara Quinn."

"Pleasure to meet you, Miss Quinn. I'm Theo."

Day 332
Friday Midday

Theo held a steady pressure on my cheek while a pattering of rain against the roof matched my rapid heartbeat. I sat silently, digging my nails into my thighs, highly aware of the tight space between us. And of how long I'd been staring at him. Too long. My tiny car felt like a matchbox with him in it. All the oxygen had been replaced by his aftershave. Ginger. Possibly cinnamon. Something warm and spicy.

"Hmm," he thought out loud. "So. Lara Quinn. That's a swish name." One of his eyebrows raised, it also lifted the corner of his mouth into a smile as though they were connected by an invisible string. "With your skills, you must be what, MI5? CIA?"

The corny compliment, and the word 'swish,' made me laugh. I liked my name. Especially the way he said it. Emphasis on the 'r,' rolling it like a growl.

I tried to look out the window, but his arms filled my whole field of vision. The view downwards was equally blocked by his chest, waist. Long, long legs... so I settled my eyes safely on his shoulder.

"I've taken self-defence classes," I said, "although, I hoped I'd never have to use them."

"They were worth it. You completely surprised me."

I'd surprised myself. "What can I say? I'm expecting a recruitment call from James Bond any day now." *Seriously?* I internally rolled my eyes, wishing to suck the words back in.

Theo chuckled. A deep, throaty hum which I felt rather than heard. He removed the wipe from my face and turned away to place it on the floor. He didn't let go of my head. Warm fingers lingered on either side of my ear, holding back my hair.

Up until now, Theo's gaze had been clinical, but when he looked back at me, something switched on. Tingly static skipped over my skin. For a few seconds of an eternity, he scrutinised every square millimetre of my face, reading me—maybe even my thoughts—the way anyone else would read a book. My flustered brain lost its connection to my mouth and went back to a mushy state of oh's, um's and ah's.

Using the excuse of turning on the heaters to dry my feet, I broke free from his gravity. "Umm, Theo, do I know you? Are you local?" I babbled while rummaging through my memory. I might have seen him in town. "Do you work in the central offices? You seem familiar."

He folded his hands away onto his lap. "I don't think we have ever met. I would remember an introduction like yours."

I began to apologise for my twenty questions, then noticed his glimmer of a smile and the way he was looking up at me through thick black eyelashes. *An introduction like mine?* Cheeky.

"Huh." I nodded as if making a fascinating discovery. "You must have hit my head harder than I thought."

"Hey, don't say that." He laughed, went serious again, scanned the floor and flicked dirt off his knee. "I feel dreadful. The last thing you need is a concussion to go with your wrist." Mouth open, he paused, undecided about what to say next. "I'm not local, but I'm working nearby on the coast, filming a new TV series."

Flashes of a movie I'd seen recently popped into my mind, followed by a name: Theodore Jackson. "You're an actor, aren't you? That's where I've seen you." A small nod confirmed it. No wonder I'd struggled to place him! Without the costumes, he looked different. *Better*. Real. "I didn't recognise you. Actually, I did, but couldn't remember why. Sorry."

"Don't apologise, I'm not offended." His eye-line dropped. "It's a refreshing change to get to introduce myself. Ah"—he ruffled his hair—"that sounded big-headed, didn't it? I don't expect or want everyone to recognise me, I didn't mean it that way."

He seemed embarrassed, but from the little I knew of him, he wasn't the shy type. Quite the opposite. He had a reputation to rival Daniel's—Rebel. Party-hard player.

Oooh. That could be why.

I knew better than to believe everything in the media though.

Theo's full attention shifted back onto me. It was like having a tonne of sticky sweet candy-floss hit me square in the chest. Weighty but soft. Slightly moreish. Okay, very moreish.

I pushed the weight aside with another grin. "Theo." I didn't know any other Theo's; I liked the way the sound rolled nicely off my tongue. "You've been so kind, but I'm fine. You don't have to worry, it was an accident."

"I may not *have* to worry, but I will. Though you hide it well, Lara, I can tell you are in pain." He gently tapped a finger on my hand. "Your wrist needs to be checked and your face needs cleaning up properly. If you won't let me take you to A&E, will you at least come to see the first aider we have on set? If he gives you the all-clear, *then* I promise to stop worrying."

There was nothing I could do to hide the traitorous heat engulfing my cheeks.

Theo pulled away with a blink-and-you'd-miss-it hint of a smirk. "I'll drive. You need to keep your wrist elevated and as still as possible. Don't worry, I'm better at driving than I am at opening doors."

I managed to smile despite the growing tension in my spine

from the thought of getting in his car and being under his control. Sweat built in my palms. I gripped the steering wheel and within seconds, my wrist burned. Driving home would be torture. *Ugh*. If I didn't go to this first aider, then Olivia would probably drag me to the hospital later anyway.

"We can take your car if that's easier?" Theo's dark stare surveyed me again, waiting for an answer. "It's okay, I've got you. Do you trust me?" he added as that string lifted his mouth into another cheesy, impossible-to-say-no-to smile.

I should be saying no. I shouldn't even have been considering it, but... he wasn't such a stranger after all, so could I trust him? I'd certainly run out of reasons to refuse him. Admittedly, the idea of seeing a 'set' also appealed to me.

Careless but kind, chocolate-eyed, and surprisingly considerate man.

My head said run. My head always told me to run away from everything.

Remnants of adrenaline trickled through my system. My gut said: "Yes."

♫

Theo started the engine. Taylor Swift automatically began singing to us about her *Wildest Dreams*. All her albums were set on a constant shuffle, plus some rock classics and random pop songs. I dug a hairbrush out of the glove box, switched the stereo off and apologised.

"I'll let you in on a secret." Theo's shoulder brushed mine as he looked out the back window to reverse. I covered up my unconscious flinch with a cough. "I'm a huge Swiftie."

Being a Taylor fan definitely helped to redeem his carelessness. I was about to say so when I caught sight of my blotchy face and smudged mascara in the overhead mirror.

"It's not as bad as it looks," Theo said in response to my groan. "It stopped bleeding quickly, so it can't be deep."

He must have thought I was reacting to the cut across my cheekbone rather than to the general state of my appearance. I didn't correct him. Blood didn't bother me anymore. Looking like a half-drowned banshee in front of Britain's rising star, however, did bother me.

We drove in silence onto the main road. I discreetly re-applied some lippy and tried, and failed, to tame my hair. The moment I finished, Theo started talking. As if he'd been waiting patiently. Allowing me the time to collect myself.

"By the way," he said, "you should probably direct me. I have no idea where I'm going."

"Oh, right! Where are we headed?"

"It's called Lan... Lanvel?"

He shook his head at his failure to pronounce the word. Welsh language one—Theo nil. So, he started to describe the place instead, giving me another excuse to look at him. Gloriously high cheekbones. Straight nose. Thick walnut hair, still wet, and just about long enough on top for it to curl. A drop of water had formed within a teeny-tiny ringlet at the nape of his tanned neck.

We approached a junction, causing his brow to furrow, in turn causing my brain to forget how to speak all over again. Not helped by the fact that his hand, now on the gearstick, was extremely close to my thigh. My heartbeat vibrated throughout my entire body.

"Umm," I mumbled, "I think you mean Llanfelinfawr. You're going the right way, stay on this road."

Llanfelinfawr—translated roughly to 'a large mill'—was a picturesque area where one of the valley's rivers met the sea. It consisted of about six scattered houses, the mill which was now a shop, a pub, and a caravan site on the headland above. What made it special was a long stretch of sandy coastline framed by tall cliffs.

Theo looked my way.

I rubbed my hands on my knees. "Sorry for accusing you of mugging me, Theo. Oh, and for thinking you were going to abduct me. I can't imagine abductors asking for directions." My attempt at making light of the situation grated against my ears. *Just stop.*

"I am in your car and you are the one telling me where to go, so technically, doesn't that make you the abductor?" He laughed. Not a wow-this-girl-is-weird kind of laugh, but an amused laugh with full-on crinkled up eyes.

Was he being polite or did he genuinely find me funny?

How should I know? He was an actor after all.

From then on, we eased into a conversation about where they were filming, how pretty he thought the area was, and that he wanted to come back and explore more of Wales soon. Even when describing places I'd known my whole life, he brought out so many details that they sounded exotic and new.

"So tell me, Lara. Lara Quinn." He quirked his brow. "What does a 007 such as yourself do when not saving the world? Do you have a normal day job, as a cover?"

Again, his humour helped to put me at ease. It sparked an excited fizzing sensation in my chest. But this was the part of introductions I dreaded, and a reason why I avoided meeting new people. Because one question *always* led to another.

I kept my answer simple, including just enough information to hopefully satisfy his curiosity. A rehearsed tactic of mine.

"Yeah," I sighed heavily. "Saving the world is exhausting, so I come back here for a break." I broke out of my mock-serious tone and continued, "I work for a construction company as an interior designer and project manager. Usually, I'm in steel-toe boots and high-vis on a building site somewhere."

I waited for the standard disbelief that came whenever people discovered that I—a 5ft woman in her twenties wearing a pink skirt—worked on a building site. Or for the look that said, '*why on earth would you want to do that?*' Neither reaction materialised.

"Pity," he said. "The boots would have been useful this

morning. You could have just kicked me. No doubt easier than the whole restrain-me-against-my-car manoeuvre."

"Not as cool though."

"No." He flashed a smile which did strange things to my insides. "Nor as much fun."

I busied myself by wiping condensation off the window and reverted the subject back to him by asking a random question—another tactic—about his first job.

♫

Twenty minutes (and one hilarious story about Theo getting fired from a deli) later, we approached the coast. An open grassy area near the mouth of the river now housed several blue storage container cabins, similar to the ones we used at work, along with a line of smaller caravans, all surrounded by temporary wire fencing. Large signs on either side of a new gateway read: Main Entrance.

As we pulled in, a security guard ran over, waving frantically at us to park elsewhere, only for him to turn a shade of beetroot when Theo rolled down the window.

"Mr Jackson," he gasped. "Sorry, didn't see you there."

"Hey, no problem. My friend here needs to see Steven, then we'll be out of the way."

That sentence landed heavily in my abdomen. Once I got passed onto Steven the first aider, my time with Theo would be over. There were still so many questions I wanted him to answer in his intelligent, enthusiastic way.

Theo's hand appeared at my door to help me out. I chickened out of taking it and instead passed him my handbag with a quiet, "Thank you."

He accepted it with a bow as if he were my butler. "My pleasure."

I couldn't help but giggle which, I discovered, is impossible to do in a mature, lady-like way.

Not that I was trying to impress him or anything.

He pointed to one of the caravans where a green First Aid sign marked our destination and walked alongside me, my handbag casually swinging on his shoulder. "Steven used to be a paramedic, so he knows what he's doing. Much better than me with a baby wipe anyway."

"You're perfect." *Crap,* that didn't come out right. "I mean, you've been so kind and, and..."

"Perfect?" He stopped at the caravan door and turned to me, his face deadly serious. "Miss Quinn, are you flirting with me?"

"Ha, what? Me... with you? No!" I scoffed. I wasn't. Was I? *As if I haven't made enough of a fool of myself.* "I just— I mean— I'm very grateful."

If I bit my lip any harder, I was going to need stitches.

The corners of his mouth twitched before releasing into a wide grin. He was teasing me.

Of course, he was only teasing me.

He'd joked a lot on the drive over, always with the same glint in his eye, but the deadpan act had taken me by surprise. The banter I used to enjoy at work felt like a million years ago. These days, people treated me differently. They always worried about upsetting me or saying the wrong thing that might bring back the past. As if I was too fragile to joke with.

A daring flicker of my old self ignited. "You're not such a bad actor, after all, Mr Jackson."

"Ah, you flatter me again." Another little head bow. "Come on, let's get you fixed up." Holding the door open, he followed me inside with a light touch of his palm on my lower back. My heart leapt into my throat. I pressed a hand to my chest, expecting the panic to hit, instead...

Butterflies took flight in my stomach.

That's new.

After my Day Zero, every new touch became amplified, I had to learn how to react all over again. Exams by doctors, hands of physiotherapists, hugs with friends, kisses from family and... other people. A huge part of communication was non-verbal. Humans touch all the time. Nudges, taps, handshakes. I didn't think twice about most forms of contact anymore.

But butterflies?

Hell, this was a whole different territory.

"Steven? I've brought you a patient," Theo called.

Opposite the door was a metal-framed hospital bed. Hidden behind a tiny desk at the far end of the caravan, sat Steven. Brown peppered hair flopped around his deeply lined, ruddy face.

His broad Welsh accent greeted me. "What do we have here then? Alright, love, have a seat."

He assessed the state of my arms and face while helping me up onto the bed. An experienced manner reassured me I was safe and his voice made me feel at home. I couldn't say the same for the surroundings. It was more a mini ambulance than a caravan, the air so saturated by antiseptic that I wanted to pinch my nose. Shelves full of boxes lined the walls, all labelled for their various purposes. Steven was rummaging through a large box for 'Wound Treatment' when a sudden bleep of a nearby machine sent my pulse rocketing.

I clenched my fists. My breath stopped.

Theo sat beside me, carefully placing a hand on my shoulder. I went rigid but didn't pull away. As the only thing in the room I knew, albeit for under an hour, his calm nature kept my mind anchored in the present.

"I'm guessing for someone who hates hospitals," he whispered, "this place isn't much better?"

I instantly regretted how my voice had risen when rejecting his offer to take me to A&E. This guy didn't miss a trick. "I don't hate them. They just bring back memories."

Noise. That was what I remembered most about being in hospital. So much noise. Chattering staff in the office, patients moaning to doctors, and visitors excitedly bringing gifts to loved ones created a buzz that never ended. Behind that, a hum of equipment, bleeps of heart monitors and Darth Vader wheezing from oxygen tanks. I rarely got more than a few hours of sleep at a time.

Olivia's visits were the only breath of fresh air. She would tell me her stories of weekend adventures and I would imagine being back at home, cosying up on the sofa with fluffy blankets and hot chocolate. Like normal. Perfectly normal. Far away from the agony, away from the nightmares, away from the buzzing and beeping of the hospital. Not having to constantly smile and tell people, 'I'm fine.' (I wasn't fine.)

Thankfully, Steven approached with arms full of supplies before Theo could ask another question.

I'd already said too much.

Day 332
Friday Afternoon

Theo recounted the morning's events to Steven in such a theatrical way that by the end, none of us could speak for laughing.

After disinfecting my face and arms, still chortling, Steven moved onto my hand. I took a deep breath to brace myself as he began methodically checking each joint. Uncomfortable but not horrendous. Until he rotated my wrist. I flinched and ducked my face into Theo's arm, begging my eyes not to water.

Theo's grip on my shoulder tightened. "It's okay, I've got you."

"All done," Steven said not a minute too soon.

I slumped against Theo's side, not fully listening to the explanation about sprains, ice, elevation and painkillers. Exhaustion from the shock had kicked in. My back ached.

"Hey, Lara?" Theo's gentle voice stirred my brain to life. "You still there?"

Steven had stopped talking and was watching me with the look of a concerned parent.

My stomach rumbled as I stood. "Yeah. Sorry. Thank you, Steven. I promise I'll rest it." We each said goodbye.

My next goodbye would be to Theo. A gaping hole opened up

behind my ribs. I wrapped my arms around my middle to stop it from expanding. *I'm hungry.* Nothing more.

"Come on." Theo hopped off the bed. "Let's get out of here. Tea? Coffee?"

The hole closed off again. For a little while at least. "Coffee sounds good." Coffee with Theo sounded even better.

We left the caravan to find the rain had stopped. Bright sunlight lifted swirls of steam from the damp, shimmering ground. I followed Theo past the cabins—main office, security, props—away from the road to a large white tent, the marquee kind people use for weddings, with windows from one end to the other.

"This is the break tent. Fancy, eh?" He showed me toward a leather sofa. "Make yourself comfortable. I'll be right back."

For a tent, it was pretty darn fancy. Carpeted floor, glass coffee tables, spectacular views over the beach. I'd seen the beach before though, so I was more interested in watching Theo. He walked to a drinks machine on the far side with his head and shoulders forward, not hunching, but as if trying to hide his height. A handful of other people were milling around and he replied to their greetings briefly. No jokes or wide laughing smiles. My stomach dropped. He was being overly nice to me, probably because he felt guilty about the accident.

On his return, I accepted the coffee along with a plate of pastries, summoning all my self-control to not wolf down the lot. He fell onto the sofa next to me and pressed a finger to his full, plump, lips—

"Right," he said, snapping me out of my lip-induced trance. "What are we going to do about getting you home?" A raised hand stopped me from interrupting. "Before you say anything, you're not up to driving. Hmm." He drummed his fingers against his mouth again. "Do you have a... someone who could drive you back?"

I didn't want to go home. I wanted to stay right there on the sofa and hear more about the amazing places he'd visited and the people he'd met. But I couldn't tell him that, so I told him about Olivia.

He looked relieved. "Great. You give her a call while I sort out one more thing. Back in a minute." He tapped my knee and hurried out of the tent.

I picked out a croissant and phoned Olivia.

"You sure you're alright?" she asked for the gazillionth time. "Why didn't you call sooner?"

"Sorry, I haven't had a chance." In reality? I supposed I hadn't felt the need. "Oh, and try to stay cool when you get here."

"What d'ya mean?"

"Umm, you'll see."

What I hadn't said was that Theo was in fact Theodore Jackson or that his friends working at the beach were in fact a film crew. She wouldn't have believed me anyway. I wouldn't have believed me. If it weren't for being in public, I would have pinched myself. Several times.

Theo reappeared with a woman whose figure would make Marilyn Monroe jealous.

"Thanks, Liv. Gotta go." I could hear her asking more questions as I hung up.

Theo stopped in front of me, Marilyn next to him. "All sorted?"

"Yep, she'll get a taxi and be here by four. If that's okay?"

"Perfectly." He crouched to my level, sitting on his heels. "Lara, this is"—the words, 'my girlfriend' flew through my mind —"May. She runs the costume department. I told her what happened and being the angel she is, she agreed to help out with some dry clothes."

Calling Olivia wasn't the only thing I'd forgotten about. I looked down at my creased up rag of a skirt and muddy ankle boots. My leather jacket and jumper were still damp and goodness knows what my hair was doing. *Eugh.* As if Theo would look twice at me in my state, or in any state when surrounded by stunningly stylish women like May.

Not that I wanted him to look.

Not at all.

His hand found my shoulder, fingertips blazing against the cool, bare skin of my neck. "I have to get back to work, so I'll leave you in May's capable hands."

I'd never see him again. All good, magically insane and impossible things must come to an end though, right?

As he stood, I said, "Wait!" At the exact same moment, he said, "Lara?"

He offered up a hand. "Ladies first."

"Oh, I just wanted to say thank you and that, umm..." How could I say it was wonderful to meet him and that I wished we had more time together without sounding like a stalker fan?

"Hey, if you want," he said, tilting his head thoughtfully and pocketing his hands, "I'll come back after and give you a tour?"

"Really?" I tried not to sound too eager. The back and forth of him leaving, returning, leaving, spun my head faster than a windmill in a hurricane. "That would be amazing. But, Theo, you don't—"

"Have to?" He finished my sentence with a sparkle in his eye. "Stop rejecting me, Lara, you're making me nervous. You two have fun. I'll see you later."

May and I watched him stride off.

"Follow me, let's see what we can do," she said, breaking the silence and eyeing me up.

Dressed in a perfectly tailored suit, May oozed chic Hollywood glamour, with a few modern twists: Pumps instead of traditional heels and rose streaks woven through her blonde waves.

We headed for the wardrobe cabin further down the field. One hell of a wardrobe. Every inch of space was filled with rails upon rails of clothes, some of which had been gathered into sections, each with a name above. Different actors or characters I guessed.

I couldn't help letting out a gasp when I realised they were Jane Austen-style costumes. "Wow, this is a period drama?" I didn't know where to look next.

"Yes," May confirmed. "I'm afraid I can't say anything else about the show as it's not gone to the press yet."

"Oh, of course." I reined in my excitement. "They're so beautiful, do you make them?"

"Most of them."

She continued to answer my questions in a concise, formal way. After Theo described her as 'an angel,' I had expected her to be a little friendlier.

Offering me a seat, she flicked through nearby rails, asking for details about how I'd met Theo, and about what I normally wore. The more we talked, the more she softened. My answers must have proved I wasn't an undercover reporter sent to dig up information.

"Here." She handed me a bundle of clothes along with an empty bag for my own. "These are perfect for you. Pop them on in the dressing room."

A small curtained off area in a far corner served as the dressing room. The curtains didn't quite reach the sides. I changed as quickly as possible, not easy with a sprained wrist, into some beige chinos and a blush-coloured, cashmere jumper. Their light colours made my fair skin glow, a hint of pink brought out the blue in my eyes and the fit slimmed my waist. *Woah*. If I ever became an actress (extremely unlikely), I'd employ May to dress me every day.

She clapped her hands together as I reappeared. "Told you they were perfect. You look lovely." After ushering me onto a chair, she blow-dried my dark hair back into waves.

I bit the bullet and asked, "Have you known Theo long?"

Her voice returned to its previous, cautious tone. "I've worked with him several times over the years. Why do you ask?"

Stupid curiosity. I tucked my hands between my thighs. "Umm. I don't know really." *Be honest.* "I suppose... he's not what

I expected? He's been so kind, I don't want him to think he has to be though." *Stop rambling.* "It was only an accident."

She thought about my reply for a second. "Theo's always kind. But he's reserved. Keeps to himself. In his position, he has to be careful." The door creaked open. "Speak of the devil."

Theo greeted us with a wave, his smile growing with every step closer. His coat had disappeared, revealing the soft grey jumper below that hugged his body in all the right places. Muscular but lean. Strong but not bulky.

"Lara." He growled my name. "I am finished for the day, which means you have me all to yourself."

My cheeks started emitting enough heat to compete with the sun and a manic grin threatened to spread all over my face. I bit it down.

Theo's eyes darkened with an expression I couldn't decipher. "So..." He exhaled slowly. "Still up for that tour?"

Theo

May caught my elbow to stop me from following Lara. "No games," she warned in a low voice. Her face pinched with worry, tainted by distrust; the same expression I often saw on the faces of my parents.

I patted her hand. "I'm not the person you knew in LA. No games."

We met during my lowest point. Back when I would have taken a bet on how quickly I could pick up a girl and get her back to my place, my car, a nearby alley or any otherwise unoccupied place. The memories made me sick. Only, they didn't feel like my memories. They felt like another one of the dark sided characters I had played, in which I then became trapped. A prisoner inside my own body. It went on for so long that I forgot where I ended and the act began. Now my name was damaged for good.

I hoped taking on this new, gentlemanly role in a sophisticated drama would show another side to me. The real side. Well, closer to the real side at least. Minus the regency clothing, lavish balls and hoity-toity language. Getting to hide out in this secluded corner of the UK was a bonus.

When Lara hadn't recognised me, the chance to start with a clean slate tormented me like a carrot on a stick. Out of reach and out of my control.

Someone like her no doubt steered clear of men with reputations like mine. She had made that clear by rebuffing my questions and ignoring my clumsy attempt to discover her relationship status. *Do you have a... someone?* Come on, I could do better than that.

Apart from when slamming me into a car, her kind of shyness wasn't something I often came across in my confined and flamboyant show-biz world. She hadn't asked any of the usual questions; no selfies or autographs. She barely spoke at all. And yet, that first moment when she had looked at me properly? Trembling with nerves while I treated her cut, crystal drops of rain caught in her long eyelashes... It felt like she had been communicating far more than words. I just needed to learn her language.

I never thought shy would be my type, but with Lara? The less she said, the more I wanted to hear.

And I'd be damned if the way she leaned into me in the first aid van, as though I was her safety net, hadn't awoken some serious caveman-protection instinct.

Was it now curiosity, or a stubborn desire to prove myself that refused to let her leave? Every time I tried, and every time she gave me the opportunity, I looked for another excuse to prolong her stay. I was attached to her by a spring that repeatedly pulled me back.

May disappeared off into her jungle of clothes rails. Lara was struggling to put on her jacket with the new strap around her wrist. My stomach churned. Thank God the accident hadn't been any worse.

Although, I smiled to myself, *I almost feel sorry for any low-life stupid enough to try and mug her.*

I approached and took hold of her collar to help pull the sleeves over her shoulders. An innocent gesture, so I thought, till Lara froze. I let go and hid my hands away before they could do anything else impulsive. "Shall we drop your bag at the car before seeing the set?"

Her small nod filled me with relief. But, was she agreeing to appease me while secretly wishing for a chance to escape? For the life of me, I couldn't read her.

And it drove me wild.

My makeshift tour involved walking the full length of the set —a row of beach huts, tents and an area of cliff face lit by industrial-sized spotlights. Along the way, I pointed out various props, types of cameras and backstage tricks of the trade. It never ceased to amaze me how much went on behind the scenes. I was an insignificant and easily replaceable cog in a massive machine.

We reached a line of short wooden posts joined by tape that marked the perimeter and stepped over. Neither of us spoke as we carried on along the beach. To most people, that might be awkward; practical strangers walking in silence, nothing but faint whooshing of distant waves and our footsteps in the sand.

Strangely, it wasn't.

Lara

I stopped to collect a pebble. Theo watched with a curious, thoughtful frown. It made him look older. Broodingly handsome. Lyrics from Taylor Swift's *Wildest Dreams* replayed through my head. There was *always* a song in my head. They had a habit of popping up at the weirdest of times.

I told him about the large glass jar in my bathroom that contained a pebble or shell from every beach I'd visited. "It's a collection of memories." I pressed a smooth black stone to my palm. "When you open the lid, it smells like the sea."

Taking the stone from me, he held it to his nose, inhaled and smiled. He started to pick out some pearly white shells, passing over any he liked for my approval. By the time we reached a tall dune at the far end of the beach, I had a pocket full of them.

Theo dropped behind to once again place a steadying hand on my lower back as we clambered up. His touch left trails of heat over my skin, a kind of heat I hadn't felt in a long time. Instead of wanting to run, I wanted to curl up and bask in it.

We got to the top of the dune, both out of breath, and looked out at the sparkling ocean spread in a wide curve before us, cradled by an arc of rusty tan sand, darkened from rainwater. Spots of sunlight highlighted random details in the distance, bringing them into brilliant focus like magnifying glasses hanging from the sky. It was one of my favourite places; that's what I was telling Theo when his phone chimed.

He read the message, eyebrows knitted together, mouth set a hard line.

Not a nice message by the look of things.

He pocketed the phone and turned away. "Yes, it is wonderful here." A new edge hardened his voice. Was this the reserved version of him that May knew?

"Theo, are you okay?" No reply, he just looked at me. I shouldn't have been so nosey. "If something's come up and you need to go, it's fine. I don't want to hang around being a nuisance. I'll wait for Liv in my car."

The last thing I wanted was for him to feel stuck with me. Helping me solely because of guilt.

He crossed his arms, deep in thought. I went to apologise again but he asked, "You mean that, don't you?"

I nodded slowly, not quite understanding the question.

His brief, thin smile made him look more lost and saddened than when he frowned. "Most people I've met would milk this accident for everything it's worth rather than worry about my feelings or being an inconvenience. Or worse." He dropped his head in a sigh. "They would outright threaten to sue me and tell the press."

May's comment about 'people in his position' now made sense. I started to see the real reason for her coolness and reluctance to answer questions.

"Then it's a good thing I'm not 'most people,'" I said. "I wouldn't do that. The thought hadn't occurred to me. Although... now you've given me ideas." Nudging his elbow brought back a smile. "Honestly, don't worry. Accidents happen, especially in my job. Last week, I literally tripped over a trip hazard warning sign."

A deep laugh shook his whole body, restoring his light and warmth as instantly as flicking on a gas lamp. I felt rather proud of my achievement.

"You should consider wearing your PPE permanently." He faced me again, a steady gaze wrapping cords of energy around my chest, like Wonder Woman's lasso. I released the tension building in my muscles by sitting down.

"And I know you're not going to sue me," he continued. "I trust you. Even if you are one surprise after another."

I tried not to snort. "Surprise? Me?"

"First of all, you overpowered me." He sat next to me, grinning as if my self-defence moves were something dangerously exciting. "You are polite, except for when you hit me with sarcasm. Clearly, you are intelligent, yet you give very little away. I can't quite make you out."

He dipped his chin to peer up at me through those infamously alluring eyelashes. I dug my hands into the sand to keep them still. I didn't want to be made out. Although, there was a part of me enjoying his efforts.

I rolled my eyes and repeated his previous tease, hoping to snap him out of this seriousness. "Mr Jackson, are you flirting with me?" It worked.

He chuckled. *"'Heaven forbid!'"* The phrase reminded me of something. I couldn't remember what. "Would it be so shocking to you, Lara, if I said, yes?"

A year ago, hearing a man say that would have filled me with a rush of joy and sent my confidence soaring. I might have sat closer, leaned my arm against his. Maybe even left my hand on the ground between us to see if he'd take it. Now, I wanted to burrow myself below the dune.

He had to be teasing me again. Surely?

Having two hands suddenly felt like one more than I could manage. I pushed them deeper into the cool sand. "No? I mean, yes. Huh?" My voice choked and squeaked. "You really must be worried about me suing you."

"You think that is the only reason why I would flirt with you?"

It had to be the only reason. It wasn't worth considering any other reason, because that would mean acknowledging the primal creature stirring in my lower stomach region.

I abruptly got up, flicking sand everywhere. "I should head back."

"Lara, please—" He caught my hand, bringing me to a stop. His grip was warm, firm. I wanted to pull away. I wanted to hold on tighter. "I didn't mean to make you uncomfortable. It's only..."

Silhouetted against the cloudy sky, he stood with one hand kneading his forehead, the other clinging onto mine. Hell, he sure knew how to create a dramatic pause.

"Do you have any idea how long it's been since I met someone and had a normal conversation about normal things?" he asked in a hurried, almost pleading voice. "Or had a conversation that wasn't planned or filmed? How long since someone *genuinely* cared enough to ask me if I was okay?"

Darkness crept over his face. Theo's moods and expressions shifted direction as easily as long grass was blown by the wind. It took all of my attention to keep up, to work out when he was teasing, when a smile was just a smile or when it could mean something else.

It must have been his job that gave him the confidence to express himself so openly. On the other hand, I wasn't sure if confidence was a skill you could learn.

Goodness knows I'd tried.

Day 332
Friday Evening

My phone pinged. Theo let go of my hand as we walked silently down the dune.

"Liv's nearly here." I passed on the message to Theo, who tipped his head in acknowledgement, half-smiling at the ground.

I didn't want the day to end with an uncomfortable silence like this. *Be brave.* I plastered on a smile. "Should I be worried about how you consider the way we met and our conversations as being normal, Theo?"

His shoulders relaxed. "I don't make a habit of knocking over pretty women in car parks if that's what you're implying."

Pretty? "Look. I'm sorry. I overreacted."

"No, I was too forward. Here I am trying to prove myself, then I go and— I am an idiot." He shrugged, head down, hands back in his pockets. "Old habits die hard."

So the rumours about his 'old habits' were true then.

Nothing of what I'd heard matched up with the man in front of me. Yes, he was confident, but so were most people compared to me nowadays. His open and blunt honesty occasionally caught me off guard. Sure, he could be a little forward. He'd also been incredibly kind and humble. The real reason for my caution had nothing to do with *his* past. I didn't want him to blame himself for my erratic behaviour.

"We all have things in our past that we'd like to change," I said, keeping my voice steady by concentrating on the words themselves, rather than on the event to which they referred. "I think it's more important who you're trying to be. And who you want to be in the future." I threw him a quick grin. "If I thought you were an idiot, Theo, I wouldn't have let you get in my car. You know I'm capable of stopping you. If I'd wanted to."

"Hmm, yes. More than capable, Miss Quinn, 007." He returned my grin and stretched out a hand to help me over a stream that ran from the river out to sea. "It's okay, I've got you."

Every time he said that line, it caused an avalanche of my internal organs. Three times so far.

Not that I was counting.

After we stepped over the water, Theo held onto my hand for slightly longer than necessary.

♫

Olivia fired off a machine gun list of questions the moment she saw me. Her interrogation ended once she was confident I'd survive my injuries.

"When you said there'd been an accident, I was so worried, hun," she said, gripping my fingers. "Like *it* was happening all over again."

I quickly shushed her by pulling her into a hug. Theo hung back while she greeted me, but I didn't want to risk him overhearing anything. "I'm okay, I promise. There's someone I want you to meet."

Brushing the fine golden hair from her face, I put my good arm around her waist and swung aside to reveal Theo. It rendered her speechless. Not something that happened very often.

Seeing the shock in her wide, watery eyes, Theo stepped up.

"Pleasure to meet you, Olivia. Sorry to be the cause of so much worry."

They shook hands. Or at least, Theo did. Olivia's arm fell limp, so he basically held her hand for an awkward second.

I swallowed a giggle. "Liv, this is Theo. He's the one who, umm, bumped into me."

She turned her head to speak to me but kept her eyes on Theo, whispering through a sugary smile. "I know who he is!"

Three people emerged from the break tent and headed our way. One of the men waved at me and called out to Theo, "Is this the poor girl you attacked?"

Theo's laugh sounded more like one of my flustered coughs. "Discreet as always, Tom."

Tom had baby blonde hair, boyish looks, and more skipped than walked, but as he got closer the soft crinkles around his eyes gave his age away. Late thirties at a guess.

After a playful slap on Theo's shoulder, he gave us an energetic welcome and introduced his companions as Becca—who I recognised as an actress—and Mason. Judging by the period costume Mason wore, he was also an actor. Or a time traveller.

"You're locals," Tom wondered, "so you'd know a good place to get a drink round here? We ain't had chance to explore yet."

Olivia answered for us, "Sure. Depends what you like. If you want something swanky, you'd have to go into the city. If you don't mind a country pub then our favourite place is down the road. It's like, tiny and quiet, but there's a big log fire." She started giving him directions.

A hand touched the spot between my shoulder blades. I instinctively crossed my arms around my waist and inhaled a sharp breath. Spice and earth filled my lungs.

Theo

Lara had withdrawn, tucking herself away behind her friend. Trying to hide in the shadows.

"Is everything okay?" I asked, reaching out to her.

She nodded sharply. "Uh-huh. Fine. We should probably get out of your hair." Her long fingers gripped the sleeves of her coat, white with tension.

In the short time of knowing her, I already had the impression that whenever she used the word 'fine,' it meant anything but. I lifted my hand off her back.

Following some of her previous reactions, I should have known not to touch her. *Dammit.* The first girl I had met in years with whom I could have a serious conversation, and I had blown it. If I kept slipping back into my old act, how would I ever prove I had changed? That I *wanted* to change? Perhaps the press was right and I deserved every damning line they had ever written about me for being so senseless.

And yet... I couldn't give up.

I smiled at Lara. "No need to rush. Hey, Tom," I added, "rather than get us all lost, why don't we ask them to join us?"

Lara glanced up at me, big blue eyes flashing with green. Oceans catching the sun.

She hadn't wanted my help originally. What if she really had been waiting for this chance to leave, too polite to tell me to get lost? I cautiously stepped closer, praying to be wrong, and lowered my voice. "I was too forward earlier. Perhaps now I am not being forward enough. I enjoy your company and would like you to come for a drink with us. With me."

She matched my gaze for longer than ever before, weaving a curl of hair around her fingers, thinking. I still couldn't interpret her expressions. Reading minds was an ability I had never wished for. Till now.

As though enjoying our peculiar staring contest, her smile

gradually returned. Finally, she nodded and repressed a laugh by sinking her teeth into her bottom lip.

My lungs grew uncomfortably large. Either that or my ribs had shrunk.

Lara

Theo's head tipped to the side. "You have to stop doing that," he said, eyes dropping to my mouth, voice dropping to a rumble.

The quieter he spoke, the deeper it reached inside me.

I blinked in surprise. "Doing what?"

His eyes lifted back to mine and with a cat-who-got-the-cream swagger, he excused himself to fetch a coat. I'm no expert, but I think he was flirting again.

Definitely. Possibly?

Olivia turned on me within seconds. "What was that?" Her jaw hung so low I worried it was broken.

I shrugged.

She glared at me. "Durr. You and Theo. What's going on?"

"Nothing. I... It's been a long day, I'll tell you later."

Before she could object, Tom reappeared with May. It turned out she was Tom's wife. They were telling us about how they met on the set of his first acting job when the others returned. While Mason and Becca filled Theo in on the afternoon's filming progress, he nodded along, asking questions, eyes repeatedly flicking in my direction.

Olivia took the lead along the narrow lane that headed inland, through the woodland running alongside the river. Tom quizzed her on all of the best places to visit, from castles and towns to bars and beaches.

May joined me at the back, linking an arm in mine. "Glad to see you again," she said, "Sorry for prejudging you earlier. I shouldn't have done that."

I was happy to no longer be under suspicion. "I get it. Theo has to be careful." I wanted to ask why she also thought he was reserved. I didn't.

Black velvet of a darkening sky draped itself over the hills into the sea. The only light came from a soft orange glow of street lamps and a sprinkling of stars broken free from their cloudy prisons. Stepping into the pub with its candles and fire burning brought on the same response from each of our group—a shoulder shake and rubbing of hands together—before heading for the table nearest the fire. Apart from the bartender and an older couple, we had the place to ourselves.

I'd been to The Cwtch more times than I could count with friends. Cwtch was Welsh for a special, loving sort of cuddle, and that was exactly what the place felt like. We liked the cosiness. There wasn't any loud music like in modern bars, so you didn't have to shout to have a conversation. It helped that the owner and his family who worked there were lovely, and the local drinks were cheap. Looking around at the rough stone walls and threadbare rugs, I realised how shabby it must have seemed to our guests. They were probably used to fine dining restaurants and the type of exclusive clubs in London that had guest lists and valets. The kind that Daniel loved. The kind I hated.

Gravitating to my favourite tweed-covered armchair by the fireside, I settled down and took off my coat. Theo pulled another armchair from a second table so he could sit next to me, although there were clearly enough seats for everyone on the other side of the fire. My butterflies returned. The imprint of his hand still pulsed on my back.

Tonight, the owner's oldest son, Ioan, was the bartender. We'd known each other for years. He bounded over when he saw us. "Hiya, Liv, Lara, how's it going? The usual?"

Olivia replied for both of us and requested menus. Ioan returned quickly and by the look on his face, was trying to figure out why the new visitors seemed familiar.

I took a menu. "Diolch, Ioan."

"Dee-olk?" Theo carefully copied the Welsh word.

"It means thank you."

I tried not to giggle as he repeated it, his mouth contorting in an attempt to mimic the new throaty sounds. We started going through other words, place names and how to pronounce different letters. Every time he laughed, he touched my shoulder or my arm and for a few jittery seconds, my voice leapt an octave higher.

"How come you know the language yet hardly have an accent?" he asked.

Be honest. I had to talk about myself at some point. "I grew up here so learned Welsh at school. After college, I got an apprenticeship in London. I guess the accent slipped. I only came back last year."

Oops. I'd left the way open for him to ask why I moved back. I changed the subject.

Over the following hours, our group relaxed into a natural chatter, bursts of laughter here and there at Tom and May's tales of being in 'the industry' with all its backstage antics. Even Ioan joined us, engrossed in a rugby debate with Mason. Becca was the only one not entirely comfortable. She rarely engaged with anyone. Except for Theo. I spotted her making excuses to talk to him, trying to get closer. *Who needs help carrying two glasses?* Theo was never rude, but each time he swiftly returned to the chair by my side, I hid my smile. I had no reason to be smiling.

Multiple drinks and several shared bowls of cheesy chips later, May yawned. "Guys, I hate to be boring and old, but we have a very early start tomorrow."

Everyone murmured their agreement. Ioan cleared the table.

Theo helped me again with my coat and my heart rate responded the same as it had the first time: as if he was *un*dressing me. The way his eyes never left mine... Etta James started singing in my head. That seductive, soulful song used in the old Coke adverts —*I Just Wanna Make Love To You.*

My thoughts were way out of control. I'd been seeing things all night that couldn't possibly be real. Heat in Theo's eyes, appraising glances my way when he thought I wasn't looking (I was always looking), half-hidden smiles every time we touched. Nope, not possibly real.

Ioan tapped my shoulder as we were leaving. "See you tomorrow then? Full band back together! It's gonna be amazing."

I peeked behind me to where Theo waited, leaning on the doorframe, one eyebrow raised, an inquisitive smirk on his lips.

"I'm not sure," I answered Ioan. "I don't play much anymore."

He tucked a pen into his Gareth Bale style man-bun. "That's too bad. Folks here have all missed you."

Like many of the locals, Ioan knew the real reason why I'd moved home.

"Thanks," I said, touched by his genuine care. "Maybe I'll come to watch. Send my love to your family."

I ducked under Theo's arm into the cold night. The others had already started walking up the lane, leaving us behind.

"Sooo?" Theo hummed, staying close to my side, our arms brushing together. "Do I sense another surprise coming?"

"I don't know. Do you?" Either it was the alcohol fuelling my newfound courage, or Theo's confidence was catching. Skipping a step ahead, I turned to face him, walking backwards. "I didn't peg you as an eavesdropper, Mr Jackson. I'll add it to your list of talents."

"I have a list?"

I narrowed my eyes. "Don't get excited. It's a small list."

"Hmm, so I'm 'not such a bad actor' with a 'small list' of talents?" He made bunny ear gestures in the air to exaggerate the quotes. "Damn. I didn't peg you as being such a harsh critic. I shall work harder in future." He flashed a smile, flicked his eyelashes. "I like a challenge."

It was difficult to walk, especially backwards, when his playful tone turned my knees to jelly. The last thing I wanted to do was fall over in front of him. *Again*. As I returned to his side, I could have sworn his hand reached for mine, only to be pulled away and shoved into a pocket at the last second. Fortunately, the darkness obscured my blushing.

"Sooo?" he coaxed again. "You are in a band? Or are you going to make me turn up tomorrow to find out?"

A million volts shot down my spine at the idea of seeing him again. "It's not anything that exciting." *Why the hell am I talking him out of it?* "Olivia's brother and a few friends have a band, they play here every month or so just for fun. Covers of popular stuff, rock classics, some old jazz. Whatever people request or we fancy having a go at really."

"And you used to play with them? Musician or singer?"

"I play the piano. If they're desperate I'll sing, but I'm not great."

"Modesty," he said, gently bumping his arm to mine, sending feathers dancing across my skin. "Another thing to add to *your* list. I told you: one surprise after another."

He didn't ask why I'd stopped playing. Throughout the day, Theo's careful questions—sometimes a lack of them completely—felt deliberate and considered. One thing I'd learned over the last year was that the most common response to any statement was 'why' or 'how come?' Hence the reason I hated talking about myself. Had Theo picked up on my self-consciousness? Or was he simply not that interested?

Not that I wanted him to be interested, of course.

Back at the car, May insisted I keep the clothes and Tom, with a parting wink in Theo's direction, said he hoped to see me again soon. I pretended not to notice it, or the way it turned my palms clammy.

Theo hugged Olivia and thanked her for coming to fetch me. Would he hug me, too? Should I go arms over his shoulders? Or down, around his waist? Oh hell. *Don't be weird.* I waited behind, stretching out every last second, running through song lyrics, frantically thinking of what to say. I didn't want to say goodbye.

"I'll like, go and get the car warmed up." Olivia grinned, as subtle as always. She may as well have said, *'I'll leave you two alone.'*

Theo stepped closer as she walked away, trying to hide his amusement by rubbing a hand down his face.

I wound the cuff of my jacket through my fingers. "I don't know where to start, or how to thank you, Theo."

"Please, don't." Another step closer. "You seem to be forgetting about this." He lifted my strapped wrist. I dropped my jacket and let my fingers slide over his hand.

Closer still, Theo began tracing the lines on my palm. "You were incredibly brave the way you tackled me. And the way you handled yourself with Steven. I twisted my ankle not long ago and yelled. A lot."

He held my hand so carefully, I felt like a priceless heirloom. *Breathe, Lara.* "Oh, it's nothing, don't worry. I've felt worse." I shuddered, my voice breaking as a memory seeped through a crack in my walls. Blocking it off, I carried on, "Despite the umm, rocky start, honestly, today was amazing. I love period dramas. So to see behind the scenes and have a guided tour from a"—*Kind? Hot? Fascinating?*—"talented actor, has been a dream come true."

"Ah, so I do have at least one useful talent on my small list."

He continued to draw invisible circles onto my skin, inching closer, a chuckle rumbling in his chest, treacle eyes trickling over my face and settling on my mouth. For a heart-pounding second, I saw where the bad-boy rumours came from. Theo's presence was so powerful and enveloping, all I could feel was him. If the world began exploding, we wouldn't have noticed.

He held me captive and I wanted to be his prisoner.

My senses were entranced by his looks, smell, sound, touch. And maybe, if I wanted it—taste.

All I had to do was lift my chin.

"Well then," he said, low and breathy, "while I'm on a roll of making your dreams come true, is there... anything else?"

Hell yes.

Heat erupted under my skin.

But, just as I was getting used to the physical contact, my double-crossing mind screamed, '*You're not ready for this!*' My mind and body were always at odds. Did they have to pick this exact second to fight? I told my brain to shut up.

Theo's breath swept my skin. Our noses touched.

Cold, shivering panic extinguished the heat in my veins.

Be brave. He was being forward again, but it wasn't him I was afraid of.

Be honest. I pushed up onto tiptoes to whisper in his ear, "I'm sure there is, but I'm not that kind of girl, Mr Jackson."

The effect of my touch made his chest expand and lips part. His grip on my hands tightened. I kissed his cheek, pulled away, and before I could change my mind, hurled myself toward the car.

Olivia scowled as I climbed in. "What are yo—"

"Just go, please."

Her face softened. The engine groaned into life.

I allowed myself to look back as we started to move. Theo stood exactly where I'd left him, shadowy in the night light, holding my gaze until we turned a corner, out of sight.

Wildest Dreams – Taylor Swift

Day 333
Saturday

The coffee pot was already full and Olivia was already sitting on one of the barstools next to it by the time I got up. She pushed a steaming mug along the counter toward me, her head cocked in a look of *'come on then, spill the beans.'*

Last night, I'd hardly said a word on the journey home. I think I'd gone into shock. So now, I spilt the beans, hoping the day would make more sense out loud. Nope. Describing the connection I'd felt with Theo made me sound absurd. Chemistry only happened in books or films. Real-life didn't work the same.

"Who says it doesn't?" Olivia argued. "It's rare, but not everyone can like, survive what you did either, but that happened." Her logic was odd, but I knew what she meant. "So anyway, we got back to the car and...?"

I flexed my fingers, still able to feel Theo's hands around mine while I replayed our last conversation. The static of his touch gliding over my palm, the electricity jumping between us. Just thinking about it made me flutter all over again.

I sighed into my empty cup. "I read it all wrong."

"No way." Olivia beamed. "Trust me, hun. From where I was sitting, he leaned in. He *more* than leaned in."

I knew she'd been spying on us. "Argh, then why didn't I kiss him? I'm crazy."

"Would you kiss any other guy the day you met him?"

Before Day Zero? Yes.

After? "No."

"There you are then. I'm proud of you for sticking to your moral guns. Then again..." She poured us both another coffee and wrapped an arm around my shoulders. "This is Theodore Jackson, the rich and famous, gorgeous stud we're talking about, so yeah, you're a nutcase."

My forehead sunk onto the counter.

She giggled and gave me another squeeze. "Look at the positives, hun. It was good to see you so chilled out. I've missed you, Laa-Laa."

As a child, she always called me Laa-Laa—yup, as in the chubby yellow Teletubbie—and the name stuck. Truth was, I missed the old Laa-Laa too.

Olivia slapped her hands on her knees. "No more hiding from now on, let's have fun tonight!"

The rest of the day dragged painfully like nails on a chalkboard. I added the shells Theo had found into my jar and stared at them, going over what I could have said or done better. I kicked myself for the cheesy jokes. And for not kissing Theo. Especially for not kissing Theo.

The old Lara would have. *'What are you afraid of?'* She would have said. *'If you like him, then what is there to think about?'* She would have made yesterday count.

I wasn't that kind of girl anymore.

But with Theo, maybe I could have been. If I'd tried extra hard. For a day.

Possibly a weekend.

♫

My house was full to bursting when the band met that evening. Guitars covered the sofas. Speakers and wires snaked across the floors. Plus there were the band members themselves: Olivia's older brother Greg (drummer) was lying on the faux sheepskin rug next to the coffee table, tapping out a rhythm on the leg of his girlfriend Sarah (lead singer). She sat crossed legged, oblivious to being used as a human drum kit, while combing a delicious smelling oil through her hair. Alex (bassist) had his head in a music book, and Caleb (lead guitarist) was huffing and grunting while trying to untangle a pile of cables.

Olivia announced to the room that I would be coming to the gig. "Operation Get-Back-Out-There starts now," she sang.

Everyone stopped to listen when I asked what she was on about.

"I'm on about you having fun, Laa-Laa. You never know"— she grinned and wiggled her hips—"he might be there." That statement sparked more questioning from the others. "Just this unbelievable guy she met yesterday who was like, *totally* into her," Olivia explained, flipping glossy hair over her shoulders.

"Since when do we live in a teen rom-com, Liv?" I mimicked her exaggerated American drawl. "He was not '*totally*' into me at all. Oh and thanks," I added on my way to the kitchen, "I'll never have any secrets with you around. You may as well tell them everything now."

"Don't worry," she whispered as I passed, "I won't give *all* the details." She may have had some annoying little sister-like ways, but Olivia knew me and knew where to draw the line.

Waiting for the kettle to boil, I kept telling myself she was being ridiculous. Theo wouldn't be at the gig. The idea lit a fatal hope in my chest. Every time I tried to blow it out, it came back brighter. Another thing I kicked myself for was not having the guts to invite him.

My brain began concocting ways to 'accidentally' bump into

him on set. *I could start jogging.* That could be an excuse for being at the beach every day.

Hell, I missed the old Laa-Laa.

I wished I knew how to get her back.

♪

I don't remember officially agreeing to go to the gig, but I ended up dressed and getting in the car anyway. I wore my best jeans, a shimmery blouse, and my favourite red lipstick. Not for Theo but because well... it had been ages since I'd been on a night out. Olivia was right; it was about time. I'd never reach my goal of rejoining the band if I couldn't even face walking into a crowded pub.

This was another step on the road back to Normalville.

Every Saturday night, local bands descended on The Cwtch, transforming it from our sleepy hideaway into an explosion of life and sound. We pulled up outside and began unloading Caleb's van. Thanks to my wrist, I got put in charge of 'the light stuff.' Tracking backwards and forwards, we walked each piece of equipment from the lane through a small side gate, ducking under the cherry blossoms that surrounded it, into a courtyard garden at the back where a small stage was set up. Large bi-fold doors had been opened, connecting this area to the cosy lounge room.

Excitement grew audibly among the waiting audience. A buzz ran through my fingertips as memories of performing here came flooding back. The thought of doing it again turned the buzz into shivers.

Familiar faces caught my eye, some people came to ask how I was doing and awkwardly welcomed me home. Others exchanged hushed whispers behind raised hands. I cleared my throat and kept my head down.

"Great to have you with us." Greg crouched next to me on the stage to plug in the last guitar. "If you wanna join in, we could do with some backing vocals on a few tracks? Have a think about it, yeah?" With a pat on my head, he disappeared to arrange his drums.

I loved my friends so much for not giving up on me and for all the times they forgave me when I snapped or pushed them away. They really had missed me. It broke my heart to see how difficult the last year must have been for them too. I was a changed person, but they'd accepted me back without question. Still, they sometimes watched me with timid expressions, waiting for me to break down at any minute.

Olivia and I pulled a small table into a corner at the side of the stage where we sang and danced along in safety, away from the main crowd. My Day Zero injuries were healed, but I'd been left with a weak spot in my lower back and stomach muscles that ached if I did too much. I didn't particularly want to find out how a blow from a stray elbow would feel.

Halfway through, I caught a glimpse of a tall, dark-haired man. The air simmered in my chest. I held my breath as he turned... it wasn't Theo. It was never *going* to be Theo. I'd let myself hope and hope was twisting my insides up.

With my track record, I should have known better.

Dancing mellowed into head bobbing as the evening slowed down. The band finished off the pop songs and moved on to folk and rock ballads. Caleb wowed everyone with his timeless Bryan Adams, *Everything I Do* guitar solo. Greg urged me to join in again when they came to the last song. Jenny's voice and the DAYS motto ran through my head. With a push—literally—from Olivia, I approached the stage.

Sarah saw me coming and screamed, "Laa-Laa's back!"

Ioan and his family, along with some of the crowd, cheered my name. Threatening tears stung my eyes. Far too many people recognised me for my liking.

"We got this," Sarah said firmly, holding out a microphone. No arguments.

I grinned back to kick start some adrenaline and wiped my sweaty, trembling fingers on my jeans. "Hell yeah."

Caleb roared into the opening riff of ACDC's *Highway To Hell*. He always liked to go out on a high.

♪

"That was amazing!" I croaked. Olivia and the band crushed me inside a massive bear hug on the stage. My hands shook with excitement, my cheeks were flushed from smiling and my throat was raw. "Oh wow, I can't breathe. Thank you so much for this, guys."

We started to pack up, randomly bursting into song followed by fits of giggles.

Movement in the corner of my eye sent my heart racing. I squinted through the darkness to see a man in a baseball cap leaning against the stone wall, half-hidden under the shadow of the cherry tree, watching me as the audience drifted away. He stepped forward into the faintest patch of light, nodded toward the gate, and walked out. High cheekbones, square jawline, long floating strides; it was him. It had to be him! My body knew it before I did. That nod? He wanted me to follow. Without a second thought, I dropped the cable I'd been winding up and ran for the gate.

The lane was empty. *What? I'm losing it.*

A long week, finished off by the sudden sprint had taken its toll. My good for nothing muscles seized up. I felt ancient. Combined with that, my disappointment made me want to collapse on the floor. I bent double, clamping my hands around my waist.

That was when I heard it. An unforgettable voice, like distant rumbling thunder. "Looking for someone?"

"Theo?" I spun around to find him tucked behind the gate and gasped, half in surprise, half due to the throb developing in my back. I covered my mouth to hide a grimace.

"I didn't mean to startle you." He took a step closer. "Car parks are dangerous places." Although hidden by shadow, I could tell he was smiling. "I had to see you again, Lara, so I thought it was worth the risk of being tackled."

I'd convinced myself his good looks had been exaggerated by my wayward mind, but good grief, he was gorgeous. I remained speechless, shivering, panting through the twinges of pain in my side.

Walking nearer, Theo tilted his cap back, carefully keeping the collar of his coat up. "I wanted to say hello sooner, but it's a lot busier here than I expected. Hey, you were fantastic. Your voice is —" His smile dissolved.

Only a foot separated us now. Even under the dim street lights, I must have looked pale. Blood drained sickeningly from my face, my hands were cold.

"Lara, what's wrong?" He drew me into a hug, the comforting way an old friend would. I didn't have the strength or the will to pull away. For some people, making contact came so easily, so naturally. I bet the feel of my head and shoulders pressing into his firm chest didn't even register with him.

"You're shaking," he said quietly into my hair.

My arms hung limply at my sides as I inhaled his earthy skin and log-smoke scented clothes. I wanted to hold him, close my eyes and rest my aching body against his.

"Sorry, I'm fine." My lie was muffled by his wool coat. "It's all the singing, dancing, and running. It's stitch, that's all." Pain easing, I tore myself away, made an effort to stand up straight and slapped on my smiling mask.

Theo squinted. He wasn't easily fooled. But, after a second of examining me, he must have decided not to ask any further questions because he said, "It appears *you* are the celebrity around here."

"Ha. Me? No." My head shook more frantically than a nodding dog on a potholed road. "Welsh people are like that. Very friendly. Everyone knows everyone. People talk." I lied again. Not completely. Not the whole truth either.

Google my name and the first results were about my job and my social media profiles. But you only had to scroll to the bottom of the page to find old news articles and court case reports about my Day Zero. From there it didn't take a genius to work out that the 'Lara Quinn, Head of Design at David Clarke Construction' and the 'Lara Quinn, only surviving victim of The London Stabber' were the same person. And unfortunately, people *did* talk. Privacy was a luxury that had been stolen. A feeling, it occurred to me, that Theo would probably understand.

I needed to change the subject. To buy time, I walked a few paces to sit on a low wall at the edge of the road. Theo followed.

"Did you always want to be an actor?" I asked, resorting back to my tactical questions. It never failed.

Theo propped one foot up on the wall, arms resting on the raised knee, and told about being at University in London. He got offered a part in a local film after being spotted in a play. A play he'd only been in because of losing a bet to friends.

"Talk about a lucky break!" I said. "So you weren't studying acting then?" Another question. Anything to keep him talking.

He explained his original plan to follow in his father's footsteps and become a doctor. But he felt the acting opportunity was too good to miss.

"The rest is history," he said, lowering his leg to take a step closer.

Each centimetre of space between us hummed. I was a radar, tuned into the position of his body, the frequency becoming louder and higher the nearer he got.

"I finished my first year but never ended up going into psychology after all," he concluded.

"Psychology?" I sounded more surprised than I felt.

"Yes." He nodded, lifting his cap to run a hand through his hair. "It's always fascinated me. Perhaps that's why I enjoy acting and the whole process of getting into a character's mind, understanding the roots behind behaviours."

"I think you'd make a good psychologist..." I let my sentence fade off, too shy to explain the theory.

He was cool under pressure, perceptive and soothing. Although, I wasn't sure his looks would be an advantage. If I was ever his patient, I'd be too nervous to speak. One look at his face and I forgot how to.

"Hmm." He pouted, a cheeky glint back in his eye. "You think so?"

"Oh, it's just... the way you stayed calm when I panicked and attacked you, it's like, sometimes, you know what I'm thinking." And feeling. Which terrified me. And intrigued me.

Mostly terrified.

A half-laugh, half-sigh fluttered out of Theo's lips and landed on my skin, sending sparks, well, everywhere. "I love watching body language. It's incredible how much you can learn to see between the lines." It was obviously a passion; his gestures became as animated as his voice. "Usually, I'm fairly good at reading people. For instance"—in one stride, he crossed the gap and sat next to me—"you don't like showing any weakness, so you hide it behind a smile and clenched fists. Yet for some reason I can't understand, you are equally embarrassed about the fearless way you defended yourself yesterday."

Heated butterflies churned in my stomach. He was close enough that his thigh touched mine and I could see every faint crease of movement on his face.

He rubbed a hand down the back of his neck as his eyes found my mouth. "You also bite your lip when you're nervous. Or perhaps... perhaps it's more when you're holding something back?" In an unconscious movement, his hand lifted toward my lips.

I jammed my hands under my thighs as my body shuddered at

the thought of being touched somewhere so intimate. Startled by my overreaction, he blinked and laced his fingers over his knee.

He noticed *every*thing. Like I was naked, my DNA on show for him to read. I dreaded to think what he'd seen between my lines during that minor meltdown. I wanted to disappear, to erase everything he knew about me and start again, but then what would I replace it with?

I knew exactly what I'd replace it with—the old me. The pre-day-zero me who didn't bite her lip, who never went shy, who didn't have the occasional urge to punch people when they got too close.

Theo looked away, a line deepening between his brows, the look of someone who'd just received devastating news. "I can't imagine anything worse than knowing what people are thinking," he said mournfully. "Being able to hear what they thought of you without cameras and scripts. The realisation of how many people you trust are lying to you. Or saying what they think you want to hear. I am happy to be blissfully ignorant."

It must have been awful, living in constant doubt of people's motives behind their interest in you. I wanted to help him. I wasn't sure how. My own emotions were kept in a locked box, buried behind a city of walls. The only way I could speak about them was by detaching myself, imagining I was talking about someone or something else.

I needed to try, or at the very least, apologise.

I couldn't fully empathise with his being famous around the world, but I did know what it was like to put on an act, to practice what to say until it sounded natural. And how it was possible to feel completely alone while surrounded by people.

When Jenny and Andrew first approached me about their charity for victims of violent crime, I'd tried to fob them off with excuses. The last thing I wanted was another room full of strangers asking about my feelings. "Thanks, I'm fine, I don't need a support group," I'd told them. Ironic, seeing as how at the time, I couldn't get out of the hospital bed without someone to support me.

"We understand," Andrew replied, his round face as smiley as ever, even though I'd essentially told them to go away. "You're recovering well. It may be though, that down the line, you might want help moving forward, like getting back home or into work?"

I nodded begrudgingly for him to carry on, then let my mind drift. I wasn't bothered about 'moving forward.' I just wanted to be able to move, full stop. Anywhere.

Jenny took up the story of DAYS when Andrew had finished. "Everyone in the group has faced an event, a Day Zero when our lives were drastically changed. But this can be a new start. A chance to be brave, be honest, and to make all the days that follow count."

On the surface, she'd seemed a placid lady with a kind smile, but as she told me her own story, I saw a strength and determination buried within. She was twenty-six when her life had changed. She'd been attacked while walking through a park on her way home from work. It could have ended so differently if not for a passing dog walker. In those days, when a woman was assaulted the way she'd been, it was often kept quiet. Seen as something to be ashamed of. As if it was her fault.

Jenny had seen through my smiling mask to the pain hidden underneath. Not because she'd read my files, but because she'd worn the same mask. Felt the same pain. With her, there was no point pretending.

"Not everyone is the same," I gently reminded Theo, keeping my eyes on an ant crawling up the wall near my feet. "I know what it's like to be treated differently because of something out of your control. But there'll always be someone you can rely on. Sometimes, it just takes a while to find them or to work out who they are."

Relief flickered over Theo's face. He stayed quiet, long enough for the ant to climb next to my hand. Now and then, it would slide back down as the stone surface crumbled beneath. But it continued to struggle and keep moving. Silently, I cheered the little guy on.

"You really are one surprise after another, Miss Quinn."

I looked up to find Theo staring at me, chin perched on his fingers, in a way that made me blush furiously.

"Argh no." I shrugged. "I'm the one surprised. I mean, it's really you! Have you been here the whole time?"

"I assure you it's me and yes, I have." He laughed but quickly muted it, pulled his cap back down and collar back up, obviously wanting to stay incognito.

The disguise must have worked. I didn't see how. Surely he stood out in any crowd? Not only because of his height. He moved with such a determined sort of elegance. When he smiled, radiant energy flowed over his skin like the northern lights. You'd never guess that secretly, he worried so much about people's opinions.

"I am impressed." He nodded slowly, lips pursed around an invisible straw. "Your band is extremely talented and has great taste in music."

I batted away his compliment with an eye roll. "It's not *my* band, but I agree. They're amazing. I still can't believe you actually came."

"Well, it seems I'm not great with rejection. And after the way you left me yesterday..."

I pressed my face into my hands.

He chuckled before carefully taking hold of my arms, lowering them so he could look at me. "I haven't been able to stop thinking about you, Lara."

Parts of my body (hopefully not anything vital) disintegrated.

I shook my head at the floor. "I don't know what came over me. I panicked. You've probably noticed that I do stupid things when I panic. Sorry." *Stupid, stupid, stupid.*

A beat passed as he glanced down at his hands encircling my

arms. "Can I tell you something? Don't take this the wrong way, but please stop apologising. I should not have been so forward again. I warned you: I am an idiot. Don't make the mistakes I did and get pushed into thinking or behaving a certain way. You're not that kind of girl, and that's not stupid. It's—" He paused. I tried to guess his next words. *Uptight? Old fashioned?* "Attractive."

I bit back the impulse to giggle like a tipsy lunatic. Not quite so attractive.

Theo's breathing deepened. A muscle twitched in his jaw, eyelashes casting sweeping shadows over his cheeks.

He was now holding my hands.

When Greg called me from the gate, I didn't know whether we'd been sitting there for ten seconds or ten years. It felt like an important moment. Why though... *hang on*, I hadn't flinched! Theo was well and truly in my space, *touching* me, but I didn't want to run away or hit him.

We both stood and took a step apart as Greg approached, which wouldn't have looked suspicious in the slightest. Theo released my hands to check his cap. I assured him he was safe, although I may have spoken too soon.

"Alright, Lara?" Greg said, slipping into big-brother protection mode. His voice sounded unnaturally deep and his Welsh accent had gone weirdly cockney gangster.

"Yeah, no problems. I just, I umm—" I stalled, unsure if Theo would want anyone else to know he was here. I glanced up, telepathically asking him what to do.

Theo answered by turning to Greg and holding out a hand. "Hey, nice to meet you. I was just telling Lara how impressed I am with your band."

Greg's tough guy act vanished, he shook Theo's hand like he'd been handed a winning lottery ticket. "Hi, wow. Thanks, man. That means a lot. Wow. I'm a fan of your stuff too. Wow." Greg was in fact a *huge* fan. His battle to remain calm showed through his fidgeting feet. "We're all gonna head off now. Unless you two wanna get a drink, yeah?" He nodded hopefully toward Theo.

"Thank you, but I can't. It's a clear forecast tomorrow so we have another early start to catch some sunrise shots."

My heart deflated. We were going to have to say goodbye all over again. *If I borrow someone's dog, that would be another good excuse for walking up and down the beach...*

"That sounds fun," I said, hiding my disappointment. "Apart from getting up at five a.m."

Theo turned his attention to me. "Precisely, so I should get going. After you put your number in here." He passed me his phone.

When I ran from the stage, I must have fallen and hit my head or fainted and this was all a hallucination because if Theo wanted my number, it meant he wanted to see me again, right?

I looked at the decision in the form of a shiny block of metal, plastic and computer chips in my hand. My fingers went numb. Was I seriously doing this?

You bet I was.

Taking the phone back, Theo called the new number until we heard music coming from my back pocket. Taylor Swift, of course.

"Just checking you weren't trying to dodge me again." Theo winked.

"Oh, as if I'd do that to you."

"Hmm." He did that one eyebrow, one-sided smile thingy. "Goodnight, Lara."

Floaty bubbles filled my body and popped all over my skin when he kissed my cheek. I watched his back fade into the darkness until I remembered Greg was still standing behind me. He stared at the hand Theo had shaken.

"You okay there, Greg?"

"I always wondered what you girls meant by swoon-worthy. But, Laa-Laa." He exhaled a high-pitched, dreamy sigh, then looked up at me with a devilish grin. "I think I just swooned."

If I'd had my bag, I would have swung it at him.

♪

Five of us were squashed into Olivia's car on the way home when Greg brought up meeting Theo. It took him ten seconds. To be fair, that was nine more seconds than I'd predicted.

"So Theo. Was here. All night?" Olivia's open-mouthed face looked at me through the rearview mirror.

Greg answered, "Yes, and he got her number. Keep up. Wow, he was so cool you know? And he loved the band!"

Sarah's hoop earrings jangled as she laughed. "Love, we know, you told us already." She dug an elbow into his ribs. "Calm down fanboy, you're making me jealous."

"Okay, okay, no matter how starstruck I am, I can be serious." Greg sighed, seriously this time, and set a hand on my knee. "Be careful, yeah? We don't really know anything about him."

While I wanted to, I couldn't disagree. I felt Theo was being honest with me, but that's all it was: a feeling.

Feelings could lie.

There was also the question of Theo's past reputation and the stories about his self-confessed old habits. Could they be the mistakes he'd alluded to? Were *all* the rumours about him true? If yes, then he might have been after something more stimulating than a conversation.

Something I would not be providing.

Alex piped up from the front seat. "We know more about him than a random bloke you'd meet at the pub. If anyone deserves some fun, it's you, Lara." The three of us stared at the back of his head, even Olivia shot him a quizzical look from her driver's seat.

Alex rarely gave his opinion on anything, let alone personal matters. When he did, he was normally the voice of reason. Look up the word 'dependable' and Alex would be the definition. He'd joined the band a month before I left for London so we hadn't known each other long. But after I came home, he'd visited me in the hospital every week without fail, despite working long hours. Apart from when playing the guitar, he hardly made a sound. So for him to suggest I throw caution to the wind and have fun was quite a bombshell.

A minute of stunned silence later, he ruffled his unruly hair and elaborated. "You deserve to find someone and have the house and kids you always used to talk about. But you're gonna get your heart broken, that's life. So if Theodore freakin Jackson likes you, go for it! Let him take you out and spoil you. No pressure, no strings attached because he'll be gone soon, and you'll have one extraordinary story for the grandkids."

We were all taken aback by how deadly serious and well-thought-out his plan was.

No strings.

Wasn't opening up and sharing your life the whole point of being in a relationship? I wanted strings, to get married one day, to have a family. At least, I had once. Before things changed. Before I changed. My strings had become a barbed wire fence that people avoided.

Greg agreed with Alex. "If Theo messes you around, I don't care who he is, I'll sort him out."

Everyone broke into hysterics at the image of Greg—placid, soft-hearted, couldn't-win-a fight-against-his-little-sister—trying to sort out the solid and probably trained Theo.

Bless. It was the thought that counted.

"None of you need to worry, or sort anyone out," I added with a pointed look at Greg. "Nothing's going to happen. Theo's only being kind." He was. Just being kind.

I laughed off the four *'yeah whatever'* snorts that came my way.

Even if Theo was interested *now*, when he found out more about me, he'd disappear quicker than Speedy Gonzales in a cartoon-style puff of smoke.

However, Alex was right that I enjoyed Theo's company. And

yes, I'd admit his eyes were more potent than a class-A drug. Because he wouldn't be around for long, I didn't necessarily have to tell him everything about my past. Or in fact, *anything*.

The old Lara would not have let an opportunity for fun pass her by. Or let a pair of addictive dark eyes get the better of her.

Maybe Theo could help to bring her back?

His confidence certainly was catching...

"Fine, look." I laughed. "I can have fun." Nobody replied. *Insulting*. "I can! If he calls me, I'll answer. If he wants to meet up, I'll say yes."

One step at a time. No strings.

Be brave. Be honest. Make all the days count. I chanted the motto to myself, turned the music up and tried to believe my own words.

The old Lara and Normalville were within sight.

Anything But Ordinary – Avril Lavigne

Theo

Half a mile further along the coast road from our film set was a holiday park, currently being used as a temporary home for cast and crew members. On weekends it was peaceful as most of them would go home to be with friends and family. At night, I could easily spot which caravans were occupied by the faint flickers of colourful TV screens sneaking through thin net curtains.

Phillip Young bulldozed his way into my caravan without knocking, roughly wiped his shoes, and dropped an envelope of updated scripts onto the small dining table. Long hours, scotch and cigars had not done him any favours. I considered commenting on his behaviour but decided it was not worth ruining my excellent mood.

"Mate, where've you been?" He grunted. "I came over earlier to bring you this."

We were not mates. A ruthless edge to his personality stung like a niggling thorn in my side. But, he was one of the best PR managers in the business. He carried a lot of influence. Influence that, unfortunately, I had needed. "Sorry. Forgot about those. I only went down the road."

"Tell me you didn't go see that girl?"

I almost hadn't. Three times I had left my caravan, returned, left again. That parting smile she gave me last night as she drove away? I feared I might have imagined it.

Phillip impatiently tapped the table.

I held my tongue, poured a drink and pictured myself somewhere calm and soothing—back home, chopping logs with dad. Or on the beach, picking out shells with Lara. If Steven hadn't filed an accident report about her injury, I would not have told Phillip about her. "I didn't realise it would be such a problem."

"Wake up mate. We made a deal; you concentrate on doing your job while I manage everything else. No distractions. I'll handle her from now on, otherwise one false move and how do you think this turns out? With you in the gossip columns again, that's how." Phillip waved a stubby finger in my face and mimed reading from a newspaper: "'Theodore Jackson Assaults Woman and Attempts Cover-up By Seducing Her.'"

"Enough." I groaned, tightening my grip on the cool water glass. "I have done everything you asked of me. I have said what you want, when you want it, to whoever you want. All I've done is work my ass off for you and yes, I'm grateful for your help with my situation. But lately, it seems neither you nor anyone else can do a damn thing about it." An invisible hand closed around my neck. "I'm tired of being everyone's puppet! I want to have a real conversation with a real person. In real life."

"Theo, mate, I get it. You're a hot-blooded male and it's been a tough year. You wanna let your hair down. But this is a tough business. Least let me look this girl up before you... go in too deep." He waggled his brows with a sickeningly suggestive gesture. "If you know what I'm sayin—"

"Don't!" I cracked. Jeez, this guy got under my skin. I slammed the glass onto the table and took a step forward. Phillip faltered and took an unconscious one back. I had played the role enough times to know how to act intimidating. Being six-foot-two with the visible strength of someone who grew up on a farm helped. "I don't want to know anything about Lara unless she is the one telling me. Leave her alone. She's genuine."

She was. She had to be. *Please, let her be genuine.*

Phillip raised his hands in surrender. "Your choice. Don't say I didn't warn you." He kicked open the door, head already back in his phone as he walked out. No goodbye.

I downed another glass of water, placed my phone on the table and stared at it, remembering the warmth of Lara's body, fitting perfectly against mine.

I had never been so nervous about speaking to a woman before.

How soon was too soon to text someone?

Day 334
Sunday

Lara

Not even the birds had stirred when the first glimmers of light appeared at my window. I lay motionless—my duvet wrapped tight up to my nose turning me into a toasty human sausage roll—questioning whether last night had all been a dream.

I started counting the lantern-shaped fairy lights that hung above my bed, already knowing there were eighteen. I'd counted them a million times before.

Mom was disappointed I hadn't moved in with them when I returned from London, but she understood why having my own place was important. I wasn't the same person that left. I was coming back for some peace and to find myself again, not stepping backwards.

That was the plan.

Getting up and down the stairs was tricky when I first moved in, so I agreed Olivia could stay with me until I got my strength back. After a few months, we'd made it permanent; she desperately wanted to move out from her mom's place anyway, and I was secretly glad of the company.

A buzz from my phone brought me out of my doze. I pulled it into the warmth of my duvet roll. '1 New Message' blurred in front of my face.

Gravity disappeared when I saw the sender.

THEO: Good morning, Miss Quinn. I appreciate that contacting you this soon and this early goes against every code of texting, but I couldn't wait any longer. I hope your wrist is getting better? Sincerely, Theo.x PS - Such a great show last night, I'm glad you were there. And your voice... Wow.

I read the text about ten times before letting out a squeal. Stumbling out of bed to throw on a dressing gown, I ran to Olivia's room across the hall.

"Liv, you decent? I'm coming in." I was still knocking on the door as I walked through it. "I need your help. Theo texted me."

She lifted her head from under the duvet, half her face covered by a veil of hair and last night's eyeliner smudged across her cheek. "He what? It's like, the middle of the night." (It was 8:34 a.m.)

She rolled over to make room on the bed. I jumped on, cwtched up to her mountain of fluorescent pillows and read the message aloud.

Her pale, sleepy face scrunched up. "Why's he calling you Miss Quinn?"

"I dunno, it's kind of a thing. The 007 joke, remember?"

"Aww, you guys have a thing!" She rubbed her eyes—smudging more eyeliner—then asked for the phone to see for herself. "He's good." She nodded. "Somehow, he manages to be respectful, funny and a bit flirty."

"All with impeccable grammar and punctuation."

She pushed the phone back into my hands with a titter. "Trust you to notice that."

I started smiling. We both whooped and screamed, pulled the

duvet over our heads and kicked our legs. For a moment, we were high schoolers again, having a sleepover, talking about the boys we fancied while drinking Lambrini; the only alcohol our mothers would allow.

My lungs reached bursting point. "Oh, I'm no good at this. What do I say?"

"You don't need my help, hun. Whatever you're doing is working. Be yourself."

Be yourself. Definition: to act according to one's character and instincts. A common phrase that was supposed to encourage and instil confidence because being yourself *should* be easy.

I mumbled into a cushion, "It's not that simple anymore."

"Yes, it is. You're the same nutty, wonderful best friend you've always been, and if he can't see how amazing you are then he's a moron. A hot moron," she said laughing, "but still a moron."

Words failed me, so I kissed her forehead. I left her room and headed for the kitchen with the promise to make breakfast and to let her know how I replied.

LARA: Mr Jackson, you are quite right, it is very early to be texting on a Sunday and therefore violates numerous codes. However, nothing so far about—

Our relationship? No, I couldn't say that. Too heavy. *Argh, stop overthinking.*

—the way we met could be referred to as conventional, so why change things now? My wrist is already much better, thank you. How was the sunrise? Regards, Lara.x

I hit send with a lump in my throat and a skip in my heart. I quickly added:

LARA: PS. I'm very glad you decided to come last night too.x

To stop me from watching my phone after breakfast, I started cleaning again; a task I enjoyed when feeling anxious. Straightforward enough for when your head was in a daze, absorbing enough that you forgot your worries. Probably why my house was always spotless.

Most of the rooms were decorated in muted whites and greys, warmed by natural materials, thick rugs and lush plants. Give me a paint sample chart and I'd be happy for hours. I loved choosing colours for clients. When it came to picking for myself? Impossible. So, I added colour using artwork and accessories that could easily be swapped around for a quick revamp, without spending a fortune.

Theo replied while I was vacuuming the sofas:

THEO: Lara, you are correct - highly unconventional, but no, I would not change a thing. The sunrise was beautiful. In fact, you can blame it for my texting so early. The vivid colours of the sea reminded me of your eyes. x

First my voice, now my eyes? All these compliments were sending me into orbit. Thank goodness it was only Henry the Hoover around to witness my celebratory dance.

Irish blue-green eyes—along with my dark hair and fair skin—were an inheritance from Mom. I liked the way the outer corners lifted to a point, making me look smiley all the time. Having the appearance of being happy reduced the number of questions about my mental state. So, I had perfected the art of smiling continually, even when my face hurt and all I really wanted to do was cry.

LARA: I'm glad we agree. The sunsets are amazing there
too, it's like the sea catches on fire. Make sure you get a
chance to see one! x

THEO: You'll have to show me the best spot to watch
them. T.x

Was that an invitation?

Over the rest of the day, we continued to text back and forth,
never more than an hour between each message. I didn't get much
done around the house after all. By the time I got to bed, I'd sent
more messages in one day than I normally did in a week.

At 10:20 p.m, I received this:

THEO: I would love to keep you up… But I realise, Miss
Quinn, you have work in the morning so I should let you go.
Talk to you tomorrow? T.x

I was not experienced when it came to text flirting or any kind
of flirting for that matter, but I think his first sentence was meant
to be a tease? I hoped it was.

LARA: Tomorrow it is then, Mr Jackson. I'll hold you to it.
Goodnight Theo.x

THEO: Please do 😊 Goodnight Lara. x

Whoa. He was good. Subtle. But good.

I held my phone to my chest. This meeting new people thing
wasn't quite so scary anymore. Maybe I *was* ready to try Jenny's
idea of dating… On the spur of the moment, I texted her:

LARA: Hi Jen, I've changed my mind, put me down for the
sponsored dating thing 😊 Why not! See you soon. xxx

JENNY: Fantastic my love! We'll arrange a meet up soon xox J

♪

The next morning, Theo's text arrived before I got to work. We carried on messaging in the same way, every day for the rest of the week.

Blank Space – Taylor Swift

Day 339
Friday

Theo

"**E**arth calling Theo?"

I looked up from re-reading Lara's texts to see Tom frantically waving at me.

Everyone else had left the beach set and were ambling up the sandy pathways to the offices or dressing rooms. I ran to Tom's side only to be greeted by a fist to my shoulder, pushing me off the path into the long, spiky grass. "Jeez, Tom!"

He laughed as I rubbed my arms and matched his pace. "Out with it, who is she?"

"Hmm?" I checked my phone again. "Who?"

"Don't be coy, I know that look."

I tucked my phone, and hands, into my pockets. "It's Lara." I couldn't help but smile when I said her name.

"Aha! The supermarket ninja. She's sweet."

"She is. She's..." A multitude of inexplicable things. I settled for: "Different."

Tom stopped outside the office, gazing out to sea. "Oh, to be young again," he said wistfully, as if being thirty-eight made him an ancient oracle. With one last jab to my ribs, he darted off toward the dressing room. "Be good, don't do anything I wouldn't!"

Another voice came from over my shoulder, "Why'd you need to be good? What are you up to now?" I didn't need to look to know it was Phillip. No one else's voice went through me in the same way.

"No reason." I shrugged and carried on walking.

Phillip must have followed, I could hear him panting at the effort of keeping up. "You're not still talking to that girl, are you? We spoke about this. Oi, Theo? Wait for me." I didn't wait. "There's things you should know about her. You wouldn't believe the skeletons in her closet."

What the?

Heat prickled over my skin. I halted, turned and glared at him. "And how exactly would you know? I won't tell you again. Leave her alone."

I jogged the rest of the way up the road to the caravan site, not stopping till I got into my bedroom where I threw off my coat, ripped open the fussy cravat and fell flat onto the bed.

Skeletons? Impossible. Lara was nothing like my ex, Yasmin. She would not do what Yasmin did. *Stop panicking, slow down, Lara is genuine.* I was the one who had made the first move and pursued her after all.

I counted the minutes between every alert on my phone. Her messages hooked me like a skilfully written script, every scene full of new twists and turns. I wanted to keep turning the pages, to understand every line, to devour every last word.

I needed to see her again. Soon.

Lara

Being stuck in the office usually sucked, I much preferred to be out buying materials, visiting furnishing suppliers or even mucking in with the decorators. Last week was different. Hours rushed by as I prepared floor plans and materials quotes for a barn conversion project. I'd challenged myself to do as much work as possible in between Theo's texts—they only paused overnight—that way I could sit and take time to read and reread them, without feeling guilty.

Theo worded his messages the same way he spoke in person. Lively and confident with moments of intensity, others of humour, making it easy to hear his voice. Low rumbles when he was serious, lighter purrs when he spoke with a smile. I confess I may have refreshed my memory by listening to a trailer from one of his older films in which he'd played the part of a morally grey, tattoo-covered superhero who seemingly didn't own any kind of shirt. Oof.

I then fell into a scrolling rabbit hole, aka Pinterest, and landed upon an image of him at an awards party with his ex-girlfriend Yasmin on his arm. Arm was an understatement. She was *all* over him. Tall, toned, tanned, with the tiniest waist I'd ever seen. Theo could probably wrap a single hand around her. He'd struggle to get an arm around me. I hated her and wanted to be her all at once. Then I hated myself for being so shallow.

Served me right for snooping.

♫

Five minutes after getting home, my phone rang. Mom called daily like clockwork to check on me, so I picked up without looking, flopped onto the sofa and answered with a sleepy, "Shwmae, Mam. You okay?"

"Very well thank you, though, I'm not so sure about the rest?"

It took one syllable to realise it wasn't Mom. I jumped up and facepalmed. Olivia, who was in the kitchen at the far end of the room, started flapping her hands about, mouthing: 'Who is it? Who is it?'

"Theo! Hi," I said. Olivia danced her way out of the room. "Sorry, I was on autopilot. Oh, and shwmae means hi. Umm, how are you?" *Hell, he's already answered that.*

"I'm still well." He was smiling. I could tell. Although we were separated by fifteen miles of town, country, road and air, it felt like he was sitting right beside me.

Over an hour had passed by the time he said, "Anyway, I called because I'm wondering if you are free tomorrow night?"

My mind blanked, what day would it be? Saturday. "The band are all coming over to mine. We get together every month, have pizza and watch a film or whatever." *Stop waffling.* "You could come too?" I desperately wanted to see him again, but it sounded like a lame idea, so I gave him an excuse. "You're probably busy though—"

"I'm not busy. I want to see you, that's why I asked."

"Oh. Okay. Well, if you want to come?"

He chuckled and sighed at the same time, the same soft little laugh he made whenever I tried to joke or flirt. It was the best, most heart-melting, stomach-clenching sound ever.

"Lara, are you inviting me to your house, to meet your friends, to eat pizza, and to 'watch a film or whatever' with you?"

Such a lame idea. "Yeah, I am."

"Then I would love to."

"Really? You do? I mean, you would?"

He did that little laugh again. *My laugh.* "I would. Text me when and where and I will see you tomorrow, Miss Quinn."

I hung up, caught my breath and jumped up and down.

Olivia ran back downstairs. "What happened?"

"He's coming." I threw my hands in the air. "Theo's coming here tomorrow!"

She joined in with my jumping. After calming down enough to stop my fingers from shaking, I texted him the details.

THEO: Will knowing the top-secret address of a 007 get me into trouble? xx T

I noticed the increase to 2 'x's.

LARA: No, the address won't. But I might… xx

Who am I? Excitement bolted through every nerve. The old Lara was still alive. And Theo had found her.

THEO: I'm looking forward to that 😉 xx T

Holy smokin bloody hell.

Mr Blue Sky – ELO

Day 340
Saturday

Theo

I t was so quiet on the campsite that I was startled by my phone ringing. Was Lara going to cancel my invitation? My heart rate returned to normal when I saw the caller: Home. With a swipe, the faces of my mum and little sister appeared on the screen.

Chloe soon pointed out my fresh shirt and the bottle of aftershave in my hand. "Going somewhere, Tee?"

"I am indeed, so can't talk for long."

"Doing an interview or something?"

"No."

She scowled. "So you're dressing up to go to Tom's caravan?" Tapping a finger to her lips, she brightened. "Ouu have you got a date?"

"Alright, Sherlock." Mum laughed. "Put your skills to good use and go find your father, would you?" Mum waited for Chloe to leave the room (which she did, after several huffs and eye rolls) then asked, "So have you got a date?"

Using the phone screen as a mirror, I fixed my collar, smiling at Mum's effort to sound enthusiastic. Worry skimmed the surface of her words like oil on water. It was always there, sometimes gathering deeper, other times separating or spreading thinner, but never dissolving.

"No, Mum. Only pizza and a film with a new friend, and some of her friends." I couldn't remember the last time I had been invited to something so normal and relaxed.

"I see. It is a girl though?"

"Yes. It's not like that…" I wanted it to be. "It's a long story."

I had woken up this morning thinking of Lara. The way she said my name, Theeooh, an exhale of breath rather than a word. And of the way she restrained her smiles. What would they be like if she fully let go? How bright would they be then?

Mum went to ask another question. I intervened, "I'll tell you everything when I see you. I have to go." I blew out a puff of air and shook my shoulders.

"You're nervous," she told me. Mothers saw *everything*.

"Sort of. Yes. A little."

"Then it is definitely a date." She wished me luck and hung up with a gentle warning to 'behave.'

Lara

Greg and Sarah arrived first, Alex not long after. I'd texted them all to come earlier than usual with the excuse of having something important to tell them.

They all sat lined up on my silver-grey sofas like a panel of judges on TV, waiting for my act. I pulled myself up straight and took a moment, the same way I would at work before addressing the team, spinning my fine gold necklace in the absence of a clipboard to keep my hands occupied.

Sarah commented on how nice I looked in my denim shirt dress. Her compliment helped me to relax, she didn't say things for the sake of it.

It had taken a shamefully long time to pick what to wear. Most of my older clothes were fitted, but now I was paranoid about wearing anything tight. Because I could feel the scarred, uneven skin around my middle, I was convinced that other people could see it.

"Okay," I started, "I wanted to warn you about an extra guest coming tonight." Olivia was directly opposite me clutching a cushion, beaming from ear to ear. Everyone else looked blank so I gave them a clue. "Someone I met recently who got my number after the gig?"

A lightbulb switched on and Greg clapped a hand to his mouth. "Noooo way! Theo?"

"Got it in one," I said, laughing at their bemused expressions. I then reminded them that Theo didn't know about Day Zero and that he was coming here as a friend, not as an actor for an interview.

To stay busy, I kept to the kitchen, put the pizzas in the oven, chopped salad, and faffed with ornaments. I caught my reflection in the glass back door and frowned. If I had the hips to balance out my er... *generous* chest and arms, I could be classed as an 'hourglass.' If I was slimmer or taller, I might have gotten away with 'athletic.' As in a boxer, not a gymnast. However, I enjoyed food, hated exercise, and was way past the growing age. So instead, my curves and I were stuck somewhere in between. Top heavy with extra bumps in the middle. Don't get me wrong, I mostly liked what I saw, but I was nothing like the goddesses Theo usually mixed with who probably all had personal trainers and dieticians. *Oh crap.*

"Stop stressing, yeah?" Greg snuck some nachos from a bowl behind me, forgetting I could see his reflection. "Everything looks great."

Growing up, people always presumed Greg was my brother because he looked more like me than he did Olivia. His ash-brown hair was a mussed-up mop of surfer curls. (He spent ages making it look messy.) His eyes were hazel, but almond-shaped and surrounded by thick black lashes like mine. I couldn't imagine having a real brother would be any better than having him.

When the doorbell rang, it triggered a mild heart attack. The type you get at the top of a rollercoaster as you're about to tip over the edge. You scream because it's terrifying and dangerous. You scream because it's exhilarating and wild.

After being faced with death at the hands of a psychotic murderer, you'd think little things like meeting a guy wouldn't scare you anymore. They did. Some survivors go the other way and become daredevils, living for thrills. Not me. I withdrew and became an over-thinker. Every little risk sent my mind on a ride through a mental house of horrors, imagining all the things that could jump out, all the dangers and what if's. Jenny said that each day after Day Zero was a new start, a second chance to live. But to live in fear is no life. So that's why we—I— had to be brave. To push on regardless of being afraid.

Easier said than done.

The room went suspiciously quiet as I hurried to the door, practising how to say hello along the way. Theo's silhouette came into view through the frosted glass of the porchway. Theodore Jackson. On my doorstep. *Crazy.* I set a smile on my face, one that hopefully would appear chilled and refined rather than frantically excited, and opened the door.

He was wearing the usual black jeans and boots, this time with a fitted shirt the colour of dry plaster, sleeves rolled up to his elbows, top buttons open.

'Hi,' was all I managed to say.

Theo noted my reaction. He was studying my every movement, a smile slowly curving his lips. His attractiveness was an undeniable fact, and he knew exactly how and when to use it. It never came across as pride though. Cheeky sometimes. But not arrogant.

"Hey." He leaned forward to give me a brief one-armed hug before running a hand through his hair.

Was he nervous? No, my imagination was being daft. Although, he did worry about what people thought of him…

I tried to reassure him. "The guys are all here, except for Caleb, he's away with his kids. Don't worry, I told them you were coming and they're on strict orders not to interrogate you, but I apologise in advance for, umm, everything they may do and say. Especially Greg. Who you've met already." *Waffling again.*

Theo stepped inside the porch and handed me a bottle of wine, fingers brushing mine, instantly spreading warmth over my skin. "You like red if I remember correctly?"

"I do. Thank you." I took a breath, moving aside to let him into the hallway.

After toeing off his boots, he circled a hand around my wrist— the good one—and stepped closer, holding my gaze. "You look beautiful." He allowed me a few seconds for those words to sink in and recover myself. "And don't worry about your friends, I can handle it."

Holy smokes, he could handle anything he wanted.

I needn't have worried. Olivia stepped up as hostess, offering Theo a seat and leading the introductions, the second I opened the living room door. Theo used the same tactic as me; asking lots of questions about their jobs, hobbies, music etc, to keep people talking. Although, I doubted he'd made a mental list on the way over the way I would have.

Everyone sat at the dining table while I served up the pizzas. Even Sarah, an unflappable fearless badass, had an adorable shade of rose covering her smooth brown cheeks. Like her boyfriend, she was a huge fan of Theo's films.

I hoped Theo didn't think my reactions to him were because of his fame.

♪

"What we watching then?" Greg asked while Olivia collected the dirty plates after dinner. "Theo, this is your area of expertise. Gotta be the new *Star Wars* yeah?"

Theo held his hands up. "Fine by me, I haven't seen it yet."

"What! That's settled then." Greg led the way to the TV.

Theo offered to help me make drinks, trailing a hand across the keys of my piano as he followed me into the kitchen. Was it normal to be jealous of a piano? I felt his watchful gaze like warm sunlight on my neck, back, waist, legs. Holding his attention made me feel... powerful. I ducked behind the fridge door to cool my face, and handed him a beer.

"Thanks, but I'm driving," he said, brushing past me to reach for a Coke, awakening my internal butterflies. In a complete moment of weakness, my body detached from my brain and I touched a finger to his smooth forearm. The more I tried to pull away, the more my hands shook, like two magnets fighting against separation. I slowly drew a line from his elbow to his hand, to the tip of his middle finger, marvelling at the contrast of his warm olive skin against my Celtic, pinkish hue.

He tracked my movement, parted his lips to breathe, swallowed, and met my eyes with a whole new kind of intensity.

Theo wasn't fazed by meeting my friends at all, but he *was* nervous.

Because of me.

What idiot invented open-plan living? I wanted there to be a wall hiding us from the view of my friends, in particular Olivia, who wasn't even trying to hide her ogling.

I handed out drinks while Theo took his seat on one end of the sofa, his arm resting across the back. Alex was at the other end next to Olivia, then a space for me. A tight space. Theo's arm would be around me. There was always my spot on the floor.

I felt that pull of a magnet and the excitement of a rollercoaster again as I got higher and higher, closer and closer to that edge...

Theo smiled as I squeezed in next to him. When Alex reached

up to turn off the lights, a shiver ran up my back. Darkness didn't scare me, however, I wouldn't normally be sat so close to a man I was attracted to. A man to whom with every passing minute, I wanted to be even closer.

The famous music from the film's opening titles filled the room. Theo's hand dropped onto my shoulder, ever so gently pulling me nearer. My left side and thigh burned from the pressure of being up against him.

"Is this okay?" he whispered.

I nodded. Hell, it was *more* than okay. All I could hear was my racing heartbeat.

I stared at the screen but I didn't see it.

Theo

I hoped Greg wouldn't ask for my so-called expert opinion on the film. I swear I tried to concentrate, but my eyes kept wandering. Seeing Lara again surpassed anything I had imagined. There were so many things to discover; the determined lock of hair which curled around her ear, refusing to be pinned up. The scent of coconut and caramel. Heaven. The husky edge to her low voice. My imagination could never have done her justice. And, since pulling that finger-drift-down-the-arm manoeuvre, the touch of her skin consumed my thoughts.

I gave in and dared to shift my hand from her shoulder to her bare neck. Her eyelids fluttered, head tilted a fraction.

Her ear was barely a hand's breadth from my mouth. If only I could— No. Too soon. Not here.

Sometimes, *not* doing anything took a lot of strength.

Lara

We all blinked as the lights came on. Theo moved his hand—which had gloriously drifted onto my neck—back onto the sofa and pulled away. I tried to sound enthusiastic about the film. I was annoyed it finished so soon.

Alex said goodnight, Greg and Sarah got up to follow while I collected up the drinks and empty popcorn packets.

"Great to see you again, Theo," Greg said. "How long are you around for then?"

I hadn't even dared to ask Theo that. The answer scared me too much. Stacking glasses into the sink as quietly as possible, I listened for a reply.

"We have three months here," Theo said, "then we head back to the London studios."

Three months! To stop my heart from escaping, I clamped a hand over my mouth and propped myself up against the fridge.

Greg smiled at me over Theo's shoulder. He was up to something. "We'll have to get together again then, yeah? Maybe you can help us persuade Lara to join in properly for our next gig?"

I shot Greg a death glare. Sneaky git.

Theo turned and caught my expression before I had a chance to change it. "Doesn't look like she's too keen on that idea." He chuckled, crossing his arms over his chest. "But I'll see what I can do."

Intriguing. Instead of asking what he had in mind, I ran upstairs to fetch Sarah's coat. Theo was already in the hallway when I returned, examining my gallery wall.

"Don't look too closely." I laughed, hanging the coat over the bannister and attempting to steer him away from the pictures.

They were mostly photos of Olivia, Greg and me at various stages of school and college. One was from a family summer holiday when we were teens. We were on a beach and I was wearing a bikini. I felt embarrassed about Theo seeing it. I didn't look like that anymore.

He pointed to the writing under each picture. "What are the songs for?"

"Oh, umm." I spun my necklace. "We kind of have this

tradition that started in school of giving our holidays a playlist and special memories their own song. Sometimes it's because the lyrics fit, or because it was playing in the background, or popular at the time." I groaned and pressed a hand to my face. "Which is very sad and embarrassing."

"Not at all." Theo smiled at me as if it were the cutest thing he'd ever heard. "Because when you hear that song again, it reminds you. It's a sort of... life soundtrack."

Huh. *Life soundtrack.* I liked that. "Exactly. That's the magic of music, it can transport you anywhere."

Honestly, I gave nearly every day a song, sometimes more than one. Fortunately, Theo seemed to accept having a soundtrack to your life as being perfectly normal. *Phew.* It also gave me an idea: I should include all the songs in my journal (when I worked myself up to actually writing it).

Theo dropped his head to the side to look at me. "Do you have a song for the day we met?"

I could have filled a whole album for that day. One song, in particular, came to mind.

"Maybe," I said.

"Are you going to tell me?"

"Maaaaybe," I teased. "Guess."

Leaning back against the doorframe, he pressed a finger to his pursed lips. "There's bound to be a song about sweeping someone off their feet."

"Oh, so *that's* what you were trying to do?"

He answered me with another smile and an enticing flick of his eyelashes as if to say, '*Wasn't it obvious?*'

When I was nine, I won an art competition and got awarded my prize in front of my whole school and a newspaper photographer. I was the bee's knees, on top of the world, giddy and blushing with happiness. I felt the same way every time Theo smiled at me. With added heat and tingles.

"There are several songs about being swept away," I said, "but it's none of them."

"Hmm. Then I'll have to think about it." He moved into the porch for his boots, pointing back at the beach photo. "You all grew up together?"

"Us three, yeah. We met Caleb and Sarah at college, then Greg met Alex through work. I was leaving for London by then, so I didn't know him well until I—" I'd almost said, 'until I was in hospital.' My eyes dropped to the floor. "Until I came back."

Heart thumping against my ribs, I twirled a piece of hair and tucked it behind my ear, waiting for Theo to ask the dreaded question: why did you move back? Theo didn't ask anything. He gently smoothed my hair around my ear, mimicking my movement, then let his fingers flow along my jawline to my chin, which he lifted, thumb skimming my lips, firing up every cell of my skin.

Being so close should have terrified me, but he had the surprising ability to slip harmlessly through my invisible barrier into the bubble where I felt light, peaceful and safe. To me, he was just Theo, a guy who bumped into me at the supermarket, a guy who made me laugh, a guy who appeared to like me.

I liked him too.

An expression flickered over his face, one I'd seen before but still couldn't work out. A kind of thoughtfulness, sadness, confusion even. What *was* he thinking about? Had I offended him somehow?

"It's a shame you're not in the band anymore," he said finally, a warm hand now on my cheek. "I would love to hear you play."

The half-melted goo that used to be my brain took a second to respond. "Oh, I'm nothing special." I wasn't bad. I wasn't great either. And I would never be a powerful singer like Sarah.

Sliding his hand to the back of my neck, Theo dipped his face closer. "I disagree."

Was he still talking about music? More to the point, was he going to try and kiss me again?

YES PLEASE!

Whoa. I seriously wanted him to. My body shivered with anticipation. But it was too soon. I didn't want to risk panicking again. One step at a time. *Be brave.*

I pulled him into a hug and pressed my face to his neck, burying myself into his spicy earth scent, mixed with the fresh cotton of his clothes and... pure man. The muscles of his back flexed under my fingers as he held me tighter, enfolding me in his heat.

"If you promise to come to the next gig," I said, tearing myself away, "then I'll get practising."

"I promise." He stepped out the door, throwing me a cheeky grin over his shoulder. "But, Lara?"

"Yeah?"

"I won't be able to wait that long to see you again."

I Think He Knows – Taylor Swift

Theo

I got back to my caravan, rushed into the miniature bed and wrapped up. My feet hung uncomfortably over the end, freezing night air turned my breath into clouds. Tonight, it didn't bother me.

I opened my music app and created a new playlist: *Lara's Soundtrack*, before scrolling down my contacts list, searching for someone to talk to about my night. My parents? No. They would worry I was getting caught up in something again. Chloe? Definitely not. A: She would tell my parents. B: She would start planning my wedding.

I stopped scrolling at the names of my school and uni mates. I hadn't spoken to any of them in the years since I had left the UK without a second glance. None of my new L.A., so-called, friends had bothered to contact me since I'd moved back. Karma was a bitch.

I needed to put things right.

If I could go back and give the eighteen-year-old-me some advice? Firstly, I would punch him for being such a gargantuan ass. Then I would tell him: *Remember who your real friends are. That voice in your head that sounds like your dad telling you to 'do the right thing?' Listen to it.*

Perhaps I would even tell him to stick with psychology.

Lara

My blood-covered hands crawled around the office floor and found a plug, the same way they did in all of my nightmares about Day Zero. I turned to aim it at my attacker's eye, only to drop it when I saw not *him*—Jeffery Smyth—but Theo sitting on top of me, pinning me down, hands slowly unbuttoning my shirt. My breath went from terrified to excited, then back again. He looked at me with pure disgust.

As he stared at my body, his face started distorting. The eyes and mouth remained Theo's but the rest—ghostly pale skin, smoke-filled breath and long nose—morphed back into Jeff.

Theo's lips whispered against my ear, "Damaged."

I woke up as they began laughing.

Day 344
Wednesday

I arrived early for the DAYS meeting and sat on a wall by the entrance, face lifted to the sun, enjoying the last of the evening light and the feel of warm red bricks under my fingers. Life had changed their surface and appearance forever. They'd been worn soft by years of people's hands brushing over them. Hands of children, dragging along into school, rushing across on their way home. Hands of parents, leaning back to take the weight off their feet. More recently, the hands of DAYS members, tentatively seeking a place of support and hope. The solid stability of the wall despite all that wear felt strangely comforting.

Thankfully, the Jeff/Theo vision hadn't returned since Saturday. My dreams were back to normal; the same replay of Day Zero, watching myself helplessly from a bird's eye view. The image of *them* was still there though, tattooed into my minds-eye.

Damaged.

That word had lodged itself into my thoughts. It was how I felt, which made it a hard word to shake off.

I needed to tell Jenny about Theo, otherwise, the nightmare wouldn't make sense. How much should I tell her? Why was I so worried? Nothing was going on between the two of us. *Errr hello,* my brain butted in on itself, *yes there is.*

There was more to my nervousness around Theo than pure attraction. My issues ran deeper. I wasn't scared of him—I was terrified of what could happen with him. Of how far things could go if I let them.

♪

Jenny ran over at the end of the meeting—her nails were rainbow colours today—and wrapped an arm around my shoulder. "Right, love," she said, bouncing on tiptoes. "Let's get these dates sorted."

Her childlike enthusiasm for everything was a ray of sunshine in what could easily have been a dark and depressive group. She treated every member like family, healing wounds that went far deeper than any knife with her kindness and love.

"Why the change of heart?" she asked, leading me over to the refreshments table.

I scrunched the lining of my pockets up into fists while chewing my lip like mad. If Theo saw me, he might have given me that mysterious, narrow-eyed look or told me to *'stop doing that'* again. "Oh, I've been thinking. You're right, I do need to start having more fun. Get out more. And, I kinda met someone. I think."

Jenny's eyebrows disappeared off the top of her head. "As in a male someone?"

"Yeah, umm, I don't know."

"You don't know if he's male?"

"Ha! No. He's *very* much male. Right up your street. Tall, dark, impossibly handsome, heart-meltingly English."

"Point me in his direction, sweetheart." Jenny posed, red lips pouted, one hand on her dipped hip.

I choked on my tea. "Easy tiger! He's incredible, but... well, complicated."

"Aren't they all?" She sighed and poured more tea; a cue for me to continue.

I told her the full story of my sprained wrist and meeting Theo, and about the nightmare.

My relationship with Theo wouldn't last, even if he was sticking around for longer than I'd thought. But wanting, *really wanting*, it to go further was something I hadn't felt in a long time. And it was down to more than his looks. He challenged me and pushed me out of my comfort zone, made me feel alive again.

It felt so good to be liked by someone for the person I was now —even if I didn't always know, or like, who that was—rather than for the person they remembered me being. Which was why I'd decided not to tell Theo about my history, because then he would see me the way everyone else did: A victim. In need of help and protection. *Damaged.* I couldn't bear the thought of him viewing me like that.

I wasn't lying. I simply wasn't going to tell him everything.

No strings.

"I mean, the whole 'someone tried to murder me' thing," I groaned. "Is that a first date, fifth date, or tenth-anniversary conversation? If you tell someone straight away, it freaks them out. If you don't tell them, it freaks them out. Either way, we're screwed."

Jenny's skin creased up like delicate tissue paper as she mulled it over. "There's no fixed solution or timeline, it differs for every person and every relationship. The only thing I *can* say for definite is that there will be the right person out there for you."

I tapped a beat against my mug. "I hope so."

"I know so." She stilled my fingers by wrapping them in her own. "Why are you so sure it's not Theo? Sounds to me that he likes you. If you expect things to fail before they start, then they will. Give him a chance."

I probably should have explained to her who Theo was.

Her face softened and smiled again. "If I'd told you at your first meeting that you'd soon be back at work as a manager, running your own office, would you have believed me?"

There were still days when I didn't believe it. I shook my head.

"And," she added, "if I'd told you a few weeks ago that you'd meet a handsome stranger who gave you the courage to take a risk, would you have believed me?"

I shook my head again, laughing.

"Look how far you've come." She grinned. "You have a second chance to live your life, so live it! There's no point trying to deny you've changed. Your whole perspective changes, but if I grab a round lump of clay and press it into a square, it's still clay and you are still you. You just have to work with the differences."

I felt like a lump of clay. Bumped, poked and prodded. Squashed and moulded. All against my will.

I remembered my first trip to a DAYS meeting like it was yesterday. I'd been in hospital for thirty-two days and frankly, I was losing my mind. Although not keen on the support group idea, I agreed to do it for Mom, who was clearly worried about how quiet I'd become. When my doctor said she'd release me from the hospital for a few hours to attend, that clinched the deal.

Physiotherapy was going okay at the time. I could stand and walk by myself, but ten metres felt like a marathon, so the downside to my outing was that I had to get in a wheelchair. Mom pushed me along the endless bland corridors and when we exited into the warm summer air, it wrapped itself around me like a comfort blanket. Gulls squawked and cried as they cartwheeled through the air overhead. I closed my eyes and breathed in freshly cut grass and damp earth—the smell of freedom.

Like a mad dog, I spent the journey with my head out the window.

Mom stopped the car outside a local school that had recently been divided into sections of offices and a community hall. Painted on one of the doors was a large yellow sun. Inside the sun, the word 'DAYS' was written in blue. More yellow signs led us along magnolia halls, covered with posters and students' old art projects, to a large hall. A murmur of voices came from within, along with chairs and shoes squeaking on polished wood floors. I fixed a practised smile onto my face as Mom opened the door.

Jenny was the first to greet us. Seeing my fear, she assured me, "Don't worry, sweetheart, you don't have to say anything unless you want to." Then she swept away to meet others, floating around the room like a lantern, bobbing up and down, sharing her light.

Mom smoothed my hair. "Oakie dokie. I'll be back in an hour, call me if there's a problem." She kissed my cheek with the advice, "Just give it a go." And then she was gone.

Being left alone in a room full of strangers made my pulse drum.

Shyness was a new experience for me.

Eager to get away from the wheelchair, I shuffled toward the only empty seat left, next to Jenny, which scuppered my plan of hiding at the back. I was sweating by the time I got halfway across the hall. Jenny looked up. I expected her to rush over and insist on helping me, however, she left me to it.

I liked her.

As I sat down, she patted my knee, her nails painted perfectly in alternate blue-yellow-blue to match the logo, and leaned in to whisper, "Do you like chocolate cake?"

I nodded, catching a waft of fancy Chanel perfume and home baking.

"Jolly good. We have plenty for afterwards," she said as if it was the naughtiest thing imaginable.

I found myself smiling again, only it wasn't a fake mask.

"Oh, and this is for you, my love." She reached into her bag. "Write in it all the things you want to say, but never will."

She handed me a book. Printed onto a blue, soft leather cover read the text: 'DAYS JOURNAL' in yellow. I clutched it like a long lost treasure.

♪

Jenny was right; I had come a long way since my first meeting. I couldn't stop now. It was about time for me to tick off another step on my plan: My journal.

When I got home, I took the advice of Julie Andrews from *The Sound Of Music* and began at Day Zero, writing my story from the very beginning.

(It was a very good place to start.)

Up & Up - Coldplay

Lara's Journal
Day Zero

It is a truth universally acknowledged that once upon a time in a galaxy far far away…

They're the beginnings of some of the greatest love stories and fantasies ever told.

Unfortunately, my story began more like a crime thriller.

The air was muggy and grey. London's traffic grumbled in the background. I unlocked the door to our construction site office, hung up my hard hat and wove through the obstacle course of furniture. First came Daniel's desk—always covered with bits of tools in various stages of repair—next came my neat desk. Then a third, shared by our trade overseers. Builders, electricians, plumbers and so on. Eventually, I reached the tiny kitchen area to make coffee. Arguably the most important task of the day.

I could have worked in our head office which had heating, soft seats and a proper toilet instead of a port-a-loo. But I've always preferred to be in the action, see the building progress for myself, help with deliveries, and get my hands on tools or a paintbrush whenever possible.

Starting early gave me time to catch up on paperwork before the team arrived and transformed our office into a bustling hub.

Hugging my warm mug, I went through schedules and risk assessments, humming along to the *Guardians of the Galaxy* album. *Hooked On A Feeling*. Classic tuneage.

After a while, I heard chains clang and rattle outside; the sound of someone opening the main gates. I presumed it was Daniel wanting to get a head start. Plus, he knew I was there alone. With a smile, I went to meet him, despite the fact we'd only been apart for an hour. Why he insisted on us being so secretive and arriving separately, I didn't understand. Most of the staff had suspicions about us anyway. (But that's another story and I'm getting sidetracked...)

My smile dropped when I saw Jeff, our new carpenter. An odd guy, though I couldn't put my finger on why. He appeared decent —well-kept clothes, light brown hair pulled back into such a smooth ponytail it made me envious—but there was something about the way he watched me. As the only woman on site, I was used to being stared at, but his stare was, I dunno? Blank. Empty.

The hair on my neck prickled. I shook off the feeling and called out a cheerful, 'good morning.' If only I'd listened to my gut.

Jeff answered me with a curt nod and I offered him a coffee. As he reached the bottom of the metal steps to the office door, I went back to the kitchen and attempted to get him talking by asking about how he was settling in. I thought he was just shy and honestly felt sorry for him.

The tapping of his footsteps paused and the door shut behind him.

"It's okay," I said, tipping a spoon of coffee into our mugs. "Leave it open, it gets pretty stuffy in here."

No response. At that point, I thought he was creepy. Still, I never expected what happened next. Who would?

Without sound or warning, a hand clamped over my mouth, another around my arm. My scream came out as a muffled whimper through his suffocating grip. Fear paralysed me. His face pressed into the back of my neck and his stale breath, thick with cigarette smoke, stung my nose. Even now, the smell makes me retch.

I writhed and kicked out at his legs, throwing the mugs, kettle, and anything else I could reach over my shoulders.

His grip tightened. "Don't fight me, darlin. Only slows things down."

That was the first time I'd heard his voice. It crawled over my skin, raspy and soulless, sticking to me like cobwebs I wanted to escape. Tears filled my eyes, blurring my sight seconds before the first stab pierced my lower back.

Shock overtook my body. When Jeff released his grip, I fell to my knees. My vision blacked out at the edges. I vaguely heard laughter in the distance. The only thought in my mind was to run and find help. I needed to get out onto the road.

Scrambling up the kitchen counter, I somehow used the strength in my arms to pull myself onto my wobbly feet. Papers, folders and pots of pens clattered to the floor, knocked down by my hands dragging over the desks. Jeff followed me, his shadow darker than a black hole. I put pressure on my back, my fingers came away wet and sticky. My delirious brain wondered, *how is it raining here?* Stumbling over some wires sent a whole computer crashing to the floor.

Again, someone laughed.

Laughter is a strange thing. It can be one of the happiest sounds; a baby gurgling, friends having fun. But marginally change the tone and it becomes terrifyingly evil.

One step away from the door, I stretched out for the handle. A wave of dizzy panic almost brought me back to my knees at the sight of my blood-soaked hand slipping on the shiny metal.

"Where you think you're going, darlin?" Jeff's words sounded distorted by his gruff croak. They've haunted me every night since.

My heavy legs gave way. I slid down the door onto the floor. He loomed above me. And he was the one laughing.

I cried for help but there was no one around to hear.

Jeff kneeled over me, a leg on each side of my hips to pin me down, the knife still in his hand. Long, jagged like a bread knife, covered in crimson blood.

Throwing my arms around and clawing at his face, I screamed, emptying my lungs over and over until I choked on my tears and my throat burned. Jeff must have gotten fed up with my fighting because he stopped laughing and plunged the knife in again, this time into my stomach.

Instead of my body reeling like the first time, it fell limp, arms thumping onto the floor beside me. I stared blankly at the ceiling, listening to my gargled, shallow breath.

Slowly, he removed the blade. I didn't think it was possible to be in so much pain and feel so numb, so unaware of anything at all.

The last of my remaining consciousness stirred up a vision of my parents' house as a policeman knocked on their emerald front door which was always surrounded by flowers. Mom collapsed to the floor when they were given the news. Panic struck again. I couldn't let that happen to them.

Hands scouring the floor like crabs in sand, I scavenged for anything to use as a weapon while Jeff's icy fingers tore at my clothes.

I... I still can't put my fear and desperation into words.

I touched something: a plug. Summoning every scrap of power I had left, I flung it forward, thrusting the sharp prongs deep into Jeff's eye socket. He yelped and fell back, cradling his face in his hands, giving me time to roll to my side and heave my weight onto my knees. I reached again for the door handle, knowing it was my only way out. My last chance to survive.

I'll admit, I felt a momentary wave of satisfaction when Jeff roared in anger, his left eye stuck shut and bleeding. *I don't go down without a fight*. He grabbed for me as the door clicked open which sent me stumbling down the steps. My body impacted the hard gravel with a thud, wiping out my last scrap of energy.

Cold. A crushing cold weight was all I could feel. Not the

normal kind of cold that comes from holding a snowball or jumping into the sea; that cold comes from the outside. This cold came from within like poison seeping through my veins, destroying everything it touched. Every breath became a battle and every heartbeat felt like a punch to the chest.

Stones cut into my back as he dragged me by the ankle over the rough gravel. My pain blended into numbness. I couldn't fight back.

This is it, I thought. *This is how I die.*

And then, everything went out of focus.

Random memories, voices, music, and even familiar smells floated through my mind. Kind of like hearing ten different radio stations in the air around you, unable to separate one from another. Then came the faces of all the people I would never see again: family, friends, and their future children I would never meet.

The sound of an engine briefly pushed away the darkness.

Clanking of metal gates.

Shouting.

Jeff kicked me in his rush to run away.

Soft and citrusy hands lifted my face out of the dirt. "Quinn? No no, look at me. Stay with me."

Indigo eyes that sparkled like dusk skies hovered inches above my own. I knew those eyes well, but I'd never seen fear in them before. *Don't be scared, Daniel*, I tried to say before my world blackened again.

I lost all comprehension of time.

At some point, distant wailing grew louder, morphing into a mechanical rhythm.

"Come on, Quinn, hold on. Please hold on, they're almost here." Daniel was so close I could feel his words and tears on my skin. "Lara, I love you. Don't leave me. Lara, please, don't leave me," he choked.

I won't leave you, I promised him with all my heart.

The warmth of his lips touched mine. The last touch I would ever feel from the first man I'd ever loved.

I longed, prayed, *begged* for one more day. One hour, minute...

One

more

breath—

Ludovico Einaudi – The Earth Prelude

Day 346
Friday

J enny had invited me to her house so we could go over our fundraising plans. Her garden was like walking into a National Trust property. Always immaculate. Apple trees lined the driveway, surrounded by rivers of golden daffodils and streaks of hot pink tulips.

I rang the doorbell, clutching my jacket tight over my chest, wishing I'd worn something warmer. Jenny appeared at the door with a bright wide smile (and gold nails). I accepted the offer for tea and followed her through pristine white hallways, across smooth flagstone floors and into the kitchen of her ex-miners cottage.

"Stuart has a driving lesson booked in for Monday." She handed over my tea in a dainty floral cup. "His family have all sponsored him, and every group member has agreed to donate five pounds for every lesson."

"That's great!" I added my name to the list of sponsors. "Oh, before I forget, these are for you." I passed an envelope across the dining table, containing some posters and leaflets I'd designed using the software at work.

"Thank you, sweetheart, they're wonderful." Jenny propped

them on her mantle like a family photo in pride of place. "Such a creative girl, you really could do anything you wanted, you know."

If I'd said that to anyone, it would have sounded patronising. When Jenny said it, I wanted to beam with pride.

She sat opposite me, chin resting on the tip of her pen, a twinkle in her light eyes. "Now as for your dates, there has been some interest." So far, three members had put their names down to take me out. "Andrew also said he will sponsor you to go out with his brother Jason. Don't worry, I've met him, he's lovely."

That didn't do much to comfort me; Jenny described everyone as lovely. Except for Daniel.

"The gals in the group"—she grinned—"myself included, will sponsor you to come for a night out on the town. Won't that be fun?"

My laugh sharply turned into a cough thanks to a balloon expanding inside my chest. None of us had socialised outside of the group before. DAYS sessions were another world, an oasis—for me anyway. It felt strange to mix them with real life. At least I could invite Olivia and Sarah along to help.

"There's something else, too." Jenny's voice lowered. She absently stirred her almost empty cup. "Andrew's been doing his thing with all the online advertising stuff. Facebook and tweety pages or whatever." I bit back a giggle, 'tweety pages' sounded so much cuter than Twitter. "He's had good responses from local papers and TV news."

"Wow, if this gets into the press you could be setting up more groups before you know it." I leaned over to squeeze her hand, unable to fathom why she looked so worried.

"Yes, well, that's the thing. One of the reporters went to meet Stuart and some of the others but..." She clicked her pen several times. "He was especially keen to cover your experience, with it being a high profile case n' all."

Oh.

I took a shaky sip of tea which was going cold, just like my hands. My story, my history and my fears would become public.

Correction: even more public.

A few minutes passed. We both looked out the window, watching the apple trees sway in the breeze outside. Jenny never impatiently rushed a silence, she allowed time for me to think, to consider new information. Theo did the same. *Theo!* What if he read the paper or saw the local news while he was here?

"Jenny, I can't— I'm sorry, I don't want to talk— I'm not ready."

"It's fine, love." She smiled and wrapped her hands around mine. For the first time, I noticed how fragile they were, pale and translucent like porcelain. The contrast between her personality and her appearance was so great that it was almost impossible to put the two halves together.

"Don't worry about it," she said with a dismissive wave. "I already told him it would probably be a no. You are far more important to me than publicity. I just wanted to give you the option." She smiled again and flipped open her diary, ready to go through my dates schedule.

She wasn't making light of it just to ease my conscience; she truly didn't care about publicity. But she did care about people. This was a huge opportunity to raise funds and awareness for her charity. A charity that I depended on.

Would I let my fear stop potential future members from being helped?

♫

"I think that's everything," I clicked off my calendar and finished my third cup of tea.

Jenny had moved on to sherry. "You're a star, thank you so much." We were walking back through the hall when she asked about Theo.

"We talk all day. Every day," I said. There was an unopened text from him waiting on my phone. "I don't know, we click but he's... I mean he's just so... he's Theodore Jackson."

"Who?"

I explained.

"Ah, I see." She nodded. "And?"

"And maybe he's changed his mind and doesn't want to see me again. He's probably got a whole list of women who would, oh, I don't know."

"Lara, don't you dare be thinking you're not good enough."

Putting his job and fame aside, Theo was spontaneous and sociable, full of energy and confidence. All the things I used to be. All the things that died with the old Lara. My worry wasn't about being *good* enough. It was about being just... enough.

Jenny lifted my hand and gave it a squeeze. "Be brave."

♪

Another reason why I wanted to see Theo again was to get the image of the Theo/Jeff monster out of my head. I walked in through my front door and checked my phone. As well as Theo's text, there was also a missed call. I returned it and he answered in a voice roughened by sleep. I hadn't realised it was almost midnight.

"Sorry," I said, "I didn't mean to wake you, I'll call back tomorrow."

"Don't go, you can wake me up anytime, I don't mind," he purred.

My blood pressure went off the charts. "In that case, would you, umm, like to meet up this weekend?"

"I would. I called earlier because Tom and May are planning a barbeque on the beach and were wondering if you'd like to join us?" When I didn't respond, he added, "Olivia can come too?" As if he could hear my brain panicking about going alone. *Sweet.*

I didn't let myself overthink, I just said, "Yes."

"Then, Miss Quinn, I will see you tomorrow."

I curled up into bed, too flustered and excited to sleep, and idly flicked through my phone's camera roll; mainly pictures of all the old buildings I'd helped to restore. As long as they were still standing with good foundations, they could be made not just useful, but beautiful again, even when others said they needed to be torn down. That thought boosted my confidence.

I was still standing.

Damage can be repaired.

Who knew what could happen tomorrow?

Tomorrow – Avril Lavigne

Day 347
Saturday

Time trickles by when you're waiting to go on holiday. Until the last hour. Then suddenly you're in a rush, frantically running around packing last-minute essentials (which I guarantee you won't use) whilst checking your tickets are safe a million times.

Well, that was similar to how my day went, and I'd just hit the frantic stage.

I finished off my makeup with a customary flick of eyeliner and stood to examine my clothes: A soft white blouse with lace around the shoulders, tucked into skinny jeans, boots, and a grey wool coat for when the sun went down.

Olivia walked into my room, looking gorgeous in a black jumpsuit. Polka-straight, golden hair pulled up into a messy, though perfect, bun. Sometimes, I couldn't help being envious. Not because of her long, slender legs and make-up-free pretty face. No, I envied her easy-going happiness. We used to be so similar.

If Day Zero never happened, we might still have been.

"You look hot," she said, skipping over the pile of clothes I'd tried on, then discarded in frustration, to get to my wardrobe. She came back with an oversized check scarf in shades of blush and tan and draped it over my shoulders. "There, perfect! Ready to go, hun?"

I added my final item to the outfit—a smile. "Ready as I'll ever be."

My butterflies evolved into a flock of swans.

On the journey, Olivia chatted away about a new TV program and various bits of gossip between singing along to the radio. She was quite happy to have a full-on conversation by herself while I watched the blur of scenery pass by, preparing a mental list of questions to ask Theo in case my mind went blank. Streets of grey stone buildings faded into an expanse of clear blue sky, dipping into green and brown fields. Puddles left by recent downpours glittered like molten gold in the evening light.

As we pulled off the road into the film site entrance, I patted Olivia's hand with a whispered 'here we go,' trying to channel my nerves back into excitement.

I got out of the car, gave my appearance one last check in the window reflection, and was about to text Theo to say we'd arrived when a short, stocky man wearing a striped suit straight out of a gangster movie waved us over to the office.

"Lara Quinn?" he asked directly when we reached the door. I nodded and held my hand out to shake, which he accepted. Roughly.

"Phillip Young. Theo Jackson's Manager." He ushered us into the office. "I'm sorry to say, Mr Jackson will not be able to meet you tonight. After a discussion, he re-evaluated the situation and we thought it best that I deal with matters from now on."

I didn't understand. Theo didn't want to see me? What situation?

"If you wouldn't mind," Phillip continued, handing me some papers, either ignoring or blind to my confusion. "There's some forms to sign. Basically, they state we're prepared to pay for medical expenses and loss of earnings incurred by your recent accident, as long as it remains private."

Oh, so *basically*, he wanted to pay me off to keep my mouth shut.

I stared at the stone-cold bribe in my hand, sticking to my skin, burning and freezing like dry ice. *You knew this would happen.* Olivia stood silently next to me. Shock and anger were the only things that sent her quiet.

"I'm sorry he took things this far. I tried to warn him." Phillip spoke about Theo as if he were a child. I pushed the irritation of that aside, he wasn't my concern anymore. "I believe it's for the best that you don't see him again. Especially in your, how can I say?" He rolled a hand in the air, stirring up his next words. "*Vulnerable* state."

There was no mistaking the piteous look he gave me.

My body froze. Phillip knew about Day Zero.

Had he told Theo? Was that why Theo had sent this guy to 'deal' with me? Or was this all his manager's decision? Why did I still care? I scribbled a poor version of my signature onto the form and thrust it back into his chest, ridding myself of the poisoned paper.

Unlike Olivia, anger did not quieten me. "You can tell Mr Jackson I don't want a penny of his hush money." I turned and strode straight for the car, knees weak, hands in solid fists.

My fingers had barely touched the door handle when Theo called my name. I hated the way it still sent an electric current through my body. He approached us from the beach path, wearing period costume. Knee-high boots, forest-green trousers and waistcoat, tailcoat slung over his arm. Bloody hell he was handsome. Which somehow made me even angrier. As did the way he greeted me; as if nothing had changed. I wanted to say so much, but shivering panic wormed its way into my system, so I ignored him.

His hand appeared on the door in front of me. "Hey, what's wrong?"

Wrong? I'd been fooled by his act. My guard had slipped. I'd been stupid enough to trust him. That's what was wrong.

He moved closer. "Lara? Where are you going?"

Infuriating tears stung my eyes. I would not appear weak or *vulnerable* in front of him. I was strong enough to know my own mind, thank you very much. A flush of hot fury swept through my veins, not purely because of Theo and his manager. I felt the injustice of having the life I'd known ripped away from me. I felt the disgust of every time I saw my scars, an evil signature carved across my body. I felt the choking rage of whenever I saw *his* ghostly white face in my nightmares. *He...* Jeff made me a victim once.

I would never be made one again.

I looked at Theo, right into his wide eyes and questioning face. *As if he cares.* "Oh, you are good. I hope you get your Oscar one day."

"I don't know what you mean?" He smiled nervously and tried to take my hand.

I slapped him.

A sharp, reflexive slap which took us both by surprise.

My palm burned. "Don't touch me!" Tears spilt onto my cheeks. "You know exactly what I mean. You almost had me with your kindness, the compliments, the flirting! Was anything you said true? No—" I laughed even though I was shaking all over. "Don't answer that, I don't care. And I don't want your bloody money."

"Money? What? Wait, Lara, slow down." He pressed a hand to his reddening face. "Where's all this coming from?"

I snapped. "Is this a game to you? What, you're bored now you've realised I'm not easy, and you're not gonna get what you want? Well don't worry, I signed your damn forms and I'll be out of your way."

I turned back to the car and forced my voice into a low,

emotionless monotone, "The stories are true then. You're not the man I hoped you were, Theo. I'm not hurt. Just disappointed."

That last line reminded me of Dad, the time I lied to him about staying at Olivia's house when really we were out clubbing. *'I'm disappointed in you, Lara. What if something had happened and we didn't know where you were?'* he'd said calmly, which upset me more than any telling off would have. I hoped in some way it would affect Theo too. Even if it was partly a lie—I *was* hurt.

Theo still had one hand against my door, easily holding it shut regardless of my attempts to pull it open. "What forms?" He rubbed his forehead, cheek, down to his chin. "What forms, Lara?"

He should have been glad I'd signed, so why pretend not to know? I looked past him to Olivia, her face a jumbled up jigsaw of emotion.

"The forms you sent so you wouldn't have to deal with me anymore," I panted.

"I swear." Theo's desperate eyes locked onto mine. "I don't know what you're talking about. Who gave them to you?"

"You did. Your manager, he said"—*breathe Lara, breathe, one, two*—"he said you didn't want to see me, that you would pay—" The hold I had over my panic attack crumbled with every second. Anger bubbled into acid that ate away at my insides and sucked the oxygen from my lungs.

Olivia interrupted, "Laa-Laa, let's get out of here, he's not worth this. He's not worth anything."

Theo's body sagged against the car. "Olivia, please, what's going on? How do you know Phillip and *what* forms?"

She scowled, dug in her pocket, pulled out a copy of the document and handed it over. I'd been in such a hurry to leave, Phillip must have given it to her instead.

As Theo read, he straightened again, muscles tense, jaw clamped. Upon reaching the last section about payment, he coughed as if the words made him physically choke, screwed the paper into a ball, held it up in a fist and looked straight at me. "When did he give you this?"

"Just now, in the office." I raised my blurry eyes to the sky, blinking to dry them quicker.

All of Theo's sharpness disappeared. He threw the paper to the floor, held my face and swept his thumbs over my damp cheeks. "I didn't do this."

"Let me go." Even as I said it, my head sunk further into his hands.

"I'm not letting you go when you're hurt," he said softly, "I didn't when we met, and I won't now."

Theo's touch made me want to cry all over again. It eroded the walls that kept me together. I didn't know him well enough to tell when he wasn't acting, but a part of me told me to stay, to not give up, to let him explain. *You don't know him at all.*

I knew enough to want to take the risk.

His hands dropped to my shoulders. "Olivia, please fetch Phillip from the office, tell him it's urgent."

She wavered. Knowing her, it was because she half wanted to see the drama unfold, half didn't want to leave me. I nodded for her to go and perched myself on the bonnet of the car. Theo stayed close, a hand hovering above my arm. His fingers shook.

"I can't believe he went this far," he whispered, more to himself than to me.

Olivia returned from the office and jogged to my side. Phillip emerged a second later. Theo took a step forward and as he moved, everything about him—expression, body, voice— became a deadly heat-seeking missile, honed in on Phillip.

"What have you done?" Theo demanded.

Phillip halted in the middle of the car park, his eyes to-and-froing between me and Theo. "Ah, come on now, we can talk about this later."

We were all startled by Tom and May appearing from the

beach path. They stopped when they saw us, as suddenly as if they'd hit a concrete wall.

Theo held up a hand, signalling for them to wait. "Phillip, I asked you a question," he growled. "What have you done?"

"Mate, come on." Phillip snorted, tugging at his shirt collar. "This is no time to get emotional. Trust me."

Theo took another determined stride toward Phillip. I must have followed him—though I don't remember doing it—because I was clinging onto his elbow, afraid of what a person with his strength could do to someone like Phillip.

"Trust you?" Theo grinned, but it was lethal. "How? When clearly, you think it's fine to go behind my back and make decisions for me. I specifically told you to stay out of this."

The suffocating chain around my chest loosened a notch.

"I'm doing what's best. I'm dealing with it, so you don't have to," Phillip argued. I guess the 'it' referred to me. *Charming*. "I'm protecting you mate. And her." Phillip turned on me, his voice slithering through a smile. "The press can be so unkind, Lara. And after everything you've been through already, if they found that you—"

"Stop!" I yelled.

Theo's arm tensed under my fingertips, poised and ready like a runner on a start line.

I pointed my free hand at Phillip, wishing I could poke my finger right into his smug face. "You don't know anything about me."

Hate is a strong word, but at that moment, I hated him. I hated the way he'd treated Theo. I hated the way he'd made me feel used and worthless in the way *he*... the way Jeff had.

"Laa-Laa." Olivia carefully placed a hand on my shoulder. "Come on, let's go."

Since living together, Olivia knew me in ways no one else did. I'd always been careful to hide any outbursts after Day Zero. I couldn't hide them from her. She heard my screams at night and understood how I had to psych myself up every time I left the house. She saw the smashed glasses or plates on the kitchen floor whenever an uninvited memory caused me to lose grip. She was also the only person who had seen me mad, and I mean *livid*, before.

"You're not leaving," Theo responded, taking my hand before pinpointing his attention back onto Phillip. "He is."

Everyone froze, waiting for Theo to say something more.

Finally, he did: "You're fired."

Those words shot the cocky smile right off Phillip's face. "Come on mate, you don't mean that."

"I mean it," Theo said. "So unless you want me to tell all of your current and prospective clients about how you acted today without my consent, you will go, pack your things and leave."

Phillip went to protest, but Theo cut him off. Instead of raising his voice, he lowered it, making every syllable clear and direct. "Get out of my sight. Now."

Shouting would not have been as powerful.

Men lost their temper all the time at work, Daniel especially. He shouted at his computer, at tools that weren't working, at anyone he felt wasn't listening and sometimes, at me. I never got used to it, I hated confrontation.

Theo's anger was different.

I remembered him saying that body language was about reading between the lines, so I studied him carefully: Quick, shallow breaths. Repeated tightening of his jaw. The hand that wasn't holding mine was clenched so tight his knuckles were white. Underneath the composed surface and cold voice—in between Theo's lines—he was furious, seething, but he controlled the emotion and allowed his head to rule his actions. I didn't know if it frightened or impressed me. A bit of both, I think.

Defeated, Phillip left.

Heavy silence engulfed us.

Tom found the courage to speak first. "Everyone alright?"

Although he addressed everyone, he spoke mainly to Theo, walking over to give him a tentative nudge on the arm.

"Yes. Thank you, Tom." Theo took a breath and smiled. It didn't reach his eyes. He lifted my hand to his chest, voice rough but gentle. "Don't go, Lara. Please. I need to talk to you."

"I don't know—"

"Not like this," he pleaded.

A numb kind of fog clouded my vision. I nodded. Theo asked Tom and May to show me and Olivia to the barbeque while he changed.

"Thank you," he added quietly, with a quick kiss on my cheek. "I'll be right there."

I followed the others down the narrow path to the beach. Olivia asked them about work in a chiming, higher pitch than normal, overcompensating and keeping the heat off me while I recovered. I wanted to hug her.

Stone gave way to dirt, dirt became sand. Salty air swept over my face. A short walk brought us to where they'd spread blankets on the sand, all surrounding a large metal bucket filled with wood. Tom busied himself with lighting it, then moved on to the barbeque.

Theo joined us, now dressed in black jeans and boots with a dark burgundy jumper. The colour suited his tan skin and dark features. He looked good in any era of fashion.

I turned away as my stomach churned and my throat tied itself in knots. I'd attacked Theo. *Again.* There was no excuse for hitting another person. I never used to be so explosive. This was a poor reflection of me and highlighted too clearly a new flaw in my personality; my mask of smiles was turning out to be a thin and fragile veil.

While Theo helped Tom set up a small table, we kept catching each other's eye. The distance between us was excruciating.

Look What You Made Me Do – Taylor Swift

Theo

Tom lifted plates out of a box of supplies and placed them on our fold-out picnic table. "Want to talk about it?"

My first reaction was: no, I did not, yet the words began to spill out as easily as water from an upturned glass.

"Whoa," Tom exhaled. "You did the right thing firing him. I would have kicked him as he passed if I'd known."

I laughed, releasing the pressure valve on my anger. "Dammit, Tom, what do I do now? Whatever he said to Lara must have been bad to make her react like that."

I looked up to see her clutching the scarf around her shoulders, clearly still anxious. Phillip had led her to believe she had been used, and she had believed him easily. Was that because of her insecurity, or my reputation? Neither option made me feel any better.

Tom randomly poked at the charcoal on the barbeque. "What do you think Phillip meant about the stuff she's been through?" he pondered.

There was wisdom and occasionally a pain in Lara's words that only came from experience. I suspected it was caused by something in her past she kept close to her chest. But I answered, "I don't know."

My attention drifted toward her again as she smiled at May. It was the kind of smile you couldn't help but return. She looked my way. *Our eyes met across a crowded room...* Yeesh. I had been reading too many romance scripts.

Tom elbowed me. "You really like this girl don't you?"

"Yes," I admitted without hesitation. "She constantly surprises me. There is so much more to—" I cut my words short as Lara approached.

Lara

I grabbed the drinks from my bag and went to add them to the table of food. A small gesture, but I needed to do something to show my remorse, and my gratitude for not also being told to get out of Theo's sight.

"We didn't want to come empty-handed so—" My voice cracked when Theo took the bottles, his fingers lingering on mine. I cleared my throat and tried again. "Please help yourselves."

Afraid of crying again, I went back to take my place next to Olivia and May on the blanket by the fire. They were talking about fashion, raving over various brands and trends. Thanks to their energy and laughter, I started to feel brighter. Brighter still when the smell of cooking floated our way.

Theo came to kneel on the blanket beside me. I kept my focus on the swaying, crackling flames, enjoying the warmth on my skin.

"What is it about open fires that makes them so mesmerising?" he said.

Olivia and May pretended not to be listening.

"It's because they look so delicate on the surface but underneath they're alive and wild," I replied. "Which I suppose, makes them kind of beautiful."

I looked over my shoulder and my heart stuttered. Theo was watching me. As if nothing else existed.

"Food won't be ready for half an hour," he said. "Walk with me?"

He stood and offered me his hand. *Be brave.* I took it.

We walked toward the dunes, watching the crashing waves as the tide came in. Brushstrokes of red sunlight shimmered over the cliffs.

How would I even begin to apologise? I needed to, sooner rather than later. Air stuck to my throat like treacle. *Be honest.* That's all I could do. My feet stopped. The effort of speaking took up all my concentration.

"Theo, my behaviour earlier was—"

"Lara, you have nothing to apologise for." Hands in pockets, he shook his head. "If I had sent those forms, then I would have thoroughly deserved everything I got."

"But you didn't, it was a mistake and that's not the point. I was wrong to blow up like that, there's no excuse." I spoke quickly, trying to get everything out before he could stop me again. "I know you said not to keep apologising, but this time it's important. Please. I am so, *so* truly sorry for hitting you."

He examined his feet. "You were already forgiven." Met my gaze and smiled. "But thank you."

Life returned to his eyes as he accepted my apology and put the event into the past, just like another piece of paper, balled up and thrown aside. Forgotten.

"Hey." His smile turned into a smirk. "You did say nothing about us was conventional." I followed as he carried on walking. "I couldn't let you leave earlier knowing you would hate me. Phillip was way out of line. I can't believe..." A huff of air finished his sentence. "I hired him to help me out of a situation which became public and created a lot of embarrassment, even for my family."

A moment passed as he kicked a few stones into the sea. "I was in a bad place. It was all my fault. But put it this way, if you had met me a year ago, you definitely would *not* have let me get in your car."

The rumours about his dodgy past were true then.

At the top of the dune, we sat amongst the swaying grass, overlooking the bay. He told me of when he got his first big acting role, of how fame and the recognition it brought hit him overnight. He later became involved with his co-star—the one I'd seen in the pictures, Yasmin—and with the life she led. Partying, travelling, always wanting to be seen, to be popular. A 'social influencer.'

"I convinced myself she loved me and that our life was normal." Bitterness chiselled the edge of Theo's words. "I listened to bad advice and acted the way people expected me to. Arrogant, hard." He passed a hand over his face and scoffed. "A bad boy."

During that time in L.A., Theo explained, he hadn't seen or spoken to his family. "Deep down I knew what I was doing was wrong. I was fooling myself. I didn't want to see their *disappointment* in me."

Dad's line had touched a nerve. I pulled my scarf tighter as Theo continued.

One night, Theo came home to find that Yasmin had yet again filled their house with a party of people, most of whom he didn't know. "I walked in feeling like a stranger," he said, describing the devastation of seeing his possessions and home being destroyed. The last straw was walking into his room to find Yasmin with another man. "She wasn't even sorry." Pain fractured his whispered voice. "She laughed at me. Mocked me for not wanting to join in with them."

My hands rose to hide the heat colouring my cheeks.

Theo jabbed at the sand with a stick of driftwood. "The tower of lies I'd built my life on collapsed. She didn't love me. I was just another prop being used to make her way up the Hollywood ladder. So I walked out with nothing but the clothes on my back and got on the next plane to the only place and the only people I had left. Home." He snapped the stick in two. "So much for my ability to read people."

Betrayal wasn't a sharp knife that left a clean cut, it was a pair of blunt scissors that tore the edges, leaving them frayed and raw.

While Theo had opened up his history, his life, and even his heart to me, I sat there barely moving so as not to distract him, telling myself not to stare, to watch the lights of the town mirrored across the sea. I never managed to look away for long. I wanted to reach out and comfort him, but my heart raced. I couldn't risk falling apart again. All I did was lean closer, touching my shoulder to his. It wasn't enough. I was so used to being split double—

feeling one way, saying or acting another—that I couldn't remember how to rejoin the two halves.

The walls I'd built to protect me made me cold. Another new flaw.

Theo carried on his story: A few days after returning home to his family the reports in the media started. Unforgiving and explicit rumours from nameless sources—Yasmin.

He smiled into the distance. "*For what do we live, but to make sport for our neighbours?*" Again, his phrase reminded me of something I'd heard before. A quote maybe? "She wanted to destroy my reputation before I had a chance to expose her. As if I would!" Theo humphed. "Anyway, that's why I needed Phillip. He had the power and connections to control the press. Which worked. For a while. Till a few weeks ago, when you and I were standing right here. I received a heads-up that Yasmin said something about me in an interview. Seems like no one can stop her."

So that must have been the text message.

Closing his eyes, Theo took a deep breath and dropped his head back into the breeze. I still didn't know what to say or understand why he was telling me so much.

Out of the blue, he leaned forward, breaking the barrier of my personal space. I let him.

"Lara? I need to know something." *Oh no, please don't ask about what Phillip said.* "Did you mean what you said before— that you believe it's more important who a person is trying to be and who they want to be, rather than who they were?"

I relaxed my vice-like grip on my scarf. "Yes. Of course, I believe it." I had to.

"Good." He grasped one of my hands. "Because you're right. I'm not the man you thought. But I'm working on it."

I wasn't the person he thought I was either. No one told strangers or new acquaintances their innermost thoughts and feelings, that was why first impressions of people were rarely accurate. Didn't everyone have a face, a persona of themselves that they put on to some extent? I supposed, for some people that persona was further from the truth than for others. A thin line ran between being guarded and being deceptive.

Theo's hands were now wrapped completely around mine, warming them in a gentle cocoon. "You have probably heard '*such different accounts*' of me that they '*puzzle you exceedingly,*' Miss Quinn."

It clicked! I knew why some of his phrases were familiar. He was quoting from *Pride and Prejudice*. "You do puzzle me, Mr Jackson. Or should I say, Mr Darcy?" I grinned.

His eyebrows shot up. "You read Austen?"

"I read a lot of things."

"Hmm. Then that's embarrassing."

"Why?" I thought it was adorably sexy.

"Because now you will realise that each time I manage to sound intelligent, I am in fact reciting memorised lines."

"I don't think you need to quote people to sound intelligent, you do it very well on your own." I gripped his long fingers to steal some of his fearless honesty. "And... we have something in common."

"A secret love for classic literature?"

I giggled. "Yeah, that. And... we're both trying to be better." Opening up to him, even just a little, didn't make me feel weak. It made me feel free.

He frowned in thought, then smiled at our intertwined fingers. "I'm afraid I'm more Wickham than Darcy."

Mr George Wickham was a scoundrel. The baddie. Darcy's nemesis, in a restrained, simmering, 18th-century sort of way.

I shook my head. "Wickham never admitted to his mistakes and never made any effort to change. So I'm sorry to burst your whole cliché, bad boy bubble, Theo, but you're nothing like Wickham."

Theo laughed, although I got the feeling he was struggling to accept my assurance. He circled a finger over my palm, spreading giddy heat from his body to mine.

"You *really* need to stop doing that," he said, lifting a hand to brush his thumb over my lip.

I must have been biting it. *What is his problem?* "Fine." Annoyed, I tried to pull my hands away, but he held on tighter. "It's a bad habit. I know."

"It's not a bad habit." He touched my chin, asking me to make eye contact. "But it could be a dangerous one."

Something about the hunger in his gaze and rumbling tone of voice made me want to find out what kind of danger. The distance between our faces grew uncomfortably small. It wasn't small enough. My stomach clenched as my breath hitched.

He leaned back with a gentle sigh. "Come on. We should get back before Tom burns everything."

Theo

We didn't talk on the way back, but Lara didn't pull away from my hand again either. I plucked up the courage to put an arm around her shoulder and held on for as long as she let me, which was till we came into view of the others, then she skipped away with a glittering, coy smile.

Beautifully wild, I thought, *just like a fire.*

Day 348
Sunday

It had gone dark outside since I'd sat on the end of my bed. That was how long I'd been there, tapping my feet to the rhythm of my music, hands drumming a beat into my thighs, engaged in a battle of wills against my phone. Every time I pressed call, I chickened out and hung up before it could ring. *Be brave.*

"Lara." Theo answered with his usual growling 'r.' I collapsed backwards onto the bouncy mattress. "I was worried I wouldn't hear from you again."

His text from earlier in the day waited in my inbox. Without a reply.

I started to say, 'I'm sorry,' then stopped myself. "I went to my parents for lunch and..." *Be honest.* "I'm still processing what happened yesterday."

His deep breath vibrated through the speaker. "Yesterday was a lot to process. I wouldn't have blamed you for not calling. I'm relieved you have, though." The relief showed through his tired voice.

Sometimes, I became so preoccupied with managing my actions and appearance to be 'normal,' that I failed to see how things affected the people right in front of me.

My way of coping was all back to front.

Theo had fired Phillip, meaning he'd been hurt enough to risk the consequences. It wasn't called getting 'stabbed in the back' for no reason. That was one thing I did understand. Literally and figuratively. Both were agonising. Both took a long time to recover from.

"What happens now?" I asked. "Will you replace Phillip?"

"No. I think it's time to take control of my own life. I'll go back to my agent for help with the PR side." He perked up. "You know, there was a minute when I thought you were going to slap him too. Now that would have been fun to witness."

"Believe me, I wanted to, I've come up against far worse men than him." A shudder crossed my shoulders. "Look, I don't know anything about PR or agents and managers, but I do know stories disappear. Especially if they aren't true. All you can do is carry on being yourself, Theo. Prove them wrong. The people who matter will know the truth."

Come on, *be yourself*? Did I seriously say that? Hypocrite.

Theo went quiet. I lay still, listening to his slow breaths. If I closed my eyes I could almost feel his hands around mine.

"You're right," he said, "I have to be patient. Something I'm not very good at. Lara... would you do me a favour?"

"Anything," I replied without thinking.

"Hmm, anything?" His deep hum charged the air. I buried my face in a pillow. "I'll remember that for another day, Miss Quinn. For now... we've been honest with each other right from the start, so promise me something?"

We had been honest. Mostly. On his side.

My insides squirmed. "Okay?"

"Don't Google me. If there's ever anything you want to know, anything at all, please ask me." A strange request, but one I completely understood.

"I promise. Long as you promise to do the same."

What a stupid thing to say! It was obvious why he should ask, but me? I may as well have told him not to press a big red mystery button because now, all he would think about was pressing the flippin' big red button.

"I promise," he said earnestly, before letting out a chuckle. "Got some dodgy photos lurking on an old Facebook page somewhere?"

"Something like that." There might have been, from my college days, if you looked hard enough.

So much for my being honest.

We carried on talking as Theo walked back to his caravan from the set, sharing stories about school days and old antics. Still lying on my bed, lazily twirling hair around my fingers, I laughed as he described trying to make a cup of tea in this tiny caravan, elbows knocking things over everywhere he turned.

"I hate to say it," he said, "but I have to go in the shower now, so unless you want to join me..."

A flutter ran from my chest to my thighs. "If it's anything like the rest of your caravan, I doubt we'd fit." Pitiful example of my flirting skills.

"Hmm," he breathed, "I'm sure we could find a way."

I imagined lifting his shirt and what his skin would feel like. Warm, smooth, firm... Liquid heat pooled in my belly, evaporating the air from my lungs.

"Lara, are you biting your lip?"

"No." I was.

"Liar."

"How did you—?"

His chuckle evolved into a groan, deliciously fading into a sigh. "Goodnight, Lara."

I put the phone down, my body full of bubbles and electricity. And fire.

Delicate – Taylor Swift

Lara's Journal
Day 3

Days one and two are non-existent.

The first thing I remember was a voice, "Lara? Can you hear me?"

It was daytime—my eyelids were red from the glow of outside light—other than that, I didn't have the foggiest what was going on.

A dull throb spread throughout my body. The light burned my eyes as I forced them open. Shapes gradually formed into recognisable things: windows, ceiling tiles, an armchair, a man.

"That's it. Try and stay awake, focus on me," he said.

He then spoke to someone over his shoulder. A pen in his top pocket caught the sunlight. Faint disco ball-like patterns shot across the ceiling. "Lara, you're safe. Your parents are right here."

As my vision cleared, I saw a badge on his white jacket: 'Mr Howard. Surgical Dept'

My initial thought was: *why aren't surgeons called Dr?* That's how delirious I was. It took a few seconds for it to click that I was in a hospital. I panicked. The aching all over my body intensified like pins and broken glass floating through my blood. An especially sharp pin made my leg flinch. With it came a second of clarity.

Jeff.

Memories raced through my mind like a video on fast forward. I tensed and blinked; I was on the office floor, terrified, readying myself for the next blow. *Where is he?* I blinked again; I was outside in the mud. *Run Daniel, we need to run!*

Someone started shouting. Mr Howard called for a nurse. They both held my arms as the shouting turned into groans. Drowsiness spun the room as the nurse pushed something into the tube in my arm and I fell under the liquid spell of drugs.

I heard Mr Howard ask my mother to come closer.

No, it's not safe. I kept blinking; Daniel disappeared. I was back in the small room, everything bright and white. My shoulders were still being held down by the nurse in green scrubs. The groaning in the background stopped. It had been coming from me all along.

Mom stepped from behind a screen wearing her favourite sunshine yellow mac, her face pale and puffy, eyes red from crying. She had never looked more beautiful to me.

My mom.

Standing in front of me.

Not a dream.

I reached out, feeling like a child again, longing to run to her so she could cwtch me up, fixing my wounds with kisses and brightly coloured plasters.

Barely able to say my name before bursting into tears, she wrapped her shaking arms around me. Dad followed behind her, turning us into a bundle of tangled limbs. I clung on, afraid that if ever I let go, they would disappear and fade into darkness all over again.

♫

Mr Howard came back later that day and asked to examine me. He checked various charts along with the readings on the screens next to me. "How's your pain?" he asked. "Scale of one to ten."

Every nerve along the path of the knife's edge burned white-hot, splitting my back in two. Easily an eight.

I looked at my parent's worried faces and gritted my teeth. "I'm fine. Six."

His black eyes narrowed into sceptical slits. "I'll give you more painkillers in a little while so you can rest," he said before giving me a brief rundown of events. "You're doing extremely well. When you arrived you were unconscious. Your heart stopped briefly due to the blood loss but we took you straight into surgery, repaired the internal injuries and stopped the bleeding. There's muscle and nerve damage but I expect you to make a full recovery. We'll talk more tomorrow." He smiled and hung my file back above my bed.

My mind repeated some of the words over and over—heart, surgery, *damage*—but they may as well have been a different language.

All I knew for sure was that I'd survived.

Genesis - Ruelle

Lara's Journal
Day 10

Tinkling cups and rattling trays signalled breakfast was on its way up the ward. The welcome smell of toast and coffee roused a grumble from my stomach. There were even mini pots of jam accompanying the toast. I tried to smile, but it felt like something my body wasn't ready for, my muscles were shaky and clumsy like a baby animal taking its first steps.

Memories of Day Zero were clear by this point. Too clear.

First, I had to recount events to the doctors, then the police, then again to another detective, forcing me to re-watch a horrific movie that never ended. Not even when I closed my eyes. I memorised the quickest way, concentrating on details, giving times and specifics so there were fewer follow-up questions. Each retelling drained my energy. My voice became so robotic and distant that it didn't sound like mine anymore.

The first question I asked was if they'd caught *him*. The police 'couldn't comment' at the time, which I guessed meant no. Jeff was still out there. Somewhere.

My second question was about Daniel, unsure if his presence had been another trick of my imagination. It wasn't. He'd travelled with me in the ambulance, waited for my parents, and stayed with them until I was out of surgery. He'd since been told I was awake so I couldn't understand why he hadn't come to see me.

At 3 pm the doctors did their afternoon rounds. I was surprised to see Mr Howard coming my way along with a woman I didn't recognise. Mom had dozed off in the armchair next to me. I gently nudged her awake.

Mr Howard greeted me with a placid smile, his granite eyes shining. "I have good news. This is Dr Carter." He indicated the woman. "She's here to talk about your transfer to a hospital in Cardiff."

A weight lifted from my chest. It meant my parents wouldn't have to stay at my little flat anymore. They looked exhausted.

Dr Carter continued the explanation, her mass of red hair bouncing with every word. "It'll be a slow recovery process, even after you leave the hospital, so we think it'll help to be nearer to your family, if that's what you want?" I agreed without hesitation. "I'll start the arrangements then."

I lay back on the hard bed, a pinprick of light and hope glinting at the end of a long, gloomy tunnel.

There was just one problem.

I waited till everyone left for the night and found my phone.

LARA: Dan, are you ok? I miss you. Please come visit soon xxx

He replied in less than a minute:

DANIEL: I am now. Be there first thing x

My heart raced with the need to see him. Tomorrow couldn't come quick enough.

It's Not Over Yet – For King And Country

Morning visiting hours came and went.

No Daniel.

Dad arrived with a bag of supplies, my favourite chocolates, and some cards that had been delivered to my flat. He then took Mom's place in the armchair while she went for lunch. Honestly, they were like my 24-hour bodyguard service. I tried to convince Dad to go back to the flat and get some rest.

"We're fine, sweetie. I wouldn't sleep knowing you're here alone." He carried on reading the paper.

Catching sight of a tall, broad-shouldered blonde man in a navy suit at the nurse's desk made my pulse jump. "At least go and have lunch with Mom. I'm not alone, look, Daniel's here."

Daniel walked toward my bed, turning people's heads along the way. The nurses couldn't take their eyes off him. That was the kind of power he had. A devil in angel's clothing. Seriously dangerous combination. When he flashed me a pure white smile, I silently begged the monitors to not show my rapid heart rate.

He shook hands with Dad before coming to sit next to me on the bed. He didn't understand the concept of personal space. Not that I'd ever minded.

Dad kissed my forehead. "I'll go join your Mom for lunch," he said, grinning as if it was his idea.

Daniel immediately dropped the bravado—the way he did when it was the two of us—and let his northern childhood accent sneak through, occasionally missing out words like 'the' and 'of.'

"I should have come sooner," he admitted, tugging at the curls on his forehead to try and smooth them. "I didn't want to get in the way with you and your family."

"You wouldn't have been in the way." I wanted him with me. I'd thought of him every minute since waking up, and of all the things I wanted to say. But now he was in front of me, my mind emptied.

It was a strange feeling; knowing someone had seen you at the worst possible moment in your life. Exposing, like sharing an intimate secret. In a way, it released me of any self-conscious nerves because nothing I did could possibly be as embarrassing as what he'd already seen.

He lifted my arm onto his lap, gripping my hands between his. "You're looking good."

My muscles finally remembered how to smile. "Ha, whatever!" I'd made an effort to wash my hair, but I looked like hell.

"Aye, well, you look better than last time." His laugh disappeared into a frown. "I shouldn't have— I'll shut up now."

If I looked too closely, I could see a reflection floating over the surface of his deep blue eyes—me lying broken on the floor, covered in blood. The memory made me shudder.

"Don't scare me like that again, Quinn," he whispered, stroking my wrist.

"I won't."

"Who else would fix my computer?"

"I only ever restart it. It's not rocket science." I lifted his hand and pressed a kiss to his baby-soft skin, wishing he would hold me so I could feel safe. But he'd never been the cuddling type. I always waited until he fell asleep, then snuck my arms around him.

When we first met, he'd had an endless stream of girlfriends, often more than one at a time. And he flirted with everyone. I'd quickly learned to ignore it. As time went on, I made fun of him for it. Slowly, I started to enjoy it. The secret wink when I arrived in the morning. The hidden hand around my waist in the office or on my knee under a desk. Our late-night *business* meetings...

"Dan," I choked on the dry air. "If you weren't there—"

He shook his head. "It were stupid to let you work alone."

"It's not your fault. Someone has to open up. It could have been anyone."

"I didn't know what to do." He leaned in closer, squeezing my hands so tightly it hurt. "Do you— how much do you remember?"

"I heard you arrive." I'd also heard him say that he loved me.

Without looking at me, he simply nodded. He didn't remind me of what he'd said. I started to question why. Did he not love me anymore? Was it a lie? Nothing more than a desperate attempt to help a dying woman?

Tears welled in my eyes. I lay back, shifting myself out of his grasp. "So what's happened since?"

"Police have completely shut down site until they finish their investigation." Golden hair flopped over his eyes as he hung his head. "I told them to take the whole bloody office container. I don't want it."

'Bloody' container was probably an accurate description.

I took a deep breath. "Daniel, I wanted to see you before I go."

He finally looked up. "Go? Go where?"

I explained about the transfer to another hospital. "They said it's going to be a slow process. I'll have to have physio, and... and other help."

Daniel knew how much I hated having to accept help. We were as stubborn as each other in that regard. He reached for my hands again. "When will you come back?"

"I don't know." I loved my job, and I loved working with him more than anything, but I wanted to feel the safety of distance and the comfort of home. The sense of calm that came from knowing your surroundings.

He looked away, using a smile to erase his pained expression, flicking his emotional switch and his focus back into boss mode. "Don't worry about work, we'll sort something out."

"You don't have to keep me on. I don't want special treatment."

"Aye, and when have I ever given you special treatment?" He said with a lopsided smirk that made my diaphragm do somersaults.

Only a month after joining David Clarke, I'd almost quit. Daniel had been drinking at the annual office party; I gave him a lift home. He invited me in. Made a move to kiss me. Yes, I fancied him, but I didn't know him, so I rejected him. Afterwards, I couldn't shake the sickening doubt he'd hired me purely because of being a woman, rather than for my actual ability. He didn't mention it the day after, so I put it down to him being drunk and hoped he'd forgotten. (Thinking about it now, it was probably because I'd embarrassed him.)

But then he changed. He... relaxed.

He gave up trying to show off.

A few weeks later on the way home from a meeting, we stopped to get dinner and talked into the night about our shared love of restoring old buildings, comparing dream houses and locations. He was intelligent and wickedly funny. He also opened up a little about his past. It shocked me, to be honest. His stepfather had been abusive and his mother—who he hadn't seen in years—was an addict who bounced in and out of rehab and prison. So he'd grown up mostly with his grandmother, who he adored.

Such a shame that it was only when he stopped trying to be noticed, that the nicer side of Daniel David shone through. That night, as we pulled up outside my flat, I leaned over and said, "If you still want to kiss me, I won't stop you again."

He wanted to. I didn't stop him.

Wow. Old Lara was bold.

Annnnyway, back to Day 11:

Daniel grinned. "I'm keeping you on because you're the best designer we've ever had. I were already planning on making you our new Head Of Design. How does that sound?"

A wave of excitement lifted me off the bed. It sounded perfect! And it was what I'd been working toward. "Are you serious? What about Peter?" Peter had been with the company longer than I had.

"He's a decent designer but he's such a suit." A twinkle—one that always made my knees buckle—appeared in Daniel's eyes. "You know what you're talking about in the office *and* on a building site. I want you, Quinn."

He already had me. Did he still not see that?

I fell silent, biting hard on my lower lip—the beginnings of my annoying habit.

"No need to make a decision now." He gently gripped my shoulder. "Think about it, eh?"

As I promised him I would, the enormity of what he was offering pulled me back to earth with a thud.

"Grand. Take care of yourself. I'll be in touch." With one last smile, he walked away, leaving me overwhelmed, excited and... disappointed.

Alone.

What About Love? – Heart

Day 349
Monday

Spring sun fought its way through fluffy clouds, warming the hidden garden in the centre of the town offices where Olivia and I sat, eating our lunch.

"I think Theo really likes you," she said, triumphantly scrunching up her empty crisp packet. "He wouldn't have bothered coming to meet your boring old mates and watch a film if he didn't. He'd be off somewhere fancy with his celeb friends."

She had a point. Although the more I learned about Theo, the more I doubted he enjoyed the whole 'celeb' part. Even so, what was he getting out of it? The memory of his hands around my face swept over my skin like a gentle breeze. Yes, I liked him and was attracted to him, *hell yes*, but I wasn't ready for... for, you know, *that*. The last thing I wanted was to lead him on.

Olivia pinched one of my grapes and flicked it up into her mouth. "I'd like, be straight with him, just ask him what he wants."

"You would because you're not afraid of anything. You know how awkward I get."

She rolled her eyes while also rolling up her sleeves and spreading herself across a bench. I felt chilly just looking at her bare arms, but in Wales, you had to make the most of every drop of sun you got.

"That's not true," she said. "I'm afraid of lots of things. And yeah, you can be goofy. Some guys find that cute, though. Daniel David. Case closed."

I resisted arguing about Daniel. All Olivia knew was that he'd once hit on me. I'd never told her what happened after that because Daniel asked me to keep it quiet. I was his apprentice back then after all. Keeping it a secret seemed exciting at the time.

Later, when it (whatever *it* was) fell apart, I was too embarrassed. And it felt wrong to bring it up now. Like when you couldn't remember someone's name, but you'd been talking to them for too long to ask. The longer it went on, the more weirdly painful it got.

Music drifted from one of the windows above us; I hummed along to the opening lines of *Wildest Dreams,* reminding me of the day I met Theo. The magic of music. I longed to see him again.

Picking up my bag and coffee mug, I tapped Olivia's head. "Time to go back to work."

"Yes, boss."

"I hate it when you call me boss."

"I know." She giggled, ducking out the way of a grape I threw in her direction.

I followed her back into the converted warehouse office block. "Remind me again how we stay friends?"

"Because you love me and rely on me for my mature advice and wisdomosity."

"Oh sure, that must be it."

We made our way up the three flights of stairs to a pair of double doors marked by gold lettering: 'David Clarke Construction.'

In the centre of our floor sat a large meeting table, around which was an assortment of mixed and matched chairs. Some of them were new, others I'd picked up second hand, then either painted or sanded back to natural wood. The walls were all a pale sky grey, decorated with abstract paintings in soft splashes of cobalt, lush green, rose pink, and coral orange—the colours of flowers and landscapes. Handmade ceramic pots containing ferns and palms broke up the rest of the space, creating a cosy garden feel. Being on the top floor meant we had a high open ceiling with skylights, bathing the room in light.

Olivia took her seat at the reception desk. I carried on through to my office. When I opened the door, I nearly flung my mug in the air.

His scent hit me first—fresh citrus—then the indigo eyes.

"Daniel!" I gasped. "What the? What are you doing here?"

He was sitting at my desk sporting my favourite combination of a charcoal suit with a baby-pink shirt, his fingers laced together on top of his head. One leg crossed, right ankle on left knee. Power pose. Body on full display, shadows of his tattoos visible through the tight-fitting shirt. Had he always been this big? Good grief, his muscles had grown muscles.

We spoke daily, but the last time we'd met in person was at his house, the day I'd left London for good. I could remember every hurtful second of it clearly. I scratched away the chill from the back of my neck. His hair had grown since, it curled back off his face like waves made of sand.

He grinned at my stunned expression, stood, and surprised me by crossing the room to enclose me in a tight hug. "Hello to you too, Quinn."

I let myself relax into his arms. I couldn't help it, it was good to see him again. "Sorry. Hi, how are you?"

"All good. So are you by the look of things?" He stepped back, hands on my shoulders, shamelessly looking me up and down.

I pulled away to hang my bag on the back of the door.

"You've cut your hair," he said, "I like it. And I like what you've done with the place. Natural. Rustic but chic. Modern. Very you."

Only Daniel could get away with complimenting a woman by comparing her to a 'rustic' warehouse.

My eyes rolled of their own accord. "And your hair's longer. Let me guess, you've been blacklisted by every hairdresser in London because you never called them back?" Several of his one-night stand's had been with hairdressers.

"Aye, you know me too well. I have to get me nan to cut it these days. She said to say hello by the way. And she still wants your Welshcake recipe."

His nan regularly dropped by the London office, always with a supply of homemade treats. A pang of guilt ran through me; I'd never said goodbye to her.

I shook myself off and skirted past Daniel to sit at the desk. It was *my* office after all, and if I wanted to get through this meeting, I couldn't afford to start reminiscing. Work and petty banter were much safer topics. "So how can I help? Or did you drive four hours just to pop by and check up on me?"

He shot me a crooked smile and sat on the desk, one foot propped on the side of my chair. "Nope. You're doing a fantastic job. I made the perfect choice when I gave you that promotion." Trust him to give himself credit. "We potentially have a huge client coming our way with a chain of bars across the country, including one in Cardiff. All of them need completely gutting. I need your help designing plans for the pitch."

"Wow, that is huge. Aren't the architectural plans your job though?" I mainly oversaw finishes—flooring, fixtures, decor—not structural renovation.

"Yeah, and I've got the drawings with me, but they won't mean anything to the owner. He hasn't got a clue about building." Daniel's knee leaned against my waist. "I need you to bring the plans to life. You know, give them your artistic touch. Show him what the finished places will look like." His smile was trying to charm me.

He didn't need to try, my head swam with ideas and my feet

tapped happily under the desk. I replied coolly, hiding my excitement. "What was that again, Daniel, you *need* me?"

His laugh boomed through the office. "Come off it, Quinn, I know inside that hot head of yours, you've already picked out stationery for the presentation."

A smile cracked through my blasé pretence.

He nudged his knee into my ribs. "Knew it. But fine, have it your way." Bringing his face level with mine, and very close, he repeated, "Lara, I need you."

He rarely called me Lara, except for when we were... well, *alone*. I wasn't proud of the flutter that ran through my chest. I looked away to switch on the computer.

"I'm glad to hear you admit it," I said, "but honestly, you had me at a bar in Cardiff."

He set a hand on my shoulder. "Awesome. We'll work on it together and I'll head back Friday. Don't mind if I crash at yours, eh?"

My mouth gaped. Not a sound came out. I couldn't say no. It was his company that renovated my place, after all. For free. "Err, fine, no problem. There's a sofa-bed in the office, nothing up to your five star standards though." Hopefully, he would change his mind and prefer a hotel with a proper bed.

"That'll do," he accepted. *Drat.* "Be like the old days again, Quinn."

No, it wouldn't. Nah ah. Nope. Not a chance.

He grinned. White and perfect, like butter wouldn't melt. "Few jobs to sort first, so see you later. Say, half sixish?"

I grimaced in return. "Yep, see you later."

Striding out of the office, he startled Olivia. She shook his hand, fussing with her hair, cheeks reddening. *Oh great.* What had I done?

In the middle of giving myself a pep talk—*having Daniel stay will be fun, we used to get on so well, we'll be busy working, Olivia won't do anything silly*—my mobile rang. Theo. My heart reacted as if it was directly connected to the phone, the vibration coming from within my ribs.

"Hi, you okay?" My eyes squeezed shut when I heard how annoyingly high my voice was.

"Hey. I am. You?"

Other than the fact that my flirt of a boss who'd seen me die, who I had a history with, and who my best friend now fancied had just invited himself to stay... "Fine," I chirped, "busy as usual. How's your day going?"

Listening to Theo talk about filming their latest scene on the beach transported me into his fascinating world filled with historic language, uncomfortable period clothes and the mad things they did behind the scenes. Using a top-hat as a target for golf practice for instance.

"I have to go home this weekend," he said. "My parents won't forgive me if I cancel, so I was wondering if you're free during the week?"

I grinned at the phone. "When were you thinking?"

"Tonight too soon?" He made it sound like a joke. I had the feeling it wasn't.

"Tonight would be perfect, but I can't." I heard him exhale. "My boss just arrived from London. We've got a big project on, I'm meeting him tonight." I didn't say it was at my own house. "How about tomorrow?" I suggested, biting a pen. Wanting to see Theo outweighed the worry of leaving Olivia alone with Daniel.

"Tomorrow's perfect. I can pick you up from work, we'll go for dinner?"

Oh, my giddy aunt. A proper date! I bit the pen again to muffle the squeak that jumped out of my mouth. Once I remembered how to speak, I gave him the office address.

He breathed softly, "Lara?" Oof. How did he always manage to make such a small word sound so intriguing and so sublimely sweet?

I hummed back, "Yeah?"

"Ignoring the whole Phillip debacle, I enjoyed seeing you again."

"You did?"

"Yes." His voice wrapped itself around my body like smooth silk. "And you were right by the way."

"About what?"

"That knowing you would get me into trouble."

"Why's that?" No one had ever accused me of being trouble before. Then again, I'd never got anyone fired before either.

He laughed, *my laugh*. "Hmm, because I've never had to be anything but myself around you. You already know far too much about me, which should scare me but it doesn't."

"I, umm...?" Being hopeless with words made phone conversations difficult. It was so much easier when I could just smile to make up for my silences. *Be honest*. "I don't know what to say to that."

"That's okay, I'm probably being too forward again. Hey, I'll let you get back to work. See you tomorrow."

My body didn't know what to do, I was floating around the office like a balloon, being blown back and forth by anxiety, excitement and confusion. Mostly confusion. I went to find Olivia to break the news about Daniel, and about my date.

♪

Olivia asked me the same question for the third time as I turned the key in our front door. "So Daniel's staying here? You're sure?"

I answered her in the same way. "Yes. I'm sure." Her enthusiasm made me more nervous by the second. "He's our boss, Liv. Be careful."

She glowered at me, offended by my lack of confidence. The expression looked out of place; even when annoyed she was pretty. It was like trying to be angry with Tinkerbell.

"Just because he's like, more Legolas than Will Turner, he's not a bad person," she said.

I just looked at her.

"Leg-o-las and Wiiill Tuuur-ner!" she repeated slowly. Because, yeah, that always made things clearer. "Two characters played by Orlando Bloom? Both gorgeous even though one's a blonde, blue-eyed fairy and the other's a dark brooding pirate."

The fact that I knew what she was getting at was a testament to our long friendship.

I kicked off my shoes in the porch. "This has nothing to do with looks and types. Daniel is a player. I've seen it. I know him." More than she knew. "Yes, he's charming and I'll be forever grateful to him, but he's not the kind you want to get close to." *Unless you want a broken heart.* I took a breath and looked her in the eye. "Sorry. I get it. Daniel is—"

"An Asgardian Thor man-mountain of gorgeousness?" Olivia supplied.

I guffawed. *She hasn't seen what's under the suit.* "Okay, yes he is. And no, he's not a bad person." Things might have been easier if he was. However, people were rarely black and white. Daniel was one hell of a grey, Thor-shaped blur.

"When it comes to women," I said, "he can't be trusted."

"Alright. I know you're looking out for me. Which is why you won't flip out when I have words with Theo."

"Words with Theo?"

"Yeah, like, the usual stuff." She shrugged off her coat and dropped it onto the stairs. "That if he hurts you, I'll break his nose and ruin his life, et cetera."

"Don't you dare!" I hung up her coat and followed as she skitted through the lounge door. "We're not a couple, nothing's going on. Liv, don't. Please."

"You seem pretty coupley to me. I know I said all that stuff about having fun, but I see the way he looks at you." She fell back onto the sofa. "It's *intense*, like, someone-throw-ice-over-the-guy intense. I don't want you to get hurt."

"I won't. I'm not expecting anything more and I won't be pushed into anything either. Stop worrying about me."

I went to the kitchen to start dinner. "Oh and, Liv? If you value your life, don't ever let Greg hear you call Legolas a fairy."

♫

By the time Daniel arrived, dinner was ready and I'd changed into jeans and a hoodie. Olivia eagerly ran to open the door. *Stop being paranoid.* Eventually, he walked in, peering around, inspecting the finished house. He'd been here once, just before I moved in.

I showed him into the office/spare room. "You hungry?"

"Always." His eyes meandered down my body. I'd seen that look before; I did not like where it was going.

I shot him a warning glare and shoved a fresh towel into his chest on my way out.

While we ate dinner around the table, I asked for more details about the new project. Fortunately, that kept the conversation going for a few hours, by which point I'd cleared the kitchen, tidied, and wiped down the surfaces (twice) trying to pass time. Daniel on the other hand had made himself at home. Bags and clothes were already all over the office floor, and he now took up the whole sofa, lying there reading a car magazine, his tie slung over the coffee table. Olivia sat on the armchair opposite playing on her phone. I noticed her makeup had been freshened up. I was too tired to worry anymore, I had to trust her. I did trust her.

I yawned, "I'm gonna say goodnight guys, see you tomorrow."

They both waved me off with a 'goodnight' in return. Daniel was being his calmer, genuine self. I hoped it meant he wasn't bothered about impressing Olivia.

I Knew You Were Trouble – Taylor Swift

Lara's Journal
Day 22

After seven hours of blissful sleep, I woke to find the rainbow garlands from the previous day's welcome home party still hanging from the bars around my hospital bed. My whole family and the band had all shown up to meet me, their expressions ranging from pure relief to happiness, to apprehension. Anxiety churned beneath like hidden currents behind calm waters. The weight of the questions they would never ask pushed me deeper under that water, suffocating me with its pressure. So, I'd kept smiling and told them I was glad to be home. The more I'd smiled, the more they believed me and slowly, the tension lifted.

My new ward was smaller, therefore quieter, than the one in London. There were six beds, each surrounded by a sickly lemon coloured curtain that reminded me of gone-off cream. They clashed hideously with the lilac walls.

Mom, Dad and Olivia arrived shortly after breakfast. Olivia greeted me with an excited but unnatural hug. It wasn't normal for Olivia to be nervous. My chest tightened as a new fear hit me—Would anything ever be normal again?

After lunch, two policemen arrived.

The taller one of the two introduced himself and explained the reason for their visit, "Miss Quinn, we've got good news. Jeffrey Smyth is in custody. He was arrested by police at an A&E in South London trying to get his infected eye injury looked at."

My body went cold when I heard the name, as instant and paralysing as an ice bath. His eye must have been really bad. A laugh bubbled up into my throat. Mom wrapped her hands tightly around mine. Dad rubbed my shoulder. Olivia sat at the end of the bed, her hands gripping my feet.

Keeping his voice slow and clear, the officer continued, "It was thanks to your description and information that we were able to identify him. We've now also been able to link him to four previous attacks."

I gasped. "Four other attacks?"

"Yes, Miss. All within the last month."

"Where?" Dad asked. "Are they okay?"

The officers exchanged a glance. It was fleeting. Barely noticeable. It filled me with dread.

The shorter officer with a beard answered, "Four women in the London area, Sir. I'm sorry to say—"

"They're dead, aren't they?" I already knew the answer. My heart felt like a brick in my chest. Solidly refusing to beat.

The officer nodded. Four women were dead. I had nearly been the fifth. In those moments when my heart had stopped beating, I *was* the fifth.

I was murdered.

Sharp pain in my back drew out a gargled sob. My hands shuddered. Black spots crept into my vision. I heard Mom shout for help, then I heard nothing at all.

♫

Olivia's petite, pale face slowly came into focus as I stirred. She jumped off her chair. "Hi, you okay? I'll go get your mom."

"No. Wait, I'm alright." I reached out for her arm. "What happened?"

"You sort of, like, panicked and pulled your stitches. The doctor gave you something for the pain, then you dozed off." Her eyes watered as she grabbed hold of my hand.

"I'll be okay," I said, squeezing her fingers. "Daniel showed up before he could— before I—" My voice stuttered, as though my brain had erased the rest of the words from existence in a wild hope it could erase the event itself.

She flung her arms around my neck. "We were all so scared. I'm so happy you're home, Laa-Laa."

I hugged her until our arms went numb with pins and needles. "What do I do now? Daniel wants to make me the new head designer. I don't know if I can go back."

"You shouldn't be thinking about work," she told me firmly.

"I have to think about something, Liv, otherwise I'll go mad. I can't sleep. I need to do *something*."

The hospital was a prison of curtains, and I was stuck in a cell with only my thoughts and nightmares to keep me company.

♪♪

Dr Carter came back later that afternoon. She re-introduced herself, although she didn't need to. Her flaming red hair was unforgettable. "Right then," she said like a sergeant major commanding her troops, "let's get you down to the gym."

I may have let out an audible groan at the thought of a gym. She ignored me and brought over a wheelchair.

The gym turned out just to be a large hall with padded mats on the floor, a few treadmills and some other strange-looking apparatus dotted about. Thankfully, there were only a handful of other patients there.

We crossed the room to an area where a bar ran along one wall with a mirror behind it. It reminded me of the dance studio I'd attended when I was little. The last thing I felt up to was a ballet lesson; they were bad enough back then. 'Lara Quinn' and 'graceful' were two things that never went together. Fast forward to my teens and I loved dancing and still do. *Nothing can keep me off the dance floor,* I thought, then pressed a hand to my waist. *Well, almost nothing.*

"First things first, we're going to do some stretches." Dr Carter crouched in front of my chair. "Then, as you get stronger we'll move on to walking and lifting. Don't worry, love, by the time you leave here, you'll have abs of steel."

('Steel' would be a huge exaggeration, but they're definitely stronger than before. Everything has a silver lining I guess.)

Within five minutes of being pushed and pulled around, I was sweating and dizzy. I knelt on all fours, panting through the pain.

Her voice softened, "You can do this, Lara."

Tears welled up with frustration. The moves were simple. A month before, I could have done them in my sleep.

"It'll get easier, I promise," she said. "From what I heard about the other guy, you're a fighter. You can do this."

~~I could.~~

I would.

I will.

In My Blood – Shawn Mendes

Day 350
Tuesday

THEO: Can't wait to see you later. I've found a place called The Mermaid overlooking the sea, I think you'll love it. xxT

LARA: Sounds lush! I'm counting down the minutes. xx

THEO: See you in 592 minutes then. 😊 xxT

The Mermaid, I'd heard, was an old hay barn, recently turned into a tapas and cocktail restaurant. Stunning, fancy, and in the middle of nowhere. Theo must have put some effort into finding it.

Hoping Theo wouldn't recognise them, I paired the trousers May had given me with a white linen shirt. Then I packed a bag with my makeup, hair straighteners, nude-coloured heels and gold jewellery ready for the evening.

When I got down to the kitchen, Olivia and Daniel were already sitting at the bar eating breakfast, chatting energetically about the news on the radio. It felt... odd. They'd briefly met before, but since when had they become such good friends?

For most of the day, I worked on the tables in the meeting area and let Daniel have my office. It was easier that way, he had lots of phone calls, plus it meant I was closer to Olivia.

"You're sure this is okay? Not too casual?" I asked her again after catching my reflection on a computer screen.

"You look gorgeous!" She beamed. "Once he's here you'll relax and you'll be fine. Stop overthinking."

Daniel joined us at the table, looking over my drawings and plans. "What you overthinking this time? Looks grand so far."

"Oh, nothing," I mumbled. "You know me, I'm a perfectionist,"

He accepted my excuse without question. "I've got some updated plans and measurements. Come take a look."

We went back to my office where he offered me a seat—my seat —at the desk so I could read the email. Shutting the door behind us, he took his usual spot on the desk, spinning the watch on his wrist while waiting. My roomy, white, uncluttered office suddenly felt claustrophobic. The walls were shrinking.

Daniel's mouth opened a few times as if to say something, then shut again with an exhale.

I was about to ask what was wrong when he said, "I wish you weren't so uncomfortable around me."

The statement winded me like a punch to the stomach. There was no point trying to deny it. He'd see through me anyway.

"Sorry." I glanced up. "I don't mean to be."

"I miss you, Lara." He gave me a raw, pained smile that stopped my breath. "I know it's been... tough. But I thought we were close."

If things had been different, we could have been. At one point, I thought we were. Until I discovered that we disagreed on what 'close' meant.

"I can't begin to explain how grateful I am to you," I said. He moaned and rolled his eyes away. I carried on. "Not just for *that* day. For my house, work, everything. But, seeing you—" I stopped talking. There was no nice way of saying his face reminded me of dying. And of having my heart crushed.

Leaning forward, he put a hand on mine. "That day changed my life, too." The office shrank by another foot. "Not that I'm comparing myself to what you went through. I just? I've never felt so helpless."

All his swagger and muscles and attitude disappeared. With his face melancholy and scrunched up, he looked younger. Angelic almost. The tremor in his voice shook my heart, sifting all my old feelings and memories to the surface.

"Is that why you said you loved me?" *Ooooh no.* Why oh why had I said that?

The question had been playing on my mind for so long that it fell out of my mouth and into the open before I could stop it. Before I knew it was even on my tongue. What surprised me most was the relief I felt washing over me. Usually, I couldn't think about those last moments with Daniel without exploding. All I felt now was tired.

He cursed under his breath. "I didn't think you'd heard any of that."

I sighed and looked away. "You mean, you wish I hadn't heard."

"No! That's not what I—" He threw his arms up and swore at the ceiling. "You were dying, Quinn! I didn't know what to—" Calming down again, he swivelled my chair around to face him. "You know how much you mean to me, right?"

Daniel did care about me. In his own way. I hoped, rather than believed, he was telling the truth about Day Zero changing him. At least then, something good would have come from it.

"You weren't helpless," I said, forcing myself to make eye contact. "If you hadn't shown up when you did." I swallowed to steady my voice. "Because of you, I wasn't alone, and that... that was everything."

He started tickling circles over my wrist. I always melted when he did that. Which he knew.

"We'll be alright, won't we?" he asked.

I pulled away. "Of course, we will. We are." The office returned to normal size.

"Grand. And to say thanks for putting me up, I'm buying you dinner tonight."

"Thank you. But you'll have to make it another night. I have a date." My cheeks flushed just thinking about it.

"A date?" He sat back, crossing his arms. "Huh. Wow. Good for you. I didn't know you were seeing anyone?"

His bewilderment offended me slightly. I went all nervous and twitchy. "Yes. No. Kind of. We met a few weeks ago and that's all I'm saying." I grabbed the printed email and walked out, feeling a lot more flustered than I should have.

All Too Well – Taylor Swift

My heels clipped against the concrete floor as I returned from the toilets to the meeting area at closing time.

Daniel stood leaning on Olivia's desk. He greeted me with a wolf whistle. "Check you out, Quinn."

His blatant approval of my appearance made my face burn, which then made me feel guilty. *Get a grip.* I quickly updated him on the planning progress, only I soon noticed his attention had wandered. He was looking past me, through the window. I turned and instantly saw the cause of his distraction: Theo's car had pulled up in the street below.

I grabbed my things. "You can work out the rest for yourself. I'm off." I wasn't about to stand around explaining work while Theo waited.

Daniel's smile became a sneer. "Hold on, *that's* your date? Didn't think you liked flashy cars?"

Ouch. Daniel's showy obsession with having new cars had

earned him a telling off from me more than once. Determined to work on my temper, I suppressed the urge to retaliate. I didn't care about the car and his remark wasn't an insult, it was a reflection of his jealousy. Without another word, feeling proud of myself, I hugged Olivia goodbye.

I ran down the stairs, with restraint so I wouldn't get a red face, and crossed the street. Theo stepped out to meet me. Any resolve to play it cool disappeared; I beamed from ear to ear.

Whenever I saw him, my vision switched from black and white to a full-colour high definition. Every tiny pixel was a hidden treasure. The softness of his light jacket. The cut of his shirt and how it tucked smoothly over his slim waist into his dark jeans. The way he smiled was like drawing back curtains on a sunny morning, opening your world to light and warmth. I studied each detail and tried to memorise them the way I would a blueprint. I would have done anything for a photographic memory.

"So," he said as we left town, "I couldn't help but notice that the sign said it was the office for David Clarke's *Head* of Design. You never mentioned that?"

I watched the blur of passing cars and buildings. "Oh, yeah. I've been a manager for almost a year now. Olivia's my assistant."

The car hummed along, quiet and smooth, making me extremely conscious of my voice. Being in such a small space also highlighted how much I fidgeted when talking about myself.

"Hey, that's incredible." Theo tapped a finger to my knee. "Another one of your surprises. For most people, being in charge, having their own office and assistant would be one of the first things they tell everyone."

Even if I didn't go around telling people, I was pretty proud of my job. My last year may have contained the most horrendous event imaginable, but it also contained a lot of good things. Note to self: make a list of all those things in my journal.

Theo shot me a sideward glance, flashing dark eyes. "Anything else you're not telling me?"

Oh, one thing.

One.

Massive.

Thing.

"If I told you everything, then how would I surprise you?" I replied, mimicking his smile. He was about to speak when my phone rang; one of our contractors. "Argh sorry, I've been trying to get hold of this guy all day. Do you mind?"

"Go ahead."

Theo

While in her world, Lara spoke with authority and confidence I hadn't heard before. She began listing various materials and tasks, most of which I didn't recognise or comprehend. Mist coats? Self-levelling compounds? No idea.

She unconsciously twisted a curl of hair around her finger, released it to fall on her shoulder, tucked it behind her ear, twisted it up again. If I hadn't been driving, I could have watched her more closely, held her hands, perhaps even kissed her. Was it still too soon?

I imagined her fingers winding their way through my hair...

I nearly missed our turning off the motorway.

"Sorry about that." Lara put her phone away. "New build starting tomorrow."

"No need to apologise, it's fascinating."

She modestly shrugged off my compliment with a giggle and looked out the window as the expanse of ocean came into view.

"Genuinely," I said, "I enjoy listening to knowledgeable people who are passionate about what they do."

The praise brought a blush to her cheeks.

Lara was nothing like Yasmin. I kept telling myself that. And I believed it, more so every day. Yasmin was all mystery and angles, Scorsese thrillers and edgy dramas. Lara was all sweet rom-coms and curves, Disney musicals and curves. So, *so* many curves.

What would it be like to hold a woman like her? A woman so soft yet so strong. A woman who could shower me with smiles. My grip on the steering wheel tightened.

Why did I have to be driving? *Next time, call a damn cab.*

Lara

Half an hour together and I already felt more like myself again.

My old self?

My new self?

Whoever it was, Olivia had been right; besides my initial shyness, I did relax around Theo in a way that would normally take me months or even years around anyone else. On paper, we shouldn't have gotten on so well because we were so different. I thought our differences would push us apart, instead, they drew me to him.

I recognised the pretty villages whizzing by as we got closer to the coast. The low sun cast shadows from the cliffs across golden sand and grey rocks below. A thin haze of cloud diffused the landscape, muting the bright greens of the fields behind us into dusky sage and the sea into watercolour washes of silver-grey and aqua.

Theo took my hand the second we stepped out of the car as if he'd been eagerly awaiting this moment for the whole journey. I know I had.

A girl greeted us at the expansive—now made of glass—barn doors. "Noswaith dda."

Theo looked to me for translation.

"Good evening," I whispered.

"Welcome to The Mermaid," the girl continued, "do you h—" She looked up from her notebook and froze mid-word. Widening eyes fixed on Theo, her mouth gaping in the need for extra oxygen and back straightening as she swept the hair from her face. A smile appeared when she recovered. No wonder Theo hadn't batted an eyelid at my reaction when we met. Compared to this girl, I was positively as cool as a cucumber.

"Theo!" she gushed. "Hi, umm, do you have a reservation?" She recognised him straight away and used his name as if they were long lost friends.

Theo's expression remained neutral. He replied formally, "I do. Under Jackson."

She checked the book again. "Of course, right this way. We have a table by the window as requested."

Not once did she look at me. I may as well have been invisible. Annoying, but then I couldn't blame her. We followed her—she didn't stop talking to Theo—to a table by, not a window, but a floor to ceiling wall of glass above the cliffs overlooking the bay. My jaw dropped. Theo broke into a satisfied smile as he pulled out a tan leather chair for me, watching my eyes jump around the building like a child in a sweet shop. There were too many things to look at. Theo included. He sat opposite and removed his jacket, rolling up the sleeves of his navy shirt.

I forgot how to blink.

The waitress handed us menus, pausing next to Theo. "If there's *any*thing else I can do for you?"

Something about the way she asked it felt like she was offering to serve him more than refreshments. Big doe-eyes, leaning forward to emphasise certain *ample* assets while gently caressing his shoulder. I wanted to swat her away like a fly. She was younger than me. Chock-a-block with confidence. Slim and toned in a way I never would be, with silky auburn hair right down to her waist. Drop-dead bloody gorgeous. I hid my reddening face behind a menu and gave my jealous self a stern talking to.

"No, thank you," Theo said. "We'll be fine."

My scowl flickered away as his hand appeared at the top of my menu, pulling it back down onto the chunky oak table. Hanging his head, he closed his eyes for a second and rubbed the crease that had formed in between his eyebrows. Embarrassed? Irritated? Both?

"Do you ever get used to that?" I blurted out. His eyes snapped open straight onto mine. "Sorry. That's a weird question."

He answered it anyway. "Not really. People say I should be flattered. Sometimes, I suppose I am. Other times, when they act like *that.*" He jutted his chin toward the waitress. "When I'm quite obviously with someone, I find it rude. Though again, it's my fault."

"But she's beautiful. I mean, you could literally take your pick of whoev—" *Where the hell am I going with this?* "I didn't mean— I just? Oh, I don't know what I mean."

He set his elbows on the table, resting his chin on clasped fingers. "The world is full of good-looking people, Lara. That doesn't always make them beautiful."

Too true. I nodded and took a sip of water. Theo remained deep in thought. I could tell because he always pursed his lips as if he was about to whistle. Great, we hadn't even ordered drinks yet and I'd completely ruined the mood.

"Sorry." I shook my head. "It was meant to be a compliment. It came out wrong."

He reached for my hands. "Lara, you still keep apologising to me." The low rumble of his voice prowled across the table.

"I know, I'm sor— Yeah." I laughed. "I do, don't I?"

"Why do you think I wanted to see you again?"

Did he expect me to answer that? He could probably feel my fingers shivering. My mouth had been stuffed with a pillow.

I distracted myself by examining a knot in the wood of the table shaped like a snail. "I don't know." *Be honest.* "There's a part of me worried you're still being nice to make up for the accident, I suppose."

He turned to look out the window. I stared at our joined hands. Some of his nails were bitten short. A small scar stretched around the side of his left thumb. As hands go, they were far from perfect, but they were his—warm, gentle, strong—which made them perfect. Seeing them around mine turned my blood into smouldering lava.

Theo spoke after a minute or so, his intensity drawing me into a bubble, fading out our surroundings. "Do you think she would have reacted or spoken to me like that if I wasn't famous?"

I didn't see how anyone could look at Theo and *not* find him attractive, but I tried to be objective. I remembered Olivia's, Sarah's, and even Greg's reaction to meeting him and replied that, no, she might not have.

"But, Theo," I spluttered, "you know that's not the reason why my hands are shaking, right? You know that doesn't matter to me?"

"I know. That's the point I'm trying to make. You never once tried to take advantage of who I am. Though I handed you a damn good opportunity to. You did the opposite and rejected me." He chuckled. "Several times if my memory's correct. In fact, I think my being famous is probably one of the things you like the least about me."

So far, it was the *only* thing about him I didn't like. It was also one of the things that scared me about us becoming closer. I admitted to him it was true.

"Most of the world sees me as Theodore Jackson, the actor they have heard scandalous things about. Yet, you didn't judge me, or presume to know me because of what you had seen. But..." he purred, "the main reason I wanted to see you, why I want to *keep* seeing you, is because you are like the fire on the beach to me, Lara. You're clever. Funny. Not afraid to stand up for yourself. You fascinate me. You're beautiful and calm. Under the surface you're strong, and perhaps a little... hmm, what was the word you used?" The water inside my body boiled over as he leaned in to whisper, "Wild."

Why did anyone bother to give him scripts when he could talk like that? His words formed and flowed like the elegant ink of a calligraphist. Sounds became cursive loops, swirling descents, whisking me away to another time, another world.

I desperately wanted to tell him I couldn't stop thinking about him, that he made me feel like there was nothing I couldn't do. But anything I said would sound clumsy now.

"Are you flirting with me, Mr Jackson?" *Oh for goodness sake,* I came across so immature.

With a glimmer in his eyes, he picked up his menu. "Absolutely. If that's okay with you, Miss Quinn?"

"Absolutely."

♫

"So in your professional opinion, did I pick a good location?" Theo gestured around at the restaurant as a waiter cleared our plates away.

Once again, the artistry of the place struck me, enhanced by lingering smells of smokey paprika, vetiver candles and champagne.

"Oh, definitely. I mean look at the view! And this building!" I pointed upwards, shaking my head in awe at the workmanship. "See the way they've fitted the new glass into the original wood frame? It's like they're moulded together. And the colours blend seamlessly into the scenery. Whoever designed this place is a genius. It's stunning because it's so complicated but looks so effortless. It adds to the view rather than trying to compete with it."

Theo's attention never faltered as he listened, watching me with eyes the colour of damp earth in the dim light. Earth that grew my confidence like a seedling, bursting further and further out of the ground with every second that passed. He reacted to my enthusiasm with one of his 'string' smiles—one eyebrow pulling up his lip. It triggered a shockwave through my lower stomach.

A flash of light over Theo's shoulder turned the shockwave

into a full-blown earthquake. The waitress from earlier, along with a few customers at another table, had their phones pointed at us.

I grabbed my menu shield. "Theo! Don't look, but I think they're taking pictures of us."

"It's okay, we'll be alright. Just ignore them."

He reacted as if it were a normal, everyday thing. Hell, what if it was? What if they'd already put the pictures online? What if I was on them? *Oh no.* No no no. The earth began splitting apart and I wanted to jump into the void. I ducked my head and tipped the menu so only Theo could see me.

"Lara?" My name was a question, asking me for an assurance that I couldn't give. Fear flitted over his face. He stood and grabbed his jacket, blocking me from the view of our spies, and held out a hand to me. "I think I need to walk that dinner off. How about you?"

I nodded and took his hand.

Theo

There were times I hated my job. This was one of them. These were the sort of stresses that never occurred to me as a teen when the prospect of fame and fortune glittered like the ultimate prize. No one warned me about not being able to take my sister to the park in peace, or about the paparazzi camping at the gates of my parent's house.

Could I not have one day? One evening of normality?

I led Lara out through a backdoor to a terraced seating area, then up a small path following the cliff edge toward a viewpoint.

The sky had turned a burning orange, reflected so perfectly by the glassy sea, it was hard to tell where they joined, as though the sky stretched all the way to our feet. Only the occasional ripple or smudge of a boat on the horizon gave the illusion away.

There was nothing but the scenery, the sound of the sea, the air in our lungs, and the two of us. I still couldn't help looking over my shoulder to see if we had been followed. It wasn't till we got the viewpoint that I calmed down. Lara hadn't said a word, but at least the colour was coming back to her cheeks.

Another night ruined because of me. I turned away to hide my anger. "I shouldn't have put you in that position."

"I'm fine."

"No, you're not, and you have the right not to be. I should have warned you about what could happen. I was afraid that if I did, you wouldn't have said yes to coming."

She squeezed my hand. "I would have said yes."

I wanted to believe she would have, but I couldn't be certain. And deep down, behind the shaky smile she was struggling to maintain, neither was she.

I let go of her hand to climb onto a small platform and inspect a rusted telescope, the kind you could operate with a 20 pence coin. They were dotted all along the British coastline at various tourist spots. When I was a child, I would eagerly run to them, hoping to find one that had been paid for but abandoned early, so I could steal its last few working seconds before the cover dropped over the lens.

"You should be able to see the film set from here," Lara said from behind me.

I attempted to point the scope at the other side of the bay and winced at the loud, whining crunch it made.

She giggled, and boy was I glad to hear it. "Although, that one sounds like it broke decades ago."

"Hmm, I think you're right." I pushed harder against the cold metal and with another crunch, the whole thing bent over. I grimaced to say *oops* and tried to pull it upright again. Lara burst out laughing and gripped her sides.

I wanted to be the one gripping her.

Our hands automatically found each other when I jumped down to rejoin her. "It is stunning here. I wish I had more time."

"You have another two months, right?" She sounded positive. Her eyes told a different story; they looked anywhere but at me.

Her ability to portray so many contradicting emotions would make her a director's dream.

She was beautiful. Unpredictable. *A fire*. At times, shyness made her hands tremble. Other times, like when describing a building, she forgot her nerves and lit up with energy. Either way, I wanted to be closer—a moth to her flame.

I nodded. "Nine weeks till we go back to London."

"I bet you can't wait to get back to the excitement."

"Not really. I feel more at home here." She finally turned to me with surprise on her face. I explained, "I have an apartment there, but I'm not from the city itself. My family lives on the outskirts. In the country. In my grandfather's day, it was a working farm." And I would never again take it for granted. *Lara would love the golden brick walls and symmetrical windows.*

"Hey," I added, bringing the subject back to happier things, "if you could build your own place, where would it be?"

"Now that's a tough question." She played with her hair again as she thought about it.

Heat ebbed and flowed over my skin as the breeze caught her sweet scent. Would she taste just as sweet? *Cool it.* I trained my focus up to her eyes.

"To be honest, I'd be more than happy with this place," she said, pointing back toward the restaurant.

"So you don't miss London either? Is that why you moved back?"

A sharp breath jolted her whole body as her gaze sprang back to the horizon. "There are things I miss. I loved working there, but something happened and... and everything changed." Her quiet, unsure voice filled the whole atmosphere. "I didn't want to be there on my own anymore. So I bought my place here, renovated it, set up the office and then employed Olivia a few months ago. I was lucky Daniel—he's my boss—kept me on."

I inched closer. Her spine straightened a fraction. To anyone not paying attention, it wouldn't have been noticeable.

I paid attention.

Her memories stirred up such deep feelings that they reminded me of her reaction to Philip and the so-called 'skeletons' he had uncovered. My inner protective caveman growled.

What had happened in London to make Lara so nervous?

Lara

Theo lifted my hand to his chest. His intensity made my head dizzy and my legs ache.

"There's something I've noticed about you," he said. My breath ramped up speed. "You smile when you're happy, you smile when you talk, and when you listen." He touched his free hand to my cheek before dropping it down my arm to hold my (thankfully, now healed) wrist. "You even smile when you're in pain." The gravity of his voice drew me closer. "Every smile is so different, there simply aren't enough words to describe them."

I smiled, then bit it down. He was right, it was my reflex, my permanent mask.

"And then." He touched a finger to my lips. "There's *that* smile."

The mysterious expression swept over his face again—strange indecision, thoughtfulness.

"Oh." I narrowed my eyes. "You mean my 'dangerous' habit?"

We were so close now I could feel his warmth, count his eyelashes. His fingers wound into the hair at the back of my neck. Fire shot down my spine.

"Extremely dangerous," he whispered, closer still.

"Why?"

"Because." Closer. More fire. "All I want to do is kiss you."

Desire. That was the expression. More accurately: desire being restrained. He wanted more. I could feel it in his touch, hear it in his voice, see it in his eyes.

It frightened me.

I wanted more, too.

It might have been a while, but surely kissing was like riding a bike? I wouldn't have forgotten how to, would I?

He kept hold of my hair while his other hand wrapped around my waist, up to my back. I tensed. *Don't panic, not now, he won't feel anything, it's all in my head.*

His lips paused above my cheek, he pressed his forehead to mine. "It's okay, I've got you. Do you trust me?"

Yes. I nodded. Lifted my chin. Fell into the spice of his skin and the salt on his lips as he kissed me.

Again.

And again.

Sun melted into the sea, turning the world into a golden orb. We didn't bother to watch. Everything fell quiet and calm like the eye of a storm. He was being careful. I smoothed my hands down his firm chest to clutch at his waist, pulling him closer. The storm hit. His kiss deepened and I drowned in his arms, my mind filling with colour and music.

"See," he said between heavy breaths, "you're even smiling now."

"I can't help it." I sighed.

Kissing *was* like riding a bike. If bikes had wings.

Oh, and turbocharged thrusters.

♪

Theo nodded toward the sporty BMW in my drive. "New car?"

"Oh, no, it's Daniel's," I replied. My brain then kicked into life so I quickly explained, "We've got a big meeting next week with a huge potential client. He's here for a few days preparing plans for the pitch. He kind of..." I exhaled. "Invited himself to stay."

"Ah. Do you two not get on?"

"We do. It's fine. He can just be"—*a pain in the ass, controlling, over-friendly*—"difficult."

Theo didn't reply.

My focus drifted to his hands on the steering wheel, then to his lips, pouted again in thought. *Make all the days count.* I wanted every second we had to count.

His thick curls tickled my fingers as I slid them into his hair, bringing his mouth to mine. I kissed him firmly this time. He responded instantly, leaning over to hold my face with one hand, the other steadying himself by gripping my thigh.

I once came unexpectedly face to face with a tiger at a zoo. I hadn't noticed it was sitting right below the window until it pounced at me. As I stared into its eyes, I knew I was safe—we were separated by thick glass and wire—and I didn't want the moment to end. Still, being close to such a powerful and deadly animal made the air quiver in my lungs. That was exactly how I felt now. Theo's touch scared and protected me all at once. The good kind of scared. The mind-blowing, life-pumping-through-your-veins kind that I could get addicted to.

His finger slipped into the gap between my trousers and shirt, onto my bare skin. The deep growl in his chest made my thighs, and pretty much everything else, clench. As he lifted his hand to my waist, he unknowingly pressed right onto my old stomach wound. A needle pain shot into my back. My body flinched.

He pulled away. "Sorry." Deep breath. "My fault." Another breath. "Too far."

Electricity sparked through my system at the thrill of having so much of an effect on him. He was always so in control, but now I'd caught a glimpse of him without restraint. A glimpse wasn't enough.

"No, Theo, it's alright." I held his face and kissed him softly. "It's not you." It was all me. "When I said, 'I'm not that kind of girl,' that wasn't me playing some kind of hard to get tactic," I confessed.

A dull ache spread from my waist down my legs. My hands dropped into fists on my lap.

"I know," he said, kissing the hinge of my jaw, "that's another reason why I like you."

I held back the impulse to ask him why. For so long I'd believed that in order to move forward, I had to go back to being my old self again. What if I was wrong? Theo genuinely liked me the way I was. Not the old me. Me. I thought I'd lost the part of myself that made me special, but Theo saw me as someone new, someone fascinating and desirable.

A trickle of pride and relief ran through my body. Tonight, I'd taken a baby step toward telling him the truth about what happened and why I'd moved home. Maybe I didn't have to hide everything after all?

He sat back and held both my hands on his lap. "However, I may have to call in that favour you promised."

I laughed. "Anything."

A second of silence passed. *Something's wrong.*

"I don't want my old ways to ruin this, Lara. I want to be better than that. I'm going to need your help. I need to learn how to behave and to... take things slow."

Although his smirk was adorable, there was a pleading seriousness in his voice and darkness over his face. What exactly had he done in his past to cause so much regret? Evidently, there was more to his story he hadn't told me. *It's all on the internet.* I pushed the idea away. I'd made him a promise—no Google. I kept my promises. Of course, he hadn't told me everything, it would be naive to think so.

And I wasn't in a position to lecture anyone about keeping secrets.

I hid my uncertainty behind my mask. "Challenge accepted,

Mr Jackson." His answering grin then made me feel like being dangerous again. "Only if you can teach me how *not* to behave."

Tipping his head back, he groaned, well and truly waking the wild creature lying dormant inside me. "Believe me, when you say things like that, you don't need me to teach you anything."

♪

That night, my dreams were the usual replay of Day Zero. I also dreamt of Theo. He was like a tree, rooted and steady, brimming with life. Solid enough to provide safety in the roughest of storms; gentle enough to give the most delicate of creatures shelter and shade.

How would it work if we were together? When and where would we see each other?

Even in my sleep, I overanalysed things.

We only had two months. Theo liked me. He wanted me. That was all that mattered.

For now.

Impossible – Nothing But Thieves

Lara's Journal
Day 34

Something I'd missed while in London was playing in the band with my friends. I watched them all surrounding my hospital bed; Sarah laughed at Greg, who was winding up Olivia. Caleb and Alex were deep in conversation planning the list of songs for their next gig. Seeing them all together made up my mind once and for all: I needed to move home.

I'd already found a house to fit my small budget. My savings would be enough to renovate it to a liveable standard and then, once I found another job, I would gradually finish the rest.

The prospect of job hunting made me nauseous. David Clarke had been my life and a home from home. Daniel's offer to become the Head of Design was the stuff of dreams. Half of my mind screamed I was crazy to not be snapping his hand off. *Crazy. Stupid. Crazy.* But even if Daniel replaced the whole office cabin, the thought of walking through those gates, across that cold rough ground, frightened and churned my stomach far more than any worries of finding another job.

I prepared what to say to Daniel before I called him, determined that—other than for the court case—I would never return to London.

He answered his phone with a yawn; probably another long day at work. "Good to hear your voice, Quinn. How are you?"

The pain hovered at around six on the scale. "Fine. Getting better."

"The guys keep asking about you. You're missed. The accountants are even grumpier than usual."

My throat tied itself in knots. Hell, it was so much harder than I'd expected. I wasn't just leaving a job, I was leaving colleagues, friends and... Daniel.

I was breaking my promise.

As much as I wanted to bury and forget London, there was a part of me—deep inside, being crushed—that didn't want to let go. Daniel and I had spent every day of the previous two years together. He was the man who'd made me feel welcome, safe and happy in a city of strangers. He got me through the most horrific day imaginable. He saved me! Although there were moments when I didn't understand him (and there still are), there were also moments when we knew each other like no one else could.

"I don't know how to say this." I pressed a hand over my racing heart. "I can't come back. I want more than anything to keep working for you, but I need— I want to stay here."

It went silent. I checked the screen to make sure I hadn't cut him off.

"Alright," he said. "I wish there were something I could do to change your mind."

At the time, there was. He could have said: *I love you, Lara. I'm sorry for not being more open. I want to make this work. Come back to me, I'll always love you.* ' But he didn't.

Instead, he said, "I know how stubborn you are, though."

I closed my eyes. Took a long breath. "True. Unless..." I had an idea.

"Go on?"

"Give Peter the role of office manager there. He'd be perfect. He literally loves paperwork. And that means I can focus on the design side from here. Most of my work is sent online, so what does it matter if I'm in London or Wales?"

"We'll do it."

"Plus it means if we have clients this way then—wait? You said yes?"

"Aye." He laughed, so loud that I had to move the phone away from my ear. "I've been thinking lately about how we could expand. This solves my problem."

"Oh. Really? You don't want to think about it first?" (I seriously need to stop questioning people when they agree with me.)

"No thinking required," he said. "You know me, I'm lazy. I'm not spending years training up another manager." Now, Daniel had many faults, but being lazy was *not* one of them. His soft voice swept my mind back to those minutes lying on the floor in his arms, "I'm not losing you, Lara."

I squeezed my eyes shut and changed the subject. "Then you'll be happy to know I've found a house. It needs some work but it has space for a home office."

"Grand. Get planning. I'll send over the team."

"What? No, I'm not expecting you to do the work."

"Don't be daft," he huffed. "You work for a construction company, of course, we're doing it for you."

"I don't know how to thank—"

"Don't thank me. Your workload just tripled. Send me the plans and I'll be in touch."

My idea went down better than I could have imagined. But was it *me* that he didn't want to lose, or only my work? I wondered why he was doing so much to help me. The work needed on my house wasn't going to be cheap. Did he love me after all? My heart skipped.

I foolishly hoped he was waiting for a better time to tell me.

Hoax – Taylor Swift

Lara's Journal
Day 50

Another physio session left me physically and mentally exhausted. I lay in a star shape on the cool plastic mats of the gym—as if I were about to make snow angels on the ground—squinting at the glare of fluorescent lights above. The room smelt like sweat and cleaning fluid. Not a pleasant mixture.

"How's the house coming on?" Dr Carter asked, trying to distract me while pressing an ice pack to my stomach. It stung like hell until the relief started to spread through my muscles. What was left of my muscles.

"All good," I gasped. "Paperwork's going through." Pant. "So hopefully." Another gasp. "I'll get the keys in a few weeks."

"I can give you more painkillers if it's that bad, Lar—"

"No! I'm fine." I sat up. "I'd rather be in pain than feel like a drunk zombie." Pain kept me in the present. Being on drugs put me in a foggy daze, like slipping away all over again, drifting over that mystical line into the darkness beyond.

She nodded. "Fair enough. Take your time, I'll come to check on you later. You're doing so well, you'll be out of here in a jiffy." With a pat on my shoulder, she left me to finish the cool-down stretches.

I could walk unaided, as well as lift small weights. Slow progress. My body was getting better every day, but my mind suffered. I couldn't wait to escape the hospital. Couldn't wait to see my house for myself, to sleep in a soft bed, to eat breakfast whenever I wanted, to leave whenever I wanted.

Despite efforts to decorate and cheer the place up with brightly coloured walls—a different colour for each ward—the hospital still felt like, well, a hospital. Bleached of any soul. Mechanical.

I made my way to the showers and undressed in front of the evil full-length mirror. I'd lost half a stone in weight but I looked swollen. My wounds had healed, mostly, and the stitches had been removed. I'd tried to avoid looking at myself (and on bad days, I still do), but I knew I had to face it. So I took a breath. Shoulders back. Chin up.

A long scar stretched from my belly button, downward through my stomach, toward my left hip. A dip followed along where the muscles had been torn. The actual cut line of the knife was raised and darker than my normal skin. It looked like a miniature Grand Canyon mapped out on my waist. I ran my fingers over it. Although I felt the pressure, the skin was numb and rough.

It didn't feel like me.

Turning to my side, I traced the mark of the first stab on my right lower back. The cut was smaller, only a few inches wide, but it had gone deeper, leaving a large dent and a radius of lined skin, like the cracks that spread outwards when a stone hits glass. No amount of exercise and treatment would make them go away.

I would never feel, or look, like me again.

Collapsing to my knees, I sobbed into my hands. I turned on the shower to cover the sound and let myself cry until there was no energy left to make any more tears. My court case date crept closer and there was no way in hell would I let *him* see me cry.

Rise – Katy Perry

Day 351
Wednesday

"Good morning, sleepyhead." Olivia greeted me in an extremely chirpy way for such an early time of the day. "What time did you get in last night?"

Both she and Daniel stopped what they were doing to look at me. Olivia held a spoon of cereal midway to her mouth. Daniel peered over the top of his magazine.

I popped a slice of bread in the toaster and acted like I wasn't bothered by their exchange of smiles and curious expressions. "Elevenish I think. What did you two get up to?"

"Not much. Ate food, watched TV, did some work." Olivia's voice became as suspiciously nonchalant as mine.

Daniel fetched another mug from the cupboard, poured a coffee and passed it my way. "Don't forget, I'm taking you both out for dinner tomorrow. Why don't you invite Mr Flashy along?"

Don't bite. I let the 'Mr Flashy' dig wash over me.

"I've some big news, Quinn," Daniel continued, "which, I think, you'll want to celebrate."

Olivia and I both asked, "What?"

"That's for you to find out. I'm just saying you might want to invite some people."

I couldn't think of an excuse quick enough.

If it meant seeing Theo, then I didn't want an excuse.

♪

At lunch, I cornered Olivia to ask how it really went with Daniel on her own. She twisted her chair from side to side, occasionally spinning it around with a wide smile on her face, as if on a teacup ride, not sitting in an office. *Aww.* She always made me laugh.

"We were fine," she reassured me. "He helped make dinner, we chatted, watched TV then went to bed." A smirk crossed her face. "Separately! It was cool."

"Thanks for not saying anything about Theo. I don't get Daniel, why is he suddenly so eager to meet him?" Other than his competitive ego wanting to compare the size of their... cars.

"Don't be annoyed. He, like, feels responsible for you." Olivia looked at the floor and tucked her hands under her thighs. She'd said too much.

"Responsible? Liv, I've told him a million times what happened wasn't his fault."

"I know, I know." She shook her head. "But you were a young woman working alone on a site he managed. You can't be mad at him forever for him feeling guilty."

I folded my arms. "You seem to know a lot about how Daniel feels."

"We talk sometimes."

I opened my mouth to ask, 'since when?' but clamped it shut again. She'd stopped spinning. Her bright, full moon eyes flicked to a spot on the floor, up to me, back down again.

In my head, I saw her as the ditsy little kid with pigtails— especially when she spun on office chairs—who followed me and Greg around. Sometimes, I forgot how much she'd grown up. My little sister wasn't so little anymore.

She watched me, picking off her nail polish, waiting for me to snap at her. I nearly had. That was the kind of friend I'd become. Selfishly expecting everyone to cope with my turbulent personality, even when I couldn't.

My knuckles were white and tingling from clenching them so tightly. "I'm sorry. I'm not mad at him. I can't explain how it feels. I don't want favours or protection because he feels guilty."

I needed to know that my place was earned. I blinked back tears of frustration. Lately, I seemed to spend most of my time apologising or crying.

Olivia wrapped her arms around me. "Laa-Laa, I know you don't *need* protecting, but that's kinda what being friends is all about. We look after each other."

I squeezed her, swaying her from side to side until we both started giggling. Then I told her everything about my date with Theo.

"Hot damn," was her response.

"Ooooh yeah," I agreed, staring blankly at the far wall, lyrics of love songs skipping merrily through my mind. I pressed my palms to my eyes and grinned.

"So are you?" she asked hopefully.

"What?"

"Going to invite him for dinner tomorrow? With us?"

It sounded like a terrible idea… but I desperately wanted to see Theo again.

"You honestly think I should?" Imitating a phone call, I lifted my hand to my head. "Hi, Theo. Just wondered if you want to come to dinner with me, my best friend and my boss? You know, just the four of us."

Dramatically throwing back her head, she groaned, "Why not? I think it'd be fun. Daniel's paying and we get to spend the evening with two gorgeous guys, what could go wrong?"

What could go wrong? Whenever you heard that line in a film, it usually meant things were about to go very, very wrong.

That wouldn't be the case in real life, right?

♫

Andrew worked his way around the DAYS group. The closer it got to my turn, the clammier my palms became. There was so much I wanted to talk about, which was a first, but so much I couldn't say.

Andrew grinned. The moment had come. "Lara, how was your week?"

I stretched the knitted sleeves of my jumper over my hands. "Fine. Same old." I answered on autopilot before adding, "Although, it was kind of crazy too."

"Crazy good, or crazy bad?" He prodded.

"Good. Both. No, good. Mostly." I looked around at a sea of confusion. "Okay, so you know I'm doing the sponsored dates?" The group nodded. "Well, the crazy thing is this week, I actually got asked out on a *real* date."

"How did it go?" Jenny piped up, radiating excitement.

"There were a few hiccups, but it was good. And I'm hopefully seeing him again tomorrow."

"Well done, Lara." Andrew beamed. "I think you can tell how happy we all are for you." He lifted his arms out to indicate the room of smiling faces.

Yeah. I did it. I went on a date that wasn't a complete disaster. *Mic drop.*

Jenny waved me over as I was leaving, insisting that I give her all the details.

"Well, of course, you did it, sweetheart!" she said, setting down her tea to cwtch me. "You're a competent businesswoman who meets and deals with people every day. I never had any doubts."

"I wish I had your confidence."

She adjusted the clip in her hair. "When people say they're scared of flying, most of the time, what is it that they're really afraid of?" Jenny's random questions usually meant she was getting at something.

I took a second to think about it. "I suppose... they're more afraid of crashing. And dying."

"So why are you afraid of dating?"

I knew the answer, but I couldn't bring myself to say it.

♫

I walked in from DAYS and went straight to my kitchen for some water. Olivia had already gone to bed; I could hear her music upstairs.

"What time do you call this?"

"Son of a—Dan!" I choked. "You frightened the life outta me." He was sitting on the sofa with his laptop. In the dark. Now laughing at me. "What are you doing?"

"Work work work."

I poured him water, took it over and sat next to him. (Mistake No1.)

"Cheers." His blurry, exhausted eyes squinted at the screen.

I shut the laptop. "You need a break."

"There you go, bossing me around." He smiled that dazzling, crooked smile of his. "I knew you still cared."

Of course, I did. No matter how many times I wished I didn't. "I don't want you to have a stress-induced heart attack on my sofa. I'd need a crane to get you out. And, I don't want you to be one of those people who get old and realise all they've ever done is work."

"You worried I'll end up alone, Quinn?" Putting the laptop on the floor, he spun his knees onto the sofa to face me. I should have moved away. (Mistake No2.) "What, no witty comeback? You're quiet. Everything go to plan with Flashy Mystery Man last night?"

"Stop it." I sighed and dropped my head back onto the sofa. "He's not flashy or a mystery. His name is Theo. We went to The Mermaid—which is this beautifully converted barn on the coast, you'd love it—and it was perfect. I just... I am quiet now." Quiet was my new normal.

"Aye get off it, you've been giving me that look all day. Same look you have when you think I'm making a mistake, or being an idiot."

Ha! Making mistakes and being an idiot went hand in hand when it came to Daniel.

"What are you really doing here?" I asked. "All this work could easily be done online. And how long have you been talking to Olivia?" Putting my thoughts together out loud started to join the dots. "The truth, Daniel," I demanded. "Do you like her?"

He swirled his watch around his wrist, brushed my hair off my shoulder and left his hand there. (Mistake No3.) "We met when you were in hospital and when she came to pick up your stuff from the office. She asked me how I was doing after everything and we got chatting. She's a nice girl. That's all."

I poked a cushion in his direction. "She is nice. She's also my best friend and your employee." Not that working together had stopped him before. "So don't you dare mess her around."

Snatching the cushion, he jabbed it to his chest, as if I'd shot an arrow through his heart. "So what you're saying is she's too good for me, eh? That really what you think of me?"

When he was being his showy self then, yes, she was way too good for him. Other times, I wasn't sure. I could see how they would fit; both social, outgoing, and fun. She was strong enough to handle him. If only he could be trusted.

"What I think of you has nothing to do with it," I said. "The point is what she thinks of you. If you hurt her—"

"You'll beat me to death with a cushion?"

My anger flared at his laughter. He never took anything I said —unless it was about work—seriously. "I mean it."

"Alright, chill out. I've another reason for being here, which you'll find out about tomorrow. But I promise you." He used my hands to pull me closer. "I'm not here for *her*, Lara."

On the surface, his promise should have been reassuring. In reality, it felt like a thin layer of paint covering up something sinister underneath. His head dipped and longing eyes looked up into mine. The gap between us shrunk as his hand slipped around my shoulders.

No no no. How had I let this happen? My heart pounded. Daniel was familiar and comfortable. I should never have let him stay. (Mistake No4.) (Or the real No1?)

Pulling my hands free, I legged it upstairs and threw myself into bed, panting like I'd run a marathon.

I hadn't done anything wrong.

The fact that I worried what Olivia or Theo would think if they'd walked in and seen us made me feel like I had.

♪

My phone woke me an hour later.

"Hey, sorry it's so late," Theo whispered. "Our last scene took forever. Tomorrow night sounds good."

The great Charlotte Bronte described Mr Rochester's attachment to Jane Eyre as being like a string underneath his ribs, tying them together. I understood why. Every second away from Theo, an ache grew as my body pulled fiercely on that string, trying to bring us back together. I missed him, and that was why I ignored the uneasy twist in my gut about him meeting Daniel.

"Great. I've found out where we're going," I said. "It's a quiet little Italian place around the corner from my office, so if you want to meet me at work again? Oh, and Greg and Sarah are coming too." I'd invited them hoping to make conversation easier and the night seem less double-dateish.

"Perfect." He chuckled. I could imagine the adorable head tilt and creases in the corners of his smiling eyes. "This time, I'll bring my cunning disguise just in case."

By that, he meant his cap. I wondered if he'd ever tried glasses, Clark Kent style. Now that would be insanely sexy.

Something else, more serious, then occurred to me. "Theo, can I ask you something?"

"Please do," he rumbled. It got even hotter in my room.

Stay focused. "So, what happened the other day, you know, when people recognised you. Does that happen a lot?"

And would they ask questions about me, to try and find out who I was?

Theo took a moment. Occasionally, when talking about himself, he became so quiet that I almost believed he was shy, too.

Almost.

"Not *that* often. People don't see what they're not looking for," he said. "I thought, with The Mermaid being out of town, it looked like a safe place... Usually, if I am noticed, people are polite and just want a selfie." He'd answered all of my questions, without answering any of my real questions.

"So if someone did see you, or saw *us?*" I hinted. Ugh, this was a weird, squirmy conversation.

"I understand if you don't want to be seen with me." His voice climbed unusually high. "It's okay, I won't come if you're worried."

I hugged an arm around my knees, curling up into the safety of a ball, mustering up the courage to be brave. "That's not what I meant, believe me. I'm more worried about whether, umm... what would happen if..." *Waffling.* "Okay. Look. It only takes a second for someone to put something online, and then they could tell other people. Like, my parents for instance?"

"Ah." He sounded relieved if still a little uncomfortable. "I swear, I won't let anyone bother you."

I believed he would do everything possible to protect my privacy, but could he guarantee it? Probably not. It was only a matter of time until the truth came out. Our time left together was short enough as it was.

If it weren't for my history, I wouldn't care if all the paparazzi in the world showed up to bother us. I couldn't tell him that though, so I plagiarised his own saying, with some poetic licence. "It's okay, you've got me. I trust you."

"Lara," he growled.

I heard the wanting in his voice and my chest tightened, too small to contain my expanding heart.

Invisible String – Taylor Swift

Lara's Journal
Day 105

Flowers lined the path to my new front door, where Mom stood waiting, holding a large sponge cake iced with the words: New Home. My house looked so stunning it rendered me speechless.

One of our builders handed me the keys with a tear in his eye. Honestly, it was like being on *DIY SOS*. Inside smelt wonderfully new. Plaster, paint, wood floors, all shiny and clean. Only this time, I didn't have to hand it over to a client, this time it was all mine! I pressed my shaky hands into my pockets.

While I looked around, a car pulled up outside. Voices floated through the open door as Dad welcomed the arrival. A hand found my shoulder; I knew who it belonged to. There was only one person I knew who wore a gold Rolex and aftershave that expensive.

"You like it?" Daniel whispered.

I looked out at the open-plan living, dining and kitchen space. I loved it. I spun and threw my arms around his shoulders, pressing my face to the black swirls on his painted neck as my willpower disappeared and the tears came.

"Take that as a yes." His hands slid around my waist and for a second, before we remembered the people around us, I thought he was going to pick me up. He cleared his throat. "And no, I won't take any arguments. You're not paying a penny. Consider this your get-well-soon and welcome-back gift from the company."

I leaned back to look him in the eyes, the same azure ocean eyes that saved me. "Daniel, I..." I cried into his chest again, but he didn't try to pull away. For once, he was the one hugging me, holding me tight, even though my tears and makeup were rubbing onto his designer shirt. I cried because the house was beautiful, because I finally had a place where I felt safe, and because he knew —without me having to say a word or explain a thing—he truly knew what I'd been through.

"Alright, alright. This is supposed to be a celebration." He stepped away, touched a hand to my damp cheek and went to talk to the builders.

Mom passed slices of cake around my packed living room. My whole family had come, plus the band and their families, then all our builders and tradesmen. I backed away toward the stairs, watching the room of people I loved like a detached spectator in a theatre, seeing a story play out from a distance through foggy glass.

Daniel caught my eye and came over. "You good, Quinn?"

"Fine. Tired. There's a lot to take in." I smiled half-heartedly.

He tugged at his hair. "Can I see upstairs?"

"Oh, of course." I was glad for an excuse to get away from the noise. "You can help me pick colours."

He supported my arms as we climbed up. I showed him the spare room, the bathroom and finally, what would soon be my room.

"So, I want to do something daring." I waved my hand around the room. "I think I might paint it black."

He quickly took in the space before focusing back on me. "Black? Aye, that is bold for you. Whatever you do will look grand. And I do like the sound of you being daring."

The air hummed with vibrations as I became aware of us being alone, in a bedroom. The only difference was that my churning insides now felt more like panic than excitement. It was Daniel. *My Daniel.* Why was I panicking?

He took a step closer and I froze as his hands wrapped around my face.

"I'm going to miss having you around," he whispered into my hair.

My breath got trapped inside my collapsing chest. I closed my eyes, willing myself to relax as he kissed me. He moved eagerly, impatiently, soon finding my jawline, my neck. *I should be enjoying this*, I thought. After all, I wanted him. Didn't I? A downward spiral of shock and confusion numbed my limbs.

He was going too fast. No one had touched me so closely since Day Zero. Panic turned to fear when he pressed my back against the wall.

I pushed him away lightly. "Dan, not now."

"Why not?" He tilted my head to kiss my ear, over my cheeks.

I told myself to *give in, stop fighting,* but I had so many mixed feelings for him swirling around. Loyalty, hurt, gratitude... love?

Laughter from downstairs snapped me back to the real world.

I pushed him again, more forcefully. "We can't keep doing this." With a huff, he stepped back and turned to leave. I stopped him before he got to the door. "Don't go, please. Stay for a while?"

A short, tight smile filtered across his face. "Sure."

He left anyway.

I didn't see him again until the trial.

Ocean Eyes – Billie Eilish

Day 352
Thursday

Daniel acted as if our conversation from the night before never happened. Or any of our previous conversations for that matter. He spent the day in one of his upbeat, cheeky moods. I'd admit, it was easier to deal with than a serious or angry one.

Olivia kicked off her shoes and lay across her usual lunchtime bench in the office gardens. Daniel took off his jacket to reveal another skin-tight shirt, showing off every single muscle. Several people spied on us from the office windows above. Neither of them seemed to mind having an audience.

My phone buzzed with a text from Jenny, asking if I was available to go on my first 'date' on Saturday. No longer hungry, I put my sandwich down. I couldn't stop thinking about how I'd turned down the offer to share my story with the local reporter. Before I knew what I was doing, I told Olivia and Daniel.

Olivia bolted upright. "So the reporter wanted to interview you?"

"Yeah, he's already met with some of the other members. He's writing the article next week," I said.

"But you refused?" Daniel questioned. "How come?"

I glared at him to say, *why do you think?*

183

"Don't worry about it." Olivia shook her head. "You want your privacy. You don't have to feel bad about that."

Daniel turned on her with a scowl. "But she's got nothing to be ashamed of." He looked back at me. "I completely get why he wants to tell your story. You're an inspiration. A survivor. Look where you are! You *should* be proud of yourself."

He meant to be kind, I think, but the way he said it made me feel like a child being scolded, stood at the front of a class and pointed at.

"I am proud of this place and what we've done," I argued. "And I'm not ashamed. But that doesn't mean I want everyone around me to—" I caught his eye and faltered. "To know everything. It was bad enough being in the news the first time."

Olivia leaned across the table to put a hand on mine. "I know you wanna help out, hun. I think the dates are a cool idea."

Daniel's reaction left me on edge. I wanted more than anything to talk to Theo about it.

But I couldn't.

♫

Ten minutes to closing time; I knew that because I'd looked at the clock so often, I was surprised my eyes hadn't worn holes in it.

Daniel and I were reviewing the day's work when Olivia knocked on the office door.

"Laa-Laa, you have a visitor." The words sang out through her wide smile.

Her delight was infectious. Grinning back, I jumped up from the desk. We were expecting a delivery of samples and new furnishing catalogues; an event we both loved. We would religiously make ourselves tea and biscuits, then sit unwrapping every delicate square of paper and fabric, swooning over every page of the new trends, spending our imaginary money to fill imaginary houses.

She grabbed my hand and dragged me across the meeting area toward the entrance.

"Calm down." I laughed. "I'm coming."

Only, it wasn't a delivery.

"Theo!" I came to an abrupt standstill and had to remember to close my mouth.

"Hey." He hugged me. Spice. Earth. Heat. Wow, he smelt good. "I was early, so hope you don't mind me being nosey?" Cocoa eyes searched my face.

Without thinking, I smiled and bit my lip.

"Dangerous," he whispered, taking my hand as I led him through the main doors to show him around.

He stopped next to the plans on the table. "You did these," he half asked, half told me.

I nodded, my chest swelling as he lifted one of the mood boards to feel the texture of a fabric sample.

"I thought so," he said. "It's your style."

"It is?" It still astounded me how much he noticed.

"Yes, it's why you loved The Mermaid. It's natural, peaceful. You love to feel like you're outdoors even when you're not. It's clever and it's beautiful." His slow, sweet smile melted my insides. "Like you."

"Didn't buy her this place for no reason." Daniel's statement startled us both.

We turned to find him behind us, leaning against the doorframe of my office, arms crossed. He approached—straightening himself up like a cat puffing out its fur to appear larger—and offered a hand to Theo. "Daniel David. Pleased and, I have to say, surprised to meet you." Theo accepted the handshake. Daniel cocked an eyebrow toward me. "Well, well, well, Quinn. How on earth did this happen?"

I confess the look on his face made me a little smug. "It's a funny story. Which I'm sure Theo won't mind telling while I get changed. He does it much better than me." I squeezed Theo's hand. "You are a *talented* actor after all."

He chuckled as I walked off with Olivia.

"Theo is like, so into you," she announced proudly in the ladies' toilets while emptying her makeup bag onto the sink counter.

If she was trying to encourage me, it had the opposite effect. I concentrated on changing into my jeans, staying on tiptoes to avoid as much of the freezing floor as possible.

Olivia flapped her hands. "Whoa, there's no rush."

"I need to get back out there before Daniel says something," I mumbled, struggling to do up the tiny buttons on my bottle-green silk top.

Halfway into her jeggings, she stopped, hovering one-legged like a flamingo. "What do you mean? What will Daniel say?"

Hell if I knew. In Daniel's eyes, money and fame made someone important, and Daniel was jealous of important people. He could get cocky and competitive. He might show off to try and impress Theo. Not to mention our history, which neither Theo nor Olivia knew about. Yet. Then there was Day Zero—CRAP. I knew this was a bad idea!

Olivia stood waiting for a response. Her balancing skills were quite impressive.

I blagged an excuse. "Nothing. I don't know. He can be a bit, you know, pushy."

She shrugged and carried on getting dressed. I darted out the door.

Theo smiled when I returned. A good sign, hopefully. He held out a hand for me, warming my entire body although the office was cool. If I was the earth, he was my sun, with the power to heat the air around me, inside me, even across a vast space.

Olivia swooped in a minute later and went straight to Daniel, excitedly chatting about the night ahead, showing him down the stairs as I set the alarm and locked the doors.

"Sorry about ditching you back there with Daniel," I whispered to Theo, in case anyone could still hear me; the stairwells tended to echo. "Please take anything he says with a pinch of salt, he can be, umm..." I fumbled with putting the keys back in my bag, unable to find the right words.

"He was fine," Theo said. "We talked about you."

Exactly what I was afraid of. I stared at my shoes and held my breath.

Theo carefully lifted my eyes to his with a thumb under my chin. "He told me how incredibly talented you are. Though, I already knew that."

"Oh, if that's all he said, I'll let him off."

"You are a mystery to me, Miss Quinn." His chuckle dissolved against my lips.

A short walk along narrow cobbled streets took us to the centre of town. Daniel and Theo were busy talking about London as we entered the restaurant. Walking in teleported us to Italy. Terracotta walls. Oil paintings of rural scenes. Mediterranean pottery hung from shelves packed with spice jars.

I discreetly asked for a spot at the back where it was more secluded. Greg and Sarah arrived as we were being shown to our table and introduced themselves to Daniel. Keeping my voice low, I offered Theo a chair facing away from the main seating area. I took the one at the head of the table. It meant that I ended up sandwiched between Theo on my right and Daniel on my left. At least I could keep an eye on them. I couldn't help but notice Olivia making a beeline for Daniel's other side.

We had made it safely and without incident onto our desserts when Greg brought up the band. "So, Lara. Decided what you're singing yet?"

My ice cream went down the wrong way. "Singing?"

Everything sounded fuzzy thanks to my last glass of wine. Or possibly because of Theo's hand on my knee.

"Yeah, singing." Greg laughed, nudging Theo's shoulder.

(Definite bromance forming.) "You promised to join in for the next gig. Remember?"

"He's right, you did." Theo's eyes sparkled my way.

I challenged Theo back. "I remember mentioning I'd *consider* it, but only if you came."

"Just you try and stop me." He pressed his beer bottle to his lips, slowly swallowing a mouthful. His other hand slid up to my thigh.

I had to clear my throat and avert my eyes.

Sarah added, "How about a Ruelle or Swift song? Or an old lil' jazzy number, you know those back to front."

"Crazy," Daniel asserted. We all looked at him. "*Crazy* by Patsy Cline. You sang it at our office do. It's perfect for you, Quinn."

That was the night I gave him a lift home and rejected his advances. If he still remembered the song, he couldn't have been that drunk after all.

"Classic song," Sarah agreed, finishing her last spoon of tiramisu.

I shrugged, wanting more and more to wriggle free of everyone's spotlight. Spinning my empty wine glass with one hand, I reached under the table with my other and gripped Theo's strong fingers.

After an assuring *'I've got you'* squeeze and a tap on my leg, Theo pushed back his chair. "Hmm. Plenty of time left to decide. Anyway. Next round is on me."

The subject quickly changed to picking cocktails. I smiled my thanks toward him. He'd read me again. And saved me.

Daniel offered to help Theo with the drinks. I used the opportunity to go for a breather in the ladies. Olivia followed me.

As soon as we were out of earshot she huffed, "What's up with Daniel?"

Daniel was acting strangely. I didn't like the way his arm kept lingering around the back of my chair. I couldn't remember him ever being this touchy in public. Or, was I only noticing it because of the way Theo's attention kept wandering toward my boss's hand every time it brushed my shoulder?

I looked into the vintage mirror at Olivia's face, her lips in a tight pout and eyes narrowed into thin streaks of blue and glittery black. "What do you mean?"

She started chewing the ends of her hair. "I don't know. He, like, keeps showing off about his car and house and stuff."

"Oh. That." I sighed. Olivia had never seen Daniel out socially before. "No, that's just Daniel."

She looked disappointed. I restrained myself from saying, *'I told you so.'*

Theo

Daniel leaned against the smooth wooden bar as if he owned it. He had removed his jacket to display an expensive watch, numerous tattoos, beyond muscular arms and perfectly manicured hands. A golden poster boy for any Hollywood action movie. No lighting, makeup or photo editing required. *Jeez.* This guy would make Chris Hemsworth, Evans, Pratt, Pine, and every other living Chris feel self-conscious.

"Sticking around for a while then?" he asked.

My gut warned me not to share too much. "A while, yes," I replied, glancing down at my own hands—weathered and rough from the outdoors and scarred from falling off a horse as a child. "How long have you worked with Lara?"

"Coming on three years. Took her on as my apprentice fresh out of college. Promoted her last year. I saw her potential."

Something about the way Daniel spoke of Lara being *his* apprentice made my jaw clench. I told myself: *You don't know him well enough to make a fair judgement on his personality.*

"We work well together. I like her style." He smirked into his glass. "Except for her black bedroom that is. Aye, that's bold even for me. What d'ya reckon?"

Why Daniel felt the need to point out he had been in Lara's bedroom, I wasn't sure. Though, I could guess. Had they been more than colleagues? *Is he the type of man she goes for?* What if Daniel was the reason Lara left London, the reason behind her insecurity?

The pieces fitted.

Stinging heat flashed over my skin. "I hadn't noticed." I shrugged. "When I'm in a woman's bedroom, I'm not looking at the wall colour." *Dammit.* I should not have said that. That was perilously close to the old Theo.

Our eyes met for a second. I had rattled him. I jammed my fists into my pockets and reminded myself: *You don't know him well enough to make a fair judgement on his personality.*

It did not change the way I felt.

Lara

Heads turned as Theo and Daniel walked back to our table. They were the same height, but that's where the similarities ended. Ha, like Legolas and Will Turner! Daniel walked with his broad shoulders back and chin high, flashing a 'hello ladies' kind of smile at anyone who looked his way. Whereas Theo carried his good looks like a discreet post-it note stuck to his back with 'handsome' written on it. Unnoticed. Unimportant. He knew first-hand the dark side of being in the limelight, so had no need or desire to draw attention to himself.

I thanked him for my mojito. He drew his lips into a thin line.

Edging my chair closer, I reached for his hand under the table. "Okay?"

"Yes." He nodded with another tight-lipped smile, swirling the ice in his Coke.

He wasn't okay. Nerves knotted my airways. What the hell had Daniel done now?

Daniel tapped his glass and winked at me. "Alright everyone, I've got some exciting news." He always had to make such a scene.

My nerves heightened into panic.

"Clarke's decided to take early retirement," he continued, setting a hand on my shoulder. "To cut a long story short. How does David *Quinn* Construction sound to you?"

Nerves and panic burst into full-blown shock. "What?" I stared up at him. This could not be happening. I was dreaming. Or having a nightmare. I couldn't decide.

Daniel's booming laugh shook the table. "You and me, Quinn. Partners. Together again."

Had I imagined the way Theo's hand just tightened around mine?

"So what's it gonna be?" Daniel pressed, pausing to take a seat and slide an arm around me in the process. "I want you, Lara."

I couldn't breathe. And this time, Theo's reaction was definitely not imaginary. He glared at the side of Daniel's head, his chest heaving, back rigid. I wasn't happy with Daniel's suggestive choice of words either and unfortunately, I understood him well enough to know they weren't accidental.

That aside, this offer was everything I wanted. My ultimate goal. Being a partner meant I would be my own boss, choosing my own projects. I wouldn't have to answer to Daniel. I'd be free.

Without breaking my promise.

"Yes," I squeaked, smiling, nodding, then laughing and finding my voice. "Hell yes!"

Theo

As we arrived back outside the office, Daniel stopped beside my car to look in through the windscreen.

"Thanks for the invite tonight," I said. "Good to put a face to the name." I refrained from saying, 'it was nice to meet you,' as it would not have been entirely true.

"Likewise. Nice wheels. Didn't fancy the newer model then?" he added sarcastically, straightening up to lean an elbow on the roof. "Aye n' by the way, no hard feelings about me staying with your girlfriend, eh?"

"None at all," I replied, refusing to take the bait.

I loved my six-year-old Mustang. What I didn't love was the way Daniel kept touching Lara. Or, if I was being completely honest, the way she didn't seem to notice or react as if she was used to it. As if it was normal.

No. Lara was not Yasmin, she was not a liar or a cheat.

Lara gave a last hug to Sarah and joined me. Olivia waved goodnight and went to start their car, followed by Daniel who hovered at the passenger door, waiting for Lara. Silently, like a spider on a web.

I pulled Lara close and tucked a stray curl behind her ear. She positively shone with happiness. "Congratulations, Miss Quinn of London's David Quinn Construction." I tried not to wince when combining her name with Daniel's. "I am highly impressed, though not surprised. You are brilliant, you deserve it."

"Theo," she sighed, no more than a whisper. I would never get used to the way she said my name. It sent shivering power through my body. "What's the matter?"

I didn't want to keep secrets anymore. Not from her. "Does Daniel stay with you often?"

Her expression turned from confusion to suspicion. "No, this is the first time. Why?"

"It's nothing, don't worry."

Either my acting was going downhill, or she was getting better at reading me. The latter, hopefully. Her jewel-like eyes, circled by smokey ink, rolled in Daniel's direction. "What did he say?"

"Nothing important." Daniel had been playing games.

"Theo?" she repeated, slower, deep and breathy.

If I didn't kiss her within the next minute, I would explode. "I can't hide anything from you, can I?"

"Nope." She grinned.

I gripped her soft waist tighter, battling the growing urge to lower my hands into her back pockets and lift her up. To feel her legs wrapped around me. To bury my face into that gorgeous spot just under her ear. It would have been incredible.

The old Theo would have done it, and far more by now. But I wanted something beyond that, something deeper and... real.

"Random question." I took a chance. "Do you have a black bedroom?"

"Huh?" Her brows pinched together. "No, I was *going* to, then I went for cornflower."

Cornflower was, I believed, a light greyish blue. Most people would say standard blue. Not Lara.

I relaxed, my mind made up regarding Daniel. I knew plenty of men like him—Phillip for one—who liked control and position. Alphas. Top dogs. The kind of men who made it hard for you to say no, and most likely wouldn't listen to anyone who did. No wonder Lara called him 'difficult.' He had probably pushed her into letting him stay.

I wasn't afraid to push back.

Across the street, Daniel was still waiting. Watching.

Let him watch.

Lara

I got the feeling Theo's bizarre interest in my bedroom colour linked in with an earlier question about Daniel staying over. Especially as he kept looking over my shoulder to where Daniel stood, his laser eyes burning into my back.

Theo held me tighter to his body as he leaned back against his car, his sun-kissed skin glowing under the streetlights. Mellow tones of a saxophone playing The Flamingos in the jazz bar around the corner drifted in and out on the breeze.

Swirling from one emotion to another, his expression changed so quickly I couldn't pin any of them down. Until, without warning, he kissed me in a way that felt far too intimate to be out in public. Firm fingers grasped my hair and around my neck as his mouth discovered every millimetre of my own. I should have been embarrassed or nervous. I didn't care.

I didn't bloody care.

Kissing him was like taking my first breath; pure exhilarating new life pumped through my veins. Kissing him was like taking my last breath; urgently, I clung to him, desperate for more.

"I'll call you tomorrow, after work?" He pulled away reluctantly, gasping, shivering, burning.

I drew a finger down the line of his straight nose, over his lips. "You better."

I Only Have Eyes For You – The Flamingos

Lara's Journal
Day 161

Every day I went to court determined to be strong, and every day I ended up hiding in a bleak corridor, fixed to the spot like a stone-cold statue. Several people spoke to me, including the police inspector overseeing my case. I don't know what they said. Their words faded into the beige carpet, beige walls and damp, musty books.

Statements from the families of the four murdered women broke my heart, not only because of their loss but because I kept imagining my parents up on the stand in the same situation. Assuming it would be better for Mom and Dad not to know what happened, I'd tried to keep as much of my ordeal from them as possible. But as we sat through hours of hearing about the other women, I realised what an evil thing your imagination could be.

After weeks of evidence and accounts from various witnesses and experts, the trial was finally coming to a close. We expected the verdict at any time. Mom and Dad sat on either side of me in the worn-out waiting area. Daniel paced up and down, the tip-tap of his smart shoes echoing up the hallway. Olivia and Greg had travelled to London with us for support and were waiting back at my old flat.

A voice came over a loudspeaker, calling everyone back to the courtroom. The jury was ready. My heart lurched into my throat as my legs refused to stand.

"I'll wait here with you, sweetie," Dad offered, holding onto my arm.

I shook my head. "I have to see this."

I needed to face *him*. To show *him* I wasn't afraid, to see *his* face as the sentence was read.

Daniel stopped pacing. "Alright then. Let's get this over with." He lifted my other arm and we all entered the courtroom together.

He, Jeff, looked different. His hair had been shaved and he wore a shirt with suit trousers, like any normal man you'd pass on the street. It made me sick to the stomach to think I'd felt sorry for him because he was so quiet. Ugh.

He didn't show any remorse. Would I have cared if he did? (Or if he ever does?) Anger and hatred ran through my blood like venom, raising my temperature and making my skin sweat. I don't know what I'd expected—some sort of closure, I suppose.

The judge gave his final comments before asking the jury for their decision. I looked up at the ceiling, trying not to make eye contact with anyone.

Most of the courtroom was an original Victorian brick building that had been added to over the decades, making it a patched-up collage of styles; Art Deco, 1970s Brutalist concrete, then some recent glass additions. An architectural history lesson all thrown into one spot. I took note of every detail to distract me from the feeling of Jeff breathing down my neck.

The verdict didn't make me feel any better.

Guilty.

Life in prison.

I wanted him to suffer the way I had, to feel the despair and pain of the families he had destroyed. I wanted him dead. I hoped prison was as bad as TV made it out to be.

A police inspector calmly read our prepared statement to some reporters waiting outside, while another officer ushered us away from flashing cameras toward a taxi.

Daniel took the front seat. My parents sat with me in the back. As we passed a group of girls, dressed all in pink out on a hen night, I smiled at a memory of a fancy dress party Olivia had been to while in college. I'd been anxious about revising for our upcoming exams but she'd talked me into going anyway. Those kinds of worries now felt ridiculously small. I never thought I could miss worrying about small things.

♪

Greg and Olivia had gone to a nearby hotel. My parents finally went to bed.

The same page of my book sat in front of me for over an hour. Every time I made an effort to read, my mind wandered away, leaving me a lifeless, empty shell. Daniel was sprawled across the other end of my sofa, absently flicking through TV channels. He didn't seem to want to sleep or to be alone either.

His witness statement was the last to have been given. The heavy wooden doors of the courtroom had groaned as I cracked them open enough to listen through the gap. He'd recalled events clearly and calmly, describing them in the same methodical way he listed out the daily tasks at work: He arrived and opened the gates, he saw the new carpenter kneeling over something in the yard with what looked like a saw in his hand. It was only as he got closer that he realised it was a person on the floor, and then he realised it was me. Jeff ran. Daniel stayed and called an ambulance as he tried to stop the bleeding.

The judge asked him about my condition and for the first time, Daniel's voice cracked. "There was blood everywhere." I heard a shaky breath before he carried on. "She were hardly conscious. White. Cold. I... I kept telling her to hold on."

He didn't tell them about the kiss.

Or that he loved me.

I guess it wasn't relevant.

"Anything to drink, Quinn?" Daniel's face flashed in and out of view from the light of the TV screen.

I pointed out the tea and coffee pots and told him to help himself.

He groaned. "I meant something stronger."

I remembered a bottle of whiskey hidden away in a cupboard. Suddenly feeling reckless, I fetched it along with two glasses.

"Aye, that's more like it." He poured us both a generous shot.

We drank in silence, slumping into the sofa, slowly letting the warm liquid sink into our bodies, breathing in heat. It was the first alcohol I'd drunk since Day Zero and it went straight to my head. And my knees.

He lifted the bottle. "Another?"

Without a word, I held my glass out. He smiled. He had a dreamy smile. I giggled. It sounded alien. I shouldn't have been giggling after our day. My hand clamped over my mouth as it turned into a choked sob.

Daniel sidled closer to refill my glass. "Today sucked." He set the bottle down, kissed the top of my head and draped an arm around me. "Heck, that's good stuff."

"I should think so," I said, tracing a finger around the outline of the birds tattooed on his torso. "You brought it, remember?"

"I did?"

"When you promoted me!" I poked his side.

He caught my hand, held it against his heart and didn't let go. "So I did. I have good taste."

"In whiskey? Or head designers?"

"Both. Obviously."

This was the side of Daniel I'd missed the most. The rare moments when he let down his guard. There had been so many times when I'd wished I knew how to break through his hard exterior, but every time I brought up the subject of family or his past, he backed further away.

Everyone had faults. If I tried harder, could I just keep ignoring his? After the life he'd known, was my wanting a public relationship and some kind of deeper commitment asking for too much from him, too soon?

Leaning into his shoulder, I looked around the almost empty flat. It felt like mine but not mine, like an odd parallel universe. "Are you going to rent this place out again?"

"Probably," he said, lifting my legs across his lap. "I were hoping you'd change your mind."

Pressing his nose to my cheek, he smoothed a hand around my face, lips brushing along my jawline. I gasped as my chest filled with a different kind of heat than the whiskey. Turning my head toward his, he kissed me. Every one of my worries dissolved; he distracted me from everything, leaving nothing but the pressure of his mouth, and the sweet, fiery taste on his tongue.

The hunger of his grip intensified. He wanted me. But did he love me? *Really?* His hand dropped from my neck to my waist. He flinched and recoiled from the shock of my rough skin. Panic shivered through me as he lifted my shirt to look.

For one heart-stopping second, his hands became Jeff's.

"No, please—" I pushed him away and covered myself up. "I'm not... I'm not the same as I—" My words were slurred and heavy. Whiskey and I have never mixed well. "You should go."

Looking like he wanted to say something, he stared at the blank TV, fingers tapping. Until his focus cleared. He stood, called a taxi and left me once again, alone.

The End – JPOLND

Lara's Journal
Day 162

I must have drifted off to sleep after Daniel left because I woke up on the sofa, wearing the same clothes. Mom clicked on the kettle.

"What time is it?" I mumbled, dragging my feet clumsily into the kitchen area.

"Nearly ten. Sorry, I tried not to wake you." She added an extra mug onto the counter and spooned in a portion of coffee for me. "Sleep okay?" Her face was red and puffy. She'd been crying again.

I shrugged while trying to smile. "Sort of."

She looked pointedly over at the whiskey bottle and glasses. "How long did Daniel stay?"

"Oh, not long." I dug some Paracetamol out of a drawer. "An hour or two."

"You know I love you, cariad." She softly touched a finger to the tip of my nose. "And I want you to come home, but are you sure this is what *you* want?" Her voice stayed calm and composed. Her eyes were afraid of what the answer might be. The same eyes as mine. Blue and green like tropical waters.

"I'm sure. I don't want to be here anymore." I wrapped her in a tight hug. "And I love you, too."

"You don't have to leave everything." I knew she was talking about Daniel.

"No. I have to." Moving away would be good for both of us.

A van arrived at noon to collect my sofa and other odd bits of leftover furniture. Greg and Olivia left to pick up my laptop as well as some photos and personal things from my office on their way home. I couldn't face walking in there.

Before leaving, I went around checking each room for any forgotten items. My flat looked the way I felt—empty, sad, worn out.

"All ready, chicken?" Dad asked as I returned to the front door.

"Almost. Just one thing I need to do."

My mind was made up.

We all got in the car and I put Daniel's address into the sat-nav for Dad. My stomach heaved when the four-story townhouse came into view. I set my jaw, clenched my fists and asked my parents to wait in the car. It wouldn't take long.

One thing Daniel and I always agreed on was design. His place was a palace, everything made from the best—stone, marble, solid oak—and thanks to his cleaner, it was always pristine. He answered the door with wet hair, wearing joggers. Nothing but joggers.

Make it more difficult, why don't you.

I rolled my eyes, steering my focus away from the birds on his abs, across the script on his arms, up to his face. "We need to talk."

With a nod, he stepped aside for me to enter the extravagant hallway, shutting the door behind me.

"I shouldn't have let that happen last night," I said, "I should have stopped you sooner and I'm sorry." I pulled at the hem of my coat.

"Lara, please." Daniel took my hands. I could smell the trace of our whiskey on his breath, sweat, soap, and... some kind of sweet lavender perfume? "It was bad timing. I didn't know how to—" He groaned. "When you come back, things'll be different."

"I'm not coming back. I'm moving and I'm not changing my

mind." I leaned against the cool, tiled wall. "I can't be here anymore."

"I'll look after you, I won't let you down again." That softer side of his voice broke through my willpower. Which was why I didn't push him away when his hands wound around my arms.

What was wrong with me? Being looked after wasn't so bad. All I had to do was sink into his strong embrace and let him take me away from all the anxiety. I was crazy to be turning down such a beautiful man.

My heart desperately wanted what we had to be enough.

My head told me it wasn't.

It never would be.

Tears threatened to fill my eyes. I looked at the ceiling. "I don't want to be looked after and wrapped in cotton wool for the rest of my life. I need to learn how to be me again."

It made more sense in my head. He nodded anyway, although I had the impression he wasn't listening. One of his hands had found its way into my hair.

"We've been through so much, Dan, and I know you feel guilty." *Don't cry,* I told myself, *don't cry.* "But we can't keep doing this because you're guilty and I'm grateful."

"You never used to worry about *why* we were together. We just were, and it works."

Our relationship was a secret. None of my friends or family knew about us. Could you truly class that as being together?

His damp hair tickled my face, soft lips brushed my cheeks. "Lara," he whispered, "stay with me."

Stay with me. My mind was transported back to the building site... the cold... the dread...

I pulled back. "Why?"

"Because I want you to."

"Why?" I repeated louder, fists tightening. I wouldn't give in again.

"Because we're good. This thing we have? We're better than good together!"

"But why? What is this thing?"

Annoyance simmered through his tightening hands. He didn't like being questioned or rejected.

After a minute of silence—during which he let go—I sighed. Over two years of 'this thing' and he still couldn't tell me. "I don't want to be with someone who can't answer that question. Not anymore."

No response.

He didn't love me.

For the third time in my life, I'd been stabbed by a brutal knife, right through my heart, ripping the breath from my lungs. I wanted to scream and fight, but I knew it was just as pointless as the first time.

My head fell against Daniel's chest. I listened to his steady heartbeat, savouring the feel of his warm skin one last time.

"Promise me you'll be careful." He murmured against my ear.

"Oh, you know how much I love health and safety." We separated, and somehow I found a smile. I vaguely heard his upstairs shower switch on. "I'll be back at work in a few weeks, and I'll let you know about any office spaces I find."

"Aye." His business face clicked into place. "I'll send over the next project info. Be good to have you back, Quinn."

And there we were, back to 'Quinn.'

For him, ending the conversation, and everything else we'd shared, was as simple as bulldozing a house made of paper.

I let myself out and looked back at him from the doorway, but I didn't have the strength left to say goodbye. Or to ask why there was a pair of women's heels by the door.

They probably belonged to the woman in the shower who wore lavender perfume.

Sometimes Love Just Ain't Enough – Patty Smyth

Day 353
Friday

"What was going on with you last night?" Olivia's voice coming from downstairs sent a chill through my spine and froze my feet to the stair carpet. "What do you have against Theo?"

She and Daniel had obviously been talking again.

"I don't trust him," Daniel replied.

Their conversation wasn't meant for me, I shouldn't have been listening. They weren't exactly being quiet though.

"I mean, Theodore Jackson?" Daniel spat the name out. "If she's happy to get off with some shallow womaniser, then fine. She sure picked a good one."

Ironic. He was quite happy for me to 'get off' with himself—a shallow womaniser. Anger bubbled in my gut.

Olivia stepped in to defend Theo. "You don't know him."

"And you do?"

"If I didn't know any better, I'd say you were jealous. If you have feelings for her..." Her voice trailed away.

Feelings? Why would she think that? If Daniel had told her about us, then she also knew how much I'd been hiding.

When Daniel spoke again, his voice was quieter. I tiptoed forward a step to hear. Not my finest moment I'll admit.

"Don't be ridiculous, Livy." *Livy?* "You know it's not like that. She... she died in my arms." A crack appeared through his words, the way it had in court when giving his statement.

I would never wish my experience on my worst enemy. I tried to imagine it from Daniel's side. Finding a friend—or whatever I was to him—in my state, knowing there was nothing you could do, desperately begging them to hold on. I wouldn't wish that on anyone either.

"I know," Olivia soothed, "but she's getting better, and stronger. You have to stop beating yourself up about it. You owe her an apology for being a dick yesterday."

Another pause. A long one. I felt even more awkward. Pins and needles tingled through my left foot, which I'd been holding at a funny angle to avoid a creaky floorboard.

"Alright, alright." Daniel was smiling. I'd been the recipient of his charm enough times for me to recognise it.

It went quiet again.

I'd heard enough. I slammed my bedroom door shut and stomped down the stairs. By the time I got down, they were both seated at opposite ends of the living room, Olivia drinking coffee, Daniel reading.

To think Olivia would always tell me everything about her life was immature. People grow, they enter new relationships. Loyalties change. After all, I'd kept things from her, choosing instead to keep Daniel's and, more recently, Theo's confidence. I knew full well Daniel would move on—it had taken him less than twenty-four hours for goodness sake—but I'd never honestly expected him to try it on with Olivia.

A sickening hole opened in my chest; I hadn't been there for her the way she always had been for me. Daniel's words, he wasn't 'here for *her*,' floated through my mind like a ghost.

What the actual hell was he playing at?

♫

Technical drawings and architect's plans were laid out on the meeting table, now surrounded by my sketches, samples and colours along with images of furniture and products, bringing our whole concept to life, ready for the final presentation. Despite the drama, good and bad, it had been a productive week's work.

Thankfully there was so much to do, I'd been able to avoid Olivia and Daniel for most of the day. They had noticed. Olivia caught my eye over the top of her reception desk. I pretended not to see her jab Daniel in the ribs.

"Fantastic work as always." Daniel came to a stop behind my shoulder. "Can I have a minute?" he asked as if I had a choice. "In the office."

Again, he offered me *my* chair. I wanted to yell, 'this is my office!' Instead, I imagined myself on the beach, in my a happy place, and let the cool sea water wash away my annoyance. Theo had been teaching me some of the visualisation techniques he used for expressing characters' emotions. It worked. I couldn't wait to tell him.

"I owe you an apology for last night and for... quite a few other nights," Daniel said, taking a seat on the desk in front of me.

Wow. Okay, I hadn't expected him to listen to Olivia. A spark of hope lit up like a match; he *could* change.

He smirked. "Theo seems like a nice guy."

That wasn't what he'd said this morning. He was lying. The match quickly got blown out.

"So, you're going to see him again?" He started playing with his watch, making out that he wasn't bothered.

I responded flatly, "Yes."

In a split second, Daniel changed because he wasn't getting the responses he wanted. He gave up on the charm.

Looking down at me like a headmaster, he crossed his arms. "Aye, I get it now. Real reason you won't speak to that reporter is because *he* doesn't know yet." He didn't give me a chance to reply. "You're so worried about Mr Flashy Hollywood finding out the truth, you'd rather lie and miss out on this incredible opportunity." He sat up straight, smug with his own apparent wisdom.

Opportunity? Ha, of course! Daniel wasn't thinking of the charity, he saw this as a chance for me to receive some kind of glory, fame even. In his mind, what other reason could there be to help?

Standing to meet his eyes, I glared at him. "This has nothing to do with Theo." Although, it did. A little bit. "You of all people should understand why I don't want to talk about what happened."

"The Lara I knew wasn't afraid of what other people thought."

My mental image of a calm beach went up in smoke.

"Well, guess what, Daniel?" I shouted, "She was murdered! So I'm sorry, but that kind of thing affects a person's confidence." All I could hear was the thumping of my own heart. I'd never raised my voice to him before.

His mouth gaped in surprise. "If you say that's the only reason, then fine. But we both know you can't keep it hidden forever." His eyes flickered down to my stomach. "He'll find out. One way or another, he's in for a nasty shock."

Nasty?

Nasty!

He was bloody lucky I'd sworn to never hit anyone again.

I forced myself to sit back down. Daniel had the look of someone who was holding onto a secret, a secret that gave him power, a secret he couldn't wait to use to his advantage.

He had said something to Theo. I knew it! It explained Theo's odd questions about my room.

"I am not going to discuss my relationships with you," I said, throwing cold daggers into my voice. "And don't ever speak to me like that. Especially if you plan on seeing my best friend again."

Did he honestly think I wouldn't tell Olivia about this? I gave a pointed look toward Olivia's desk and the realisation he'd overstepped a line finally dawned on his face.

"Now, if you don't mind." I clicked open my emails and made myself busy. "I have work to do, so I would like *my office* back. Safe journey, and don't forget the presentation folder on your way out."

Hell, that felt good.

He left without another word—like usual—crossed the reception, picked up the folder and headed for the exit. He stopped only briefly to say goodbye to Olivia. She stared after him, arms drooping by her sides. Hopefully, I wouldn't see him again for a while, which meant neither would she.

Her pained expression tore through my anger; I remembered what it felt like to be disappointed by Daniel.

These days, I expected it.

Dreams – Fleetwood Mac

Theo

With a deep breath of hay-scented air, I stepped out of my car onto the driveway of my family home and stretched my legs. The lights of London sparkled in the far distance.

Chloe ran to meet me, nearly bowling me over with a hug. She held no grudge for my missing out on years of her life. It was in the past, completely and truly forgiven. The regret still ached inside me like a broken bone that wouldn't heal. I hugged her back, holding her off the ground till she started laughing and kicking her legs about.

Our parents waited by the door. A year ago, when I arrived back from L.A. and turned up unannounced at three in the morning, they too had welcomed me home with open arms. Nevertheless, a lake of unease surrounded each of us, filled with distrust, unspoken hurt, and disappointment. Some days the lake would shrink, on others it would refill again. I feared it would never dry up completely.

We ate dinner together around the table in the kitchen, catching up on the events of the past weeks. It didn't take long for Mum to ask about my date, her sharp eyes dancing with curiosity. I glanced toward my father, who wore a forced smile that scarcely masked his worry. Another bucket of water had just been added to his lake.

Christopher Jackson saw me as the kind of person who would never walk when I could run, or like when I could love. I considered loyalty and passion as strengths. But Dad had seen how they could also be weaknesses when blindly misplaced. Because of them, I had done some foolish things and believed some dangerous lies.

The only thing I could do to prove myself now—as Lara said —was to be patient, carry on being honest, being myself, and then the people who mattered would know the truth. The people who mattered to me were all right here. *Almost* all the people.

I took Lara's advice and told them about her. Everything: How we met, her work, the band. Phillip.

"Glad you got rid of that odious bloke," Dad said.

Chloe snorted. "Such an arsehole."

Dad gave her that warning look which only a parent can but laughed in agreement. "On that note, I'm heading for bed." He clapped my shoulder. "Nice to have you here. Hey, maybe we'll meet this girl soon?"

His genuine interest gave me hope. "Soon," I said, grinning.

Thanks to Lara's advice, the edges of our lake were slowly evaporating again.

I couldn't wait to tell her.

♪

"Come ooooon, Tee, gimme some details," Chloe nagged while helping carry my bags upstairs. "You really like her? What's she like? When can we meet her?"

"I said soon. Perhaps. It's only been a few weeks, I don't want to scare her away."

"We're not scary!" She dumped my bag unceremoniously on the carpet and hopped onto my bed. "Come on, what does she look like, you got a photo?"

"Hmm, no I haven't."

I stopped unpacking. Lara had never once asked me for a picture. As far as I knew, she hadn't told anyone, apart from the friends I'd met, about knowing me. I smiled at the balled-up socks in my hand. Lara didn't view me as some kind of trophy to be bragged about, that was why.

Glued to her phone, Chloe started whispering to herself. "Wales. Construction. Interiors... Yes!" She skipped over. "Is this her?" She waved around a picture an inch from my nose of Lara on Instagram.

"That's her. How did you find that so quickly?"

Chloe pulled a face at me as if that were the dumbest question ever. "Err, it's called the internet?"

The phone got whisked away again. I wished I had taken a longer look at the picture. How would Lara react if I asked her to send me one?

"She's cute," Chloe said, jumping back onto the bed. "It's a private account though, so I can't see anything else, I'll have to follow her—"

"No!" I launched myself at the phone but Chloe was too quick and hid it behind her back. "Don't do that. Please, Chloe, she'll know I've been talking about her." And we had both promised: No Googling.

"Okay, okay, I won't. Jeez, chill."

We stared each other down, till I let Chloe win and turned

back to my unpacking. Otherwise, we would have been locked there all night. She always won anyway.

"Whoa," Chloe said a minute later, "another Lara Quinn got attacked by this guy called The London Stabber and *survived*. How freaky is that?"

That truckload of information slammed into my chest at a hundred miles per hour. My hands fuzed to the handle of the wardrobe.

Heart still thumping, I formed my expression back into one of mild interest. "Hmm, yes, freaky." I dug an elbow into Chloe's ribs to nudge her off the bed. "Come on, I think that's enough snooping for one day. Get outta here, I'm shattered."

"I'm gooooing." She giggled in between trying to fend off my hands as I playfully pushed her into the hallway, where she then started dancing, wrapping her arms around her waist, pretending to hug someone. "You just wanna be aloooone so you can call Laaaaara," she sang.

As I took a step forward to grab her, she made a run for it down the hall, shrieking with laughter.

I shut the door and lay down, staring at all the film posters covering the walls, mentally listing what I knew:

One—*The London Stabber*. I remembered it being in the news last year. The timeline fitted. London was a big place though. And yet... Lara Quinn wasn't exactly a common name.

Two—When we met, her initial instinct was to defend herself against an attack.

Three—Something happened in London to make her return home. Something she didn't like talking about. Something that made her physically nervous.

Four—She'd asked me not to Google her. Was this why?

Five—She lost her temper when Phillip alluded to an event in her past. Had he discovered the same information as Chloe?

Ridiculous. It had to be another person. It couldn't be the forever smiling, gentle and strong Lara I knew.
It couldn't be *my* Lara.

Could it?

Day 354
Saturday

Soggy cereals were disgusting. I hadn't meant to let them go soggy, but after taking one mouthful—about fifteen minutes ago—I felt too sick to eat anymore.

Following Daniel's abrupt departure yesterday, I'd kept myself busy, then gone to bed early to avoid Olivia. I heard muffled sounds of her talking on the phone late in the night in a way that made me uneasy. And guilty. She was talking to Daniel. Either that or she'd met someone else I didn't know about.

She knew what I thought about Daniel. I had to let her make her own choices, her own mistakes. Only, she didn't know *everything*, did she? Who knows how he might have spun our story. Oh hell, if I told her the truth now, would she think I was the jealous one? That I was telling her out of spite? It didn't matter, one way or another I had to tell her. I'd already been hiding too much from too many people.

Theo would know what to do. He'd have the perfect words to say without causing any more problems. I wished I could ask him, but that would mean telling him about Daniel, too.

Every day I told myself to be brave and honest.

Every day I ignored myself.

A buzz from my phone interrupted my idle cereal stirring.

THEO: Morning, beautiful. Arrived safely back home and I've already been interrogated about you 😊 Off to meet some school friends today. Call you later x Wish you were here, babe. I miss you already. xxx

A tear dropped into my bowl of oaty mush.

"Laa-Laa?" Olivia rushed over. I hadn't heard her coming down the stairs. She came to a standstill at the other side of the table when she saw the phone in my hand. "Oh, hun. What's happened?"

Sitting beside me, she slowly and carefully put an arm around my waist, as if I was made of cracked glass and she was afraid of shattering me completely.

I slid the phone toward her and she read, her breath quickening as a smile appeared. "I don't get it? That's like, so sweet. Why are you crying?"

I rubbed my wet face with my sleeve. *Attractive.* "Because I miss him too. And I... I genuinely like him, but he doesn't know me." I sniffed. "I wish he'd stop calling me beautiful. He wouldn't say it if he saw—"

"Don't say that. You're beautiful, get that into your head. You have to just tell him. Rip the plaster off and get it over with. He likes you. Like, a lot. I mean, he told his family about you! But if he can't deal with your past then he's not the right guy. It's not like he's squeaky clean either." Her head dropped. "I'm sorry I pushed you into this."

"You didn't. I thought I could keep my distance and now—argh I'm so stupid. We all knew it wouldn't last, even Daniel said... he thinks I'm..." Nasty. *Damaged.*

"Don't listen to Daniel. Forget about him, he's just jealous," Olivia hissed. I didn't dare ask what he'd done to annoy her. "Anyway, we have TV to catch up on, then you have a date tonight." She got up and headed for the sofa. "With a guy from DAYS, yeah?"

I slumped over into the brace position. "I'd forgotten about that. It's Andrew's brother. "

"It's only coffee." Olivia laughed. "You'll enjoy it, you won't have to stay long."

"I suppose so." I joined her on the sofa, ready for an episode of *Friends*. (The one where Joey gets his head stuck in a turkey.)

Best friends really were the best.

I *had* to tell her the truth about Daniel, for her own sake, even if she would hate me for it. I tried not to think about it as we started singing along to the theme tune.

Scars To Your Beautiful – Alessia Cara

Theo rang as I arrived at the coffee shop for my fake date.

"Mr Jackson," I answered with a smile.

He chuckled, "Miss Quinn, what are you up to?" His deep voice filled my insides with heat, his question filled me with ice.

I'm seeing another man. "Just meeting a friend for coffee. You?" It wasn't a lie. Not exactly.

He briefly told me about his day and about the huge mountain of a dinner that he was now expected to eat with his family. What was it about parents and their constantly wanting to feed you up as if you never ate without them? I laughed as his warm, purring tone put me at ease.

A man who looked like a younger, slimmer version of Andrew stopped at the crossing further up the street. "My friend's here, I better go."

"Enjoy. Hey, are you free to meet up on Monday when I get back?"

"Definitely." That gave me time to work out how to start telling the truth. "At the beach, after work?"

"Perfect."

I grinned and tapped out a rhythm on my arm. "Okay. I'll see you there." I couldn't help being excited, even if it meant a difficult conversation. "Oh, and, Theo?"

"Hmm?"

I doubted myself, then closed my eyes and went for it. "I miss you, too."

He hesitated. "You do?"

"Yes." How could he not believe that?

"Lara..." He exhaled a long, slow breath. "How am I going to survive till Monday?"

♪

Jason was a sweet and friendly carbon copy of his older brother Andrew. He introduced himself with a handshake, held the door open for me like a gentleman and pulled out a chair at one of the small round tables near the window. He also had Andrew's trait of being a chatterbox, which meant all I had to do was come up with a question now and then to start him off, then he would carry on about his sales job, his family, et cetera. Before I knew it, two hours had gone by, along with several cups of coffee. My head buzzed from all the caffeine.

Surprisingly, though, I was enjoying myself. He was a kind soul and, obviously, he knew all about DAYS and my reason for being there, so I didn't have to worry about what I could, or could not, share. *The way you should feel around friends.*

When had I turned into such a secretive person?

Jenny called when I got home to find out all the gossip. She then asked what I thought about having some sort of public open day or celebration at the end of our fundraising activities, to which we would invite everyone who'd supported the charity, along with past and present members. I told her it was a great idea and that I'd do everything I could to help; it was the least I could do for not meeting the reporter.

Day 356
Monday Afternoon

Rainy Days and Mondays – The Carpenters

Most of my Sunday had been spent going over what to say to Olivia about Daniel. A copious amount of chocolate had been harmed in the process. Plus there'd been lots of singing along to every kick-ass, confidence-boosting song I could find.

Typically, we were flat out at work all morning. I visited a new site to do some measuring up. Once I got back, every time I tried to start a conversation with Olivia, one of our phones would ring.

I checked my watch again. 4:35 p.m. Time was running out.

Olivia stopped in the doorway of my office, watching me, watching my watch. "Stop overthinking. You'll be fine." She'd presumed my nerves and jittery behaviour all day were due to my meeting up with Theo.

All I needed to do was say, 'Liv, I need to talk to you.' But whenever I tried, my throat dried and my mouth sealed up with glue.

"What's that saying you have?" she asked, then answered her own question. "Be brave, honest and make it count, yeah?"

I nodded. She was the one who deserved my honesty. *Be brave.* "Liv, I need to talk to you. It's about Daniel."

Her nose wrinkled. I pushed out the chair opposite my desk and asked her to sit. *Right,* I could do this. If I thought of it as a business meeting, I could present her with the truth the way I would a building plan, explain events as they happened and the reasons behind them.

"There are some things I never told you about him, about us, that I should have," I began clumsily, clasping my cold hands in my lap.

She sat quietly as I went back to the beginning: How Daniel and I became involved, what happened before, on, and after Day Zero. I kept my voice steady by watching a paper bag blowing around outside the window. One look at her big watery eyes would have broken me.

By the time I'd finished, she'd sunk in her chair, sleeves pulled over her hands, arms crossed over her chest.

"Liv?" She hadn't spoken for a full ten minutes. I dared to look up at her blank face. She looked so delicate. Like a china doll, which I'd just smashed. It was worse than anger or tears. "Liv, please? Shout at me or something. Anything."

"I'm not going to shout at you." A half-smile fluttered in and out of focus. "You better get going. I'll lock up."

She wanted to be alone, which meant one thing: she was angry.

Olivia was a lot better at controlling her temper than I was. Instead of yelling (or slapping people) she would go quiet and disappear, usually into her room, surrounded by loud music.

I gave her shoulder a squeeze as I walked out. "I'm sorry." *Please forgive me.*

Halfway to the beach, my hands started shaking so much I had to pull over. Seeing Olivia's pain, partly caused by Daniel, had brought back my own all over again. A tiny box crushed my heart, and the first person I wanted to talk to about it was Theo. And that scared me even more.

I was starting to depend on him, sharing everything that happened throughout the day, even silly things like hearing a new song on the radio. He did the same, telling me about the scenes they were filming, practising his lines with me before he went to bed. Even though they were supposed to be top secret. A constricting ache ran deep into my chest. Just when I needed him most, I was on my way to reveal a truth that would send him running.

I counted to ten with my eyes closed, then pulled down the mirror, brushed my hair, tied it into a high bun and put on my favourite red lipstick. Mom called it my war paint.

Theo was walking up from the beach as I pulled into the film site entrance, still wearing his period costume. I nearly stalled the car. *Oh come on!* I was about to break up with my very own Mr Darcy. *Be brave.* He might not break up with me. He might just turn and walk away without saying a word, the way Daniel always did when he didn't get what he wanted.

I stepped out and Theo jogged over. No matter how much my head told my mouth to cool it, I ended up grinning. Full-on Cheshire cat style.

"Hi, Th—"

He took the words out of my mouth by crashing our lips together, his warm hands slipping around my neck and waist. I fell back onto the side of my car with a sigh, the hard weight of his body pressing against the full length of mine. His kiss strayed to my jaw, throat, back to my face. After the warm day, he tasted like sun and salt. His breaths were quick and hot. He seemed to be all over me, all at once. Hell, he knew what he was doing.

To slow him down, I pressed my hands around his face, dragging a thumb over his lips to wipe off the lipstick smudges.

"I've been waiting to do that all weekend," he murmured against my cheek.

I held him close, willing myself to remember this moment forever. To remember the softness of his voice, the fluttering swirl of inner heat, the glow in his eyes as we breathed in each other's air. I pulled back and drank in every inch of his face. It wasn't enough. I wanted more time.

I *needed* more time.

"Lara?" Sweeping my fringe to the side, his brow creased. "Too much?"

"No." *Not enough.* An even smaller box squeezed my heart.

He pressed his forehead to mine and took my hand. "Come on, I'll get changed and we can go to The Cwtch. I'm ravenous!"

After that kiss, so was I.

We walked the road to the holiday park, snaking up a steep hill, following the edge of the growing cliffs. Thank goodness for my flat shoes. Theo untied the collar of his loose shirt. The cotton turned almost see-through when the sun caught it. Tiny curls of hair looped behind his ears.

I could look at him for the rest of my life and never have enough.

He recounted the weekend meet-up with his school friends, some of whom he hadn't seen in years. The happiness and relief he felt from their reunion radiated from him like, well, a radiator. If you could imagine the heat as bright white waves and explosions. Their evening ended in their village pub singing karaoke.

It didn't take long for his joy to infect me. I cracked up at his impersonation of his cockney, tone-deaf friend Lucas trying to sing Robbie Williams' *Angels*. Their day out sounded like the kind of thing my friends would do. *Not very 'Mr Flashy,' eh, Daniel!*

At the top of the hill, we stepped off the road and through a wide, rickety gate, tiptoeing over a cattle grid.

Theo pointed out the third caravan in a line of about ten, on the right hand side of the small field. "Here we are, home from home."

On the other side of the field was a matching line of caravans. The perimeter was marked by a moss-covered dry stone wall. A small, simple brick building that housed a few extra showers and washing facilities had been built in the centre of the field. It was basic, but people didn't come here for luxury, they came for the views over the bay—shimmering calm water held in by a horseshoe of golden sand, pale cliffs and emerald fields—and for the peace and quiet.

Theo unlocked the door of his caravan. Uh-oh. I hadn't thought this through. I stuffed my shaking hands into my pockets, unsure of what to do next. Should I follow him? It would look odd if I hung around outside.

"Wow, you weren't exaggerating about it being small," I said, stepping inside, my heart hammering in my chest. "It's lovely, though."

He stopped in front of me in the narrow hallway, which doubled as the kitchen, his head brushing the ceiling. "It does the job. And now that you are here..." He ran a finger down my arm, took my hand. "It has everything I need."

My blood pressure shot through the tin roof. I dragged my eyes from his, held my breath and made myself walk to the other end of the caravan, where I sat on the bench sofa underneath the window. Theo excused himself and disappeared into what I presumed was the bedroom, the door to which was no bigger than a standard wardrobe door. He had to duck to get through. Our connecting string tugged my rib cage, pulling me to follow him again.

I fanned my face with my hands (no help in the slightest) and distracted myself with my favourite hobby: being noscy. Although incredibly tiny, the caravan did have everything a person could need. Dining table, gas fire, TV, bookshelves, mini versions of standard appliances. All decorated with shades of white, cream and blue, giving a relaxed, beach hut vibe.

One of the nicest things about this particular spot was a nearby oak tree. Gnarly branches stretched over the roof so that if you looked up out of the window, you could see right through the leaves into its canopy. A flock of small birds hopped tirelessly through the branches.

"Better than TV, isn't it?" Theo's low voice thrummed through the air and over my shoulder.

I nodded and spun around, only for my answer to disappear completely from my mind. He stood three feet away, halfway through pulling on a T-shirt. The low light from the windows turned to liquid as it met his skin, pouring itself around every curve of his chest and line of muscle, bathing him in a honey glow.

Breathe. My lower stomach flipped and clenched, like that moment on an aeroplane when the engines burst to life and you're thrown back into your seat by pure unrestrained power. A smile twitched the corner of Theo's mouth as I forced my eyes back to the window.

"Way better than TV," I agreed. "It's like watching a whole city up there."

Footsteps came closer, his arms came into view, leaning on the windowsill as he sat next to me, T-shirt now fully on. Sadly.

I watched him as he looked curiously up into the tree, eyes jumping left to right, following the movement above. I loved the way he always seemed so fascinated by the world around him, noticing tiny things most people wouldn't give a second thought. He caught me watching him and shifted to face me.

This was the most private place we'd ever been alone together. A fact that short-circuited my brain. Gripping tightly onto my knees, I shied away from his gaze as a tingling blush returned to my cheeks.

On the table, a familiar shiny black pebble was being used as a paperweight on top of what looked like a script. Oh! It was the pebble I'd picked out the day we met. He'd kept it?

My heart splintered into pieces.

The longer we were together, the more I felt like I was no longer hiding something but that I was outright lying to him. I desperately wanted to tell him what happened with Olivia and about my argument with Daniel. But Theo wouldn't understand my loyalty or connection to Daniel unless I told him about our history, and in turn, about Day Zero.

All I'd wanted was to keep one day, one event to myself. No drama. No strings. Not to end up spiralling into a pit of secrets.

If I told Theo everything, my fears would come true. He would treat me differently, be completely freaked out and walk away, or be angry that I kept it from him. In short, our relationship would be over.

If I *didn't* tell him, then I was digging myself further into my pit by pretending to be someone I wasn't. I would never be able to talk about anything real so eventually, everything would fall apart anyway. Again, our relationship would be over.

I needed to decide which path I'd regret the least. Quickly.

Deep down, I already knew which one it had to be. So had Jenny. That was why she'd asked me about the fear of flying. The real reason dating terrified me was because I was terrified of opening up. And ultimately, of being rejected. Of being viewed as damaged.

If I kept on hiding from Theo, then I would always be left wondering: What if I'd just told the truth?

The truth hurts. Like hell. But it wouldn't claw at my insides the way the guilt of lying would.

Theo was studying me, I could feel his eyes on me, then we were staring at each other. For too long. It felt more intimate than when we were kissing.

Theo

Lara blushed and looked away. I used to think it was shyness, but after the way she kissed me earlier, and the way her eyes just ate me alive? She wasn't so shy around me anymore. It was more of a deliberate, guarded restraint. Self-protection. *Fear?*

No. She wasn't the Lara Quinn from the news. She couldn't be.

The thought of someone hurting her... it wasn't worth thinking about.

She glanced at me again, blushed even deeper. I didn't take my eyes off her. The dress she wore—smart, business-like but modern—was my favourite one yet. Which, I swear, had nothing to do with how much of her legs it showed. She reminded me of a golden age Hollywood star. Audrey Hepburn perhaps. Somehow, she looked equally as good in leather and denim whilst singing AC/DC.

The old Theo blazed inside me. I wanted her mouth on mine, her body under me, her skin in my hands. *Take her, make her yours.* All I had to do was lean forward, sink myself into her soft—I pulled the brakes on that train of thought.

I did want her. But not just for one night. I wanted all of her. Her smiles, her jokes, her secrets, darkness, light and life.

Patience.

I wanted her in a way that neither of us was ready for.

Yet.

Lara

"Come on," Theo said, hoarsely clearing his throat. "Let's go get some food."

On the way down the hill, we passed some other members of the cast and crew. I expected Theo to let go of my hand. Instead, he held it tighter and met everyone with a nod or wave. He wasn't trying to hide us being together. It felt good. Not like when I was with Daniel, who'd even made me hide in his room the one time his nan popped over unannounced. With him, everything was cloak and dagger, mystery and shame.

Shame?

Daniel never kept any of his flings or one night stands with glamorous socialites quiet. So why me? He'd said it was because I was his apprentice, but... was he embarrassed of being seen with someone ordinary like me?

An empty, sickening ache rolled through my gut. Daniel was the one who had made me secretive. He was one who had put a wedge between me and Liv, then sat back and let me hammer it in.

I needed to tell Theo soon. I couldn't go on like this, even if we only had a matter of weeks left together. I didn't have the strength to jump out of my pit of secrets in one go, but I could dig myself out, one truth at a time.

"So, have you decided on whether or not you're rejoining the band?" Theo asked as we passed the entrance to the film site.

I hadn't thought about it since the night out at the Italian. "I'm not sure. I'd like to, but it's been so long since I played in front of anyone."

"Anything I can do to help?" His cheeky eyebrow wiggle made my foot stumble and my heart stop.

"Oh? What did you have in mind?"

We took the left onto the smaller lane through the woodland and, with an arm around my shoulder, he pulled me closer. "I have a few ideas, but..." His voice deepened. "You're not that kind of girl, remember."

I was starting to regret ever saying that.

His hand found the small of my back and guided me into the warmth of The Cwtch, then toward one of the small sofas near the fire. I felt at home surrounded by the crackle of burning logs, the subtle scent of wood smoke and the feel of Theo's arms around me.

Ioan took our orders and brought over our drinks. Theo thanked him in Welsh.

"You've been practising," I commended.

"I have a good teacher. Although there is one subject I'm struggling with." His string smile made an appearance.

"Which is?"

"Hmm." He brushed the stray hair from the back of my neck

and ran a finger down the top of my spine. "She said she would teach me how to behave. But whenever I'm around her, I seem to get worse."

"Maybe she likes the way you behave," I said, taking his hand. "No improvements necessary." Ou-er. This third-person flirting thing was fun.

I leaned closer, as if to kiss him, but pulled away at the last second to take a sip of wine.

He laughed gently, head tilted to the side. *My laugh.* "You certainly are trouble and fire, Miss Quinn."

♪♪

"Did you really tell your family about me?" I asked, finishing the last of my dinner. After not eating since breakfast, I could have eaten it all again.

Theo offered to get me another wine, but I refused; I needed a clear head. And to be able to drive home. Unless... *No.* For goodness sake, I was the one who needed help with behaving.

Theo grimaced. "Yes, I did. Too forward again?"

"I didn't expect you to but no. It's very sweet actually."

"Well, I took your advice, to be honest and patient. It helped. Though, I'm still working on the patient part." He sagged under the weight on his shoulders. "I thought things were getting better, but it's as though they expect me to disappear again at any second."

Reaching out for his shoulder, I moved closer as he took another strained breath.

"They don't trust me, not completely," he admitted. "I can't blame them. I know I made mistakes and wrong choices but that's not who I am now. It wasn't truly me all along. But how can I prove this is me when I'm famous for pretending to be other people?"

We had the same problem, only in reverse. His family worried about him going back to old ways, mine worried that I wouldn't.

I hugged his arm. "There's nothing more you can do. After all the things we say about change—change is good, people *can* change—that doesn't make it any easier to accept when it actually happens."

"I'll keep working on the patience then."

"You and me both."

Time ticked by and I still hadn't told him one truth about myself. I was failing. And falling. Falling further into my pit of secrets, which was quickly becoming a cavern. Panic knotted my throat, my hands shivered. I tucked them under my thighs.

"You can talk to me, you know," Theo said, putting down his glass to carefully recover one of my hands. "About whatever it is that's bothering you."

Be brave. One secret at a time. I wished I could be more like him, fearlessly able to open up instead of being a shaking mess. *Be honest.* "I argued with Daniel before he left. It was"—*nasty*—"Bad. Now Olivia's angry with me and she's upset because of him."

Theo kept his expression neutral, tipped his head, nudging me to keep going. Classic psychologist move.

I gripped his hand. "I told her some things from our past that I should have told her a long time ago."

Theo wrapped both his hands around mine, giving me time to put my thoughts into words.

I looked at the fire. "I worry that some people don't want to change. That they just get better at hiding who they are. I never thought Daniel would be stupid enough to try it on with my best friend, though." I sighed. "I dunno. Maybe I shouldn't have said anything at all."

"No," Theo said finally. "I believe you did the right thing."

"You think so?"

He smiled. "If you hadn't, it could have been worse. Though, I am surprised."

I squinted, confused.

He chewed his bottom lip ever so slightly. "Correct me if I'm wrong, I'm filling in the blanks here, but I didn't think Olivia was the one he was after."

My head fell forward. Theo really did notice everything. He had a natural ability to see past words and understand behaviour. I envied him.

"Were you..." He shuffled in his seat, voice quiet, squeezing my hand tighter. "Were you and Daniel together in London? Is he the reason you left?"

This was my chance; another truth.

Daniel would probably have described our past as hooking up. Friends with benefits. *Ugh*. That wasn't how I felt. I always hoped it would become something more. I thought it *was* something more.

"When I met him," I said, "I'd never been away from home, then all of a sudden I was alone in London and he... Well, he's Daniel. If there's anyone here like the charming Mr Wickham, it's him. When things got tough, he moved on to the next person. I felt like I'd been cheated on. Not that we were ever properly together. It was always a secret. I didn't even tell Liv, which is why she's angry. And I deserve it."

The more I thought about it, the more I saw how much I'd been used. I'd watched Daniel cheat on other women after all, but stupidly thought he would change for me. *Such a fool.* A young, naive fool. Daniel had convinced me that keeping us a secret was to protect me; The only person he'd really been protecting was himself. My not telling Olivia had nothing to do with work, it was because I was ashamed.

I rubbed my tired eyes. "Whatever it was, it's over. Long over."

Theo's jaw and back relaxed. Only then did I realise how tense he'd been. With one finger, I drew around the outline of his hand on mine.

"That's good to know." His smile returned but quickly dissolved. "Not about the way he treated you, or what happened, but I mean, it's good to know that you— That he? That you're?" he stuttered. "Jeez, I'm not explaining myself very well, am I?"

Tapping the floor with one foot, he stared at the table, pulling a hand free to palm the back of his neck. I'd never seen him look so awkward before. If I hadn't been so worried about what he was thinking, I would have said it was extremely cute.

"It's okay, Theo. Just say it."

He stayed silent. If he lived by a motto, I think it would have been: If you can't say anything nice, don't say anything at all.

I inched closer and whispered his name. I'm positive it made him blush, so I said it again. He closed his eyes, swallowed, clenched his jaw, hummed out a growl.

When his eyes opened, they had turned into the eyes of an animal. Wild and hungry.

A few deep breaths later, he was human again.

"It's not my place to say anything," he said.

I sat up straight, pulling his hands onto my lap. "I'm asking you, so yes it is. You understand people." I rolled my eyes. "I don't."

"Yes, you do." He chuckled. "You understand me."

"Because you tell me things and I trust you. I can't read between the lines like you do."

The way he looked at me was like the way I looked at a blueprint. With wonder and awe and excitement of the things to come. "You see things differently, Lara, that's all. You see details. You describe things as cornflower instead of plain blue. You can also pull your emotions out of situations to see the bigger picture. That's how you were able to tell Olivia the truth, even when you knew it could hurt your relationship."

It didn't surprise me that he noticed those things. It did surprise me how he thought of them as positive things.

I shook my head. "What good is knowing details, like being able to tell you how a building was built, if I can't tell when people are about to stab me in the back?" My spine flinched at the accuracy of the expression. I shut my eyes to a wave of nausea. "And bigger pictures are useless when you can't see what's right in front of you. It's like me buying wallpaper before any bricks to build the actual walls." Theo was smiling at me. "Sorry, I know, I sound stupid."

"I like it when you talk construction. And you never sound stupid. Never."

"I do. You're just too nice to say it, Theo."

One of his hands wandered onto my thigh. "My name and 'nice' are not usually two things I hear in one sentence."

"Then I'm not the only one who can't see what's right in front of them, because you are nice."

"How nice?" he purred, lips brushing my neck.

I swivelled to face him, daring to cuddle up to his side. "*Too* nice."

"I can be even nicer if you want me to be." His chuckle disappeared into my hair.

Butterflies violently pummelled the inside of my chest, my stomach and... further down.

"Stop changing the subject," I said as firmly as I could through a giggle. "I want to know what you think. Seriously. You're the expert on people."

"Hmm." He sat back and thought about it. "The way Daniel acted. The way he spoke about you. It was... possessive, almost. As if you belong to him. That you're already his. In his mind, it's not a case of *if* but *when*."

I knew Daniel could be a control freak, sometimes to the point of being a bully, but possessive? Of me? There had been a few slip-ups, moments of weakness, but had I given him the impression we were still a... thing? I thought back to all the times I'd told Daniel how grateful I was, and how much I owed him for everything.

No. Theo had it wrong this time. It wasn't his fault. He didn't understand or know Daniel the way I did. Daniel wouldn't use our connection from Day Zero to manipulate me. *He wouldn't.*

Tension tightened Theo's face as he watched the cogs turning in my head. I remembered his questions after meeting Daniel about the colour of my room and him staying over. The look on Theo's face when he saw Daniel's arm around me. The reactions to Daniel's innuendos. *Jealousy?* A little. More like insecurity. Probably because of what Yasmin did to him.

Theo tipped his glass to his lips even though it was empty. "I shouldn't have said that. It's not any of my business."

Seeing Theo this way—anxious, self-conscious, unsure of himself—made my heart melt for him.

I took his hands back. "I am not Daniel's. I was young, and believe it or not, I wasn't always this shy. Then everything changed. I've changed." Theo met my eyes again, relaxed his face. "I knew he would say something to you. He's such a, such a—? Ugh, I can't even think of the word!"

Theo smirked. "I could provide a few."

I laughed, relieved to see his sense of humour returning. He wrapped an arm around me, flicking off any of his doubts and worries like dust from his shoulder.

"Don't worry about Liv," he said. "She's hurt, yes. Perhaps embarrassed. But give her time, she will understand once her anger dies down." His face snuggled into my neck. "After all, '*what are men to rocks and mountains*' and friends?"

"Was that *Pride and Prejudice* again?"

"Dammit. I'm going to have to find a book you haven't read."

I slid my arms around his waist and felt his chin rest on the top of my head. A happy warmth filled my body. I'd told him the truth. Some of it at least.

"Theo?"

"Hmm?"

"I don't mind being your business. If you know what I mean."

His lips found my ear. "I would like nothing more than for you to be my business."

Day 356
Monday Evening

I listened to Theo repeat his lines for the next day. I wanted to stay in this spot for the rest of time. A few minutes went by before I realised he'd stopped talking. Then I worked out why; I was unconsciously winding his hair around my fingers.

Dropping my hand, I mumbled, "Sorry."

"Don't be."

His eyes pierced through my skin. The word 'brown' did not do them justice. Brown was the colour of work boots and envelopes that contained bills. His brown was a whole forest of colour. Black earth, auburn bark, amber and rust of autumn leaves dancing in the air.

I had to remind myself again: *I'm here for a reason.* The truth.

The door of the pub opened. I was surprised to see Theo's colleagues Mason and Becca walk in and sit at the bar.

Theo's muscles stiffened as he leaned away. "Hey, shall we walk? I know how much you love sunsets," he whispered.

I agreed and grabbed my coat.

Compared to the fireside, the air outside was crisp and chilly. Theo tucked me against the warmth of his side, his brow was creased, eyes distant, lost in his thoughts.

We wouldn't have been able to talk in company anyway, but something was up. *Don't get sidetracked.*

"Don't you like Becca?" I pinched my lips and pulled my collar over my mouth, but it was too late.

Theo sighed. "It's not that I don't like her. I don't entirely trust her. She's friends with Yasmin. The last thing I want is her reporting back on me and starting new rumours. Especially now they can affect more than just me."

He must have meant his family, right? Yasmin wouldn't be bothered about me.

We cut down a narrow pathway through the wooded area and came out onto the beach near the dunes. Reflections from streetlights of the town on the other side of the bay bobbed about like fireflies across the rolling surface of the sea.

"Theo, you didn't do anything *that* bad, though. Did you?" By the time I'd finished the question, I'd changed my mind about wanting to know the answer.

Glancing at me, he slowed his pace, thinking, deciding. "You honestly haven't read up on me, have you?"

No secrets in Hollywood it seemed. "You asked me not to, so, no."

He stopped walking to look me in the eye. I thought he was going to kiss me again. I wanted him to, I really wanted him to. But I was afraid that if he did, I'd completely forget my purpose in coming here—to tell the truth—so I dropped my head.

"Thank you," he said, brushing his hand along my jaw to lift my face.

"What for?"

"For trusting me. For giving me a chance." He drew me into his arms. "For just being you."

Hell, his smile should be illegal. And his eyes. Maybe his hands too.

Definitely his hands.

I pulled away with a grin and carried on walking, dragging him along with me.

We'd climbed up and over the dunes before he came back to my previous question. "It was only ever drinking, and girls, really. Everyone suddenly wanted to be my friend, the attention was overwhelming. After I met Yasmin, the girls stopped. I was a lot of things, but never a cheat."

He shot me a nervous look. "As her behaviour got wilder, so did her choice of friends. Her drinking got out of control and escalated to drugs. I got home from filming one night to find my house full of police. Some of the neighbours had called them." He stopped walking to rub a hand down his face. "The house was in my name so I was the one who got carted off to the station for a night. Some of her friends, it transpired, were underage. Some of them were wanted; dealers, assault, mostly drug-related. But, the week after, she did it all again. That was the night I left and well, you know the rest."

I started walking again, my heavy feet sinking in the sand. The shock must have shown on my face.

"I swear, Lara," he said, catching up with me. "I never got involved in anything like that. But she was, she still is terrified that I'll expose her because she could lose her modelling contracts and a lot, I mean *a lot* of money. So she started the rumours, made out I was the one pushing her into doing drugs. She also *'accidentally'"* —he air-quoted while barking a cold laugh—"leaked my prison trip to the press. She's clever. She always includes just enough truth to make everything believable."

I pushed the words 'modelling' and 'clever' out of my head. "Why haven't you said something? Defended yourself?"

"I tried at first. She denied everything, and I had no proof. I came off looking like a bitter ex-boyfriend. So I learned to ignore it all, or at least, pretend to ignore it." With a sigh, he came to another halt. "It was my own fault for being so blind. I have to handle the consequences. As you said, the people who matter know the truth." He reached for my hand. "That's why I wanted you to know."

I mattered to him. I couldn't get my head around that. Not all of the time.

We got to the stream that flowed from the woodland river out to sea. On our previous walks, the tide had been out so it had been easy to walk across. Not this time. I looked down at my pumps; I was going to have to take them off to wade through.

Wearing a dress had been a bad idea.

Theo rolled up his jeans and crouched in front of me. "Come on," he said, offering a piggyback.

I laughed. "You won't be able to carry me over there." I was no size 0 model.

He passed me his shoes to hold. "Ye of little faith. It's okay, I've got you." His lips curled into a grin. "Don't you trust me?"

I stepped forward to loop my arms around his neck. He lifted me up, hands gripping firmly under my thighs. My *bare* thighs.

Wearing a dress had been an amazing idea.

Halfway across—where the water came to Theo's shins—he stumbled. I slipped to the side, squealed from the shock and tightened my legs around his waist, at which he burst out laughing and bounced me back up straight. When I realised he'd pretended to fall, I threatened to drop his shoes in the water.

"Don't you dare!" He held my legs closer and started to run.

I threw my arms in the air as the wind blew the hair from my face and cold water splashed my skin.

Theo

I had never heard Lara laugh the way she did when I ran with her through the water, so I kept running until I couldn't breathe.

Eventually, I collapsed onto the cool sand, a hand pressed over my thumping, giddy heart.

She placed my shoes down carefully next to me, shifting her

weight from foot to foot, fighting with her nerves again. I wanted her to fall onto my lap so I could disappear underneath her.

She sat to enjoy the sunset. I propped myself up on my elbows to watch her face.

Beautiful. That was still the only word to describe her. With the amount of reading I did and all the lines I had learned, I should have been able to think of another word, something superior and unique. But every other word floated straight out of my head every time she smiled at me. Every other smile, every other laugh I had ever known was wrong. No one else did it properly.

Being able to talk to her was like finding a waterfall in a desert, and earning her trust in return was like cracking a safe. Each time she opened up, I heard another click of the dial, another barrier unlocking. It took time. *Patience.* I was willing to wait because the treasure inside was worth it.

I kept telling myself that her bad experience with Daniel must have been the cause of her insecurity and yet the words, 'London Stabber' refused to leave my mind.

A breeze picked up. She tucked that strand of hair behind her ear, the one which persistently refused to be tamed, and her fingers brushed that soft spot I still longed to kiss.

To hell with it.

I held back as much as possible, touching my mouth to her skin so lightly it felt like a dream. Her eyes closed as her head fell to the side, letting me in, allowing me to go further, and oh lord the sound she made—an almost inaudible sigh —filled me with a fiery need so strong it hurt.

My body ached for her. I wanted the pain. I wanted to burn in her fire until there was nothing left.

I am in so much trouble.

Lara

I knew as soon as I'd seen Theo—lying on his back, grinning in between gulps of air, his powerful legs stretched out, creating two little mounds of sand by his feet—that sitting next to him would put me in danger of getting side-tracked again. I sat there anyway and could feel him watching me. I could always feel him.

He moved closer to kiss my neck as his fingers teased the band out of my hair to let it fall. The gentler his touch, the more intense it became. Instantly, my body responded, goosebumps appeared over my arms as I sank into his embrace.

I couldn't help but think fleetingly of Daniel. He was my only real point of reference when it came to men, after all. To me, Daniel was like Chopin score or a gothic cathedral. As much as I could appreciate the complex beauty, I could never fully understand it. It wasn't... me.

But Theo spoke my language.

Theo didn't lose patience if I slowed him down. He didn't get annoyed when I laughed and flicked his wandering hands away from my thighs. He liked it when I took control. He especially liked it when I rolled him onto his back so I could slip my hands under his shirt and trail kisses down his neck.

The Start of Something Good – Daughtry

"Stay right there," Theo said, reaching into his back pocket to retrieve his phone.

I was in too much of a delirious daze to reply. He clicked open the camera and pointed it in my direction.

My hands sprang up over my face. "What are you doing?"

"Stop, wait." He pulled them back down. "Look at the sun again."

I frowned.

"Please?" He kissed my palm. "I want a picture of you."

With a shaky breath, I turned away. The phone moved up and down behind me. I tried to forget he was there. Impossible. He kissed the back of my neck again. I grinned and looked over my shoulder, right at the camera.

"Got you!" he said victoriously, sitting at my side, one of his knees supporting my back.

He handed me the phone and I swiped through the pictures. The backlight from the setting sun created a glow around my profile, bringing out golden highlights in my hair. I returned to the last picture again. He'd caught me just as I turned, hair flicked up in mid-air as if I was standing in front of a fan on a shampoo advert. And I was smiling. Really smiling.

No mask.

I stared at it for longer than I should have.

Since Day Zero, I hadn't kept any pictures of myself. All I saw in them was a ghost of the old me. A waxwork copy. Accurate but missing life.

"Beautiful," Theo whispered, as I blinked a warning sting from my eyes.

"It's not fair." I nudged him. "You're not in any of them."

His arms swallowed me up against his chest. "You have the whole internet full of pictures of me."

"Oh, so I have your permission to look now?"

"You don't need my permission to do anything," he said. I raised my eyebrows. "Okay, you can look. Actually. No." A chuckle shook his body. "Perhaps that's not a good idea."

"Something you don't want me to see?"

His eyes followed the movement of his finger as he touched it to the hem of my dress, painting circles of heat on my knee. "I am more than happy for you to see *every*thing, Lara. But I'm right here. You don't need the internet."

It was incredibly hard not to watch his lips as he spoke. Damn those lips. The camera snuck into my peripheral vision again. I turned to look, but as I did, he kissed me. All thoughts of anything else vanished.

He pulled me to my feet when it started to go dark. "Are you busy Wednesday?"

Wednesdays were DAYS meetings. Jenny was eager to set up our girls' night, as well as the open day/party event, so I couldn't miss it.

This was my chance. Another secret, another step. "I am. Sorry. I help out with a local charity and we're meeting to arrange our next fundraising event."

He looked impressed. *"I am all astonishment."*

Good grief, I wished he would stop quoting Austen. (No, I didn't.) It did, however, make it very hard to concentrate.

"You never cease to surprise me," he said, bending over in front of me to tie his laces. I tried not to stare at him like a brazen predator. "What's the charity?"

I gave myself a mental slap with a wet fish to calm down. "It's a support group called DAYS. Jenny—she's the founder—wants to be able to start up more groups around the country."

He straightened, holding a hand out for mine which I took without hesitation. His touch still made me a little nervous, but it was a fear that I longed for.

Lara Quinn: adrenaline junkie. Ha!

"That's fantastic." He grinned. Getting praise from Theo made me want to skip everywhere for the next thousand years. "So what kind of event is it?"

We started walking and I explained the overcoming everyday fears concept, and Stuart's driving lessons, along with some of the other members' activities.

Theo agreed it was a clever idea. "It's genuine, people will relate to those kinds of fears."

Back at my car, he lifted my hand, swinging me around like a ballroom dancer to face him again. "You still haven't told me what *you're* doing. What is your great fear, Miss Quinn 007?" The air between us buzzed with electricity.

"Oh." I squirmed. "It's sort of embarrassing."

"I won't tell a soul."

My fingers trembled again. After his reaction to finding out about Daniel, how would he feel about me going on dates? Even if they were fake.

"Okay. So. Umm. I sort of agreed to a *50 First Dates* kind of thing. Sponsored, and all just with, you know, friends. Four booked in so far. One of them is a girl's night out so that's not really a date. Not that any of them are real—"

"Lara, I get it. First dates are petrifying."

To him? As if! "You're just saying that."

"Hey, trust me, I'm not. I was in a right state before taking you to dinner."

I pulled a face which said, *'Yeah, whatever.'*

"Seriously!" He laughed. "I wanted to impress you. In case you haven't noticed, I have been trying to impress you ever since we met." He blinked and looked at the floor, hands finding his pockets. "I'm worried someone will say something, the way Phillip did, and you will try to run away again."

The glow of his confidence faltered, its power interrupted by another ripple of insecurity.

I held my palm to his cheek. "You don't have to *try* to impress me, Theo."

"I needn't worry about any of these dates whisking you away then?"

A dark sparkle returned to his eyes as they lifted and in the literal blink of an eye, he switched from adorably innocent to meltingly sexy. I grinned and brought his lips to mine.

I only had him for another eight weeks. I wouldn't risk it. *Make all the days count.*

My final secret could wait for another time.

Or never.

♪

I got home and found Olivia lying across the sofa, wrapped in one of our chunky knitted blankets. I made us both a hot chocolate and sat next to her, tucking my feet under the blanket.

"So how'd it go?" she asked hesitantly. "Did you tell him?"

I held my mug under my chin, letting the cocoa steam fill my nose and warm my face. "Not everything. I told him about Daniel, DAYS and the dates, but… I couldn't do it, not all at once." She sat up, I rested my head on her shoulder. "I'm so sorry, Liv. For keeping things from you, for being snappy and angry and distant and selfish, for not being the friend I used to be. For everything. I'm so sorry."

"That's enough, it's ok—"

"No, it's not. And you can't keep letting me off every time I screw up because of what happened. I know you do. You all do."

"Alright, yeah." She shrugged my head off her shoulder. "I was mad at you. I can't believe you never told me. I'm more mad with him though. He swore you were only ever friends, that you were just close because of, like, you know… Zero."

I took a deep breath and a sip of chocolate.

Olivia did the same. "You don't have to tell me everything, I get that. And I know you never lied, but for crying out loud." She put her mug down to wave her arms at me. "Sleeping with your boss for two years is not nothing!"

"It didn't mean anyth—"

"Listen to me," she interrupted with a pointed finger. "Yes, it did. Maybe not to him, but it did to you. I know you. I just—" She threw her hands up and slapped them down on her legs. "I can't— Argh men!"

We both took another sip of chocolate.

She blew out her cheeks. "I get why you warned me about him. Don't worry, it was only a few flirty texts. Until he left and ghosted me." She groaned and shuddered as if she'd seen something disgusting. "Now his behaviour makes sense. He was, like, all over you."

I pinched the bridge of my nose. "That's kind of what Theo said."

"He did? You know, I had a feeling he didn't like Daniel." She gave me a coy, sideways glance. "Hun, have you considered that Theo *really* likes you? Properly like-likes you, not just for fun?"

"I'm trying not to, he's not here for much longer so... there's no point getting carried away." No matter how much I wanted to imagine a future together. "Besides, Theo's life is so on show, and I can't even tell that reporter about me because I'm too scared of what people think. Daniel's right, I'm not strong enough."

Olivia's eyes widened into huge blue globes. "Rubbish! Telling a reporter your life story or not has nothing to do with you being strong."

With a tired smile, I nodded, wanting to believe her. We drank the rest of our chocolate and watched another episode of *Friends*.

A buzz in my pocket then made us both jump.

DANIEL: Quinn, good news, we got the new client. I'll pop down soon for us to go over the contracts and plans. Dd

Oh, yippee.

I showed Daniel's text to Olivia.

She punched one hand into her other palm. "Tell him to get lost."

"If only."

I didn't want to ruffle any more feathers before the partnership paperwork was finalised, so for now, I had no choice but to get on with him.

After that: freedom.

Lara's Journal
Day 212

Rhys, a guy that Olivia and Sarah had set me up with, was late for our third date. I bounced on my toes, scrunching the fabric inside my pockets into fists. A taxi pulled up outside the bar. I stopped bouncing. It wasn't him. The bouncing restarted as I checked my phone for the hundredth time that minute.

Nothing. I felt so angry about being stood up and blamed it on the way I'd jumped a mile when he'd tried to hold my hand the last time. I was mostly fine with friends and family, but being touched by strangers made my skin itch.

The man who'd gotten out of the taxi walked toward me at the bar entrance, stopping at the other side of the door to light a cigarette. The smoke strangled me, like a thousand snakes slithering over my body, tightening around my throat.

Someone touched my shoulder, I bit my lip to hold in a scream.

"What the?" Rhys stepped back, rubbing a hand over his velvety buzz cut.

I laughed off my fear and apologised for acting crazy.

Rhys squinted before placing a hand on my lower back and

leading me into the bar. I ducked away from his touch, the smell of smoke still fresh in my nose, and my memory.

"So, how's work?" he asked.

"Huh? Pardon?" I took off my coat and sat at the table opposite him.

He squinted at me again, brow wrinkled like the damp sand nearest the sea, pressed into the shapes of waves. "What's up with you? Have I said something?"

He ordered us wine. I felt like I'd already drunk a bottle.

"No, it's not you." I tried to fix my smile. "I'm fine. Just hungry! Let's get some food." I made a show of excitedly picking up my menu. Rhys nodded and followed suit.

I already knew what to order, but it gave me a moment to calm down.

Breathe, in one-two, out one-two. None of my calming techniques worked. With every breath, I felt more like I was going to be sick. The smoke had gone into my bloodstream. My hands shivered uncontrollably. I began mentally reciting the lyrics of a Taylor Swift song.

That didn't help either.

"Umm, Lara?"

I looked up, straight into Rhys' vivid green, and very freaked-out eyes.

"Err, you were singing? Out loud?" He glanced around to see if anyone else had heard. They had. Several people were staring my way. *Mortifying!* "You sure you're okay?"

I made an excuse about not feeling well and needing some air.

Without waiting for an answer, I charged for the doors. Big mistake. I stepped out into another cloud of fresh smoke. The cloud morphed into solid walls, boxing me in, tighter and tighter. Pain seared through the back of my head and down my spine as shivers became shudders. At some point, I must have started screaming. Somebody tried to help me, but I wasn't there; my mind was back in the mud of the building site, rough stone snagging my skin, warm blood soaking my clothes. *His* hands on my chest.

The last thing I remembered was the thud as I hit the pavement.

Everything went blank for a while after that.

Black. Grey. Voices. Spinning. Black.

Until a woman said, "So what's your relationship?"

"I told you, we met for dinner," Rhys replied. His bright red face came in and out of focus. Anger? Embarrassment? Probably both. "She said she wasn't feeling well. She went outside. When I heard shouting, I came to check on her and this is how I found her."

I was sitting on the floor, my back against the wall of the bar. Cold damp from the concrete seeped into my skin, numbing my bum and hands

The police officer carried on asking Rhys questions. It didn't sound as though she believed his story that a sober woman would face-plant the curb for no reason.

"Oi, Jones, she's waking up." A voice to my right made my heart lurch into my throat.

I looked up to find the olive, leathery face of a man dressed in green. Paramedics uniform.

He grinned, dimples forming in one cheek. "Alright, love, you'll be okay. "

The officer, Jones, came over to kneel at my other side, still eyeing up Rhys. I pushed myself forward.

"Take it easy." The paramedic put a hand on my shoulder to steady me. "It's Lara, isn't it?"

I nodded. *Ouch.*

"Can you tell us what happened? A witness said you screamed?"

I stole a glance toward Rhys; biting his nails, bright red, dazed. "I had a panic attack. I came outside to get air but I... I think I fainted."

Jones jutted her chin toward Rhys. "And you know this man?"

"Yes, we'd just met up." I caught Rhys' eye and whispered an apology. He carried on biting his nails. I quickly explained the attack had happened because of a previous experience and told them to check my medical records if they didn't believe me.

I'm not sure if they did check, but after confirming I didn't have a concussion, Jones finally dropped her suspicion of Rhys and let us go.

"I'm so sorry," I told him.

Rhys started walking me toward the main road. "What happened? One minute you're singing, the next you've disappeared." His face was red again. Definitely anger and embarrassment—anger that I'd embarrassed him.

"I'm sorry. The smoke reminded me of something." I stopped and gave him the short, clinical version of Day Zero. As I did, his arms crossed tighter over his chest. Face turned away.

He shifted his weight uncomfortably. "So. You? Did he..." He couldn't look at me. "I mean were you—How do you...? Holy—"

"Yeah, I know. It's a lot. But I'm fine now. Well, apart from the occasional fainting spell." I laughed, high and humourless, trying to make light of everything and excuse my behaviour. Pushing against all my fears, I reached out to touch his arm. "Let's go for a drink?"

He pulled away. A shadow spread over his expression, draining his skin of colour, sapping any kind of interest he might have had in me.

I had my answer.

I shrugged, put my smile back on and let him go. "Although, I should probably go home." (Watching people squirm isn't fun, so I'm used to giving them excuses.)

When I asked about seeing him again, he gave me *that* look. The one where I'm a wounded animal, mangey and covered in fleas; he felt sorry for me, but at the same time, he didn't want to get too close.

"It's not you but, Lara, I don't think I can deal with all of this."

Has a sentence starting with, 'it's not you, but' ever ended well?

What I wanted to say was: *'Ha! Who can?'* Instead, I clenched my fists. "Okay. I'll see you around then. Take care, Rhys."

I turned and walked, not knowing where to. Olivia was staying with her mum for the weekend. I didn't fancy going home to an empty house, so I wound up outside a tiny bar called 'Jazz' which, surprise surprise, played jazz music. The deep notes of a saxophone, along with the smell of bittersweet coffee, whiskey and leather drifted through the doorway.

Be brave, I told myself.

I stepped in and absorbed the dimly lit atmosphere. Industrial style bulbs hung randomly from what looked like scavenged driftwood. The sax player stood in the far corner, swaying from side to side, eyes closed, lost in the music. A woman wearing a spotty '50s tea dress took my order as I hauled myself onto a bar stool. She hummed along to the song while mixing my Dark and Stormy cocktail.

Delicate swirls of pink roses climbed up her neck and draped down her arms; some of the most amazing tattoos I'd ever seen. They were so realistic, I would have believed her if she said she'd sat in a garden for a decade and let the plants grow all over her.

"Here you go, chick." Her sparkly brown eyes hovered over my face. "I know you, don't I?"

I dipped my head and took a sip. Our town newspaper had recently covered my story with a picture of me leaving the London courthouse on the front cover. 'London Stabber Convicted After Citywide Manhunt' read the headline. The article went on to explain how a local-born businesswoman (me) had survived his final attack.

"I work around the corner, maybe we've passed each other," I said, pointing at her arms to change the subject. "They're beautiful."

"Aww, thanks!" Twisting her wrists, she proudly showed off her personal artwork before being summoned to the other end of the bar.

I called Greg and told him what happened. He immediately offered to pick me up on the way home from work. It meant I'd have to hang around for a while, but I didn't mind. I idly browsed Instagram, scrolling back through people's lives and all the things I'd missed. What struck me was how normal everything was. While my life fell apart, the rest of the world carried on.

My next drink was a straight up-whiskey.

"Rough day, chick?" The rose lady asked, sliding a glass of amber liquid toward me.

"I got dumped."

"Been there, done that, got several t-shirts." She topped up my glass to a triple shot.

By the time Greg arrived, I felt pleasantly light and floaty. He pulled out the stool next to me with a *chin-up* kind of smile. My head slumped onto his shoulder while we listened to the music.

The saxophonist was joined by a bassist and singer. Their soft notes lulled me into a daydream. I was in a boat, drifting down a bubbling river, dappled sunlight warming my face, cool water gently lapping around my hands and toes. The magic of music. And yes, quite a large quantity of alcohol.

Greg twitched his shoulder. "Let's get you home before you fall asleep on me, yeah?"

On the way to his car, I kept insisting that I wasn't drunk. I wasn't! Just tipsy. He didn't argue, not even when he had to help me find the door handle.

"What's wrong with me?" I babbled as he got into the driver's seat.

Okay, so maybe I was a *little* drunk.

He plugged in my seatbelt. "Nothing. There's absolutely nothing wrong with you."

The car chugged into motion. I hugged my arms around my chest and pressed my face to the cold window glass.

When we got home, Gregg walked me to the door. "Straight to bed, yeah? And don't ever let anyone make you feel there's something wrong with you. Okay?"

I angrily kicked off my shoes, almost falling over in the process.

"Lara? Promise me."

"Fine!" I shouted, hands shaking again. "Then stop treating me like I'm sick! I know you're trying to help and, and..." *What was I saying?* "You don't even joke anymore. You used to make fun of me all the time and yeah, I know it's stupid but I miss it. I just? I miss... I miss everything."

He pulled me into a hug. I wanted to scream at anything or anyone. Poor Greg got the brunt of it. The more I struggled and cried, the tighter he held me, swaddling me like a baby until I eventually gave up and calmed down. We just sat there, squashed onto the bottom step in my tiny hallway.

"I'm sorry." I sniffed. He loosened his grip when I looked up and smiled. "I love you."

"I know," he replied in true Han Solo style. He pointed to the makeup smeared on his shirt and made a joke about me being a messy crier. He was trying.

I nudged his ribs. "You have a real way with words to cheer people up."

"Sure do. Did you know I'm writing a book?"

I leaned back to see his face. He looked deadly serious. Swaying around (that was probably me) but serious. "Since when do you write?"

"Ah, it's an idea I've had for a while now. It's about reverse psychology. Yeah, you really *don't* wanna read it." He pumped his eyebrows.

"Oh, come on," I snorted. "That's terrible."

"You said you missed my legendary humour, so... I did learn one thing though."

I was almost too afraid to ask: "What?"

"That there's no point if you're writing with a broken pencil."

"Ha! Okay, I take it back. I do not miss your jokes."

I waved him off, then slowly and clumsily made my way to bed, a smile still on my face. *I will be me again.* Someday. I just needed a plan.

♫

A small earthquake hit my house. It turned out to just be my phone, buzzing itself around in circles on my side table, hitting the base of the glass lamp. I rubbed my face. 1:12 a.m.—people didn't call that late unless there was an emergency. Or someone had died.

"Daniel?" I croaked. "What's wrong?"

"I got your message."

"Message?" *Oh, hell. What message?*

He laughed a deep humming sound, reminding me of the saxophone from Jazz. "Have you been drinking, Quinn?"

I must have rung him before Greg arrived, or before I fell asleep, I couldn't remember. I remembered feeling angry though. Anger was good. Much better than the all-consuming, hollow, twisting pain that was there before.

I pressed a hand to my pounding head. "Whatever I said, ignore it."

"You said something about whiskey? And you want me to come over and distract you..."

It all came flooding back; I'd rung him from the bar. It was the damned whiskey's fault; it tasted like him. Sweet. Hot.

He huffed another saxophone laugh. "Tell me something. You still sleep in that old Pink Floyd tee?"

It wasn't *old*, it was vintage and had belonged to my dad from his bygone rocker days. I smoothed a hand over the soft cotton and made a mental note to buy proper pyjamas.

Daniel started laughing again. My silence was a big fat admission of guilt. "I like that shirt. Especially the way it rides up yo—"

"This is not work-related." My body heat and temper were rising. I wanted to rip the T-shirt off. But then I'd be talking to him naked, and that would be worse. Much worse.

"Aye, don't be like that." He sighed. "I wish you weren't four hours away."

If I was in London, he wouldn't have called; he would have turned up on my doorstep.

If I was in London, I would have let him in. Poured us wine. Loosened his tie...

"Why?" I breathed, caving into his deep, whispering charm. "What would you do?"

"I think you know that one, Quinn..."

A tear sank into my pillow. I missed him.

I hated it.

Moral of the Story – Ashe

Day 358
Wednesday

I spent the morning visiting two of our local projects and even managed to do some painting. It put me on such a high that not even a text from Daniel confirming his visit for Friday got me down.

Theo rang at lunchtime while I sat in the cafe opposite the office. He soon had me in stitches. He'd accidentally fallen into the sea while filming. It must have been freezing. He also sent me the photos from the beach. First, the one of me looking away, then the one of me smiling into the lens. I stared at it again. Maybe it was knowing who was behind the camera that made me love it so much.

Next came a few pictures I didn't know he'd taken. My heart bounced around my ribs as I went through them. One was of us looking at each other. Another was of me laughing when he kissed my neck. I touched a finger on the screen. I could feel the pressure, the warmth, the tickle of his hair on my skin.

Now I knew what he felt like, I would never stop wanting to touch him.

A text popped up:

THEO: Last but not least. My favourite 😊 T xxx

And there it was, on my screen.

Me.

Kissing Theo.

Not a full-on wahey, kinky picture. It was sweet, intimate, that first second when our lips touched, his hand around the side of my face. He looked so happy.

The internet could keep all its photos. Yes, even the shirtless ones. This was my Theo. Not the aloof, acting, pretending Theo; the Theo who was kind and gentle, warm and smiley, who hid his hands inside his pockets when he was shy.

After a minute of me not replying—I couldn't stop looking at the picture—he texted again:

THEO: In case I haven't made it clear enough—I like you,
Lara. Really. A lot. T xxx

Then again:

THEO: I mean A LOT. In fact, a ridiculous amount. T xxx

And again:

THEO: Immensely. Exceedingly. Tremendously. *T* xxx

I cracked up like a madwoman. Eventually, I managed to squeeze in my reply, inspired by one of Mr Darcy's famous lines:

LARA: Mr Jackson, *in vain, I have struggled. It will not do.
My feelings will not be repressed.* You must stop texting me
so quickly (!!!) and allow me to tell you… I like you, too. A
LOT. xxx

THEO: Babe, you're killing me! Why am I only now finding out about your ability to quote Austen off the cuff? You have no idea how much more I like you now. T xxx

LARA: Surprise! I quote Austen, Friends, T.Swift, Tom Jones —you know, all the classics. I was just imagining you in costume and it reminded me. xxx

THEO: Were you now??? You cannot be this perfect, there has to be a catch. Do you snore? Are you secretly a werewolf? No, wait, that would be hot. The werewolf thing, not the snoring. Not that I mind if you snore, anyway… If I steal the Darcy suit for our next date, will you talk more Austen to me? 😊 T xxx

If I laughed any louder I'd get thrown out of the cafe.

Unfortunately, though, there was a catch. He just didn't know about it yet.

♫

Andrew had started his routine of going around the circle of members, asking each one about their week, when I rushed in. More than a few grins came my way as I attempted to tiptoe to a seat across the squeaky wood floor while wearing clumpy, steel-toed boots and a high vis jacket that rustled like a crisp packet. I may as well have announced my late arrival on a loudspeaker with a trumpet fanfare, accompanied by a marching band.

Andrew tried his best not to laugh. "Lara, good to see you. How's your week been?"

Still shaking plaster dust out of my hair, I smiled back. "Good, thanks!"

Expecting that to be it, he turned to the next person.

I surprised him by carrying on. "Very good, actually. My dates are going well. Your brother is so sweet, by the way. Oh, and I'm singing on Saturday with my friends in my old band. I'm super nervous, but I'm looking forward to it."

Someone went berserk with the remote that controlled Andrew's expression, flicking it back and forth between pride, happiness and shock.

Finally, he settled on happiness. "Wonderful, I'm so pleased. Jason said it was lovely to meet you. You're doing a fantastic job, as is everyone with their sponsored events!"

He continued giving an update on the fundraising progress, then the room erupted into a discussion of ideas for the celebration. Afterwards, I headed straight for Jenny. The warm smell of baking surrounded me as I held her in a hug.

"Hello, my love!" She beamed. "Look at that face, someone's had a good day."

I grinned, shrugged a nonchalant shoulder, and poured us both tea.

"Fantastic to hear you're getting back with your band," she said. "Here's an idea: Why don't we combine the girls' night out with your concert? I'd love to hear you play."

A flutter swept up through my stomach. I leaned my weight back onto the table. Theo would be there. And my friends. The line between keeping DAYS and this side of my life separate was becoming even more blurred.

"Umm." I stumbled. "Theo's coming and well... he doesn't know everything yet."

"Don't worry, sweetheart, we can leave it for another time."

"Oh, what the hell!" I said, riding my wave of excitement. "Let's do it." Theo's texts and those pictures had more of a reckless high effect on me than whiskey did.

I couldn't imagine Jenny in the crowd at the pub, though. Merely the way she called it a 'concert' made me worry whether she knew what she was letting herself in for.

With a gentle arm around me, she squeezed my ribs. "I can't wait to meet this man of yours."

I laughed. Was Theo *my* man? *Not for much longer.*

Jenny winked. "Speaking of men, I spoke to the caretaker and booked this hall for our get-together."

I made a note of the date as we said goodnight and went to see how Stuart and his driving lessons were going.

Theo

Olivia opened the door of their house looking shocked but pleased.

"Hey," I said awkwardly, "I know you're not expecting me, I tried calling Lara. Is she home yet?"

"Not yet. She's probably driving." Olivia checked her watch. "She won't be long, though. Come in, you wanna drink?"

I followed her in, scanning the pictures of Lara with her friends and family on the wall as I passed, thinking it strange how there were no recent pictures. My attention was caught by one of her, Olivia and Greg all dressed as Star Wars characters at a party, dated five years ago. Her joyous smile back then was the same as the one in the pictures I'd taken at the beach.

It was unfathomable how seeing her, even in a photo, could make me feel like there was a river of fire flowing through my hands, a bolt of lightning in my stomach and a cymbal clashing in my heart—burning, thundering, vibrating—but it did.

I took a seat at the kitchen counter. Olivia filled the kettle and chatted away about her day. She reminded me of Chloe. Full of energy, with a voice that sounded like laughter. A flush of heat swept across my palms. If any guy ever tried to mess with my sister...

"I'm sorry about what happened with Daniel," I said, then paused. She might have been annoyed with Lara for telling me. "None of it was your fault," I added. The more I learned about

Daniel, the less I liked him. "Believe me, I know. I used to *be* a Daniel." And that was why I didn't trust him.

Fortunately, Olivia didn't seem bothered by my knowledge.

She smirked and handed me a coffee. "Thanks, hun. He's a real jerk. It's gonna be so weird when he comes back Friday."

"He's back so soon?"

Her lips pinched together. "Only a flying visit, just to drop off some contracts or something." She sat opposite and quickly shrugged it off. "As Lara's best friend, I have to ask. You're like, genuinely not that kind of guy anymore, are you?"

I looked up from my cup, catching the tail end of Olivia's apprehensive expression.

"No," I replied honestly. "At least, I spend every day trying not to be."

She nodded. "Good. Because if you hurt her, I'll go totally Liam Neeson on you and hunt you down.'"

"I don't doubt that for a second," I confirmed with a quick grin, pressing my hands onto the cool stone of the countertop. "The last thing I want to do is hurt Lara." I hoped Olivia could see how much I meant it. "She has been through enough already."

I was purely referring to how I met Lara, her wrist injury and then what happened with Phillip, but the reaction from Olivia— an unconscious flinch of her back, flash of fear behind her dilating eyes, intake of breath—made me think of something else: the *other* Lara Quinn from the news.

Another piece of Lara's puzzle slotted painfully into place.

Lara

My heart bolted out of my throat like a pinball flung from its machine when I saw the Mustang on my drive. What on earth was Theo doing at my house? *He's here to end it.* I rummaged through my bags for any makeup. All I found was an ancient sticky lip gloss. I put some on anyway and scraped my hair up. There was no way I could sneak in and change without them hearing me. I was just going to have to walk in wearing my work clothes. Mud, plaster, paint and all.

I huffed.

This was me, and this was how I looked most of the time. If Theo didn't like it? Tough.

His voice floated toward me as I stepped in. I opened the living room door and my legs went heavy. Would I ever get over the surge of excitement and pure energy every time I saw him? I hoped not. If anything, he got better looking.

Long strides brought him to my side. "Hey, I thought I would surprise you for a change."

Slipping off my coat, I put down my hard hat and bag of paintbrushes. "This is definitely a surprise." I nervously smoothed a hand over my straw-like hair.

Theo kissed my cheek with a grin, a grin that soon spread onto my own face as I relaxed. Olivia boiled the kettle, then suspiciously had to answer a phone call so headed upstairs. (I hadn't heard a phone ring.) I carried on where she left off and made tea, watching Theo as he leaned back to rest on the counter, eyes down, thumbs tucked in his pockets. My cup slipped in my clammy hands. He was here to end it after all.

"Everything okay?" Forcing the words out was like pushing a boulder uphill.

"Perfect," he replied. An easy smile made its way back to his face. "I wanted to ask you something and found myself driving here."

"Oh!" I breathed a sigh of relief, bit back my grin and sat on one of the bar stools, gripping the cool metal legs.

Standing so close in front of me that my knees were pressed against his waist, he picked up my paint-splattered hands. "Why? What did you think I was here for?"

The inch between us felt like lightyears. I resisted the desire to wrap my legs around him and grab his arms. Arms that could hold me carefully and pick me up easily, arms that could be strong, maybe even carry me upstairs...

If only I could make his black T-shirt evaporate. *Calm it down!*

"I'm not sure," I said.

He laughed—an exhale, chuckle, smile, head tilt—*my laugh*. "Hmm, I wanted to ask what you were doing next weekend? It's my parents' anniversary. Chloe has organised a bit of a party and..." Turning to look out the window, he hesitated and swallowed hard. His Adam's apple bobbed up and down. I could almost hear him telling himself to *'be brave.'*

I'd always viewed Theo as a beam of unstoppable, confident white light. For a split second, though, a glass prism dropped into that light and I saw him in a whole new way. The light divided into a hundred rainbow shards—insecurity, love, kindness, passion, strength—each one a facet of his personality. The open honesty he showed didn't come from being fearless, it came from courage. The courage and determination to redeem himself and show the world, *to show me,* who he really was.

There were so many things I didn't know—favourite colour? Was he a clean freak? Did he like *Friends*?—but they didn't matter; they were details, the accessories that got added to a house over time. In that second, I saw *him*. Plans, foundations, framework; his heart, motives, truth.

He turned back to me and the prism disappeared, all the colours joining once again to form into his warm, constant glow.

"I was wondering if you would like to come?" he said. "With me. To stay. For the weekend. I can drive."

My lungs exploded as he kissed behind my ear. I think he had a thing for my ears, or more accurately, the part of my neck behind my ears. Not that I was complaining.

It wasn't until after I'd said yes that the panic set in.

He wanted me to meet his family.

Then there was the whole, you know, staying overnight.

Breathe. My plan to keep my distance had well and truly gone out of the window in a ball of fire.

Since opening up on Monday, something between us had shifted. I could feel Theo struggling to maintain control whenever he touched me. A part of me now wanted him to let go.

"But, Theo, will your parents mind? I mean, they don't know me, and umm... what do they think I am?" *What do they think I am?* Flip, my brain had turned to mush.

Theo's soft chuckling breaths warmed my skin. A low, delicious sound that made me think of hot chocolate and a lion purring. I'd never heard a lion purr. But I would bet it sounded just like that.

"Miss Quinn, is that your way of asking me where this is going?"

I remembered asking Daniel something similar. He couldn't answer me. Could Theo?

"I think so," I said, looking directly at him, his nose resting on mine. "Yes. It is."

"Well, my sister's dying to meet you. They all are. And I..." Theo searched my face. "I would like to introduce you as my girlfriend. But if it's too soon?"

Girlfriend! Okay, so Olivia was right again. This was more than a fling. Way more than Theo just being kind. He did like me. *Like* like me. For reals.

Oh my word, I'd reverted into a teenager on prom night.

Seriously though, was I ready for this step? Not sure.

Was I ready for this step with Theo? I wanted to be.

But... '*You can't keep it hidden forever.*' Daniel's voice echoed around my head. '*Mr Flashy Hollywood.*' People with cameras followed Theo around. '*He'll find out. One way or another, he's in for a nasty shock.*'

I rested one hand on Theo's shoulder, the other on his chest. "I just—How will we?" *Be brave. Be honest.* "There's something we need to talk about."

He held my face. "I know. And we will. I'll explain everything. But for now, please don't worry." He kissed me again, hands dropping to grip my hips. I lost all my willpower and restraint and hooked my legs around his waist.

"I've got you," he whispered. "Trust me."

I did.

I was the one with secrets.

At some point later, Theo pulled away, covered in the dust from my clothes.

"On a side note," he said, carefully flicking a spot of dried paint from my nose, "is it weird how I find you incredibly gorgeous when covered in dirt and paint?

"Yes!" I laughed, planting kisses all over his cheeks. "You're such a weirdo."

"I swear to steal the Darcy suit for our next date, *only* if you wear these overalls and talk Austen to me."

"I also have a tool belt."

"Damn, Lara..."

False God – Taylor Swift

Day 361
Saturday

Put people in front of me—and the thought of Theo watching—and it felt like I'd never seen a piano before, let alone played one.

With the band all squashed into my living room, we went through my song a third time. I missed a note on the second verse and slammed my hands on the keys. "I CAN'T do this!"

The room went deathly quiet. Caleb bit his nails. Alex flipped through a music book. Sarah, Greg and Olivia shot me furtive glances from the kitchen.

"I'm sorry," I mumbled, getting up for some water. I drank a glassful. Held my hands under the cold flow of the tap. Was tempted to stick my head under.

Greg came to my side. "Don't worry about tonight. If you don't feel like it, then we'll skip the solo. Stick to the backing, yeah?" One side of his face lifted into a teasing smile. "I hear Theo invited you to meet his family? That's pretty big."

"Shut up," I teased.

"You'll be fine. You've always been the tough one."

"Right."

"You have!" He laughed. "Remember when we were like,

eight, and you punched that boy in school 'cause he was bullying Liv?"

I dragged a hand down my face. "Thanks for reminding me." Maybe my temper wasn't such a new trait after all.

He rolled his eyes, just like Olivia. "You say you can't do stuff but when it comes to it, you don't back down. You can do this. Bee-tee-dubs, I'm not just talking about the band." He clicked his tongue and threw me a wink.

"Oh, thanks, Dr Love."

"Anytime my young Padawan. Promise me something though, yeah?"

"What?"

"That I get to watch when you tell your dad about your new boyfriend."

Oh, hell. My parents didn't know Theo existed. Dad was beyond over-protective, which made him intimidating. I was his only child. A daughter. A daughter who nearly died.

After Greg and Olivia's father left when they were young, Dad took them under his wing, loved them like his own. Even so, Greg was still scared of him. Especially because when we were sixteen, Dad got it into his head that Greg and I were secretly going out together. For months Dad would interrogate Greg whenever they met—where he was going, what he was up to—looking at him with an *'I-don't-trust-you'* and *'I'm-watching-you'* sort of face. Poor Greg, he had to put up with that right until he met Sarah.

I poured us both another drink. "I'm thinking I'll tell Mom, then let her handle it from there."

If I told Theo the truth tonight as planned, it might not get that far. *He won't stick around.*

A void opened behind my ribs.

♪

With each minute closer to the gig, the more my legs resembled bendy spaghetti. I tried to keep busy by focusing on rehearsals, tidying, and making gallons of coffee, but I kept finding myself standing in random places, not knowing how I got there, staring into a jumbled blur of space. I used to thrive off these nerves. Even look forward to them. *Mental.*

Tremors ran through my hands as we packed Caleb's van with the equipment. Shaky, sweaty, slippy fingers were never a good thing for a piano player.

When we pulled up outside The Cwtch, I saw Jenny and three of the girls from DAYS—Bethany, Emma and Ffion—going in through the gate to the courtyard. I swallowed the lump in my throat, gripped my leather jacket and forced on a smile.

"Laa-Laa?" Olivia stopped the engine to look at me, her wide eyes wrapped in shimmering silver ovals of eyeliner. "You sure you're okay? You like, haven't said a word all afternoon?"

"Yeah, of course. I'm fine."

She chewed the inside of her cheek. Thinking about my nerves made them worse so I hurried out to help unload the van. Alex passed me the two guitars, then followed with an amp. We ducked under the gated arch and stepped into the courtyard where rivers of fallen, sugary pink cherry blossoms swirled across the purple slate ground like a subtle impressionist painting. An occasional petal danced through the air, glittering in rays of golden evening light. Any other time, I would have paused to take a photo, but I was too afraid to stop moving. It put me at risk of being swallowed by fear.

I caught Jenny's attention and waved her and the girls over to the stage. While introducing them to the band, I saw Theo walk in. His cap was on, tilted low to cast a shadow over his face, along with his uniform of biker boots, black jeans ripped at the knees, and a long coat with an upturned collar.

He slipped through the growing crowd with all the stealthy poise of an undercover agent.

In a word: hot.

I imagined myself running to meet him, throwing my arms around his neck and kissing in front of the cheering crowd, the way couples did in the movies the moment they realised they were in love. *Whoa, hold on.* Love?

He jogged the final steps to enclose me in his arms, every inch of him smiling. "Hey, beautiful."

I swallowed the acid building in my throat. As Theo greeted the rest of the group, my weight sagged into the support of his arms. He could probably feel the sweat gathering on my back through my thin blouse.

Fifteen minutes until the band started.

I needed air. Mad considering we were already outdoors.

Not daring to look up, I mumbled the excuse of helping Greg and bolted for the gate.

Shadowy tentacles tightened around my body, blurring my eyes with dizzying speed, making me gag. I just about made it to the van as my panic attack took full hold. In a wave of nausea, I tumbled against the metal side. Alex jumped out looking startled, caught my arms, and gently lowered me to sit on the floor of the back section.

I gasped for breath. A bitter taste of salty tears filled my mouth.

Alex pulled my head onto his shoulder, gently rocking me from side to side. "Alright. Deep breath. You're alright."

In one-two. Out one-two.

Theo

I caught sight of Lara talking to a group of people near the stage. Heat climbed from my toes to my chest, filling me with a need to have her in my arms.

"Hey, beautiful," I said. It still wasn't a big or worthy enough word to describe her.

She was dressed all in black—heeled boots, slim jeans, a strappy top that floated like liquid over her fair, creamy skin—with her hair pulled up. Strands of broken-free curls teasingly caressed her neck.

Her replying smile was fleeting and small, distracted and nervous. I hoped it was because of the upcoming performance; not because of my decision to pop the 'girlfriend' and 'meet the family' questions all at once. *Idiot.* Being my girlfriend wasn't easy. A whole list of complications tagged along like an unwanted third wheel.

I hated having to talk about such serious things so soon but Lara deserved to know what she was getting into. Especially after the incident at The Mermaid.

With my place in L.A. sold, I now worked mainly in the UK, and I had assured her our lives could be kept private. Yet, by explaining as much as possible, I may have unwittingly overwhelmed her. I could feel her closing off. Putting up walls.

A shiver ran up my spine.

Did she care about me and trust me enough to take on the challenges?

I gripped her waist, afraid to let go. Trembling, she leaned heavily into my side, then unexpectedly excused herself to help Greg. I moved to follow but was stopped by an older woman who was dressed more for a night at the opera than for a local gig.

"Hello, I'm Jenny." She adjusted her floor-length camel coat and held out a hand. "You must be Theo."

"Pleasure to meet you, Jenny." I shook her hand and tried to push aside my worries. Lara probably wanted some space and a quiet moment to prepare.

Jenny hadn't let go of my hand. "Pleasure's all mine, love. Lara wasn't exaggerating about you, *very* handsome indeed!" Her energy sparked over her skin, lighting up her bright eyes.

"Hmm, she said that, did she?" I flashed a crooked smile, sending Jenny's cheeks the same colour as the blossoms covering the floor. "I've heard all about you, too. Lara tells me you're hoping to set up more locations for your meetings?"

Jenny's face set with determination. "Yes, exactly. I want to train more leaders and spread the groups across the country."

Olivia ushered our small gathering to an empty table tucked in at the side of the stage.

I pulled a chair out and offered it to Jenny. "Are the groups for a specific purpose?"

"They're mainly for victims and witnesses of violent crime. Although I would never turn anyone away." She carried on talking about how the group started, but her voice slipped into the distance.

Violent crime? Images of Lara screaming hurtled through my imagination. A million emotions poured down my throat, choking and dragging me underwater. Lara had been helping DAYS for the past year. It was a year since the *other* Lara Quinn had been attacked. My legs felt detached from my body. *Please, God, no.* Not my Lara.

The final piece of her puzzle had clicked into place, and as much as I tried to reject it, so much started to make sense.

I drowned.

The band was due to start. I scoured the crowd. Lara wasn't anywhere to be seen. Olivia had disappeared too.

Jenny was waiting with an expectant expression; she must have asked me something. "Sorry, Jenny, have you seen Lara?"

"I think she went that way."

By the time Jenny's hand pointed to the gate, I was already running. I ducked through and saw Olivia by the side of a small white van across the street.

"Liv!" I called, jogging over, straining to keep my voice steady. "Where's Lara?"

The street was quiet now that everyone was inside waiting for the music to start. Quiet enough for me to hear a soft cry and

Lara's muffled voice from inside the van: "Don't let him see me like this."

Lara

Theo stopped abruptly next to Olivia, I could see him through the gaps in the door hinges. His body became a motionless statue, except for his panting chest. He looked pale.

Olivia tried to stall him, badly, by telling him we had a problem with some equipment. No way he wouldn't see through her terrible acting. All I wanted to do was kiss him until he smiled, tell him this wasn't his fault.

I dried my cheeks, shook out my hands and checked my face in the reflection of my phone screen. Alex stayed by my side.

"It's okay, Liv," I said, sounding weaker than I would have liked.

Theo immediately came to the door. He swayed forward, wanting to step closer but not sure if he should. It scared me to see how much I could affect him. How I, for some inexplicable reason, had the power to crack his outer defences and interrupt the current of his confidence. Scared and bewildered.

"Sorry I disappeared," I muttered into the floor. "Alex, you better go and get ready." I turned to smile at him. "Tell Greg I'm sorry."

Alex stood, squeezed my shoulder, patted Theo's, and walked back across the street, taking Olivia with him.

"Hey," Theo whispered, carefully sitting next to me, hands outstretched as though ready to catch me.

He didn't bother to ask if I was okay; it was pretty obvious that I wasn't.

I couldn't look at him. If I did, he would see the mountain on my shoulders, the weight of my past and my secrets pushing me into the earth. He would see how the pain of losing him was already ripping me apart because I knew it would happen as soon as he found out the whole truth. It was as good as done.

I set my elbows on my knees, my face in my hands. "I panicked. I'll be alright." *But when?* "Sometimes, I have these meltdowns, and it's... it's exhausting."

"I didn't mean to put pressure on you, Lara." His voice was low, kind.

"You didn't. It's not your fault. I just can't do this. It's too much and it's been a long time."

He slowly dipped his chin. A thin streak of light cut through the shadows across his face, highlighting one feature at a time—stubbled chin, sharp cheekbone, a flash of golden caramel when it crossed his eye.

"I understand," he said. "My life is all over the place. It comes with baggage that I don't blame you for not wanting to deal with. I wish I could be some guy from town who bumped into you, who can take you out for a drink without wearing this ridiculous hat, who could ask you out and everything would be simple, but I'm not and I can't. Asking you to be my girlfriend and expecting you to accept everything that comes with it so soon was selfish of me. I know this isn't the kind of life you would ever choose to be involved with." All of that came out in one quick breath.

"Wait, what?" Did he think I was trying to break up with him? I sat up to look at him. "No, Theo, you've got it all wrong. I mean, yeah, it has been a long time since... never mind." I waved that dangerous thought away. "I was talking about being back with the band. About playing tonight."

While he silently processed that, his eyebrows raised, then frowned, mouth opened to speak, shut again until finally, a smile crept in. I'd never met anyone before who could show so many expressions in such a short space of time. I loved watching them.

"So," he wondered, taking my hand. "You *do* still want to go out with me?"

"Yes!" I started grinning. "Theo, right now, wanting you is the only thing I'm sure of." Even if it scared the hell out of me every time he tried to explain about schedules and press and agents.

I wound my fingers between his. "I am freaking out a bit though. Actually, I'm terrified." I exhaled and shook my head. He looked worried again. "But it's not because of you. It's everything else. Every day."

I expected him to give me some sort of *'what on earth are you on about'* look. He didn't. He nodded, listening, waiting for me to carry on. A surge of gratitude pushed up through my chest, lifting the weight on my shoulders. *I can do this.* I could tell him about me. Not because I had to. Because I wanted to.

I laughed at myself and the floodgates smashed open, allowing me to breathe and a year's worth of cooped up words to flow. "I'm tired of being so scared. I never used to be, you know. I would've been straight up on that stage, literally buzzing from the atmosphere. But I can't do it anymore. I've changed, and I don't know how to go back. It's like...? It's like I don't know how to be *me* anymore."

His eyes never left my face. They told me more than words could—he understood how it felt to be lost, to lose yourself.

I grasped both of his warm, rough, perfectly imperfect hands between mine. "Theo, I get what you're saying. Being your girlfriend comes with unusual complications. But, if it means I get to be with you, then I'm willing to carry a whole load of baggage because trust me, I already have a shipping container full, so what's a bit more?"

That gorgeous string smile of his appeared, dispersing any clouds and darkness from around us. Determined not to get distracted, I turned away as he leaned closer.

"There's something else," I said, "I should have told you sooner. I've tried. I've really tried, but I'm a coward and I don't want to lose you." *Not yet.*

"You are no coward," he argued, urgently lifting my chin and my eyes back to his. "And I'm not going anywhere. Please believe me."

I failed miserably to stop him when he leaned in again to kiss me—A delicate, tortuous whisper of a kiss.

Until my hands found the back of his neck.

In one swift move, he hoisted me up to straddle his lap, holding my body so not even a breath of air was left between us. It still wasn't close enough. I tightened my legs around his waist, rewarded with a moan from deep inside his chest. His hands explored my thighs, under my top, skimming up my back—he didn't flinch in disgust—as he kissed along my jaw, down my throat. When he reached my collar bone, my head fell back with a gasp, my heart beating like the wings of a hummingbird, so fast it became one continuous, indistinguishable haze of movement.

Music filled the air as the band started playing. My band. I was supposed to be supporting them, not making out in the van like a groupie. I was also supposed to have told Theo about Day Zero.

Again.

I pulled away, the taste of Theo's sun-kissed skin clinging to my lips. "I should go and join the guys. I did promise."

His fingertips drew circles on my shoulder blades. "You don't have to do it for me."

"I know. But I think I want to. That's the effect you have on me, Mr Jackson," I teased. "I feel like I could do anything right now."

"Anything, huh?" He laid back, slowly stretching his arms to clasp his hands behind his head, revealing a seductive slither of boxers and firm skin. I became highly aware of what was between my legs.

Oh. My. Life.

I stood and waved a pointed finger. "Lesson Number One in learning how to behave, Theo. Stay clear of dodgy vans."

"Hmm, noted. Then, let me give you Lesson Number One in

learning how *not* to behave." He tilted his head, beckoning me to come closer. "Get back in the damn van, Lara."

His growling voice reeled me in, and his body—all muscle and rollercoaster power lying in front of me—almost made me change my mind. I saw myself pulling off his shirt, smoothing my hands up his chest, down his abs...

The guys wouldn't miss me that much, would they?

Theo was watching me with a smile. He knew exactly what I was thinking; the heat in his eyes told me so.

I hooked my fingers through his belt and pulled him upright. "Come on, you," I said, leading him away with a deliberately bitten-back smirk.

We walked across the courtyard to join Olivia, Jenny and the DAYS girls. Greg waved, and I gave him a thumbs up. I pulled Theo's face to mine for one final kiss, which took him and my friends by surprise.

Sarah did her little *'you go girl'* jig as I joined her on stage and sat at the piano, ready for the next song. (Stevie Nicks. What a legend.) My heart pounded in my throat. My fingers turned icy. *Be brave.* I could do this. Just like old times. Alex and Caleb began the opening riffs, my foot tapped out the tempo. Knowing Theo was watching warmed my skin as if his arms were wrapped around me.

I started on cue. Hit every note. Found every chord. Loved every single second.

Edge of Seventeen – Stevie Nicks

Several times over the evening I saw Jenny and Theo talking. My cheeks flushed, guilt gnawing my insides. Once again I'd failed to tell him about the biggest part of my life. I *was* a coward, terrified of losing what I wanted:

The man I was falling in love with.

Day 365
Wednesday

"He hasn't even called me. How can he not call me?"

"He knows?" Olivia answered, glancing up while still managing to write an email.

"How could he forget?"

"I'm lost? So you, like, told him then?"

"Told him?"

She stopped typing and spun her chair to face me. "Yeah, told Theo. About Zero?"

My confusion passed over. "Oh, no. Not yet. I meant Daniel."

"Oh." She slumped. "Why do you care?"

I folded my arms. "I don't."

She went back to typing. I went back to my office.

Everything was fine until I went to write the date on an invoice. I got to the last letter of the month before the pen slipped, shaking itself free from my chilled, sweating hand. My parents had already called numerous times throughout the day. Mom tried to sound casual, always with some sort of excuse (she needed to borrow something, she couldn't get her computer to load a file) when the real reason was to check up on me.

A buzz. One New Message, this time from Caleb. They were

all concerned. They'd probably reminded each other of the day: 365.

One year.

I grabbed my phone from the desk and held a finger over the power button, my breath catching when I saw a message waiting from Theo. He didn't know; it wasn't his fault.

The only person who hadn't contacted me was Daniel.

Come on, what did you expect?

I threw my phone across my office.

Olivia burst in through the door looking fierce, ready to ambush whoever had broken in. Her scowl dropped when she saw it was just me. Then she clocked the phone on the floor, picked it up, and placed it gingerly on the desk. The screen had a new crack, but it was still working.

"I'm okay," I said, panting, forehead pressed to the desk.

"I've finished everything for today and we don't have any more calls scheduled," she said quietly, walking on eggshells. "Why don't we go grab a coffee before you go to DAYS?"

I closed my eyes, wanting to cry, scream, wrap my arms around her, swing her around, laugh and thank her all at once.

♪

I updated the DAYS group on how another one of my 'dates' had gone the previous night. So far, our fundraising was a success. Stuart's story had been published in the newspaper, sparking more interest from local news and TV. Several reporters were scheduled to come to what was now known as the 'End Of Campaign Celebration.'

Ffion cornered me at the end of the meeting, immediately asking about the gig, gushing about how much fun she had, and repeatedly asking if I was going to be at the celebration. Ever since Saturday, she'd been texting to see how I was and if I wanted to meet up for drinks.

Funny. She'd never bothered with me before. Something made me think her newfound friendliness wasn't all down to me.

What Ffion *really* wanted to know was if Theo would be there at the celebration with me. The question bobbed around in her mouth like a cuckoo waiting to burst from a clock. I clamped my jaw and chewed my lip. The thought raised my blood temperature to a steady simmer. It was a glimpse of how people's behaviour could change around Theo, I supposed.

I was starting to wonder if he was the one who needed to feel safe and protected, not me. I heaved a sigh of relief when Jenny came over and asked to speak to me.

Gentle porcelain hands with pink nails wrapped around my elbow and led me to the small kitchen area at the back of the hall, where I helped her make tea and cut up cakes. Chocolate cake, of course.

Before she could ask, I told her, "I'm fine." I laughed. "My beat-up phone wouldn't agree, but honestly, I'm... better."

"Good." She set the kettle down to hold my hands. "I'm so proud of you, sweetheart." I shook my head. "I mean it. You were fantastic on Saturday." She gripped my hands. "It was rather wild. I haven't had that much fun in ages." She went back to making tea, humming happily.

Jenny had every right to feel bitter after what happened to her. Instead, her kindness had grown beyond measure. The world needed more Jennys.

Although Theo and I spoke every day and had met for lunch yesterday, I admitted quietly to Jenny's back, "I still haven't told him."

She knew who and what I was talking about. "You will. The time will come and you'll be fine. You're stronger than you know, Lara. I see it, and that man of yours sees it."

♪

That night I went to bed but didn't sleep. I looked at the photos from the beach, imagining Theo's arms around me, hearing his voice tell me, *'It's okay, I've got you, go to sleep.'* Then my mind would drift back to Daniel—Jeff—Daniel again.

One whole year and not so much as a call to say hi.

Not even a text.

If I could fight a knife-wielding killer, why couldn't I get past my anger toward Daniel?

He didn't love me. He never had. I could see that now. And even though I no longer wanted it to be true, it still hurt. All that we'd shared before, on, and after Day Zero had been easily forgotten like it meant nothing to him, and that made me feel... worth nothing.

Over the last year, I'd blamed all of my insecurity and fears on what Jeff did to me. What if the seeds were already there and Day Zero had only made them grow?

What if they had been planted by Daniel?

Not long now, I told myself, *not long, and I'll be free of him.*

Dancing With Our Hands Tied – Taylor Swift

Day 367
Friday

The reflection of my weekend suitcase in the rearview mirror taunted me.

I'd crammed so much in that it looked ready to burst. Smart jeans, heels, blouse, jacket and cocktail dress for the party—I didn't know how formal it was going to be—along with casual day clothes. Plus practically every bit of makeup I owned because, you know, just in case. Toiletries, hair straighteners, phone charger. The list was endless. Then came the different types of underwear Olivia had insisted I take. *Flippin' heck.*

I wasn't sure what worried me the most, facing Daniel today, meeting Theo's family tonight, or spending the weekend with him. The combination of all three was an anxiety cocktail. Stress crushed my sides like rubbish in a compactor, squishing me into an inanimate and numb brick.

Daniel called just after 1 p.m, by which point I felt nauseous.

He greeted me in his usual way. "Quinn. I'm nearly there. You both in the office?" I answered yes, even though Fridays were *supposed* to be my day off. (Which he knew.) "Grand. Look, Lara." Uh oh, he called me Lara, not a good sign. "I feel bad about our, ah, misunderstanding. Let me make it up to you. How much have you raised on your dates?"

Misunderstanding? Was that what we were calling it?

"Six hundred and fifty so far," I replied.

"I'll double it. And I'll buy you lunch."

I couldn't turn that money down. "Fine. But if you cancel or you're late, you're still paying up."

"Aye, you drive a hard bargain. It's a date, n' Quinn?"

My lip was stinging from being bitten. "Yep?"

"I won't let you down." *Too late.* "Meet me in the cafe opposite in fifteen. Bring the contracts."

He may have been good at hiding his working-class roots behind a fancy new accent and gold Rolex; he wasn't quite so good at hiding his desire to avoid Olivia.

When he walked into the cafe—wearing a suit that cost more than my car—I felt jittery, the way you do when you're about to have an injection. Waiting for pain.

Why hadn't I asked for the money without lunch? Was I that easy to manipulate?

We went over contract details along with schedules, budgets and project plans. It took longer than I'd hoped, especially as Daniel kept ordering more coffee and food. Theo was picking me up at 5 p.m. *Thirty minutes to go.*

"Am I boring you, Quinn?"

I looked up from my phone to see Daniel leaning on the table, staring at me.

Being awkward around him wasn't a new feeling. But there were different kinds of awkwardness. In the beginning, he made me nervous because I wanted to impress him and earn my place. Then, as we worked closely together, I was constantly aware of where he was, looking out for him, finding ways and excuses to be nearer, to be alone. Now I wanted the opposite.

I sat as far back as my chair allowed without it tipping over. "I'm not supposed to be working today, remember?"

He dropped his head back with a tut. "You're my partner now, you can't be having days off when I need you."

'Partner' didn't mean lap dog. "I'm not even going to respond to that." I gathered up the paperwork. "Theo's picking me up soon, so if we're—"

"You're still seeing him then?"

I nodded.

His mouth tightened. "Hmph."

"What's that supposed to mean?"

"Didn't think it was serious. That's all." He shrugged.

"Oh, because why would Theo be interested in me and my 'nasty' surprises, right?"

He huffed and shook his head. "What are you on about?" Did he genuinely have a selective memory? "I just didn't think you'd waste your time on a guy like him."

My spine stiffened. "Like him?"

"You know he's going back to that supermodel to film a sequel next year." His eyes narrowed. "Weren't they *living* together?"

No. Not possible. Theo wouldn't want anything to do with Yasmin. Daniel must have made a mistake. Or he was saying it for a reaction.

"Aye, I get he's got the whole bad boy thing going on," Daniel scoffed, "but since when has that appealed to you? You've dragged me over the coals enough for it over the years." My mouth fell open, too shocked to reply. "He's done way worse things than I ever have, Quinn. Apparently being famous means you'll overlook it." He sighed dramatically. "I gotta say, it's pretty shallow."

"Shallow?" I said bitterly. "Seriously?"

"You shouldn't trust him."

"That's rich coming from you. Theo's the first to admit to his mistakes. At least he's learned from them and is *trying* to be a better person. Unlike some people."

"That's not fair. You know me."

"Yeah. You're right, I do now." I clenched my fists to stop the tremors. "You're the one who wanted to keep us a secret, probably so you could play around and cheat on me like you did with all the others. You're the one who kissed me and then ran off to someone else the night of the trial. The one who tried it on with my best friend. And you're the one who told me you loved me, then walked away. You always walk away!" *Don't you dare cry.*

He closed the gap between us, reaching over the table to grab my arms and pull me closer. I winced but he didn't let go.

"Lara, I don't understand? There was no one else," he pleaded, voice dropping to a whisper, indigo eyes swimming with concern. "When I found you like that, torn to shreds, I... I couldn't cope."

Unable to look at him for another second, I shut my eyes.

How had I been so blind for so long? I never thought he would go this far and use the one memory he knew would break my resolve. Break *me*.

I felt exhausted. "There was a time I thought you were changing. Letting me in. Letting me see the real you. Now I realise you were just changing your tactics."

Theo's car pulled up across the street.

I snatched my arms from his grasp. "This time, Daniel, I'm the one who gets to walk away."

Theo

Lara appeared from a cafe across the street, flushed and distracted. She waved and signalled she would be back after fetching her bag. Then I saw the cause of her distraction; Daniel exited the cafe in the direction of his car, which was parked a few spaces behind mine.

I nodded as he passed. *Keep walking, keep on walking.* The damn man stopped.

Reluctantly, I rolled down the window, but I did it with a smile. "Hey, how are you?"

Daniel also replied with a strained, clearly false, smile. He was no actor. "Grand. You off out then?"

"We're going away for the weekend."

A flash of surprise passed over his face.

I felt guilty for enjoying it. Only for a second. "So, you're headed back to London?" I asked.

"Not yet. Just stopped by to sort a few things. And I'd promised to take Lara out for a lunch date." Leaning on the window frame, he sniggered through his nose. "Most expensive date yet. Worth every penny." He looked at me like he was waiting for the words to settle in. Testing me to see if I knew about the dates. *Sly.*

The old Theo might have knocked him out by now.

I didn't bite. "Well, thank you. It's for a good cause."

He straightened and stepped back, annoyed that his plan had failed.

"Don't let me keep you, Daniel. I'm sure I'll see you around again."

He carried on walking.

I uncurled my white knuckles from the gearstick.

Lara

Theo opened the back door so I could put my bag inside and touched a hand to my arm. "Can I help?"

He wasn't talking about the bag. With a jerky head shake, I rushed to the front passenger seat before my legs gave way, trying to mould my face into something happier. I failed.

Theo got in, started the engine and smiled at me, but there was no light. No sparkle. "What did he do this time?"

"Nothing. It doesn't matter." It did. And I couldn't keep it together any longer. I turned away to wipe my eyes. "We argued again. I lost it, and then he... he grabbed me—"

"He WHAT?" Something inside Theo snapped. "I'll fu—" He

flung his door open and jumped out of the car, marching straight for Daniel's BMW further down the street. Flaming hell. *Do something!* I ran after him.

"Theo, stop! Please." I grasped his sleeve and spun him around. "I'm okay. It wasn't like that. Wrong choice of words. He held my arms when I tried to leave, that's all."

"That's *all*?" Theo encircled me, burying his face in my neck. "He can't do that, Lara."

"I know. It's okay, he's gone now." I held Theo tight, letting his breath slow and muscles relax.

Would it make me a pathetic weakling or some kind of anti-feminist to admit that his protective instinct made me feel all fluttery inside?

When he did eventually look up, I ran my fingers through his hair. "What exactly were you planning on doing?"

"There wasn't any sort of planning or much thinking involved." He kissed my forehead. "I'm sorry, *'angry people are not always wise.'*"

If he was going to start quoting Austen with that little frown creasing his eyes, I was going to rip his shirt off right there and then in the street.

♪

Theo started to drive. We were nearly at the motorway, a point of no return, looming closer and closer. Shivers sailed over my skin and a cold sweat swept up my back. I couldn't keep on hiding the truth and lying. It was killing me. And I wasn't one to throw that expression around lightly.

"Theo, wait." My tongue felt like a razor blade.

He glanced over. "Forgotten something?"

Oxygen escaped me, the claws of panic around my neck. "I can't do this, I can't let *you* do this. You need to know—" *I can't breathe.* "Stop the car. Please. Stop the car!"

Theo

I recognised the pain and fear in Lara's eyes, churning her calm blue lagoons into dark whirlpools. I had seen it before. When we first met. In the first-aid trailer that reminded her of a hospital. When Phillip almost exposed her. On our first date when she talked of leaving London. Most recently, when she panicked at the gig. I reached across to hold one of her cold, trembling hands.

The anguish of her voice crushed my heart as she fought to speak, gasping for air, waves of panic crashing her against the rocks, over and over. I realised now that she had been trying to tell me the truth for so long.

I pulled over at the next possible place—a small dirt track into a field—and folded her into my arms. All I wanted was to end her struggle. For her to know that she didn't need to be afraid anymore. To keep her safe whilst setting her free from the walls that caged her. Her tears spilt onto my collar.

"Lara, it's okay, I've got you. Shuuuuush it's okay, babe. You're alright. You don't have to talk about it, I already know."

Cool—but now steady—hands pushed my chest away, her breath slow and intermittent. *I already know.* What possessed me to say that? Those words threatened to destroy a future that had barely begun.

Anxiety tore through my veins like a raging bull.

Lara stared at me. Her fear had been replaced by fire.

A thousand words flew through my mind—when, why, how, *liar*—I wished she would say any of them, all of them. I whispered her name, not knowing what else to say, being careful not to move or push her, preparing for her anger. Would she lash out at me again? I wanted her to. Anything but this painful silence. Anything but her running away.

Slowly, she began to blink the fire away, extinguishing it with her long, damp eyelashes.

Lara

The car slowed. Stopped. Theo's arms found me.

I wanted to run so I could cry on my own but my hands refused to release Theo's shirt.

For every thought that passed through my head, telling me not to let him see me fall apart, there was now another one that argued, *don't let him go*. Because underneath the fear, I wanted him to see me more than anyone else. Old me, new me. All of me.

Every damaged and crazy and broken part.

"Lara, it's okay, I've got you. Shuuuuuush it's okay, babe. You're alright. You don't have to talk about it, I already know."

'I already know?' Those words smacked me like a baseball bat to the head.

I flattened a hand over his chest and pushed. His heart pulsed wildly under my fingertips, the only thing to remain alive while the rest of the world fell into an eerie quiet.

He knew. How? Had someone told him or had he broken his promise? How *long* had he known? Did he know when he first kissed me? When he asked me out? I didn't know which question I wanted to be answered first. If any of them.

"Lara?" he said, a helpless whisper, a brush of a feather across my face.

My muscles tightened, itching to jump out of the car and flee the confined space. I blinked the last of my tears away. Confusion dulled my senses as I sank deeper into an expanse of emptiness.

"I need some air." *And to think.* I got out and walked away from the car to lean on a wire fence which creaked and wobbled under my weight. The noise startled a cow who'd been sleeping on the other side.

Theo followed me, I knew it without looking; as if I were a Jedi and could sense the force of his presence. The thought reminded me of Greg doing a Yoda impression—he would have been proud of me for making a *Star Wars* reference—which made me smile and distracted me long enough to catch my breath.

"When?" I croaked, turning back to Theo. "Phillip knew. Did he tell you?"

A grey haze over the fading sun painted the lines of Theo's brow and the curve of his lips in silvery light as he shook his head. "He tried to, said you had secrets that I should know about, but I didn't let him."

"Then when?" I sounded stronger than I felt.

He rubbed a hand over his head. Slipped his fingers into his pockets. "When I told my family about you, my sister was asking questions. I didn't have any pictures of you then so she looked up your name." With a hand pressed over his heart, he looked into my eyes. "I swear, I didn't know she was going to. She found your Instagram, then said something about there being another Lara Quinn from London who survived an attempted murder."

An echo of the icy blade sent a shudder up my spine. I turned away.

"She doesn't know," he said, "she doesn't even know you lived in London, I didn't say a word to anyone. Then, when Jenny told me more about DAYS, things well... clicked." His voice faded into the wind.

That meant he'd known, or at least suspected, for a while. I leaned back against the fence and took a deep breath. The wire was sharp and uncomfortable, but I couldn't trust my legs to hold me upright. Theo didn't try to approach me or push me to speak.

I wanted to run into his arms. I also wanted to pound my fists onto his chest.

Why hadn't he said something?

Why, why... *why?*

And how had I not noticed? Not once, not for a second in any of his vast expressions had I seen so much as a glimmer of *that* look, the one I knew all too well—pity, sorrow, sympathy—not even any morbid curiosity. "You still wanted me to come with you this weekend? Even though you've known all along? It doesn't bother you?"

"Bother me?" He kept blinking, shaking his head. "Lara, I didn't say anything because I shouldn't have known. I know what it's like to have people invade your privacy. But bother me?" His hands fisted. "Of course, it bothers me."

Ah. There it was. Any second now would come: 'Why didn't you tell me?' 'Why did you cover it up, hide, lie?'

I waited. Vaguely aware that a growing number of cows had gathered to watch us.

Theo took a step closer. "I presumed everything you said about London was because of Daniel. Especially after seeing the way... the way he treats you—Argh." He threw his head back, laced his fingers behind his neck, flexed them out at his side. "The thought of someone hurting you, Lara. Of how he's *still* hurting you."

Still hurting me? Jeff... or Daniel? I sank into a crouch, head in my hands. Theo could have been talking about either of them. And that made me feel sick.

"Dammit, Lara. I could..." His voice dropped to a low thunderous growl. "I could *kill* him." Theo was infuriated, shaking with frustration.

But it had nothing to do with me hiding anything.

He moved to within touching distance and knelt at my level. "I can understand why you wouldn't want to tell me, but if it's because you think it changes the way I feel about you, you're wrong." His hands found my face, surrounding me with heat and deliciously earthy skin. "Since the second we met, you are all I think about. The first thing when I wake, the last before I sleep. You, and everything about you. The way you see the world, the way you're always surprising me. Your passion. Your fire." He pressed smiling lips to my forehead. "I'm not going anywhere because when I'm with you, my past disappears and I know exactly who I am and exactly who I want to be." He lifted my chin. "For as long as you want me, I am yours."

The world had been continuously spinning while I focused on what made us so different. Now, it skidded to a brutal halt and a revelation hit me with the full force of its gravity—we were the same. Hardwired into thinking we weren't enough. Both of us were hiding and scared and damaged in our own ways.

My hands wound their way over his back with new confidence. I wanted to know, feel and understand every part of him. "Theo, I will always want you."

Then—on the side of a road, in the middle of nowhere, being watched by a herd of cows, our feet sinking into mud and icy wind whipping at our clothes—the world began spinning again and he kissed me. So tender, yearning, needing. So raw and breathless that I wanted to cry with happiness and relief.

In that moment, it felt like we had found our true purpose for being alive.

To complete each other.

Space – Biffy Clyro

Day 368
Saturday Early Morning

A woman's voice lifted the darkness. "Did she say yes? Is she coming?"

I half expected to be on my sofa with the TV left on. Then I heard the thrum of the engine, the whoosh of passing cars, and felt smooth leather against my face. I yawned, glanced at the dashboard clock (12:18 a.m.) and rubbed away the weight holding my eyes shut.

Theo noticed I was awake and took my hand. "Yes, Mum. She's here and she can hear you. We won't be there till after one. Traffic's bad," he lied with a sneaky wink at me. "Don't wait up, we'll see you later."

"Alright, I've made up the room in the guest wing for you, Lara. Help yourself to anything you need."

Wing? Good grief, how big was their house going to be?

I thanked her feeling a ripple of embarrassment, grateful she hadn't presumed I'd be sleeping in Theo's room. No matter how much I may have dreamt about it, I still wasn't sure if I was ready for that. Theo said his goodbyes, then slowly passed a hand through his hair. The ripples grew into waves of lava, rising, falling, rising, falling.

"Not far now," he said, spreading a hand over my thigh. I didn't bother trying to hide the untamed, blushing effect it had on me.

We carried on talking about his family, home, and memories from growing up. I absently traced a finger over the fine hair on his arm, around his hand and wrist, plotting out each tendon, freckle and curve of skin.

Occasionally, he would start a sentence and I'd brace myself, waiting for a question about what happened to me. I'd never known anyone to find out and not immediately want to know more. If it was the other way around, would I be curious? Absolutely. So why wasn't he saying anything? *He's waiting for you to tell him.* Of course, he was. He was so unbelievably understanding and kind, I couldn't even think of a word to describe it.

I leaned over to kiss his cheek.

He stopped mid-sentence and chuckled. "Hello, what was that for?"

"Can't a girl kiss her boyfriend for no reason?"

"Yes. Anytime she wants. Please."

♪

An aged wooden signpost for 'Oakriver Farm' pointed us down a single track lane.

After a minute, Theo stopped the car and got out to open a gate, and I realised it wasn't a lane at all but a private drive. He'd said his home used to be a farm; this must have been it. I grabbed my handbag from the seat behind, found my hairbrush and powder, and freshened myself up. I wouldn't be meeting his family until the morning—later in the morning—but I still felt nervous. As if I had to make a good impression on the house itself.

It was Theo's home. A place he loved. A place where he felt

protected from the world and its prying eyes. A place he wanted to share with me, trusting me to keep it secret.

Blackness swayed and swirled around us as we disappeared into a tunnel of trees. I couldn't even see any stars. When it eventually opened out, we were on a gravel clearing. A Victorian-style lamppost glowed ahead of us, next to an arch shaped doorway. Even in the shadowy light, the house was exquisite. It emerged into view like a scene from a film noir. Elegant, dramatic, mysterious.

We unloaded our bags and I followed Theo, both of us treading as lightly as possible across the stones. He stepped inside and flicked on a few lights, revealing a hall and living room that were large enough to fit the entire ground floor of my house.

Everything about it sang, 'welcome home.' Slate flagstone floors, silvery blue walls, plump sofas with huge cushions, oak shelves stacked with well-loved books and trinkets. Grand but cosy.

Theo stood watching me again with that enticing, curious smile of his dancing over his lips.

"Sorry," I whispered, "You know I love old places."

"I know." He held out a hand. "Come on, this way."

The tone of his voice brought my butterfly friends back to life. They started using my heart as a trampoline.

He led me down a long hallway, past a door to the kitchen—I caught a glimpse of navy units and marble tops—through another door into a bedroom.

All four walls were deep forest green, instantly making me feel cocooned and wanting to curl up with a book and glass of wine. It was much darker and more traditional than anything in my own home or anything I would design, but wow. It was stunning. Most of the room was simply styled—off-white painted furniture, gold-framed pictures, candles on the window sill—except *the* bed. A four-poster draped in luxurious velvets, linen sheets and tasselled cushions. A rush of energy pumped through my legs as I imagined running and launching into the mountain of softness. I restrained myself and settled for stroking a hand across the squishy quilt.

"I hope it's up to your designer standards." Theo's breath on my neck sent a melting tingle of static down my spine.

Heat flooded over my skin. I turned, dropping my bag. He was just as irresistible as the bed. I used his belt to pull him closer, any previous desire to sleep now gone.

I wanted him so much I ached all over.

A good ache, the way you feel after a run, only this ache spread further than my legs. It flew through every nerve and every cell. I'd never felt anything like it before. He slipped off my jacket and let it fall to the floor, his hands drifting from my shoulders to my neck, down my back, waist, searching for a way under my top.

Automatically, I twitched away.

Theo's breaths were quick against my face. "Did I hurt you?"

"No. No." I kissed his jaw. "It's like a reflex. I don't— I'm no good at this."

"Yes, you are." His teeth teasingly nipped my ear. "You're too good. It makes it *very* difficult for me to behave."

His smouldering eyes confirmed it. He was hungry.

Breathing him in, I wrapped my arms around his neck. I couldn't go any further without warning him. "I was stabbed. Twice."

He tightened his grip around me. "It's okay, you don't have to expl—"

"I need to," I interrupted, "I don't want you to be shocked. Or... disappointed." *Or have a nasty surprise.*

I sat on the edge of the bed. Theo followed my lead, sinking into the space beside me.

"His name was Jeffrey Smyth. We thought he was a carpenter. I was the fifth." I choked and gripped Theo's arm for strength. "I was in hospital for a long time, it took months for me to get back to normal."

I glanced at Theo, his tight jaw, furrowed brow and pinched lips.

Lifting one of his hands, I touched it to my lower back. "This was the first one." Anger flared behind his eyes before he reined it under control. I guided his hand to my stomach. "This was the second one. They don't hurt. But I do ache, especially my back, and..." My courage ran out. I stared at the dark parquet floor. "And I'm not beautiful."

This was the point where most people crumbled. The moment where I could practically watch their minds backtracking, grasping for anything to say, some way to change the subject or escape. In truth, I didn't expect people to have any profound words of encouragement. Simply listening and being there was enough. What had surprised me though, was the way some people backed off, horrified, as if I had a contagious disease.

Silently, Theo sat still, processing. I should have told him sooner. What if he was regretting everything he'd said, trying to think of a way out? How would I get through the weekend knowing he didn't want me there? I'd have to call Olivia to pick me up. I wrung out my hands. Chewed my lip.

Theo swept the hair from my forehead, fingertips trailing across my cheeks, over my lips, reading my skin like braille. "You know it utterly ruins me when you do that."

I couldn't help but smile as his mouth met mine.

"And how you smile when I kiss you." His warm hands found my waist. "And the way you always manage to get paint on your nose when you're working."

I laughed and in a surge of power, lifted his T-shirt right over his head.

Holy hell.

I wanted to make him step back so I could take in the image of his body and give my mind a chance to come back from the whirling, swimming, soaring place it had disappeared to. But by the time that idea had fully formed, he was kissing me again, lowering me backwards onto the bed.

Now he was the one biting my lip.

He stopped to add, "And the taste of your skin."

My hands clawed over his shoulders, exploring his back as his kisses worked their way to my collarbone, to my chest, each one setting off an explosion of heat and colour and sound. He was delicate, steady, and judging by the low growls in his chest, enjoying every second. I was trying not to grin or laugh or scream his name.

I flinched again when he went to lift my shirt.

He pulled me up to sit with my legs around his waist, holding my shaking hands, his eyes reading mine.

"I want you," he breathed in his visceral purr, "so much." Butterflies the size of eagles pounded my ribs. "But I will wait as long as—"

"No!" I blurted, more forcefully than I'd meant to, which made him chuckle. "I'm not scared. At least, in my head, I'm not."

I wasn't, not anymore. I felt the same way I always did around him. Like there was nothing I couldn't do, nothing that could stop me. "I know what I want. Sometimes the rest of me just doesn't listen."

He gripped my hips, kissed my throat and drew me closer so I could feel the proof of how much he wanted me. "Then tell me what you want, and I will listen."

"You," I said, unbuttoning my shirt. "You've got me. I trust you."

His gaze became molten sugar on my skin. It flowed into my soul, melting every last wall I'd built as if they were no more than a thin layer of frost. As I dropped the shirt from my shoulders, he touched a hand to my waist, smoothing it over the lines and dips of my scars. Only, under his fingers, they transformed into threads of golden script. A reminder, not that I'd died, but that I was alive.

Very much alive.

"Lara, you are beyond beautiful." (I couldn't help noticing his eyes were now on my sheer lace bra.) "And if I have to keep telling you that every minute of every day till you believe me, then I will."

He kept his word.

He told me in between every consuming kiss, every fragile new touch, every glorious breath and every beat of my heart.

Under The Table – BANKS

The faint sensation of something landing on my shoulder stirred me. I twisted onto my back, pulling the duvet with me, in that state of half-dream, half-waking, when everything glows in a sun-drenched haze and you're afraid that if you move, even a fraction, nothing could ever feel as comfortable or as perfect again.

The gentle pressure landed again, this time at the top of my forehead, wandering down the line of my nose, onto my lips and under my chin. I opened my eyes when it tickled across my middle. Theo was propped up on one elbow, his hand now splayed over my hip. Glimmers of morning light bounced off the contours of his shoulders, arching over his waist.

He took my breath away. I tried to think of all the places or buildings I'd seen that had done the same. Nothing came close. He was designed, not by some mortal architectural genius, but by God himself.

I was overwhelmed by a compulsion to bury myself under the covers, petrified that in the daylight he'd see how plain and ordinary I was, and how little I deserved him. But that wasn't what made my heart stumble and miss a beat. It was the fact that *he* was looking at *me*—a hesitant smile, crease in his brow, a flicker of eyelashes—in a way that made me think, almost, maybe, that he felt exactly the same.

Theo

I watched Lara sleeping. Was that creepy? I didn't care, she was incredible.

The most beautiful thing I had ever seen.

And to think she'd worried about me being *disappointed?* I

trailed a finger lightly across her shoulders—she turned onto her back—down her face, over every mesmerising climb and descent of curves to her waist. I wanted to get lost on the terrain of her body.

I would never be good enough for her, which only made me more determined to try.

Her eyes flickered open, the lines of ink along her dark lashes now smudged into sultry charcoal clouds. She disappeared under the sheets with a shy giggle.

I pulled them back down to kiss the tip of her nose. "Good morning. As much as I wish we could stay here all day, I should go and say hello to everyone." I tipped my head toward the door.

I *really* didn't want to go. Not that I didn't want to see my family, but I could feel the heat coming from Lara's body, nothing but a cotton sheet keeping me away.

She sighed. Nodded. Reluctantly, I got up.

As I walked around the room picking up my clothes, Lara watched me. She recharged my energy. Lit me up. I bent to pull on my jeans and flashed her a look over my shoulder with a quirk of an eyebrow that made her bite her knuckles to stifle another giggle.

Jeez, if I didn't make it out of the room in the next three seconds, then I never would.

Lara

I showered in the ensuite and dressed as quickly as possible, floating a few feet off the ground. I didn't want to waste any time but couldn't help stopping to look around the room properly.

The pictures on the walls were family photos. One was of a couple at their wedding. Judging by the style of fashion and the man's deep brown eyes, I guessed it was Theo's parents. Then there were a few of the same couple in various places, with a baby, then a young boy and another baby; Theo and his little sister. Further along the wall was one of Theo on his school-leaving day, celebrating over the results slip in his hands. He was slimmer then, hair buzzed short, long limbs he hadn't quite grown into. Still handsome. I stared at it for a few minutes, then told myself it was weird to fancy the sixteen-year-old version of my boyfriend. *Boyfriend!* I laughed, moving on to the next wall of photos.

At any second, I expected someone to appear around a corner and tell me to leave. To tell me off for peering into another facet of Theo's life without him knowing. Was this how Elizabeth Bennet felt when curiosity got the better of her and she visited Pemberley for a nose at Mr Darcy's house?

A grin spread across my face when I discovered a later picture of Theo at university, playing the guitar.

Three words sang in my mind: *I love him.*

Oh. Wow, okay. I pressed a hand to my stomach, feeling the memories of his kisses over my scars as he told me I was beautiful.

I loved him.

♫

Venturing out of my room, I heard voices coming from the kitchen. I could feel myself starting to sweat, but set a smile on my face and opened the door, immediately swathing my senses with the lush smell of growing things. Tomatoes, greenhouses and fresh lemons.

"LARA! Yaaaay I'm so glad you're here!" Chloe half ran, half skipped over to hug me.

Even without seeing the photos, I would have recognised her. She had lighter eyes than Theo, hazel merging into grey, but they shared the same high cheekbones and full lips. And the same hair, though hers was long, falling into chocolate ringlets at her waist. She scooted me toward a bench at the table in the centre of the room, talking the whole way there, asking questions without waiting for any answers. I only caught the odd word clearly. Her energy reminded me of Olivia.

"Theo's gone to help Dad out, he'll be back in a minute," she said, taking a seat next to me, which thankfully also slowed her down. "But it's cool because it means we get to talk about him." She leaned in closer as if to tell me a dangerous secret. "He's never brought a girl home before, you know."

He'd lived with Yasmin, but she'd never met his family? My smile faltered as I glanced up and noticed his mother standing on the far side of the room, leaning against the sink, watching us, watching *me*, a potato and peeler in her hands. I could see the worry that Theo had talked about. She smiled back, but it didn't fit comfortably, slipping off like a jacket ten sizes too big. Similar to how May first greeted me.

She didn't trust me.

"Thank you again so much for inviting me, Mrs Jackson, and for letting me stay." I fell into my usual waffling, only this time in my highly polished English telephone voice. "Your house is stunning." *Relax.* It sounded like I was auditioning to be the Queen for an episode of *The Crown.*

"Our pleasure to have you. Please, call me Alison." Her expression lifted. "And don't worry, you'll get used to Chloe's hyperspeed." She shot her daughter a look to say, *'calm down.'* It was a look I knew well from my mom.

"Would you like a drink?" she asked. "You had a long night."

Although I knew she was talking about our journey here, heat flushed over my cheeks. Fortunately, she'd already turned away to fill the kettle. I offered to make the coffee myself and volunteered to help with the preparation of jacket potatoes and their various toppings, ready for the evening. Alison seemed surprised but I insisted. Keeping busy would ease my nerves, and it wasn't like I could whip out ol' Henry the Hoover and randomly start cleaning their house.

Working together at the sink, we talked about the farm and its history. As I was asking Chloe about school (exam finals coming up, plus she was taking a fashion design course), Theo opened the back door. A sack of logs was slung over his shoulder. His hands, white T-shirt, jeans and boots were covered in splinters of bark and wood dust. A grin split his face when he saw me.

He was handsome whatever he wore, so perfect that every glimpse made my heart explode into a million tiny hearts. But this was *him*. I'd never seen him so relaxed. Everything I saw finally matched up to the person I knew on the inside.

"Hey," he said, dropping the logs to put an arm around my shoulders. "I didn't expect you to be up so soon. Sleep well?"

I stealthily dug a finger into his ribs, warning him to behave. It might have worked if I hadn't been biting my lip and blushing.

"So," he said, "you've met Mum, Chloe, and this is my dad, Chris." He stepped aside so I could see the man coming through the door behind him, carrying another box of potatoes.

Chris introduced himself with a kiss on my cheek and apologised for the state of his mucky hands. Maybe it was because of the eyes and familiar mannerisms but, despite a tense gravel edge in his voice, I instantly warmed to him.

I lifted my own hands, dirty from the potato peelings. "Don't worry about it."

"What?" He laughed. "Not been here a day and you're already working?"

"Oh, I don't mind, honestly, I like working."

Theo's arm fell back around my shoulder. "She's not being polite, Dad. She means it."

A look of pure pride covered Theo's face as he told them about my promotion to partner. Although part of me wanted to cringe with embarrassment, another part listened in a dazed stupor, floor spinning below, my lungs swelling with his praise. How I managed not to grab his face and kiss the life out of it, I do not know.

Alison asked Chris and Theo to start setting things up in the barn. Theo took my hand and led me outside with them.

Next to the house was a garage filled with chairs and tables, all of which needed moving to the barn at the back of the house. Theo started on the tables while Chris and I moved the chairs. By the time we carried the last of them out, we'd talked about everything from cars to music, gardening, and his attic conversion project.

"I can take a look up there if you want," I offered, "check the roof structure, see how much space you'd have."

Chris stopped to look at me. "Really?"

"Yeah, of course! I'd be happy to."

Theo set down the final table next to us. "All done. Come for a walk?"

I turned back to Chris on our way out of the barn. "Let me know. Whenever you're ready, okay?"

Chris nodded and waved us off with a grin.

Theo chuckled. "Dad's always changing something in the house, you may have just landed yourself a full-time job."

"I don't mind, really, I like to help."

"I know. It's another item on the list of things I love about you."

Oh, my days. My heart stuttered. *He used the L-word.*

He pulled me to his side and led me across their field-sized lawn into the woodland that followed the route of the driveway. I asked about who'd be coming that evening. He listed off a few names: aunts, uncles, cousins, plus a few of his parent's friends from work. Roughly thirty people altogether. The air started to freeze as I breathed it in, shrinking my throat.

Theo picked up on how quiet I'd gone. "Hey, if it gets too much and you need to leave at any point, tell me. Please. It wouldn't be a problem if perhaps"—he shot me a disarming smile—"we went back to our room..."

My knees turned to jelly, my brain to candy-floss, my blood to electricity. An echo of the word 'love' on his lips bounced around my mind.

"As tempting as that sounds," I mused, tapping a finger to my chin, "I'm looking forward to tonight. I want to meet them all. I can do this." I could. For him. For me.

"Do you—" He coughed like he regretted saying anything.

I let him stew on it for a while, partly because I loved watching him pout to think. "Theo, it's okay, I won't be offended." He lifted an eyebrow. "I promise!"

"Okay, well." He swallowed. Hard. "I was wondering if you have panic attacks often?"

"Not so much these days," I said, relieved by how easy it was to talk to him. "Mostly I just get nervous and shaky. It passes if I take a minute. Sometimes, it's like I can't breathe, and I go dizzy. I feel like I want to run away, but I never know where to."

We came out of the woodland by a small stream and a lichen-covered bench, where we sat and I carried on. "Occasionally, something like a sound or smell triggers a memory and I feel like I'm there, living everything all over again. Cigarettes normally. Jeff was a smoker." I took in a lungful of fresh air. "Thankfully, that hasn't happened for a while."

Day 368
Saturday Afternoon

Like pieces of a jigsaw that were made to fit together, I relaxed against Theo's side, my head and shoulder moulding into the curves of his arms as he listened to my story about the disastrous last date with Rhys.

"So now you also know," I said, "the reason why I'm scared of dates."

"Well, if you ever panic again, you have somewhere to run to now." He twisted my hair through his fingers. "You can run to me."

I fell for Theo all over again.

Song lyrics sprang to mind—Bryan Adams, *Run To You*—the way they often did. I started humming the chorus. Theo sang the rest. He had a good voice, gravelly and low. I turned to watch him, genuinely impressed.

"Soundtrack of the day?" he asked.

"It is now."

He laughed. "Hey, you still haven't told me what the song was for the day we met?"

"Because I'm still waiting for you to guess."

A grin wrinkled his eyes. He carried on humming as we walked back toward the house.

Summer had skipped over the horizon. Warmth spread through the breeze, bringing with it a heady smell of blooming flowers and sun-dried grass. I wanted to bottle it like perfume so I could spray the memories across my skin every day for the rest of my life. Not just the scents, but the way the sun filtered through the trees, the touch of Theo's arm around me, his side pressed against mine, close enough to feel him laughing, breathing. The sensation of being light enough that I might float away at any point, every image crystal clear, bright and perfect like a photograph.

We could see Chloe in the barn, hanging fairy lights across the backs of chairs, from the beams, over the doors, basically everywhere she could fit them. Chris was outside the doors, talking to the driver of a vintage VW camper that had been sprayed duck-egg-blue and converted into a mobile, hire-out bar.

Theo slowed to a stop. "Speaking of dates." We hadn't been for some time, but I knew he'd been thinking about something. "I was wondering if there is a way I can help? I would like to give something and I know people who can help spread the word about DAYS."

His kindness and generosity wrapped the kind of warmth around my heart that made me want to jump up, fold my arms around him and sing at the top of my lungs. "That means so much to me, thank you! But I don't want to take your money."

I wouldn't want anyone to think I was using him. I had to consciously stop myself from looking toward his family.

"You're not taking it, Lara, I'm offering. If I can't use what I have, or the position I'm in to help the people I... *care* about, then what good is it?"

The hesitation before the word 'care' was minuscule; it was enough to send my pulse rocketing into space, taking my brain with it.

I pretended not to notice.

"Please," he continued, "think about it. Talk to Jenny and let me know. Hey, we could go on a date? I'll even wear the Darcy suit."

Oh, yes, please. "Honestly, Theo, you already give me enough." He was enough.

His hands shot back to his pockets. "But it's okay for Daniel to help?"

I froze, mouth gaping.

Theo closed his eyes and rubbed a hand over them. "Sorry. I didn't mean that." He swallowed and took a breath. "I saw him yesterday, as we were leaving. He said you'd been on a lunch date. I know it's not real, but why didn't you tell me?" His expression tightened with nerves.

"I don't know," I said honestly, shaking my head. "We were working over lunch. He offered to make a big donation, so I couldn't say no."

"And yet, you say no to me?"

"He's my boss, it's difficult."

"The boss who you used to be involved with, who stays in your house, who sits with his arm around you while messing about with your best friend. Who seemingly can treat you however he likes but is still allowed to help?"

An underlying current of hurt eroded Theo's words, sharpening them at the edges as his voice deepened with anger. Tension grew in his arms. He pinned them down to his body.

"You don't understand, Theo." As soon as that left my mouth, I knew it was the wrong thing to say.

He took a step back, head thrown back, panting as if he'd just run for miles. "Then, please. Help me understand."

Grabbing a handful of his shirt, I pulled him across the lawn, out of the eye-line of his family. He let me—he was plenty strong enough to have stopped me if he wanted to—but he still wouldn't look at me. I wanted to shout back, to accuse him of not trusting me. I couldn't. He'd been cheated on, used and betrayed. It may not have been caused by a physical knife, but that kind of damage also took time to mend.

I cupped his fragile face. "He was there."

Theo's eyes lifted to mine, widening, anger instantly dispersing when he realised what I was talking about.

"Daniel was the one who found me. I died, Theo. My heart literally stopped and Daniel was there. If it wasn't for him, I would have ended up like the others and—" The memories sent a chill through my body.

Theo pulled my head onto his shoulder with one hand gripping my neck, the other anchoring me at the base of my spine.

"I should have told you." I looked up, crumbling when I saw his watery eyes. "I should have told you everything right from the start. There's so much I don't know how to explain, and when I try, people change. They treat me differently. Or they... they leave me." *They walk away, like Daniel.*

Still holding onto his shirt, I pressed my face to his chest, breathing in the spice and earth to steady my voice. "We have a motto at DAYS: Be brave. Be honest. Make all the days count. I kept repeating it to myself every time I saw you, but I was so afraid of what you'd think of me. But I don't want to hide anymore. Even if being with you means people find out who I am, I don't want to be scared anymore." I started smiling. Theo did, too. "I don't want to let you go."

He kissed the left corner of my mouth. "Then don't." The right corner.

"Even if I have to fight off every girl on every date, in every restaurant who tries to flirt with you, I'm not letting go."

Another kiss on my nose. "Then don't." More kisses over my cheeks.

"I mean it, Theo. I like you, a lot, exceedingly, tremendously, and I don't go down without a fight."

"I believe you." He chuckled, pausing the kisses long enough to say, "I've experienced your fighting skills first-hand, remember. You are the strongest person I have ever known. My fire and trouble."

"Well, then, Mr Jackson, that's because *'my courage always rises at every attempt to intimidate me.'*" I quoted Elizabeth Bennet and got the reaction I wanted; a deep groan vibrated Theo's chest.

"Well, then, Miss Quinn, you should know that if you are going to talk Austen to me, I will take you down with or without a fight. Right here. Right now."

Well, then.

I quickly recited every quote I could think of.

♪♪

We entered the barn—my lips tingling from the effects of Theo's stubble—to find Chris laying the tables; he called Theo over to help. I went to join Chloe, who had finished with lighting and was now onto flowers.

I held my arms out to relieve her of the monstrous bunch of pink roses she was struggling to carry. Stopping at each table, she would pick out five and place them into a tall glass vase. Once the roses were gone, we did another lap of the room, this time lighting a white candle jar for each table.

When we'd finished, we stood back to admire our handiwork. The barn filled with the delicate scent of rose and vanilla. The walls glowed with flickering light.

I gave her a nudge. "It looks amazing, Chloe."

"Thanks." She beamed. With a pointed look in Theo's direction, she whispered, "He *really* likes you, you know. They don't say much, but Mum and Dad like you, too."

I hoped so. His mom had been especially quiet. I could feel her watching me every time I went near Theo, waiting for some kind of sign that I was an imposter. Ready to catch me out for trying to steal her son away and drag him back to his old ways.

Theo caught my eye and flashed a grin. Since being home, his energy seemed to have multiplied by a thousand. Chloe gave us a *'get a room'* eye-roll.

We did have a room... maybe that explained Theo's chipper mood.

Chloe took my hand. "Now, it's time for our makeover! Come on." She pulled me toward the house, shouting over her shoulder to Theo and her father that we'd see them later. I got the feeling arguing would have been pointless. Goodness, if she and Olivia ever got together they would be unstoppable.

Fortunately, though, Chloe's idea of a makeover simply meant going through the clothes I'd brought with me. I laid out my options on the bed. She immediately picked the cocktail dress. I'd bought it for my cousin's wedding a few years before. I wasn't as self-conscious back then, so with any luck, wearing it again would bring back good memories. Maybe even a little of my old confidence.

From the front it was a simple shape, lightly fitted, finishing at my knees. At the back, the neckline dipped into drapes and folds of fabric at the bottom of my shoulder blades. The cherry-red, shimmery silk was what made it special. It was one of those dresses that, as soon as you put it on, you had to spin around to watch the way it swished and fell.

Chloe left me to get herself ready. I moved on to my hair and makeup, still humming.

Run To You – Bryan Adams

Theo

Our guests, most of whom I hadn't seen since leaving for L.A., were already gathering in the barn. Their possible reactions to my being home made me restless. I took long strides across the driveway, breathing deeply, repeatedly clenching and stretching out my hands. If Lara could face them, and they were strangers to her, then I could.

Thinking of her, the sweet smell of her hair, and the softness of her skin under my fingers, filled me with a sense of calm. Being with her made everything else clear. Past, present. Future.

"Theodore!" My aunt called out the second I stepped through the barn doors, inadvertently announcing my arrival. Faces turned to see for themselves; an icy silence rushed through the room.

I gave her a thankful hug for the way she struck up a conversation as if our years apart had only been a day. My father, her brother, came to join us a minute later. The surrounding noise swelled again, though there were still furtive glances being thrown in my direction. Glances that put the hairs at the back of my neck on end. I was being talked about. I expected as much. It didn't stop it from hurting.

The room stirred again, this time because of Chloe's entrance. She threw up her arms and sang: "Let's get the partaaay started!"

Lara discreetly followed Chloe, candlelight painting flames across her face. My awareness was drawn to her by an invisible force. She walked straight, shoulders held back, her forever-present smile lighting her eyes. Only her hands, clasped together in front of her waist, gave her nerves away, and the occasional bite of her lip.

One of my cousins—Harrison, attractive, *single*—immediately made his way over, giving a hurried hello to Chloe before introducing himself to Lara. *Watch out,* I thought, *she won't take any nonsense.* I watched with amusement as Lara held out a hand for Harrison to shake, subtly yet firmly, keeping him at arm's length.

A tap on my shoulder called for my attention.

"She's a lovely girl," Dad said.

"Does your opinion have anything to do with her offer to plan the attic?"

"Perhaps." He chortled. "She's a keeper." His chin dipped to give me a stern look. "So for goodness sake, go and rescue her."

After a firm clap on my back, he walked away with a grin. I rubbed the relief from my face. They may not have sounded much to anyone else, but I knew those words were the sign of my father's approval and forgiveness. The lake between us, filled with waters of the past, shrunk further than ever before.

A step behind Lara, I paused. Her dress rippled like a waterfall cascading down her back.

I loved how polite and thoughtful she was. I loved how her fears made her strong yet empathetic. To me, even the scars she hated were another sign of her courage. They were stories of the bravery she showed every single day written on her skin. I loved her fire.

I loved *her*.

So damn much.

Reaching out, I breathlessly skimmed the back of my hand down her spine. Instead of tensing, she relaxed at my touch and leaned into my arms.

Lara

Theo arrived just as his cousin asked if I wanted to get a drink from the bar. I was glad of the timing. Harrison was sweet—confidence and charm were obviously Jackson family traits—however, he stood a little too close, and his eyes wandered downward from my face whenever he thought I wasn't looking.

The nimble touch of Theo's hand on my back awoke every cell and once again my world shifted from black and white to dazzling colour. *James Bond, eat your heart out,* I thought, taking in Theo's slim-cut tux.

He shook Harrison's hand. "I see you've met my Lara."

My Lara.

He said it so casually, so naturally, like the words were ready on his lips, waiting his whole life to be spoken.

I'd never believed in soulmates or fate. Our lives were shaped by the choices we made. Sometimes bad things happened because you were in the wrong place at the wrong time. Sometimes good things happened because you were in the right place at the right time. (Like running into a car door on a rainy Friday morning.) Olivia didn't agree. She firmly believed that there was a special person who you were destined to meet, the yin to your yang, your other half. Or as she, in true Olivia style, once said: the bacon to your eggs.

Who would ever have thought the man of my dreams—who wanted me, who could read me, understand me, who found my awkward, clumsy shyness and ability to quote from *Pride and Prejudice* attractive—would come in the form of Theo?

Nope, not me.

Not in a million years.

♪

Music started after dinner. *Three Times A Lady.* The first dance song from Chris and Alison's wedding. Theo put his arm around Chloe as she started crying, watching their parents on the dance floor.

Halfway through, Chris pulled up his sister. Alison grabbed a very reluctant nephew. Chloe found her grandfather.

Theo stood and held out a hand. "Dance?"

One word was enough for my heart to take flight. And to then plummet through my stomach. "I don't know how." My kind of dancing never involved a partner.

"Good," he said, one corner of his mouth lifting into that smile I couldn't resist. "It means I get to teach you." He rolled up the sleeves of his shirt, took my hands and led me to the floor.

The pressure of people watching us vanished like smoke into the air when Theo guided my one hand around his waist and lifted my other. With my cheek to his, I followed his steps. Swaying and floating, gliding and skipping. I laughed as he twirled me and pulled me back into his arms.

"Theo?" I said, head against his chest, listening to his heart. He hummed in response. "Do you ever feel like you're living in one of your movies?"

"In what way?"

"Because sometimes things feel just... too much, to be real?"

"If by 'too much' you mean too perfect, then yes, right now I feel like I'm living in a movie."

Honestly, this guy! "You should seriously be writing your own lines." I slid my arms around his neck. "If this *was* a movie, what would happen next, Mr Director?"

"I would spin you again"—he spun me—"during which we would cut to a musical montage of us dancing the night away. Then I would kiss you"—he kissed me—"and whisper in your ear how beyond beautiful you are." He gripped my waist and held me close.

"Oh, you like my dress, then?"

"Very much. So don't be offended"—I looked up in surprise, but he was still grinning—"when I tell you, that I can't wait to take it off."

I rolled my eyes as if I were chastising him when really, I couldn't wait either. "Behave, you."

"Hmm." He found his favourite spot behind my ear. "I think it's a little late for that, don't you?"

Before I could think of anything to say—which would have required restarting my brain—Chloe, Harrison and some others joined us on the dance floor.

Cue the montage.

Day 368
Saturday Night

As darkness fell, so did the temperature. Theo's parents and the handful of others who were left retreated into the warmth of the house. I stood outside the doors of the barn, leaning against the VW bar, regretting my decision to wear strappy heeled sandals. My feet were freezing but my soles burned. Hell, it felt good to dance again though.

The top few buttons of Theo's shirt were now undone, bow tie hanging loose around his neck. Who invented such a bizarre item of clothing that only became attractive when worn incorrectly? The carefree way it draped over his chest turned it from the accessory of a stuffy professor into the lure of a hunter. I wanted to grab hold of it, bring him closer. *Later*, I told myself.

He addressed me in his best Shakespearean English. "Red wine for m'lady?"

Goosebumps appeared on my arms as I took a glass from his hand. "Why, thank you, kind sir."

"I confess," he sighed, "I have ulterior motives."

"Never!" I took my time kissing his jaw.

He chuckled, a rumbling growl, his lion's purr. "Lara, that was not what I meant, though... No. Stop distracting me." He pulled himself away with a grin. "Please remember how kind you think I am, and how much you like me at this moment, because I am about to ask you to do something for me."

"Oh?"

"Come on, I'll show you."

Skipping on tiptoes so my heels wouldn't disappear into the grass, I followed him into the house. My heart rate increased as I tried to guess what he wanted from me. We entered the living room. Empty. Voices came from a room further on, where I hadn't been yet.

Theo stopped to open the door. "After you."

What could he possibly want me to do in front of an audience? I held my breath and stepped forward. My question was immediately answered.

In the centre of this smaller sitting room was a baby grand piano, black and glossy and divine.

Theo stood behind me, hands on my shoulders. "Would you play for us?"

I glanced around the room, counting eight people dotted around on armchairs, chatting while drinking. I'd played in front of ten times that, but it wasn't the quantity that scared me. Theo, his parents and his family were people I cared about and I wanted them to like me.

"What about that song Sarah mentioned?" Theo coaxed. "The one she said you know back to front."

Crazy by Patsy Cline.

It was actually Daniel who'd brought up that song on our night out. I wondered if Theo deliberately left him out. Anyway, it was one of my favourite songs to play, and the one I was supposed to have performed solo at the last gig.

Theo lowered his hands over my arms, gently hugging me from behind. "You want to slap me again don't you?" He kissed my cheek and pointed us toward some empty seats. "Don't worry, another time."

Polished ivory keys called to me. The difference between playing on a grand and playing on my digital piano was like tasting an aged fine wine straight from the cellar of a French vineyard, compared to a five quid bottle from a corner shop.

Nothing felt like the real thing.

I caught Theo's hand. "One song?"

"One." He smirked mischievously. "Then I'll stop nagging you."

"Promise?"

"Cross my heart."

I glanced back to the piano. "Alright."

Waves of electricity sparked over the surface of my skin as I took a seat. Butterflies battered the inside of my chest, drunk on the large gulp of wine I'd just taken, praying it would calm my trembling fingers. I stroked my hands over the keys and positioned a foot over the sustain pedal.

Thankfully, I couldn't see any of the audience behind me, except for Theo, who'd relaxed into a seat on the far side of the piano.

My first few notes came out feeble and unsure. Two bars in, I hit a low note and as its deep reverberation filled my body, I felt my cheeks tightening, pulling my mouth into an unconscious smile. Then I astonished myself—I started to sing.

In the second verse, my voice wavered. Bad choice of song.

Very bad.

Like most people, when I first heard it, I thought it was a love song. And yes, I suppose it was, but not in a happy-endings kind of way. It was a woman singing about her heartbreak over a man who she knew she was going to lose. Therefore, she was the crazy one for ever thinking she could keep him.

In less than six weeks, Theo would be gone.

He would leave me and carry on with his life. I'd known that from the start.

But I'd let myself forget. I'd let myself wonder what our life could be like.

My eyes flickered over Theo. He'd told me he was mine for as long as I wanted him. *What if I want him forever?* Pools of water blurred my vision and in the last line, I caved. I met Theo's intense gaze.

I was the crazy one. Crazy for letting myself fall in love.

Crazy stupid crazy.

Recognition flashed over his face. A sharp breath inflated his chest.

A hand on my shoulder made me jump. "That was wonderful, Lara." Alison grinned, melting the ice from her voice. "Won't you play some more?"

The instinct to run pulsed through my legs. My knees shook, fighting to get off the chair. *Be brave.* I couldn't run away from her, not when she was finally letting me in.

I kept my head down. "Thank you. I would. But, I'm sorry, I'm so tired." I blinked the last tear from my eyes and grabbed hold of Theo's hand, which had appeared on my other shoulder. "Thank you again for having me. If you don't mind, I think I... I'll say goodnight..."

Theo practically picked me up off the chair, his expression telling me, *'It's okay, I've got you.'* But now even that—the connection, the closeness, the way we could communicate without words—scared me.

When we got to the hall, I pulled away from him, rushing to my room.

"Wait!" Ragged fear in Theo's voice brought me to a standstill outside my door. "Lara, please. You're not crazy."

My heart lodged in my throat.

Walking along the dimly lit corridor, his tall body pushed away the shadows until he was close enough for me to hear him whisper, "You're not crazy." He lifted his palm to my face. I wanted to fall into it, curl myself around him, inside him. "Lara, I—"

The words he was about to say hung in the air between us. The same words that filled my own body: *I love you.*

But I couldn't bear to hear him say them, because six letters divided and broke those perfect words apart. And I hated myself for it.

D-a-n-i-e-l.

Only one man had ever said he loved me, and I'd clung onto it like a lifeline, like a miracle that could save me. Deep down, I hadn't let go.

Tumbling further and further, I peered into Theo's eyes, searching for a sliver of doubt. There was none. If Theo told me he loved me, he would mean it.

It didn't change the fact he was going to leave me.

Time was repeating itself.

Losing him would leave me more broken and damaged than ever before.

I pulled his mouth to mine and kissed him with all of the desperation I'd felt when taking my last breath. I needed him the way colour needed light. The way tides needed the moon. The way humans needed air—one could not exist without the other.

I frantically grasped his hair and swept my tongue over his lips, forcing his heated breaths to quicken and deepen against my skin. I didn't want his delicacy or restraint anymore. He felt it. Solid fingers gripped my thighs. He lifted me off the ground, coiling my legs around his waist, pressing my back to the wall so he could free a hand to open the door and carry me inside.

Like You Mean It – Ruelle

Theo

I had played the scene in a hundred films, in a hundred ways, from a hundred different time periods, but falling in love with Lara was nothing like in the movies.

If you were to ask me *when* it happened, I couldn't tell you; it dawned slowly and silently like a sunrise. If you were to ask when I *realised* it, then I would probably tell you of the first time she visited my family. When we danced in the barn. When she sat at the piano, lamplight drawing shadows from her long eyelashes over her face, the blush on her cheeks, her voice singing through my skin, flesh, bone, and into my soul. The night her fire turned into a furnace.

I fell in love with Lara note by note until her melody became my oxygen. Until her rhythm became the beat of my heart.

She was the only music I ever wanted to hear.

Day 383
Sunday

Over the weeks since visiting Theo's family, he barely went to his caravan other than to pick up new script pages. We spent every moment we had left together. My house, my room, my bed smelt like him.

This weekend, he'd combined a meeting in London with visiting his family, so I'd invited my parents over for Sunday lunch, then roped in Olivia to help me cook. I wanted it to be special. Neither Mom nor Dad had said anything, but I could tell my mysterious absence had been noticed.

Mom entered the living room first and when she saw the table laid with fancy napkins and candles, her face glowed.

Dad looked scared stiff. "Special occasion I don't know about?"

"No, Dad. Don't worry."

Relieved, he relaxed, sat at the table and unfolded the newspaper from under his arm.

Mom liked to occasionally remind Dad about the year he forgot their anniversary, usually whenever she wanted new shoes. Not that Dad ever complained about her buying things. He worshipped the ground she walked on. It was embarrassingly cringy. And incredibly sweet.

An hour later, my phone buzzed.

DANIEL: Quinn, I'm still waiting on Hoffman's reno plans. Needed them yesterday. Dd

Two weeks ago, a new sign went up on my office door for 'David Quinn,' reminding me every day that I was now an official partner. If it weren't for that, I would never have known. Instead of being allowed to pitch for my own projects and manage a team, Daniel was controlling my work more than ever. I felt more like his PA than his partner.

I put my phone down without replying. He could wait until work hours.

Mom touched my wrist. "Okay, baby?"

"Fine. Just up to my eyeballs with work."

"I'm sure it'll settle down once you get into your new role," Dad said encouragingly, in between eating and still reading. "Daniel's been very good to you."

Yes, Daniel had. In some ways. I sighed. Of course, Dad would love him. The man who rescued his daughter. My knight in shining Gucci. "More wine, Mom?"

She had a mouthful of peas so gave me a thumbs up.

Olivia accompanied me to the kitchen. "So," she whispered, "they don't know about you and Daniel either?"

"Nope." I poured myself a large glass of wine and immediately took a gulp.

"Or about Theo?"

"Nope."

She sucked in her lips and took the wine bottle from my hands. "I'm gonna need some of that."

We dished up our desserts and took them back to the table.

"Is all this work the reason we haven't seen you?" Mom asked.

"Umm. Kind of."

Dad laughed. "I'll have to have words with that boss o' yours."

Daniel was not supposed to be my *boss* anymore. That was the whole point. Olivia cleared her throat and gave me a pointed look. I followed her glare down to my hands where, unknowingly, I'd screwed the table cloth up into my fists.

I flattened it back out. "The reason I've been AWOL is, I'm seeing someone."

Dad choked on his Yorkshire pud.'

"Oh, wow!" Mom gushed. "That's lovely. Tell us all about him."

Where to even begin? Theo was everything and more. He'd brought me back to life, revived parts of myself that I thought I'd lost forever. With him, I felt protected and safe, but he didn't do it by keeping me to himself in a secret box. He gave me the freedom to be me again. With him, I could glimpse a future of happiness and love and adventures.

Until I remembered he was leaving.

Four weeks.

Then my heart would stop beating all over again.

It was cruel if you thought about it. I'd been stranded in an ocean of mundane, surviving by treading water, then he came along and threw out a rope to pull me to shore. But just as the golden sands and tropical paradise were on the horizon, he was tossing me back out to sea.

Olivia filled the silence. "He's dreamy."

"It's Daniel, isn't it." Dad smacked his paper onto the table with a satisfied grin. "I knew it!"

"He's definitely a hottie." Mom agreed, although not sounding quite as enthusiastic.

"It's not Daniel," Olivia blurted.

My head fell into my hands. *Make it stop.* What was I thinking, telling them this now and getting their hopes up, only to have to go through the whole, 'he left me' conversation in a few weeks?

All three of them stared at me, their faces a picture of confused concern.

"Theo," I said, wishing he was here. No, actually, I'd rather teleport myself to him and out of this mess. "His name is Theo."

I dusted off my familiar old smiling mask. "It's nothing serious," I added offhandedly. "He's moving away soon, so it won't go anywhere. But I just wanted to let you know, and apologise for not being around."

Dad didn't look happy in the slightest. "Then why are you seeing him?"

Because I didn't think I'd be stupid enough to fall in love. Because I... didn't think.

No strings.

Ha! What a lie.

I shrugged and thankfully, Elton John interrupted the conversation by singing his song: *Daniel*. Guess who I'd set that ringtone for? At least it was an excuse to leave the table. Taking Daniel's call was the lesser of two evils.

"Sorry. If I don't answer, he won't stop." I picked up just as Elton got to the chorus and took the stairs two at a time. "Hi—"

"I know you saw my message, Quinn. You ignoring me now? I get it's Sunday, but this is what you wanted."

This was not what I wanted. For the first time in my life, I hated my job. "And yesterday was Saturday. Some people have lives outside of work." *That was harsh.* But he'd promised me taking on the partnership wouldn't mean working weekends.

I waited for his cutting, sarcastic reply. It didn't come.

"Lara, please. I'm counting on you. I just need those files finished."

He sounded exhausted. More than exhausted... stressed. Daniel never sounded stressed.

The Hoffmans and their chain of hotels were one of his first clients. Surely, they wouldn't threaten to go elsewhere? "Is everything okay?"

He inhaled. Slowly let it go. "No."

Crap. "The floor plans are done. I've got to finish the costings, but I can get it to you tonight."

"Cheers. It's not that."

"Then what?" I paced the length of my room. "I'm doing my best here. I can't go any quicker. Don't they like the concept?"

"No, no. They love it," he said. So why the hell was he harassing me on a Sunday afternoon! "Nan fell down her stairs."

I stopped pacing, my heart missed a beat. "Oh, Dan, I—"

"She's alright," he interjected. I let out my breath. "But she broke her ankle and dislocated her shoulder, so I've moved her in with me. And they're doing tests for... other stuff." I sat on the edge of my bed and closed my eyes. It was hard to be angry with someone who loved their nan so much. "That's why I'm behind on work. I know I'm putting a lot on you, Lara, but I... I'm relying on you."

"Of course. Anything you need, I'm here."

That was what partners were for, right?

Friend – Gracie Abrams

Day 384
Monday

Using the dressing table mirror, I watched Theo behind me while he examined my bookshelves, head tilted to the side to read the spines, his hair still dripping from the shower. It was even more gorgeously curly when wet.

"You're worried," he said, half question, half fact.

"I'm fine."

"She'll be alright." He gave a comforting smile, referring to Daniel's nan, and waited for me to elaborate. When I didn't respond, he went back to my books, running a hand along the top shelf which, for me, would have required standing on the end of my bed to reach. "Have you read all of these?"

"Ninety-nine per cent."

"Austen, Hoover, King and... *Twilight?* Hmm, you certainly have a varied taste." He chuckled and slid out a book.

"There wasn't much else to do in hospital, so I tried everything. Oh, except that." I pointed to the one in his hands. "That's from my A-level English. I've never liked Shakespeare."

"Have you seen any at the theatre?"

I shook my head.

"Then that's why." He smiled. "As soon as I have some time

322

off, we will go to Stratford and see a play."

My chest imploded and exploded at the same time. Why was he planning things for the future? *A future that will never happen.*

Opening the book, he sat on the nearest corner of the bed and started to read. Rumbling vowels poured over my skin. "*'My bounty is as boundless as the sea, my love as deep; the more I give to thee, the more I have, for both are infinite.'*" The lines were from Romeo and Juliet and he knew them off by heart; he only looked at the page once. "Lara, I—"

I leaned over and kissed him to stop him talking. He didn't respond and when I pulled away, he stayed silent, watching me, thinking.

I finished straightening my hair. "Okay, I have to get going."

"Why do you do that?"

"You don't like it straight?" I frowned.

He scrubbed a hand down his face. "Why do you stop me every time I try to tell you that I lov—"

I slammed my drawer shut and stood up.

Of course, he'd noticed. He always noticed everything like that. He saw between the lines and heard my unspoken words. It was one of the many things I loved about him.

Theo hung his head. "Do you still love him?"

"What?" I choked on my tightening throat. "Daniel? No!"

"The fact you know who I'm talking about suggests otherwise." He blew out a breath, then whispered so faintly I almost didn't hear, "You call his name sometimes. In your sleep."

I went cold. "It's not like that. I have nightmares. I can't—I don't want to talk about this now."

"Then when?" Theo held my eyes. "You don't talk to me at all anymore."

I didn't. I couldn't, because every day that passed was another day closer to him leaving. I was preparing myself, building my walls back up like a fortress around my heart. He'd noticed that, too. So why couldn't he see that he was going to break me?

"I'm not going to talk about this because you don't understand." I stepped away to pick up my bag. "Daniel told me he loved me. Then he left, okay? He left me." My pain funnelled itself into anger, raising my voice and emptying my lungs. "And now you're leaving me, too. So I can't—I can't do this again. I don't know what you want from me." My heart might never recover again.

"I live in London, not on another planet." He stood and carefully took hold of my arms. "All I want is you. For you to trust me. I'm not leaving you. Why do you think I've been trying to explain everything?"

He had explained. He'd been completely open about his work and living situation.

He hadn't mentioned anything about any sequels in L.A. with Yasmin though. Had Daniel seriously made that up? If it was true, then I couldn't for the life of me work out how to feel about it. It might only be a movie but... would Theo have to *kiss* her?

"It doesn't matter," I snapped. "You'll go back and you'll forget about me." Theo's hands and eyes dropped. I'd hurt him. It crushed me. "I just want things to go back to normal. It wasn't meant to be like this. You weren't supposed to..." *Breathe. Slow down.* I wasn't making any sense. Arguing never made any sense. "I'm sorry. This is why I didn't want to tell you everything."

"No." Theo wrung his fingers as pained resignation seeped into his low voice. "Don't apologise for being honest. At least I know where I stand." He turned his back to me, looking out the window. "You think I can walk away like this never happened because it *'wasn't meant'* to be real. Is that what you're saying?"

I couldn't speak. The more I tried, the more my throat knotted. I went to take his hand, but he tucked them into his pockets.

"So, it was never your plan for this to be more than temporary," he said, black eyes finding mine, boring holes into my heart. "What was I, an experiment? A way for you to test the water with no strings or risk? Because the whole world knows I'm not capable of anything serious or feeling anything deeper. Is that it?" His chest heaved as his control buckled.

No strings. What had I done? I could see him shattering to pieces right in front of me and each piece cut deeper into my soul. "Don't say that. That's not what I mea—"

"You say you trust me but you don't. Not really. Not enough. Otherwise, you wouldn't be giving up." He screwed up his face, fighting tears. "I know it won't be easy but I thought, I genuinely thought we would work it out. Together." He reached out to me. "I am not Daniel. Lara, I—"

"Stop it." I pressed a hand to his chest to keep him at a distance. "I'm sick of everyone talking about Daniel. This isn't about Daniel."

Obviously, it was about Daniel. The man who supposedly loved me, then walked anyway every time I needed him the most. The man to whom with my dying breath, I'd made a promise to never leave. I hated the way I felt the need to defend Daniel. Hated the way I'd used the pain he'd caused me as the concrete to build my walls.

I loved Theo, and although I could see myself pushing him away, destroying him with my words, I couldn't stop myself. This whole situation felt unreal. "You don't understand. Daniel saved my life, he was there."

"And he will *always* be there!" Theo's brow furrowed as he shook his head. "Can't you see how he's using that? You're there at his every beck and call, Lara."

Theo was probably right. But instead of listening to him, facing my fear and admitting to just how naive and blind I'd been, I dug my heels in. "Oh, no. No, no. You don't get to psychoanalyse me." I waved a finger. "You talk about experiments and trust, but when were you planning on telling me about going back to work with Yasmin? Back to playing happy families and making love for the cameras? I guess that's all pretend to you, though, so I'm supposed to be fine with it?" I huffed a bitter laugh and rolled my eyes away. "You know you're right, there's a lot of things I don't understand because maybe, Theo, I don't want to."

Theo

I crashed.

The way an old computer does when it can't process any more information. Alarms rang in my ears. Error messages popped up all over my body as cell by cell, I began to shut down.

It wasn't right. It wasn't fair. Lara wasn't Yasmin. So why, how, was this happening all over again? I had willingly given everything of myself to another woman and once again, she had used me for what she wanted, taken what she needed, leaving what was left of me to fall apart.

It *wasn't meant* to last.

She wanted *normal*.

The elusive normal life. The thing which happened after a director called 'cut' on a happy ending.

To me, the ending was the real beginning. So what if all the meet-cutes, first times and secret plot twists were in the past? The exciting part was what came next. Making a home, washing dishes, taking a bath with a good book, curling up next to the person you love. All the things I had been given a taste of while being here with Lara.

Normal life was the adventure I had been waiting for my whole life. And yet... it tore my heart when I realised: A normal life was the one thing I could not provide her.

Lara stood her ground, shaking from head to toe with fire and —something I had never seen before—*hatred* in her eyes. I didn't know this Lara. She felt like a stranger.

I backed further away, struggling to steady my breath. "How do you know about the sequel? I thought we promised to be honest and not use Google?"

"I didn't. Daniel told me."

I bet he had. That clever, sly bast—

"It's true then?" Lara demanded, in a cold and alien voice.

If this was how she truly felt, then I didn't see the point in telling her that I had already started legal proceedings to end my contracts. She should have asked me. Instead, she chose to believe Daniel.

How would I ever compete with the man who saved her life?

Daniel kept her hanging with his claws in so deep, she couldn't see them. She refused to see them. And I wasn't going to be the one to make her. Sometimes, we have to see things for ourselves— the hard way.

Daniel and Yasmin would make a good pair.

"If he told you," I scoffed, "then it must be true."

Lara exhaled her frustration and headed for the door. "I'm not going to argue with you."

Air dried to dust in my throat. I followed her out of the room onto the stairs. "You promised you wouldn't run away from me again."

Lara had promised me open honesty, to not hide or run, to not let go, to fight. Yet here she was: closed off, hiding, running and giving in.

What more could I do? I couldn't force her to love me or order her to trust me. And without trust...

I pressed my hands over my face to wipe away my feelings.

One thing I did know was how to act.

Lara

Theo followed me out of the bedroom. "You promised you wouldn't run away from me again."

I stopped at the top of the stairs, gripping the handrail for support as his voice tore away my strength. "We'll talk later, okay?" I said.

He tipped his head with a shrug and spoke like nothing that just happened bothered him. "Go on. You'll be late for work."

I should have stayed.

I should have talked.

I should have kept my word by being honest, trusting him and fighting for us.

But... I didn't.

My heart was going to be broken again. *Why delay the inevitable?*

Afterglow – Taylor Swift

Pulling up onto my drive after work, it occurred to me that the prospect of having your figurative heart ripped out was frighteningly similar to having your literal heart stop. If I were a songwriter, I probably could have come up with some poetic way of describing how I felt. But alas, I wasn't, so the best I could come up with was: downright miserable.

And after a whole day spent thinking about how to face Theo, I still didn't know where to start.

Mom surprised me by opening the front door as I stepped out of my car. A dark spiral of hair escaped her ponytail as she bobbed her head, eagerly waving me over. I sank into her warm cwtch, burying my face in her hand-knitted jumper and homely scent. I wanted to cry, to tell her everything, but I didn't want to spoil her happy mood. "Caru ti, Mam."

She cupped my face. "Love you, too, sweetie." She then whispered, as quietly as someone could when bursting with excitement, "Hope you don't mind I let myself in to borrow a phone charger. Why didn't you tell us?"

"Tell you what?"

"About your Theo being, you know, *the actor.* Goodness me, he's even more handsome in real life!"

She glanced behind and sure enough, there was my handsome

Theo sitting on the sofa. My insides lurched like I'd been dropped from a great height. Mom linked my arm and escorted me into the living room. Theo started smiling as she sat down.

This was not how I wanted them to meet. To be brutally honest, I hadn't wanted them to meet at all. I knew Mom would love Theo. I didn't want her to be hurt again either.

Life was falling apart so, in true British fashion, I offered them: "Tea?"

Theo joined me and filled the kettle.

"What's going on?" I mumbled, sounding much more accusatory than I meant to.

"She answered the door when I got here. Where were you?" he said, low and growling, but with a perfect smile on his face for Mom's benefit. "I've been calling you. Are you okay?"

"I dropped Olivia off at Greg's." And drove the long way home via the quiet coast road to try and clear my head.

Cups clattered onto the surface thanks to my trembling fingers.

Theo tried to help, but I stubbornly ignored him. His hands went to his pockets.

"How was work?" Mom asked.

I thought I'd gone past my days of having to fake smiles. Fortunately, I could still remember how to. "Fine. Busy."

"Any news on Daniel's nan?" Theo added.

"She's better." I nodded, then hissed, "Don't pretend like you care."

What's gotten into me? Theo wasn't the one I was angry with. His expression was as hurt and as shocked as when I'd slapped him. If not more.

He grinned, exaggeratedly, eyes wide, voice a pitch higher than it should be. "I'll leave you two to catch up then. Pleasure to meet you, Mrs Quinn."

I hadn't noticed on my way in that Theo's bag was already by the front door. Packed.

He slung it over his shoulder.

"Theo, please! I said we can talk."

"And if I talk, will you believe me, Lara?"

"I—it's just so complicated."

A moment of painful silence passed as he glanced away and tried to smile.

Before I knew what was happening, his lips melted into mine.

Pulling my body flush to his, he clung to me for dear life, fingers grasping my hair into fists so tight it almost became painful, building and deepening and wild. Until he released me and wrapped his hands delicately around my face to kiss my temple. Tender and raw. No sound except our ragged breaths.

His kiss told me all I needed to know. That I was everything. That he would pour his soul into mine and give me every last drop of himself if he could. It cried out for me to hold on. It said goodbye.

It set me free.

Opening his eyes, his voice shook with the effort of stepping away. "I've left something for you upstairs. Think about it. Please. That's all I ask."

I watched him leave. Walked back inside. Sat next to Mom. Burst into tears.

This time, I told her everything.

♪

On my bed was a square, black velvet box. My bones turned to solid steel. It looked like a ring box.

Inside was a pearly-white, spiralled shell. Wrapped around the shell was a gold chain necklace, finer than anything I'd ever seen. I lifted it carefully, afraid of breaking the fragile links in my clumsy, undeserving fingers. Hanging from the chain was a pendant in the shape of a flame.

Underneath the box was a letter:

Lara,

I planned on giving you this necklace to celebrate some upcoming news, but I want you to have it now anyway. I may not have a life soundtrack but since you gave me the idea, I have been making a playlist for you. For us.

Chasing Cars — Snowpatrol
Ironic if you think about how we met, but also, can't we just forget the world?
Lady In Red – Chris De Burgh
Yes, I know it is as cheesy as Wallace and Gromit's fridge, but whenever I think of that night we danced in the barn, this is the song I hear.
Grow As We Go — Ben Platt
Despite the highs and lows, we helped each other grow.
You are in Love — Taylor Swift
*Because **A)** I knew you would never listen to a playlist which didn't include at least one Swift song and **B)** Because I could hear it, feel it, see it. Couldn't you?*
Turning Page — Sleeping At Last
Because you are every page, word and note to me.

When I saw this shell, I remembered the day we met as clearly as if it were yesterday and, Lara—my Lara, my beyond beautiful Miss Quinn—I realised something: I was falling for you even then.
I don't know whether you can ever find it in your heart to truly trust that I am yours. I hope that you can. I hope that you will because all I do know is this— Lara, you are the fire that burns in my heart, and I am in love with you.
For as long as you want me.

Theo xxx

Day 385
Tuesday

I told myself I'd call him at lunchtime.

Then I told myself I'd call him when I got home instead.

Every time I opened my mouth, I wanted to scream. I hadn't even eaten all day. What would I say? Nothing had changed. He was still leaving. *Three weeks.* I'd never known any long-distance relationships to end well. Especially not ones with famous heartthrobs who had women throwing themselves at them.

If I called Theo, it would be to say goodbye.

I couldn't do it.

Be brave. I wouldn't let a man break me again.

Here I Go Again – Whitesnake

<h1 style="text-align:center">Day 386</h1>
Wednesday

When Andrew heard my old standard reply of, 'Fine. Same old,' his face stumbled and lost its smile.

Congratulations, I thought, *you've even made Andrew miserable.*

Yup. Everything was back to the same old normal. Same old life. Same old work. Same old Daniel. Who, despite having moved his nan into a new care home, was still dumping more and more work on me. When I'd suggested to him about getting an assistant so I could go back to my (proper) job, he'd laughed and completely disregarded the idea.

Andrew went to ask another question, I grabbed my coat and walked out of the hall. Not even DAYS meetings felt like my safe place anymore. Nowhere did.

Theo was my safe place.

Snap me in half and you'd find his name written through my soul like a stick of Brighton rock—*Theo Theo Theo.*

Light footsteps chased me outside. I slowed down. "Jenny, I don't want to talk about it."

"Then we won't talk about it, my love. I only wanted to check if you're coming on Saturday?"

"Yeah. Sure." I leaned onto the side of my car, oblivious to the drizzle slowly soaking into my hair. No matter how much I wanted to hibernate, I wouldn't miss the campaign celebration. Jenny and DAYS deserved it.

"As we're here, would you mind giving me a lift home?" she asked.

I nodded, unlocked the doors and walked to the driver's side. "What about the meeting?"

She waved a hand. "Andrew can cope without me for one night."

It wasn't until we pulled onto the main road I wondered, "Has something happened to your car?"

"No," she chimed, "the car's fine. It's me that's broken down." I caught a glimpse of her in the wing mirror, lips twitching as she chewed her cheeks. "It's my eyesight. I'm not allowed to drive anymore."

"Oh, Jen, I'm sorry. If you need anything, you know where I am."

"Thank you." She patted my arm. "But I'll be putting my bus pass to good use from now on. Did you know I can go right across the country on this thing? For free!"

Although she sounded happy, her eyes were tired, staring unfocused out of the window. She loved her car; a vintage Beetle that her late husband had restored. His pride and joy. Her freedom. We stopped at traffic lights and I gave her hand a quick squeeze.

"Never mind." She shook her shoulders and snapped back to the present. "Life has a way of throwing things at us, doesn't it, love?"

We drove the rest of the way in silence.

The Beetle sat on Jenny's drive. It put my poor car to shame, despite being ten times its age.

Tapping her silver nails on the door handle as we stopped, Jenny hesitated, "Will Theo be coming on Saturday?"

A sharp pain ran through the gaping, Theo-shaped hole in my chest. How was I supposed to start picking up the pieces of my heart when they all belonged to him? "No."

"Shame." Jenny sighed heavily. "Lovely young man." She pointed to her car. "I suppose I should sell her now."

My head shot up. "You don't have to do that, surely?"

"Cars are designed for driving."

"But... but you love it. You have a garage, don't you?"

"Yes, where she'd rust and be no good to anyone."

I looked helplessly at the pristine, shiny red Beetle. Jenny should have been the one crying, not me. Why the hell was I crying about a bloody car?

"I've made up my mind," she said, back straight, hands clasped on her lap. "It's time for her to go and make new memories, and to make someone else happy. We can't hold on to the past." Her hand settled on my knee. "You know, after my Day Zero, I spent years thinking I could pretend it never happened. I fought against everything kicking and screaming, but the only person I hurt was me. I was stuck. It took me a long time to realise: you can't walk forward if you're holding onto something behind you."

I dried my eyes. "How do you do that?"

"Walk forward?"

"No," I exhaled, half laughing, half still crying. "How do you always manage to talk about things without talking about them?"

She grinned. "Shush. It's my superpower."

Fear Of Letting Go - Ruelle

Day 388
Friday

Theo

I ached all over with a hunger only Lara could fill. My heart refused to believe she was gone. Each time I closed my eyes, I saw her. When I woke up, I could smell her coconut shampoo on the pillows. I would turn, expecting to see her there, only to be crippled by the empty space all over again.

Had she not read my letter?

Or had she read it and decided not to respond?

That was worse.

Lara

Why was it that whenever you felt so much, you felt nothing at all? And whenever you had so much to say, no words existed?

What could I do?

He was the one who walked away.

They'll always walk away.

Sad Beautiful Tragic – Taylor Swift

Day 389
Saturday

Thanks to a glorious sunny day, we moved the campaign celebrations outdoors. Jenny and Andrew handed over the last DAYS certificate to Stuart, setting off another burst of applause and flashes of cameras.

The crowd drifted away from the temporary stage, back to the buffet tables set up underneath gazebos on the sports field, next to the school hall.

Dad lay an arm across my shoulders and squeezed, almost pulling me over onto our picnic blanket. "I'm so proud of you, sweetie."

"Thanks, Dad." I tried to smile. Even my well-practised mask wouldn't work anymore.

My certificate and bunch of flowers sat by my side, the lines under my name read:

Thank you for your achievement and continued support of DAYS.
Without your courage and generosity, we would not be here.

Courage? Me, the woman who couldn't make a phone call? Ha! I didn't deserve it.

Greg joined us on the blanket, a mountain of food on his plate. Olivia edged away, looking disgusted.

"What?" he spluttered through a mouthful of crisps. "I'm hungry."

She slapped him hard on the shoulder. "Eugh, you're so gross."

Greg turned to Sarah, who merely raised an eyebrow. "Don't look at me," she said, "I'm not going to defend you." At which, Olivia carried on winding him up and stealing his food.

If Theo were here, he would have done that rumbling little chuckle.

If Theo were here, he would have had his arms around me and Dad would have been watching him like a laser-eyed hawk.

Theo Theo Theo.

I'd lost count of the number of times I'd gone to text him about random things—like finding a hedgehog in my garden last night—and had to remind myself that I couldn't.

Olivia froze, her finger still poking into Greg's chest as she glared over his shoulder. "What's *he* doing here?"

We all turned to look. My hand clamped around a clump of grass, ripping it clean out of the ground.

"Did you invite him?" Olivia scowled at me, her fine eyebrows bunched in the centre of her face, creating little creases across her forehead.

"No." I most definitely did not. "Stay here, I'll sort it."

As I approached, Daniel folded his arms across his incredibly tight shirt. It always surprised me how different he looked in casual clothes. He rarely wore anything other than a suit. His business was his life after all.

"What the hell are you doing here?" I said.

"Aye, Quinn, that's not a nice way to greet your biggest sponsor."

Of course. Andrew had sent automatic invites to everyone who had donated.

I took a second to compose myself. "Sorry. You're right. Thank you for your support. But this is a long way to com—"

"I fired Peter."

Shock thumped me in the chest, physically pushing me back a step. "Peter? But, why?"

Daniel shrugged. "He was slow, always did things his way."

Peter had been hired by Clarke, the partner before me, and he'd been in the building trade for longer than Daniel. I knew they clashed, but he was damn good at his job.

"He had more experience than you," I said, my calm composure dwindling. "You can't fire people because you don't want to listen to them. You should have spoken to me about this."

"I knew you'd say no. I say yes. And I get the final say, so..." He lifted his hands, using them to weigh up the argument. "If it makes you feel better, I told him you didn't agree. Anyway, that's why I'm here. I need you to come back to the London office and take over. I'm shutting this one down."

Fireworks exploded in my mind. "What? You can't do this!"

He took a step closer, a hand finding my arm. "Quinn." His voice softened, "Lara, it's been over a year. We both know it's time for you to come back."

Oh, we knew that, did we?

'Not a case of if, but when,' Theo had said, *'You're there at his every beck and call.'* He was right. About everything. My skin crawled. No. Not this time. Gone were the days when I'd run back to Daniel's smile after he shouted at, undermined, belittled or disrespected me.

"So you do remember then?" I replied coolly.

He checked his watch, annoyed by the questions wasting his time. "Remember what?"

"That it's been over a year. You never called me. Just another day for you."

He slid his hand up my arm, onto my neck. "I should have called."

I remembered how much I used to crave his touch. Only a few months ago, I would have believed him, taken his hand and given in, convinced myself that this gentle side was the real him. I had it all backwards.

Now I knew how it felt to be touched by a man who truly loved me.

Theo loves me! At least... he had. Would he still?

As for Daniel ever considering me to be an equal partner, that was a joke. He just wanted someone who he thought he could walk over.

The old Lara might have let him.

I wasn't the old Lara anymore.

I had stood up to a murderer. I didn't just survive, I fought back! And I was prepared to stand up to far worse for the people I loved.

Daniel's hand tightened on my neck. "Come on, Quinn. Don't argue again. You're coming back. You said you'd be there for me."

I pushed him away, groaned up at the sky in anger, fists clenched. "All this time, I've done everything you asked, tried to impress you, tried to understand you—" I choked. *Be brave. Be honest.* "Jeff was an evil person who did an evil thing. He stopped my heart, but you? You were the one who broke it! I trusted you. I loved you. But the way you always left me made me feel worthless. Like I wasn't worth fighting for. Like no one else would want me."

There. I'd said it: My truth. My fear.

I didn't love Daniel, I hadn't for a long time. But I'd been holding on to a rose-tinted memory of all our fun times.

The idea of freedom when working for him was an illusion because there would always be a part of me that felt indebted, connected and tied to him. "Dan, I'm not doing this anymore."

"Lara, come on. What are you talking about? Please, I need you." His voice cracked, the way it did when he'd found me on the floor and when he gave his witness in court. The way it did whenever he was *actually* telling the truth. And no matter how much I wanted to hate him, I couldn't.

We were all damaged. Only, it wasn't the damage that defined us; it was the way we dealt with it. If we weren't careful it could make us distant, hard and selfish like Daniel. Or we could become more determined to change and better ourselves like Theo. To show kindness, empathy and love like Jenny.

With a deep breath, I let go of the last of my anger. I let go of Daniel.

I met his eyes. "If you ever cared about me—"

"How could you say that?" His head shook as he reached for me again.

I held him at arm's length by pressing a hand to his chest and jutted my chin toward the gazebo. "That's Jenny and Andrew. Please go and talk to them. Tell them everything about your past and what we went through. Let them help you to be happy." I smiled.

That was my final thanks and the best advice I could give. Whether he took it was up to him. My debts were paid.

"Goodbye, Daniel. I quit."

As I walked away, I didn't look back.

I'd done enough of that.

♪♪

Olivia pounced on me as soon as I got to the blanket. "What happened?"

"Won't Daniel be joining us?" Dad asked.

"No. He's leaving," I said. "We won't be seeing him again."

Mom dug her fork into Dad's knee and shot him a warning glare when he tried to ask why. Olivia started grinning. It was catching. She hugged me as we burst out laughing.

Until all of the air and blood abruptly vanished from my body. "Oh hell, what have I done? I've screwed everything up."

I'd shut Theo out, pushed him away and let him leave without a fight. By refusing to trust him, I'd practically called him a liar. I was no better than Daniel.

Olivia looked furious. "Don't you dare go back to him."

"Not him." I waved in Daniel's direction, although he'd already left. No surprises there. "Liv, I need to borrow your car."

She hesitantly handed me the keys from her pocket. Something clicked in the depths of her silvery eyes and her smile grew again, stretching across her face. It was like watching a flower bloom in slow motion.

"Be brave!" she sang out as I legged it across the field.

Revolution – The Score

I jiggled frantically in the driver's seat as if that would make the car go quicker. Town eventually faded into green hills. When I reached the open road to the beach, I put my foot down, turning the sheep in the fields into fuzzy white blurs.

The gate to the caravan site was locked. Probably to stop crazy people like me from getting in. I didn't care. I climbed over, ignoring the needles tingling through my back, swung my leg over the top, and ran for the caravan under the oak tree. The tree that reminded me of our first kiss and that feeling of being perfectly safe but completely free.

How could I ever have doubted that Theo loved me?

Hot metal, baked by the sun, stung my knuckles as I knocked on the door. *Please be here.* What if they'd finished filming early and I was too late?

It cracked open.

"Theo!" Oh, thank you, universe.

He frowned at my breathless, and in all likelihood, bright red face, and carefully stretched out a hand toward mine. "Lara? What happened?"

He should have been angry after the way I'd ghosted him, but there he stood—gentle and strong, insecure and kind, imperfect and perfect—worrying about me.

I loved him so much.

Taking a few steps back, I bent over and leaned onto my thighs to pull myself together. Theo moved forward to help.

"I'm okay, just, argh, one sec," I panted, "I have to tell you something."

He stopped by the doorway, arms hugged across his chest, eyes down.

Right. *This is it.* My last chance to be brave and honest. I had to make it count.

"I didn't come here expecting you to forgive me," I began, "but I need to say how sorry I am because you deserve that much at the very least. It wasn't your fault. I did everything I promised you I wouldn't do."

Being so close to him put my body in hyperdrive. My arms were gesturing all over the place of their own accord. "I've been trying to think of what to say and how to say it ever since you left. Going over every book and every line of every song, but *A Million Love Songs* later and I still don't know how. And yes!" I exhaled with a grin. "Ironically, that is actually a song."

A glimmer of a smile twitched the corner of Theo's mouth. Or had I imagined it? I wasn't sure; he was still looking away. From his pouted lips, I could tell he was listening though.

"I've been holding on to the past, Theo, because I was afraid of losing who I was. I never used to get scared, or shy, or angry, or panic. I thought I could go back to normal. It's taken me this long to realise: I don't *want* to go back."

His head turned a fraction.

I edged closer. "I know I'm gonna be stuck with these faults for a long time, maybe forever. But I'd rather have them and be here with you than be the old me without you. So here I am, fighting for us."

He glanced my way, arms softening.

Please look at me. "I quit my job," I blurted out in desperation.

"What?" He flicked over another glance. "But you love your job."

Hearing his voice made me want to cry. I dared to step closer. "No. I enjoyed my job. I love *you*, Theo."

Finally, his gorgeous eyes found mine.

I nearly collapsed on the floor. "As of about half an hour ago, I'm officially unemployed and..." My nerves faltered. I looked away, pulling at my sleeves. "I doubt I'll be getting a good reference."

"Then that makes two of us."

Huh? Theo was watching me, properly now, the way he always had. Searching. Reading. Like I was the only thing worth looking at.

He raked his hair and explained, "I received a confirmation letter yesterday that I'm being released from the contract to film with Yasmin. I've also filed an official harassment complaint against her. She won't be talking about me again."

Something melted into a gooey mess inside my chest. "You're not going to L.A. then?"

"Getting out of those contracts was another reason why I hired Philip. I was never going to go back, Lara. This was the news I wanted to give you with the necklace. I should have just told you. I shouldn't have walked out the way I did. I..." The familiar scent of earth, sun, spices and unmistakable *Theo*, filled my lungs with every step closer. "I needed you to believe me. But not because I could prove myself with a piece of paper, but because you *trusted* me."

I took his hand, gazing hopefully into his eyes. Eyes that always told the truth. Eyes that understood and accepted me with a raw kind of love I never thought I'd find. "I know. I trust you. With all my heart."

He touched a finger to my chin. "I love you, Lara. You are my future. In fact"—One eyebrow lifted the string connected to his lip. Hell, I'd missed that smile. I could live off that smile—"Miss Quinn, you are my *Wildest Dreams*. Which, I believe, was the song for the day we met?"

Hardly able to speak through all the butterflies and fire and electricity, my head jerked in agreement. "You knew that all along, didn't you?"

He shrugged a *you-caught-me* shoulder.

I flung my arms around him. I'd never let go again. "Maybe it was that bump on the head, after all, Mr Jackson, because I've been falling in love with you ever since."

His hands disappeared into my hair, feather-light kisses landed over my neck. "I did hit you pretty hard," he purred.

"Head over heels."

As my lips found his, I whispered his name (the way he liked it).

He groaned in response, drew me closer, nipped at my lip. "Lara, do you ever feel like you're living in a movie?"

"With you?" I laughed. "Always."

"Then... what happens now?"

"Oh, it should be raining for a start."

"Because all wonderful and romantic new beginnings happen in the rain?"

"Exactly." I stood on tiptoes, slipping my fingers under his shirt and over his strong back. "Then you'd lift me up and carry me off into the sunset. Or at least into your caravan, where we can talk Austen all night long and live happily ever after."

"Hmm. Well, I can't do anything about the weather. As for the rest..."

When Theo picked me up, he started to laugh.

My laugh.

Wildest Dreams – Taylor Swift

Day Five or Six Hundred and...
Something?

(Six Months Later)

THE DAILY LONDON

Exclusive interview with Lara Quinn, an ambassador for the charity DAYS, who support victims of violent crime. We talk love, journals, and surviving an attempted murder.—**By Cassie Kowalski.**

I meet Lara in the modest suburban house she shares with her partner—actor and director, Theodore Jackson.

She immediately offers me a drink and leads me into a stunning kitchen. Not surprising, considering she runs a new interior design studio (Livara) with her best friend.

Cassie: Okay, Lara, the obvious question is: How do you move on after what happened to you?

Lara: I've tried to answer that in different ways. Ultimately, the only answer is: You just do. *(She smiles and hands over my coffee.)*

I suppose it's similar to how you cope with heartbreak, or even grief. Everyone is different. You get up in the morning, go through the motions and survive another day. After a while, you stop surviving and start living again.

"Surviving is instinctive. Living takes courage."—Lara.

Cassie: You've been careful to stay out of public view. *(I point to the ring on her finger, hinting at the secret engagement.)* But now you're helping to expand the DAYS groups and have even agreed to publish excerpts from your personal journal. Why the change?

Lara: I started writing a journal,

like Jenny *(the DAYS founder)* suggested as a form of therapy, to express things I would never say. Writing down your thoughts and fears is a way of confining them. They lose their power over you and morph from dark, heavy clouds that blacken your mind into tangible lines and curves of ink on a page. Once captured on a page, you choose what to do with them. You can analyse and face them whenever you're ready. You can scribble over them and correct them. Hell, you can even rip the page out and burn it if you want.

For a long time, I couldn't talk about what happened to me. And I've shied away from chances to help DAYS in the past. But as time passed, I stopped wanting to erase my thoughts and memories.

I no longer measure out my life as before and after Day Zero. There's no 'old me' or 'new me.' I wasn't broken or damaged beyond repair.

I was different. But I was still me. So I guess, this feels like my next step forward.

"Sometimes we can mend on our own, other times we need help. Admitting you need help doesn't make you weak."—Lara.

Cassie: So now you're recovered, you want to focus on helping others?

Lara: I wouldn't exactly say I'm recovered. There will always be days when Theo and I have to forgive each other, push each other, pick each other up and remind ourselves of who we're trying to be. But that's okay. *(At this point, Theo edges into the room behind Lara to listen.)*

Love is not blind. Love is seeing someone with all of their ups and downs, mistakes and victories, good and bad, but loving them anyway, despite all of those things. Because of all those things.

But yes, I hope that sharing my experience can, even in some small way, help someone else.

(Lara grins and points over her shoulder.) He thinks I haven't heard him, doesn't he? *(I nod. Theo laughs, comes to shake my hand, and teases his fiancé about being 'a Jedi,' then Lara continues.)* I know I'll always be okay because we've got each other. I trust him. We'll be brave. We'll be honest. We'll make all the days count.

The book - *All The Days* - comes out next month.

It contains excerpts from the journal of Lara Quinn along with experiences from other DAYS members.

Acknowledgments

Diolch yn fawr, a big thank you to you, my lovely reader.

I sincerely hope that you've enjoyed spending time with Lara and Theo as much as I have. If you did, then please drop by to say hi and tag me on your socials @ByElleJayce

All indie authors like me are literally fueled by you folks leaving reviews for us on Amazon, GoodReads, on your blogs, or those funky TikTok's that I can't get my head around! It really does make our day. All The Days 😊

Now, there's a saying that goes something like this: 'Be careful of what you say/do near a writer, as you may just end up in their next book.' And it's true! Every story contains a part of the writer and their life, and this brings me to my second thank you—My Hubby. All the anxiety, nerdy-ness and crazy music-loving habits come mainly from me. But all the good stuff—kindness, forgiveness and love—that all comes from him. Babes, you are my world, my rock, the murmzeep to my jinglepin, and a million times a million love songs.

Third—Dad. Dad wasn't born; he just rocked up one day on a motorbike with a journal and pen. He taught me what an incredible thing it is to keep learning. With a book in your hands and words at your fingertips, you have a life ahead full of adventures, mystery, romance, and galaxies far far away. Thanks for giving me all that. Miss you.

Fourth—Mum. Your strength is an inspiration. The words 'thank you' will never be enough, even if I say them every minute of every day. Plus your cooking is legendary! Wuv ou.

Then there's the amazing Bookstagram and Writing

Community where I found some of the greatest beta and arc readers, writers, and friends. Margaret, I'm so glad our obsessiveness over fiction and cleaning brought us together. You are officially my BBFF—Bestest Bookish Friend Forever.

Isobelle at Inspired Creative Co, Angela at A. H. Joy Editing, plus Amy Trent, Erin Thomson, Megan Beth Davies, Katie, Chloe, Effie (just to name a few), and everyone who answered my many, maaaany, 3 a.m rants/breakdowns about blurbs—you are all stars.

The #Sanditon squad. Honestly, if you mad lot hadn't introduced me to the world of fanfiction, this book wouldn't be here. And hey, we saved it! I know it's bittersweet, but I'll never forget how you guys kept me laughing through the lockdown. Well then... 😉

I can't *not* mention the music of Taylor Swift. She's a favourite with many writers because secretly, we envy her talent for telling intricate, heartbreaking stories within a few minutes of a song.

Finally—Be Brave. Be Honest. Make All The Days Count.

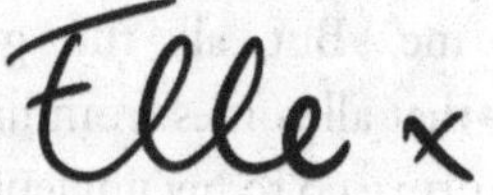

P.S Don't forget, the full playlist for *All The Days* is on Spotify. And if, like me, you really aren't ready to let go of Lara and Theo yet, you'll be pleased to know that they, and some other familiar characters, might be showing up in a sequel... Stay tuned via social @ByElleJayce or on my website, ellejayce.co.uk